# Knight

The Abled Chronicles: Book Two

R. G. Hurley

Hurley Books

# Contents

| | | |
|---|---|---|
| Prologue | | 1 |
| 1. | Chapter 1 | 7 |
| 2. | Chapter 2 | 20 |
| 3. | Chapter 3 | 31 |
| 4. | Chapter 4 | 36 |
| 5. | Chapter 5 | 41 |
| 6. | Chapter 6 | 48 |
| 7. | Chapter 7 | 57 |
| 8. | Chapter 8 | 61 |
| 9. | Chapter 9 | 75 |
| 10. | Chapter 10 | 87 |
| 11. | Chapter 11 | 101 |
| 12. | Chapter 12 | 106 |
| 13. | Chapter 13 | 113 |
| 14. | Chapter 14 | 127 |
| 15. | Chapter 15 | 131 |
| 16. | Chapter 16 | 143 |
| 17. | Chapter 17 | 149 |
| 18. | Chapter 18 | 159 |

| | | |
|---|---|---|
| 19. | Chapter 19 | 176 |
| 20. | Chapter 20 | 185 |
| 21. | Chapter 21 | 189 |
| 22. | Chapter 22 | 193 |
| 23. | Chapter 23 | 198 |
| 24. | Chapter 24 | 207 |
| 25. | Chapter 25 | 215 |
| 26. | Chapter 26 | 222 |
| 27. | Chapter 27 | 226 |
| 28. | Chapter 28 | 237 |
| 29. | Chapter 29 | 245 |
| 30. | Chapter 30 | 259 |
| 31. | Chapter 31 | 267 |
| 32. | Chapter 32 | 278 |
| 33. | Chapter 33 | 286 |
| | Authors Note | 293 |

# Prologue

The summer sun beat down on Maria's back and warmed the soil under her hands. She'd always enjoyed working outside in the soil; it was a love that had served her well when she had met a certain botanist who would become her husband, and later when successfully growing food meant the difference between life and death for their family.

As a family, they'd certainly eaten a lot of homegrown potatoes during the Hard Times. In hindsight, it really wasn't all that hard to guess why they were one of Nova's least favorite foods, but potatoes were easy to grow if you knew what you were doing, and about as nutritious as it could get.

While Maria still enjoyed the sense of independence and security that a thriving kitchen garden gave her, now that she knew that her family wasn't in danger of starving she much preferred growing beautiful things. As she surveyed the variety of flowers surrounding her and noticed just how many of them were edible, Maria smiled—it was true that old habits died hard.

She had just bent down again to weed around a patch of red carnations when the terrified screams of her granddaughters shattered the soothing melodies of bird song. Maria was already moving towards them before she'd even consciously processed what she'd heard.

Maria might have been in her sixties, but a lifetime of work had kept her body strong, and Maria's legs pumped hard as she sprinted towards the small creek where the two little girls had been playing. Snake sightings were rare this far up north, and poisonous snakes were almost unheard of, but Nova and Caleb had taken the family car into town for work, and if one of the girls were bitten they'd lose precious minutes waiting for an ambulance. A second scream rent the air and Maria began to worry that perhaps it wasn't a snake—a ravenous coyote or stray dog were also possibilities. She tried not to think about what she would do if it was a two-legged assailant. Nova and Caleb had hidden their identities well, but the fear always remained that they would be exposed, and that Kaleo and Katherine would be in danger.

She scrambled down the small bank of the creek, gripped her pruning shears tightly, and mentally prepared herself for the possibility of having to do something very unpleasant to protect her granddaughters.

Another scream, sounding like it came from Katherine, was surprisingly followed by Kaleo's laughter. Maria breathed a sigh of relief, although it was soon replaced by anger at the scene before her.

"Take that, you non-Abled scum!" Kaleo screeched as she threw a hand-sized rock at her sister.

"Stop throwing rocks at me, Kaleo, and let me get in the water. It's hot out here and the bugs keep on landing on me," Katherine whined. "I don't like this game anymore. You're being mean."

Katherine took a step into the creek, and Kaleo retaliated by throwing a tree branch at her. The stick was much larger than the rock, and even as Katherine screamed and threw her hands up over her face, it smacked her across the side of the head and knocked her onto her back.

Maria judged that she had seen enough. "Kaleo, you stop that and come here right now," she ordered as she bent down to comfort the crying Katherine. The poor girl had fallen on several sharp rocks that had scraped her hands and the backs of her legs, and the cut from the stick on her forehead was beginning to bleed.

Kaleo scrambled out of the creek and ran over to Maria and Katherine. "Katherine, are you okay?" she asked in a concerned tone in a complete reversal from her earlier calloused words.

"No, she's not okay, you made her bleed," Maria said. She loved Kaleo to pieces, but sometimes the girl just had no clue. Katherine only continued to cry. "What were you even thinking, throwing rocks and sticks at your sister like that?"

Kaleo at least had the good sense to look ashamed. "We were playing a game, Grandma. I had abilities and Katherine didn't, and I was keeping her out of the creek."

"And why would you play such a silly game?"

"Because everyone knows that Ableds are more special and better than non-Ableds," Kaleo said.

Katherine hiccupped. "Kaleo told me that if I let her be the Abled first, then we would switch, but when it was my turn to be the Abled she wouldn't get out."

"That's because I remembered that Katherine didn't deserve to get in the creek because she didn't have abilities, and abilities aren't just something that you can develop all of a sudden once you already don't have them," Kaleo said.

A chill ran down Maria's spine. She'd heard the kind of talk that Kaleo was spouting, but it wasn't common and it certainly wasn't a view that she would have heard from anyone in their small family. "Who's been telling you these things, Kaleo?" she asked as gently as she could, knowing that the little girl didn't understand the damage the type of talk she was repeating could cause.

"Ms. Sandra tells me and Katherine about it all the time. She says that since Momma and Daddy have abilities we should have them too, and that we're special and should act like it."

Sandra Warminghill babysat Kaleo and Katherine a couple of times a week to give Maria a break and let her socialize with her quilting club. When Nova and Caleb had decided to settle down, they'd picked a piece of property far enough from town to give them some privacy and keep any prying eyes from looking too closely, and they'd taken great care to choose an area that had a good mix of Ableds and non-Ableds of all types. Sandra was an acquaintance they had made early on after their relocation and had come highly recommended by several other friends of her daughter and son-in-law. The young woman's own ability had been a particularly helpful one for a nanny: She could make her voice extremely soothing.

Not that she would be taking care of Kaleo and Katherine anymore; Maria would make sure of that. She knelt to look Kaleo in the eyes.

"Abilities or no, you should never treat someone in such a horrible way," she said. Katherine sniffled and Maria removed the handkerchief she had pressed to the little girl's head to stop the bleeding.

"But Ms. Sandra said that only the strong survive, and that Ableds are the strongest," Kaleo said, still trying to reconcile the two viewpoints.

Maria chose her words with great care. "Do you think that I'm strong, Kaleo?"

"You're very strong," Kaleo said proudly.

"That's right, I am. Much stronger than you are right now." Maria playfully poked Kaleo's arm. "But one day you may very well be stronger than me. When that happens are you going to start throwing sticks and stones at your old, weak, non-Abled grandma?"

Kaleo shook her head, aghast at the idea.

"And what if you don't end up having abilities and Katherine does? How would you like it if she didn't want to be your sister anymore because she thought that you were too weak?"

"I wouldn't like that." Kaleo reached out to hug Katherine. "I'm sorry, Katherine. I didn't mean to hurt you. We won't ever play that game again. Do you want to play in the creek with me? I can help you find pretty rocks for your collection."

Katherine nodded and returned her older sister's hug, and Maria felt her heart melt. They were both such sweet, caring girls, if a little misguided at times. However, she wanted to make sure that she drove her point home where they would never forget it. She sat on one of the large rocks at the bank of the creek and pulled the two girls onto her lap. They were almost getting too big to fit, but for now she would gladly pay the price of a little discomfort if it meant they would remember the lesson.

"Now, you two, listen to me very carefully. Abilities are a gift from God, a calling from Him to protect the weak and helpless, not to take advantage of them. They are to be used to help others, not to hurt them. If you both forget everything else that I ever say, remember this: If either of you does ever get abilities, you must use them for good, for protection, not to hurt others or prey upon the weak. Strength is about what's inside of you and how you face the challenges that come your way, not about what abilities you have or how much you can hurt others."

"What kind of challenges?" Katherine asked.

Maria kissed the top of their heads. "Any type of challenge. My prayer for you both is that you learn to be adaptable and able to roll with the punches. Strength is being able to get knocked down and not letting your failures define you, but instead learning from them and letting them fuel you to grow and become a better person. True strength is found by getting knocked down, getting back up again, and continuing to fight the good fight and defend the helpless even when it hurts or gets hard. Never forget that."

**PART ONE**

# Chapter One

*16 years later; 5 Years Post-Betrayal*

Kaleo pulled into the parking space at the Professors' training facility and turned off her car. A black motorcycle drove past on the side street next to the parking lot, and her mind turned to memories from the night before. She checked the time on her watch and saw that she was early and still had a couple of minutes to relax before her match. She leaned against the car's headrest and cast her mind back to the night before with a smile.

"New beginnings," was what Stefan had said in an almost reverent tone before kissing her tenderly, as if her lips were cotton candy that would melt away at the first touch. His kisses had made Kaleo feel giddy and light-headed, and she'd been grateful for the added support when he wrapped his arms around her. Then he'd pulled back and studied her face again, and the look in his eyes made the extra time she had spent touching up her hair and makeup before his arrival well worth the effort.

After that, Stefan had donned his protective gear and helmet, and left with promises of a truly romantic first date. Kaleo's smile grew wider as she replayed the memories in her head. She might have only known Stefan for three months, but she felt as though it had been much, much longer, and she was definitely looking forward to their date that night.

But first things first. She got out of the car to head inside. She'd followed the Professor's directions to the letter and parked in a different area of the training facility at his request. As she had driven past the main parking lot, Kaleo had noticed that several more cars were parked there than usual, but thought nothing of it—it was her first time being there on the weekend, and she was sure that the Professor had other pupils with busy schedules.

A couple of weeks before, Kaleo had been given a tight, black, short-sleeved shirt, black pants, and black athletic shoes so that she could practice under the conditions of the upcoming match. The most disconcerting part of the uniform was the black full-face helmet with its mirrored visor, which the Professor had explained was used to keep the combatants anonymous and remove any biases or prejudices during the match.

Dressed in the uniform, a bag packed with a change of clothes slung over her shoulder, Kaleo entered through a side door and found one of the Professor's assistants waiting. She was shown to a changing room where a black jumpsuit and helmet were already laid out on a bench, waiting for her. The jumpsuit hadn't been part of the practice sessions, but the assistant explained that the Professor had decided to require it for increased anonymity reasons. Once Kaleo had zipped it up and placed the helmet over her head, the assistant led her into a separate waiting room and shut the door.

After a few minutes, she heard a soft knock on the door and the Professor walked in. He surveyed her costume and nodded in approval.

"It needs one more thing," he said as he stuck a fabric patch on each of her shoulders. When Kaleo looked in the mirror, she admired the colorful patches; each depicted a red and yellow bird rising from flames.

The Professor nodded as he admired his handiwork. "I took the liberty of assigning you a codename for anonymity purposes; given your circumstances, Phoenix seemed fitting."

"Because you expect me to crash and burst into flames?" she couldn't resist asking.

He shook his head. "Because I expect you to rise to the occasion. Now it's time."

The Professor led her out the door, down a hallway and then into the facility's arena. Large wooden boxes that varied in height from a mere couple of feet tall to towering over her head had been scattered throughout the room, giving it a decidedly warehouse-like feel, and a curtain against one of the walls had been pulled away to reveal a mirror running the length of the room.

Kaleo pressed the button that turned on her voice modulator. "I see that you've redecorated." The voice that came from the modulator was deep and metallic.

"Your opponent will be in shortly. When you hear the bell, it's the signal to start. All weapons have been blunted or replaced with wooden versions to prevent any serious injury, although if you do somehow manage to hurt yourself, we have a doctor on standby," the Professor said before walking back through the open doorway with no further instructions. The wooden door shut behind him, and a second metal one dropped over it.

Kaleo walked over to one of the boxes. Even with all her weight pressing against it, the box refused to budge. It seemed sturdy enough, but when she leaned over the top and lifted her feet off the ground she felt her abilities falter. With a sigh she turned away; there would be no jumping around on boxes today.

After she'd satisfied her curiosity, she sought out the energy patterns in the room and began to feed her abilities. Within a minute, Kaleo had created enough of a buffer to form a shield attached to her left arm, that was large enough to cover her torso. She'd done enough shield transformations to know that she could easily enlarge the shield at a moment's notice, but she didn't want to give away her hand too early in the game.

The door across the room opened, and her opponent stepped through. The person wore the exact same jumpsuit and helmet as she did, and Kaleo couldn't make out any identifying features of weight, body type, or even gender. The only thing that she could tell for sure was that the opponent seemed to be a little taller than her and had some type of black and white patch on their shoulders.

As she kept an eye on her opponent, Kaleo walked to the center of the room, where a large space had been left clear, and withdrew her baton. Her opponent didn't move, but as she reached the center, she was just able to make out what looked like two handles jutting out over their back.

"Are those swords? I feel cheated; all the Professor gave me is a baton," she called out.

The figure opposite her said nothing and settled into a defensive stance at the edge of the room. Kaleo wished that she hadn't spoken and did the same; the silence unnerved her. She calmed her nerves by focusing on the few energy patterns that eddied around them.

The sound of a bell rang clearly through the space, and before the sound waves had faded away, her opponent made their first move.

They seemed to pull two knives out of thin air and threw them at her. Kaleo hardly had time to react; even as the knives were speeding her way, the figure began sprinting in her direction. She immediately crouched down and raised her shield to protect herself from the projectiles. Both knives made contact with her shield and fell to the ground, and the energy they imparted made the yellow light of the barrier grow brighter. With a glance, Kaleo registered that each knife looked like it was made of a dark, polished wood. She was sure that if the knives had been actual metal and gotten past her shield, she'd have been killed before the match even truly began. She turned her mind back to the matter at hand as her opponent reached the center of the room. They didn't stop or even pause to take stock of the situation, and instead drew swords and charged directly at her.

Everything was moving faster than Kaleo had anticipated, and she realized that she was still crouched to defend herself from the knife attack, which wasn't an optimal position for close-quarters combat. She reacted by instinct and drew a bubble of energy around herself just large enough to allow her to stand up and evaluate the situation. Her opponent stopped just short of the barrier and slashed at it with one of their swords to no effect.

"Well, at least this will stretch out for longer than a minute," Kaleo said as she surveyed her adversary from the safety of her bubble. She knew that she couldn't maintain the bubble for long due to its high energy drain combined with the relative lack of energy sources in the room, but her endurance workouts had paid off and right now she needed a plan more than she needed an abundance of energy. As her mind raced, her eyes fell on the patch on her opponent's shoulder, which was a simple black X on a white background.

"So, what should I call you? X? Cross? Railroad?" she asked as her opponent prowled around the outside of the bubble.

"My name is Strike. Now, are you just going to sit there and relax, or are we actually going to do something? I have a date tonight, and I'd much rather be getting ready for it than playing this waiting game with you." The voice from the modulator was distorted and high-pitched, but the mocking tone was unmistakable.

Kaleo took a deep breath and snapped the bubble back into a compact shield, settling into a defensive stance as she did so. "Fine, I'd hate to ruin your plans with your hot date. Your move, princess."

They closed quarters. Kaleo managed to protect herself from Strike's attacks by catching most of them on her shield and knocking away the others with her baton. However, try as she might, she couldn't land a solid blow. Strike always sidestepped or twisted out of the way at the last possible moment, so the rare hits Kaleo landed were only glancing in nature. Several times the two of them came together, traded blows, and then backed apart. Even when they were separated by the diameter of the circle, Kaleo had to stay on her guard. Her opponent seemed to have an ability to close short distances with superhuman speed, and only sheer luck had enabled her to counter the onslaught.

After the third or fourth round of attacks, Kaleo could feel the sweat dripping down her face. She knew that if she didn't go on the offensive and end the match soon, she'd run out of stamina. All the blows to her shield had kept her energy reserves well stored, but maintaining such a large shield for so long in combination with the fight had severely begun to test her endurance. In her sparring matches with Nicole, she had always had a couple of moments of respite to catch her breath; she was afforded no such luxury here.

As she watched closely, Kaleo noticed that Strike was beginning to slow down as well. There were no more fancy sword tricks or dancing footwork, and the time between the charges was slowly lengthening. She briefly considered erecting another bubble barrier to give herself a chance to catch her breath, but decided that it was too risky as it might also give her opponent a break to recover. After the next charge and subsequent retreat by Strike, Kaleo followed.

To her surprise, Strike turned and ran away from her into the obstacle field. She hesitated at the edge of the clearing—in a field of obstacles, any ability that imparted even a modicum of increased reaction time would be to Strike's advantage.

The hesitation proved to be her downfall. Out of the corner of her eye, she saw a blur of movement. Kaleo jerked her body to face the threat, but she was too slow, and one of Strike's dark wooden swords swung down towards her unprotected forearm. Then several things happened at once, and time slowed to a snail's pace.

The sword made contact with her arm and Kaleo heard a loud crack. She watched her forearm bend in a place where there was no joint, and pain blossomed where she'd been hit.

The shockwave from the hit combined with the pain, and the new sensation vibrated throughout her entire body as though she were a tuning fork. The vibration traveled to her toes and then back up to the point of contact. From there it took on the form of an electric arc that sparked from her arm straight to her opponent's helmet.

The force of the electricity threw Strike several feet away where they landed flat and lie still.

The vibration that exited Kaleo's arm created an exquisite pain immediately followed by the loss of all sensation around the break. Completely overwhelmed, Kaleo fell to her knees.

Again acting more on instinct than conscious thought, she created a protective bubble with whatever energy she had left while cradling her arm and gritting her teeth to keep from crying out. After she had taken a moment to recover and process what had happened, she realized that Strike still hadn't moved, and she began to worry that she'd seriously injured them.

Her fears were allayed when she heard Strike slap the ground and start shouting in a foreign language. The electricity must have knocked out the voice modulator, and they stopped abruptly, but it was too late. Kaleo smiled through the pain—she hadn't understood the language, but the voice had definitely been male and all too familiar.

The Professor's voice crackled over the sound system in the arena. "That was quite the educational match. Both of you, head on over the infirmary; the doctor on duty will meet you there. Strike, you'll have to show Phoenix the way. Good work; I'll go over the match with each of you at a later time."

Kaleo took a deep breath and released the barrier, letting the light slowly fade into the air. She watched Strike stand and gingerly take a few steps, and then rocked to her own feet, taking care to keep her broken arm as still as possible. Strike gestured to one of the doors and she followed him. With a heave, he rolled up the inner metal door and pushed the wooden one open before leading her down a hallway to what she assumed was the infirmary. Kaleo barely got a chance to look around the small space lined with doors when two assistants appeared and attempted to lead them into separate rooms.

Kaleo turned off her voice modulator. "Had any good oranges lately? Maybe gone bird watching?" she asked as Strike started walking away without a backward glance. Her words had an immediate effect, and his head jerked around.

The second assistant was motioning sternly for Kaleo to go into a separate room. "I don't think that'll be necessary," she said as she turned to look back at Strike. "If you're who I think you are, I'd think that you'd want to be in the same room for this."

The two assistants looked completely lost at the unexpected turn of events, but Strike waved them away before grabbing Kaleo's hand and pulling her into one of the treatment rooms. He shut the door behind them and turned to her. In the reflection of his helmet, she could only see her own face plate.

"What did you just say out there?" he asked.

"I think you heard me perfectly fine. Do you still not know my voice? I'm hurt," Kaleo teased as she looked around the small room. There was a generic picture of a flower bouquet on one of the walls, and the furniture consisted of a treatment table, a couple of chairs, and a small cabinet overhanging a countertop crowded with jars full of medical supplies.

Strike pulled off his helmet and placed it on the countertop. Stefan's green eyes were filled with concern, and his eyebrows were furrowed together in a frown. "Kaleo?"

"You'll have to help me get the helmet off; I'm afraid that I'm a little disadvantaged at the moment," she said with a shrug of her injured arm. The adrenaline from the fight had begun to wear off, and she swayed on her feet as the small movement caused the pain to flare up again.

Stefan guided her to one of the chairs and helped her sit down. Then he knelt in front of her and gently removed her helmet.

"Surprise," she said.

Stefan frowned. "How'd you know that it was me?"

"I didn't know anything until you started yelling, and it sounded remarkably similar to what you say when someone cuts you off in traffic," she said with the best smile she could muster, but another sharp pang raced up her arm and she grimaced instead.

"Does it hurt badly?" he asked as he looked at her arm.

"I would think it does," Katherine said as she opened the door and sailed into the room. She looked at them and put her hands on her hips. "Well, well, well, what do we have here? I thought anonymity was the name of the game today," she scolded with mock severity.

Kaleo's eyebrows rose in surprise. "You're the doctor that the Professor was talking about?"

"The one and the same. That was some match that you two just had. I think that I could hear the snap from your bones all the way in the viewing area." Katherine handed Stefan a large jug of water and shut the door behind her.

"The viewing area? We were being watched?" Kaleo asked.

Stefan groaned and slumped in the chair next to Kaleo. "How many people were there today?" he asked before he took a big gulp from the jug.

Katherine finished washing her hands and dried them off on a towel. "Just about the entire task force. Some of us made a good amount of money too." She turned to look at Stefan and her sister. "You're up first, Stefan. Take off your shoes and that ridiculous jumpsuit and let's have a look at you."

"I'm not hurt that bad—Kaleo's the one with the broken arm. Take care of her first," Stefan protested.

"I need to make sure that Kaleo's little firework show didn't do anything to your nervous system, or anything else for that matter. It won't take long, and Kaleo's treatment isn't going to be nearly as simple."

"I'm fine, Stefan. I've had worse," Kaleo said. Stefan glanced at her, the bewilderment evident on his face, but then he did as Katherine asked.

Katherine put one hand on the top of his head as the other tapped each of his toes and fingers. Then she had him wiggle his toes, smile, roll his eyes, and stick out his tongue before delivering her verdict. "You're fine. Looks like the voice modulator is the only thing that got fried after all. If you start feeling any weird aches or pains over the next few days, let me know."

Next, Katherine turned to Kaleo and helped her sister unzip the jumpsuit. Pulling the jumpsuit off her injured arm wasn't easy, and Stefan winced as though each of Kaleo's whimpers of pain were dealing him actual physical blows. Her forearm had already begun to swell and turn a dark red color, and Katherine whistled when she saw the injury.

"You sure did a number on this arm, Stefan. What pain level are we at, Kaleo?"

"Pretty bad."

"You know I need a number."

"I don't know... it's faded a little bit. Maybe a six or a seven? It's more dull and achy now."

"And what was it right when it broke?"

"More like a nine and really sharp; a solid ten when I shocked him."

Stefan winced again.

"Sounds about right." Katherine turned to Stefan. "Are you okay, Twitchy? Need to leave the room for a little bit?" When he shook his head, Katherine turned back to examining Kaleo's arm.

Kaleo looked at Stefan. "Why were the task force members watching today?"

"I'm a member," he said.

"He's actually one of the two mission leads for the task force. No prizes for guessing who the other one is," Katherine said. She glanced at Stefan, who made a face from behind the water jug, which he had raised to his lips, and shrugged.

"I'm trying to help you out here, buddy. Kaleo's not dumb; she was bound to figure it out eventually."

"Do you often spar with the Professor's students?"

It was Katherine's turn to look at Kaleo in surprise. "Didn't you know that the Professor is all but the official teacher for the task force? He takes very few private students."

Kaleo sighed and put her good hand over her face. "I'm going to kill Nicole. No wonder Mom and Dad were so encouraging about my lessons." She looked suspiciously at her sister. "And I take it that you're the official doctor for the task force?"

"Close, but not quite. The official doctor, Dr. Fields, is my supervisor, but he has no problem letting me do most of the work. They wanted the best of the best when they recruited me, and even made it part of my training. After another year or two, I'll be a full-fledged doctor."

"So am I the only one in our family who isn't a part of the task force?"

"Pretty much. You know that Mom's going to try and recruit you again after today, right?"

"Why would she?"

"Stefan here is too modest to admit it, but his record when it comes to matches among the task force members is almost perfect. As far as I know, today was the closest I've ever seen him get to actually being beaten by someone who isn't a former Savior."

Kaleo frowned. "I see. So I take it that the Professor said that I didn't actually beat him?"

"I believe it was officially ruled a draw, pending my findings. They may change it to a technical win by Stefan considering the nature of your injury." Katherine trailed off as she focused on Kaleo's arm and then shook her head. "But looking at this injury, I personally wouldn't blame you if you gave him another good shock right now just to get even."

"I didn't know who I was up against," Stefan interjected.

"No, duh, you didn't. That's kind of the whole point of the jumpsuits and helmets, isn't it?" Katherine turned back to Kaleo. "You want to know what's going on with your arm?"

"Of course."

"Good or bad news first?"

"Bad news."

"I'd need an x-ray to be certain, but I'm almost sure that you've got an ulnar break, and some other minor injuries."

"That's all? I thought you said it was bad," Kaleo said with a weak laugh.

"The good news is that once I get it set properly, I can speed up the healing process quite a bit and you won't need surgery, but you'll still have to be careful with it. I can promise that you won't be doing any more matches for at least a couple of weeks."

Kaleo scowled. "I've got to keep up with my training; I've been making good progress and can't let it go to waste."

"I'm sure the Professor will be able to work around a broken arm." Katherine grabbed a splint and a sling from one of the cabinets. "Now hold still, I've got to put these bones back where they belong. This may hurt a little."

"Can't you call Apathy in?" Stefan asked.

"I could, but you know what the side effects of him using his abilities are."

Kaleo looked between the two of them. "I don't. Is Apathy a person or is it just Katherine's codename for when she finally ditches all her emotions and embraces her inner sadist?"

"I see that your injury didn't affect your awful sense of humor. No, Kaleo, Apathy is the alter-ego of my coworker and supervisor, Dr. Fields; he can numb your nerves where you won't be able to feel any pain... but you'll also lose most of your emotions until it wears off. Usually, it takes a couple of hours but can last up to several days depending on how much pain you're in," Katherine said.

Kaleo glanced at the clock on the wall and then at Stefan, weighing her options. Her arm really hurt, but their match had been scheduled in the early afternoon, and if they wrapped things up quickly, she'd only have three or four hours before it was time for their date. She remembered the butterflies in her stomach the night before when they had kissed, and swiftly came to a decision. "Don't worry about it, I'll tough it out."

"Kaleo—" Stefan began, but stopped when she shook her head. He reached out and placed her good hand on top of his. "If you need something to squeeze, don't worry about hurting me."

She nodded in response.

After Katherine had set the bones, splinted Kaleo's arm, and placed it in the sling, she sat back on her stool. "I can give you some pain meds that should help to take the edge off today, and I'm going to need to stop by your house tomorrow and work on it some more, but I think if you promise to be very careful, you should be able to just wear the splint on Monday under your suit jacket."

"Thanks, Katherine."

"No problem. Now, what are you doing after this? It's been a while since we last hung out and I'm off for the rest of the day," Katherine asked as she tidied up the room.

"Actually, I was going to take Kaleo out to dinner tonight... That is, if that's what she still wants," Stefan said uncertainly.

"I see. Good thing that important date wasn't with someone else; you might have really gotten electrocuted then." Katherine pulled a pad of paper out of her white coat and scrawled several things on it before handing it to Kaleo. "Here's your prescription. Any of the pharmacies around here should have it in stock, although I wouldn't mix it with alcohol if I was you."

"No alcohol? How else am I supposed to get through this date?" Kaleo shot a teasing glance at Stefan, who still looked much too serious.

A corner of Katherine's mouth twitched. "I'm sure that you'll manage just fine. Kaleo, take care of that arm. Stefan, you have my number—if anything weird comes up, let me know." And with that, Katherine gave her sister a final hug before excusing herself from the room.

After Katherine had left, Kaleo and Stefan sat for a moment without saying anything.

"If you've changed your mind about us, I will completely understand. I know that this was a lot," Stefan said quietly into the silence.

"Change my mind? After you just broke my arm?" Kaleo shook her head and laughed. "No, sir, you're not getting out of this now. You are going to get to spend a lot more time with me over the next few days and assist me with my cooking, my cleaning and anything else I need help with. Then I'll decide if I want to keep you around or not," she said as she nudged his side with her good shoulder and smiled at him.

# Chapter Two

After Katherine released them, Stefan walked Kaleo out to her car and confirmed the time of their date. She drove home slowly, only making a quick detour to the local pharmacy to pick up her pain medication. Once she was home, Kaleo swiftly found out that only having the use of one arm made everything much more difficult, and she had barely enough time to shower and get ready before Stefan stopped by. He drove them to a nearby park that usually wasn't too busy, and parked the car in a secluded area.

"I hope you don't mind; I know that I promised you a very romantic date, and I originally had other plans for tonight, but I thought that we might want more privacy than a busy restaurant could provide," Stefan said as he opened the car door for Kaleo.

He produced a blanket and large picnic basket from the trunk before leading her to a flat spot in between several trees.

"That's okay, we said the second date is when we tell each other all of our secrets, right?"

Stefan grinned as he settled the blanket on the ground and placed the food containers on it. "I hope you feel like Italian food."

"Italian sounds lovely."

"I wasn't sure what you wanted to drink, or if you'd taken that medication yet, so I got us both lemonades."

"How thoughtful of you."

They ate in silence for a few minutes.

"How's the food?" Stefan asked.

"It's delicious."

He looked at her slyly. "That's good to know. I'd hate to strike out now."

Kaleo felt her nose twitch and he seemed to take it as a sign of encouragement.

"Of course, I hope that if it had turned out horribly you would have given me a second chance to see if I could rise from the ashes of my failure," he continued.

"You? Fail? That'd be quite shocking."

Stefan laughed, lounging on his side. "So, I assume that you do, in fact, have abilities?"

Kaleo nodded and told him all about her lessons with the Professor, how she'd been training with Nicole the past several weeks in preparation for the match, and how her abilities had transformed from the Russian roulette of Canary to the much more stable energy manipulation that she had recently mastered.

When she asked Stefan about his own abilities, he shifted uncomfortably. "You'll have to forgive me; I'm not used to talking about them. Between my two brothers and me, only one of us has abilities, and neither of my parents do. Basically, my ability lets me speed myself up. As you saw today, when I really get going I can almost become a blur. If I'm just running off my own energy, I only have about a minute and a half before I get tired, but if I'm in a fight I can let myself get hit or shocked and somehow my body uses that energy instead. If I'm worried about being in a serious fight, I'll carry a taser and pre-emptively give myself a shock."

"You didn't bring a taser today? I'm hurt," Kaleo teased.

"Yeah, well, to be honest I wasn't expecting to have that much difficulty today and thought that my own power would be enough." He made a face. "Of course I was sorely mistaken and unprepared. It could have been worse, though. If I try and push it too long, or go too fast, sometimes there are consequences that are less than fun."

"Consequences? Like what?"

"You know how if you sprint as fast as you can for a quarter of a mile it feels like your heart is about to give out and you're about to die? Something like that, but even worse, and that's just for the short-term side effects."

"It's a wonder that you're able to do anything at all then—I'd be terrified of a heart attack."

Stefan shrugged. "I try not to get to that point. I've learned how to supplement just enough to give me an edge in actual combat, and I always try to hold something in reserve." He took a sip of his lemonade and raised his cup to her. "But I will say that you almost got me today. If you'd been even a couple of seconds faster and I had hit that shield of yours again, I'd have been done. It seemed to suck the energy right out of me. I'm sure the Professor is very pleased with himself—he's been trying to find me a challenge for several months now." He took another sip of his drink. "In my defense, I've been rather distracted thinking about how to impress a very attractive young lady and may not have been in top form."

Kaleo blushed at the compliment and changed the subject, unused to being the object of such flattery. "I'm surprised that some of the other members of the task force don't give you more of a run for your money."

"You know how abilities are. We all have a special niche, and mine just happens to be much more combat oriented. Nicole is the closest non-Savior, and even she has trouble getting the explosives near enough to me to cause damage without risking herself, although I'm sure if Nicole was actually trying to kill me and didn't care about her own life, she could just blow us both up."

At the mention of Nicole's name, a thought occurred to Kaleo. "Nicole is part of the task force then? I remember her saying that she took a couple of classes from you."

"I'm not supposed to say anything, but considering how she was the one who gave you the Professor's number, and what she told you... I think you can figure it out for yourself."

"And the other people who you always sit at lunch with? Those 'co-workers,' as you put it?"

"Audra and that group, you mean?"

Kaleo nodded.

"Can't tell you unless you join the task force."

"Me? On a team with Audra? I'm sure that would go over well." Kaleo snorted.

"I know that you two got started off on the wrong foot, but I promise that she's really not all that bad."

"She said that I should be ashamed for not having abilities and that I was an embarrassment to my family."

Stefan frowned. "She has some views that I certainly don't agree with, but she's our top mediator and negotiator. I'm sure that once she finds out about your abilities she'll calm down and be nicer."

"I still don't want to tell her."

"Why not?"

Kaleo turned to look him fully in the face. "Why didn't you ever tell me that you're Abled?"

He shrugged. "Some people would treat me differently if they knew. Dating an Abled guy is all that some girls care about, and I wanted to make sure that you liked me for me. As the daughter of Sifter and Architect, I thought that if you didn't care about dating a non-Abled, you were probably pretty special."

"Especially as the non-Abled daughter of Sifter and Architect, right?"

"Don't change the subject, you still haven't said why you don't want to tell the others about your abilities. To be honest, it'd probably throw Audra through a loop."

"You sure are talking a lot about Audra."

"You were the one who brought her up. Do I sense a little jealousy there?" A grin creased Stefan's face as he teased her.

"Jealousy? Not in the slightest." Kaleo's carefree tone sounded a little too forced even to her own ears.

Stefan's grin grew wider as his eyes softened and he took her hand in his. "If I told you that you're the only woman I've been able to think about these past few months, would you believe me?"

"I'm sure that it would break your mothers' heart to hear that you haven't given her a single thought in so long," she replied dryly, and he chuckled.

After they finished their food, they lay watching the clouds in the deep blue sky until the sun began to set. Kaleo helped Stefan clean up as best as she could and he drove her back to her house. Like the gentleman he was, he unlocked her front door for her and lit a couple of candles so that she didn't have to fumble with the match box or use any of her energy credits on electric lights.

"Are you going to be okay tonight with your arm?" he asked as they stood in her living room.

Kaleo rolled her eyes. "It's just one broken arm; I'm sure I can manage."

"If you need anything, don't be afraid to call me."

"I'm fine, Stefan, don't beat yourself up over it. It was an accident, and for the record, I was completely joking earlier about making you help me. I didn't actually mean it. You don't have to do anything else."

"Shhhh," he said, and placed a finger to her lips to quiet her. "This gives me the perfect excuse to see you more often without being weird about it."

Kaleo sighed. "Fine, but only because you insist. I need to go grocery shopping tomorrow. If you really want to help, you can drive me to the store and carry the bags."

"That would be my pleasure. What time?

"Right after lunch? Early afternoon? It shouldn't take too long."

"I'll see you then. Sleep well tonight, beautiful." Stefan kissed Kaleo's cheek goodbye and left.

Stefan was true to his word, and the next day he chauffeured Kaleo to the grocery store, insisted on pushing the cart, carrying the grocery bags into the house, and helping her put everything away. Just as they were finishing, Kaleo heard someone walk onto the porch and open the door.

Katherine's voice floated out from the living room. "Kaleo, is someone else here? Whose car is that out in the driveway?"

"We're in here!" Kaleo called out.

Katherine walked into the kitchen and smirked. "Ah, Stefan. I was expecting to see Kaleo's other boyfriend."

"Don't listen to her, she's joking," Kaleo said from the fridge where she was storing the last of the produce.

"And here I thought that I could put my intelligence connections to good use for once," Stefan deadpanned.

Katherine raised her eyebrows and leaned against the kitchen countertop. "Oh, really? Have you ever—?"

Kaleo closed the fridge door and leaned against it, also watching Stefan.

"Have I ever what? Stalked someone for personal reasons?" Stefan snorted. "Of course not, that would be highly unprofessional... and creepy on so many levels."

"Have you ever been tempted to?"

"Perhaps. Are you here to see Kaleo?"

"Whatever would make you say that?"

Kaleo sighed and turned to Stefan. "Thanks for all your help today, Stefan. I won't ask you to stay any longer. I'm sure you have your own things to get caught up on, and Katherine is in one of her moods."

Stefan took the hint graciously and left. After he was gone, Kaleo turned to her sister.

"Other boyfriend?"

Katherine tossed her wheat-colored hair over one of her shoulders with a flip of her hand. "Can't let him get too comfortable. Sometimes it's good to keep them on their toes."

"Yes, because you have so much experience in the romance department."

"You know, I would have thought that you'd be nicer to me considering how I'm only here to help your arm heal faster," Katherine retorted as they sat down on the couch.

Katherine spent the next hour working on Kaleo's arm. By the time that she was done they were both feeling drained, but Katherine declared that as long as Kaleo continued to be careful, she would no longer need the sling and could make do with only the splint.

"Of course that's assuming you want to keep your identity secret. The only people who would even be suspicious are the other task-force members who saw what happened."

Kaleo shrugged. "We'll keep it on the down low for now. I've gotten used to people thinking that I don't have any abilities, and in some ways it's kind of nice—helps weed out some of the more insincere people."

"Whatever you say. You going over to Mom and Dad's for family dinner? I think that tonight we're supposed to have enchiladas."

"I was planning to. Can you drive me since I'm on your way back anyways?"

"I suppose I could do that, but I want to hear all about you and Stefan as payment."

"You already know everything. We talked just a couple of days ago about it and what happened at Adrian and Kiana's wedding, remember?"

"No, we talked about how you were finally going to tell him that you wanted to actually officially date him instead of whatever it is that you two have been doing for the past couple of months."

"We've just been good friends."

"Yeah, sure, you keep on telling yourself that. I've seen you two together; he's never looked at you like a 'just friend' would, and you act differently around him."

"What do you mean by that? Are you saying that I'm faking my personality around him?" Kaleo was mildly offended at the insinuation.

"Not at all," Katherine said as they walked to her car. "When he's around, or when you're talking about him, you're just different. Happier I guess, a little more relaxed. Not as angry at the world."

Kaleo buckled her seatbelt. "I'm not angry at the world."

"Angry at the world... angry at yourself. One of the two." Katherine shrugged. "It's okay if you are, you've been through a lot. I get it."

"I don't think that you do."

"Are you kidding me? C'mon. I'm a doc in a hospital. I see pain and suffering every day. The world isn't a nice place, and I see every shift just how much it can chew someone up and spit them out. You've always been so good about picking yourself up and dusting yourself off no matter what life throws at you, but that shield you've got isn't easy to get past."

"As Stefan found out yesterday," Kaleo said with a smirk.

"No doubt in more ways than one."

They pulled into their parents' driveway and parked behind two other cars. "Looks like family dinner this week includes the extended family," Katherine remarked as they got out of the car and walked up to the house.

"Of course it does. How many of them were watching yesterday?"

"Mom, Dad, and Mod, so it's a safe bet that Sniffer and Wiper probably know by now too."

Kaleo and Katherine walked in and were greeted by Mod and their mother, who were sitting in the living room. Kaleo swiftly found herself wrapped up in her mother's hug.

"The fighter of the hour," Mod crowed, and raised a glass to Kaleo. "We've been trying to find someone to give Strike a run for his money for quite some time now. That was an excellent first match, very promising."

"Is your arm feeling okay?" Nova asked, her voice laced with concern.

"I fixed her up pretty good, Mom. Don't worry, she even got some pain medication. Just try not to squeeze her too tight. And you can drop the pretense, Mod. Kaleo knows that it was Stefan yesterday. I caught them getting pretty cozy in the treatment room after their match, if you know what I mean," Katherine said as she kicked off her shoes.

"He was helping me take my helmet off because I couldn't do it myself. Stop implying things that didn't happen," Kaleo complained, and Katherine smiled and stuck her tongue out at her older sister in response.

"Wiper and Sniffer are in the kitchen with your father finishing up the enchiladas. You know how your dad gets about his homemade salsa," Nova said, ignoring her daughters' good-natured bickering.

Almost before the words were out of her mouth, Caleb poked his head around the wall that separated the living room from the kitchen. "Kaleo, Katherine, perfect timing. The food's ready, come and eat!"

As they moved into the kitchen where the enchiladas and sides were set out in a buffet-style line, Kaleo hugged Mod, who was dressed in a pair of jeans, plain black t-shirt and looking particularly androgenous. "How have you been, Mod? Up to anything interesting lately?"

"Not that I can really tell you about," Mod replied a little sheepishly.

Kaleo nodded. "Ah yes, the task force. I understand."

Wiper overheard what she'd said. "The task force? Who let that cat out of the bag?"

"I did," Katherine admitted. "Well, to be fair, Kaleo recognized Stefan's voice and they had a little face reveal before I could even get into the room." She shot Kaleo a mischievous grin and raised her eyebrows as if to say more, but refrained when Kaleo glared at her and shook the enchilada spatula threateningly.

"Speaking of Stefan, how's he doing? Have a good date?" Sniffer asked from his seat at the table.

"How'd you know?" Kaleo asked Sniffer, feeling a blush begin to creep over her cheeks as every eye in the room turned to her.

"I can smell him on you," Sniffer said simply before taking another deep sniff. "And do I smell food from Valentino's? That was a good choice."

Kaleo frowned and sniffed her shirt. "There's no way you're that good. I showered."

"Their marinara sauce uses a special kind of garlic that makes sweat smell differently. Don't worry, it's faint even to me."

"So it's official now? Why didn't you invite him over tonight?" her father asked as he finished placing the toppings on his enchiladas and sat down. "We always have more than enough, and you know that Sniffer's food never disappoints."

"We've only been on two dates. I'm not inviting him over to meet the family so soon."

Caleb scoffed. "Two *official* dates. You two have been spending quite a bit of time together for the past couple of months. Plus, he already knows just about everyone here with the exception of Sniffer, so why be nervous about it?"

"I know him too, I've worked with him before. Director Stone requested my nose for a couple of very sensitive cases, and I talked to Strike a little bit on the way to Adrian's rescue mission, remember? He's a nice guy," Sniffer said.

Caleb nodded. "See? Everyone knows him, and we all like him. Should have brought him around."

"Oh, stop that, Caleb, you know family dinners are different from just another day at the office. Let them get to know each other a little first," Nova said as she dipped a tortilla chip into the salsa bowl.

"Yeah, can we please talk about something else besides my new boyfriend?" The words were out of Kaleo's mouth before they had fully registered, and it was obvious that only the daggers in her mother's eyes were keeping her father from making another teasing comment.

"Sure, let's talk about when you're joining the task force," Wiper said brightly.

At his words, Katherine snorted into her drink and Nova sighed and shook her head. Nova had been trying to recruit Kaleo to join the Midwestern Pact Abled Task Force ever since she had regained her abilities several months before, to no success. Wiper looked around and saw the reactions that his words had engendered. "... or not. Sensitive topic?" He turned to the youngest Savior. "What about you, Sniffer, how's your family doing? Any news about your brother?"

Sniffer shrugged. "Jeffery's doing fine. He just graduated high school and is thinking about what to do next. We're still not sure where Eyes is, but I keep on hoping that he'll show back up one of these days."

Wiper frowned. "I'm sure that he'll come around eventually. Is Jeffery planning on going to college, or is he going straight into the workforce?"

"He's going to try to get some more school, but between you and me, I don't think that he's quite cut out for it. You know how he is when he gets really focused on something."

Kaleo looked around the table as she dug into her plate of food. Wiper had started retelling a story from the old Savior days, with Mod adding in the occasional relevant detail. Her mother and father were smiling across the table at each other, still obviously very much in love after so many years of marriage and two grown children. Katherine and Sniffer were in deep discussion over what Kaleo assumed was something medical considering the brightness in Katherine's eyes as she talked animatedly, and the way that Sniffer's nostrils flared whenever he got excited.

The atmosphere in the room was warm and bright, and she smiled to herself. Perhaps her father was right: She'd have to invite Stefan to a family dinner sooner rather than later.

# Chapter Three

The next day when Kaleo got to work, she found an unexpected message from the director of the Midwestern Pact Intelligence Agency on her desk that asked her to stop by his office for a meeting at her earliest convenience. Kaleo checked her schedule, saw that her morning was free but her afternoon completely booked, and decided to make the trip upstairs while she had the time.

As she walked up the stairs, Kaleo reflected that she'd never actually been to the department where Stefan worked. She hadn't even realized that the intelligence agency offices were all the way on the fifth floor, and a warm feeling sprang to life in her chest when she thought of just how many times Stefan had made the trip up and down the three flights of stairs to her office.

Kaleo found the Intelligence Department with little trouble and was greeted by a stern-looking receptionist with a name tag identifying him as "Brian" sitting at a desk in front of a blank gray wall. When Kaleo handed the receptionist the message that she had received, he took the paper with a frown and made a phone call. She stood awkwardly and looked around as he spoke into the phone in a hushed voice. After a minute, he hung up the phone before standing from his chair and gesturing for her to follow him back.

Beyond the entryway, Kaleo was immediately struck by the open-floor plan of the space. The building itself was part of a long-gone university that had folded during the Hard Times, and her own department occupied the former faculty offices. The Logistics and Trade Division, where she worked, was made up of a series of offices connected by a hallway or two, and could best be described as nice and cozy on good days, and almost unbearably cramped on others.

Instead of cramped offices and blind corners, the Intelligence Department sat at the other end of the spectrum, with very few partitions between desks. The walls along two sides of the room had several doors with name plates on them that Kaleo assumed opened into the offices of the department management. Through the internal windows of several meeting rooms, she could see out to the city beyond.

Her guide led her to a large office in the corner and knocked on the door. When the occupant inside called for them to enter, the receptionist opened the door and motioned for Kaleo to walk through.

"Thank you, Brian, that will be all," an older man sitting behind a desk said, and Kaleo heard the door close behind her.

"It is nice to officially meet you, Kaleo. I am Director Jason Stone. Please, come in and sit."

He gestured towards one of the chairs in front of his desk, and Kaleo did as he asked. It took her a second, but she finally recognized him as the thin man who'd been at the meeting with Governor Hamilton after she had helped stop the kidnapping attempt on Adrian several months before.

Director Stone's office contained several large wooden filing cabinets, a few chairs, a couch, and some rugs, all in varying shades of brown, tan, and gray. A large bank of windows ran the length of the outside wall of his office and afforded a nice view of a park that was just down the street. Kaleo appraised her surroundings with a couple of discreet glances before sitting in one of the chairs across from the director.

"I received your message." she said, placing the paper on the desk.

"I appreciate your promptness in answering it."

Kaleo shrugged and leaned forward. "I was booked for the rest of the day. Now, what can I help you with?"

"Direct and to the point. I like it." The director leaned forward to mirror Kaleo's own body language. "To be perfectly frank with you—which is a pleasure that I don't often have in my line of work—I have heard of your recent... accomplishments and would like to extend an official offer to join with the Midwestern Pact Abled Task Force."

"Why the offer now?"

"After your performance on Saturday, I'd think that would be obvious."

"I was under the impression that was completely anonymous."

The director waved his hand. "Anonymous to most people."

"You're aware that both of my parents, and my mother in particular, have already tried to persuade me to join multiple times?"

"Yes, I am. However, I think I may be able to provide both some insight and a new argument that they've been overlooking."

Kaleo raised an eyebrow. "By all means, then, please do explain."

Director Stone leaned back in his chair and picked up a wooden ball from his desk that he twirled in his fingers as he spoke. "I get the sense that your hesitation in joining stems more from a desire to set yourself apart from your parents and make a name for yourself than because you have no desire to go back out into the field."

"What would give you that idea?"

"I requested your file from your parents after the incident with Adrian. Your stated motivation for creating your team—your "Flock" as you referred to it, was that you wanted to stop the rash of kidnappings and murders that had been plaguing the Abled community, correct?"

Kaleo nodded.

"Then why the added layer of secrecy between you and your parents? Why the memory wipe?"

"If something had happened to me, I would have been a liability to them."

"Yes, but why even create the team? Why not work for your parents and only have your relationship with them wiped? Alternatively, why not work for someone your parents knew? They've been able to maintain their secret identities while also remaining in contact with a network of allies and sources for decades—you could have had your pick as an intern, or more, at any of the private companies or agencies that they have connections with."

He paused and watched Kaleo as she considered his words. "I don't know. I'm sure that they mentioned it, but it never seemed like all that great of an option to me."

Director Stone tossed the ball up in the air and then caught it and pointed at her. "It's my belief that you didn't want to ride on their coattails; you were seeking to make your own way in the world and wanted as little assistance as possible. Of course you had to depend on them and some of their connections for the funding, but the memory wipe? The secrecy and added security in between your base and their headquarters? Everything points to the fact that you were trying to separate yourself from them."

"I love my parents," she said defensively.

"That doesn't mean that you don't want to be independent of them. Why be so hesitant to join the task force otherwise?"

"I chose not to join because I didn't know what the extent of my abilities were, I didn't want my mother to be accused of nepotism, and I didn't feel like it would be fair to my teammates if I ended up being deadweight."

"I'm sure that your mother told you that we have non-Abled support staff; you could have easily joined in that capacity."

Kaleo shrugged and said nothing.

"As for being deadweight—if your performance on Saturday is any indication, I can assure you that you won't need to worry about that." Director Stone shifted in his seat and set down the wooden ball. "In addition, we are in need of the expertise that you have gained through your work."

"Planning infrastructure and trade doesn't sound like something your task force would be interested in... and even if it was, I'm sure you could figure out a way to find whatever information you needed easily enough."

"On the contrary; infrastructure and building plans, trade patterns, ship and train rosters are all things that you deal with every day, and that would provide us with a potentially valuable source of information that we have been lacking so far. Unfortunately, neither I nor anyone else on our team has any experience in those things, let alone a desire to learn more about them."

Something about Director Stone's serious nature made Kaleo sit back and organize her thoughts. "What would the task force expect from me? I'm already working overtime some weeks; combine that with the training I'm sure that I'd need to do, any missions I may be needed for, and whatever information I would need to analyze... That all adds up to a very busy schedule."

"Many of our members are able to integrate some of their work with the task force into their daily jobs, but I do agree that you may have some difficulty with that given the nature of your department and its current funding level. I won't lie to you—long hours may become the norm for you in order to keep up with everything."

Kaleo nodded. "I was afraid that you'd say that. Unfortunately, I don't think that it'll work then, but I thank you for the offer."

"Afraid of a little hard work?" Director Stone smiled, but his eyes challenged her.

Kaleo didn't back down and met his piercing gaze with a cool look of her own.

"All due respect, sir, if you really saw what happened on Saturday, and spoke to the Professor about my abilities, then you should understand why I have no desire to become overwhelmed in any aspect of my life."

A genuine smile played at the corners of his eyes and mouth. "Rightfully so. Nevertheless, my offer stands. I'll send you more information about the job, and you can think about it as long as you'd like."

The director stood from his desk and walked around to shake Kaleo's hand. "Now, I understand that you wish to preserve your anonymity for the time being. Don't be concerned as to anyone thinking that the timing of this meeting was suspicious. I've had it on my schedule for the past week, and if anyone suspects anything, I'll say that I have possibly found a break in the Adrian Hamilton case and wanted to interview you to corroborate my new source."

"The past week? What if I had done poorly on Saturday?"

"The Professor seems to believe in you; maybe you should start believing in yourself."

# Chapter Four

After Kaleo walked out of Director Stone's office, she paused. Her lunch and afternoon schedule were completely full of meetings, but she still had plenty of time until they started, and she'd already completed all her last-minute preparations.

She decided that it was high time she visited Stefan at work for once. The only problem was that she had no clue where to find his desk, beyond a vague idea that it sat near a corner. She looked around at the bustling room, couldn't spot his face, and felt more than a little lost.

"Can I help you?" A feminine voice asked just as Kaleo was about to give up and go back down to her office.

Kaleo turned her head to locate the speaker. The voice belonged to a brunette woman almost as tall as Kaleo, who carried a large cup of coffee. The woman's face was familiar, and Kaleo placed her as one of the people who sat with Stefan at lunch

"Yes, sorry. I was looking for Stefan. Is he here right now? I don't see him."

"Stefan? He's probably in his office. Usually, he's one of the first people in. Follow me and I'll take you there."

The brunette led Kaleo down to a corner office on the opposite side of the main room. The door was open, and her guide walked through without hesitation. Kaleo paused at the doorway, suddenly unsure of herself. The office was almost as large as the director's, and much more sparsely decorated with only a desk, a couple of chairs, and a gray couch. A large blue geometric rug lay in the center of the room, and several windows ran along the side wall overlooking the city skyline.

Stefan sat across from them, behind a large desk made from dark wood. His head rested on one of his hands as he pored over the documents in front of him, completely lost in thought and unaware of their presence.

Kaleo's guide coughed politely. "You have a visitor, assistant director."

Stefan looked up, peering at the newcomers through a pair of black narrow-frame glasses. The frown on his face was replaced by a smile when he saw Kaleo. "Thank you, Laura. I'll take it from here. Would you mind shutting the door on your way out?"

After Laura left, Stefan rose from his chair and hugged Kaleo, taking care not to press too hard on her injured arm.

"I wasn't expecting to see you. What are you doing here?" he asked as he led her over to the couch.

"I just had a very interesting meeting with your boss." Kaleo looked into his face and lightly touched the side of his glasses. "I never knew that you wore glasses. In fact, it seems that there are a lot of things that I don't know about you, *assistant director.*" She looked around his office again and raised an eyebrow. "As I recall, you said that you were jealous of my office because you 'had a dark desk in a corner.' Now I'm beginning to think that you were just making fun of me."

Stefan pursed his lips. "Usually I prefer contacts, but my prescription ran out and I forgot to get a refill. And I will have you know that, to be fair, I wasn't technically lying about the office. My desk is both dark brown *and* located in a corner." He kissed her hand, and the crinkled skin around his eyes told her that he was aware that his excuses were flimsy. "But if it helps, I am jealous of how much more welcoming and inviting your office feels."

Kaleo wasn't going to let him off the hook so easily. "And what was that about being two steps above an intern?"

"I may have been slightly underexaggerating."

"Anything else that you've been underexaggerating that I should know about? Number of girlfriends? Wives? Children?"

"A dozen of each."

"Well, as long as it's only a dozen, I suppose I can live with that. That's it, though; any more and it would be absolutely scandalous."

Stefan looked down at their entwined hands. "You really don't mind that I didn't tell you about everything earlier?"

She shrugged. "You told me that there were lots of things I didn't know about you. To be honest, I thought you were talking about things like eating your steak with ketchup, but I can't say that you didn't warn me; it's not like you could just tell your brand-new girlfriend everything about your abilities, the super-secret task force you led, and then tag on just a little mention about being the second most important person in the MidWestern Pact Intelligence Agency. To be honest, in hindsight it all makes sense. I'm more concerned that I've known you for... how long? Three months? And that I'm just now finding out that you need glasses."

"Girlfriend?" Stefan's eyes lit up as he savored the word, apparently not hearing the last half of what she'd said.

Kaleo felt her face flush. "I'm sorry, I didn't mean to assume anything, I just thought that since we've kind of started dating... and I didn't know what else to call it..."

"No, no, don't worry. Calling yourself my girlfriend is perfectly fine with me." Stefan smiled, and then his face took on a more serious expression. "I promise I was going to tell you eventually about my job. There just never seemed to be a good time, and it always felt a little bit too much like bragging, and the glasses thing just never seemed like a big deal. Like I said, I rarely wear them."

"Don't worry about it, I understand." Kaleo glanced at the time on the clock and stood up. "I just wanted to stop by and see you since you always seem to be the one coming to visit me. I should let you get back to whatever you were working on. It looked pretty intense."

"Can I stop by later and see you?"

"I'm booked solid for the rest of the day."

"This evening?"

"Dinner with Lin." She paused. "Speaking of Lin, what are the rules as to what I can tell her about Saturday? She knows about how I was scheduled for the match, and about my abilities, but not anything else."

Stefan shrugged. "You can tell her whatever you want to. Lin seems nice. I don't mind if she knows and technically the identities of people on the task force aren't top secret—most of us just don't talk about it, and we don't release names and faces to the press for privacy reasons."

"Okay, thanks."

"Busy this afternoon and dinner with Lin this evening then? That sucks. I've got a full day tomorrow including an evening meeting that I can't miss." Stefan ran his hands over his face and glanced at Kaleo. From his expression, she hazarded a confident guess that the meeting was for the task force. "What about Wednesday? Wednesday dinner? I'll pick you up and we can eat wherever you'd like?"

"Wednesday works. I'll see you then." Kaleo kissed Stefan on the cheek and turned to leave.

After the match on Saturday, she felt that their relationship had both taken a large leap forward and noticeably regressed. It was almost as if now that they knew more about each other, they also realized just how much they hadn't known before. It felt like they were walking on eggshells when it came to physical affection, as if they were unsure as to where exactly they stood with each other.

Stefan's voice interrupted her thoughts. "I've got a little bit of time; let me walk you down."

"You don't have to. I'm pretty sure that I can find my way back."

He took her hand in his and held the door open for her. "I'm sure that you are more than capable of that, but this way I get to show my beautiful new *girlfriend* off to the office. The water cooler gossips haven't had anything nearly this interesting in weeks, and I've got to keep their appetites satiated or they'll start making up horrible rumors, like that I put ketchup on my steak."

Kaleo laughed and let Stefan guide her with his hand on the small of her back across the busy room full of people starting their day. When they walked past the reception desk, Stefan paused and led her over to Brian.

"Brian, have you met my girlfriend, Kaleo?"

Brian's face was almost completely impassive, but Kaleo thought she detected a muscle in his forehead twitch. "Yes sir, earlier when she had her meeting with Director Stone."

"Glad to hear that. For future reference, if she ever comes back up here to see me, you can send her directly to my office unless I'm in a meeting."

"I understand, sir."

After Stefan had walked Kaleo to her office and hugged her goodbye, she got back to work.

# Chapter Five

That evening Kaleo met Lin at a small cafe that was well known for both the selection of their soups and the wide variety of their salad bar. The atmosphere was relaxed and comfortable, and they loaded their plates before finding a table near one of the windows. The view overlooked a patio filled with a variety of flowers growing in pots and a small bubbling fountain.

Kaleo was always grateful for the chance to catch up with her friend. Lin had been swamped at work, and they hadn't been able to hang out lately over lunch.

"How has work been?" Kaleo asked as she dug into her food.

Lin blew on her soup. "Busy, obviously. We're trying to get a head start on research for some new bills that have been rumored to come down the pipeline soon. With the economy doing so well there's been talk of adjusting interest rates which means more work for us, and the Fraud Department has been practically on fire with how much they've been having to deal with."

"And you have to help out with all of that?"

"I'm usually more on the analyst side of things, but I've got enough experience with accounting that if fraud needs an extra set of hands or eyes they pull me over to help out." Lin took a cautionary spoonful of her soup, wrinkled her nose, and reached for the salt.

"I've been missing you at lunch, but it sounds like they probably need you more than I do," Kaleo said.

"More like they just don't want to pay me more for having to work the evenings," Lin grumbled.

"At least you get paid extra if you have to stay late."

"That's very true. Speaking of lunches, how have those been going?"

"I've been eating at my desk or with my coworkers if I happen to catch them on their way down."

"Not with Stefan?"

"Eating lunch with Stefan would be great... it's just some of his friends that are the problem."

"Ah, what's-her-name. The bottle blonde with the attitude. Ava? Amelia?"

"Audra."

Lin snapped her fingers. "That's it, like the car."

"... not quite." Kaleo laughed.

"Is she still being rude?"

Kaleo frowned. "The time I tried to eat with them most recently, she oscillated between being sickly sweet and making little barbed comments and backhanded compliments."

"Like what?"

"She told me that she liked the 'just rolled out of bed' casual look I had going on that day and that she admired that I had the self-confidence to try to pull it off." Kaleo wrinkled her nose. "I believe the precipitating factor was that I wore my hair down and it was more curly than usual."

Lin almost choked on her soup. "She said that while Stefan was there?"

"No, that was after he had gone to refill our drinks."

"I hope you put her in her place."

Kaleo shrugged as she finished chewing a bite of her salad. "I played dumb and thanked her very nicely for the compliment. Starting the drama isn't worth it, especially with me being the new person in the group and all. Right now it's much easier for me to just avoid that situation, especially because I get the feeling that if she crosses the line while Stefan is there he's going to say something, and then she'll dislike me even more. It's better to just avoid the confrontation for now." She took out some of her pent-up aggression by stabbing a piece of bacon. "Anyways, enough about me. What about you? Anyone on your radar since you broke up with Adam?"

"Not really. I still can't believe the nerve of that guy."

"What was it that he did again? Cancel a date because he was late to a doctor's appointment or something?"

"He canceled a date last minute because he had to get a haircut, and then later he tried to 'make it up to me' by having me host a party for him and all of his friends for the Abled fight championships, which included the expectation that I'd dress the part in a hideous kimono that looked like one of the costumes that the ring girls wear."

"Gross. The nerve."

"You can say that again. He expected me to do all the clean up too. Plus, after all that, he didn't even understand why I was breaking up with him. I'll never understand what it is with some guys and their stupid Asian fetish or whatever it is, especially when the only really Asian thing about me is my looks. For all anyone knows, my family could have been Americans for the past two hundred years."

Kaleo grimaced in sympathy. "Did you ever find out any more about your family? I remember that you said you thought you had a lead the last time we talked.

Lin shook her head. "It turned out to be another dead end. I'm still just as much of an orphan as ever."

"Only an orphan in name. You know that my family loves you, and if you weren't so old I think my parents would offer to adopt you to make it official," Kaleo teased. Lin had become a regular fixture at the Hughes' weekly family dinners since they had reconnected, and had only missed the one earlier in the week due to a lingering sinus infection.

Lin smiled, and the light in the room lightened a shade. "Hey, if your parents want to adopt me, tell them that I can bring the papers over anytime. I've always wanted to have sisters."

After her dinner with Lin, Kaleo drove to the training facility for her first lesson with the Professor since her match with Strike. The Professor was waiting for her and took her back to one of the private training rooms immediately.

"Katherine has informed me that you are expressly banned from all activities involving physical contact until your arm heals. Fortunately for us, Saturday exposed some deficiencies that we can now direct our attention to."

"Before we begin, Professor, I have a question," Kaleo said.

The Professor looked at her with one eyebrow raised, waiting for her to continue.

"Have you been training me this entire time for the express purpose of joining the task force?"

"I see that you've been talking with a few of my colleagues."

"You could say that."

The Professor shook his head. "When I took you on as a student, I had no ulterior motives; your story about your abilities intrigued me. What you do with the knowledge that you gain during your time here is completely up to you."

"You invited the task force members to watch the match."

"Any time one of their own is in a match, some of them show up; especially when it's one of their leaders. Is that all?"

"For now, yes."

"Good, then we can get started. What do you think was your biggest problem on Saturday?"

"Beyond being slow and letting my arm get broken?"

The Professor waved her words away. "That was strategy and lack of experience, which are things that we can fix with more practice. If you had more patience, you'd have had a much better chance. Surely you've figured out by now that your abilities are defensively-centered; when you go on the offensive, you risk losing your edge."

Kaleo pursed her lips. "So what was my problem?"

"What concerns me the most was the electric shock you delivered to Strike. I believe that was an accident, correct?"

"Correct."

"Please, tell me what it felt like to you."

The Professor listened intently as Kaleo explained what she had felt when Strike had surprised her and hit her arm. When she finished recounting her story, he nodded and walked over to a side counter where someone had set out a tray with several items on it. He first held up a clear bag full of water.

"The energy that you control is like the water in this bag, and your abilities are the bag itself, through which you can shape the water into whatever form you wish."

He squeezed the bag in the middle to create an hourglass shape and then set it down on the table and squished it flat to illustrate his point.

"Your abilities have grown to the point that you are now able to easily mold the water if you have time to prepare. However, sometimes events out of your control overwhelm you and even your powerful abilities are not enough to keep the water within its proper sphere." He pressed one hand against the bag until all the water was forced to one side and slammed a fist into it. The bag split open and a gush of water splashed them both.

"As you can see, when the container becomes overwhelmed, the results are not easily controlled and may get very messy."

Kaleo tilted her head to one side. "Would it be possible to strengthen the metaphorical bag that the water comes in so that it doesn't split open as easily?"

"Yes, but that only solves part of the problem—if you have any desire to ever seek out difficult situations or get back into the field, I can all but guarantee that you will eventually encounter a force larger than you can tolerate. Keeping that in mind, what other solution would you suggest?"

She thought for a second. "Perhaps trying to figure out a way to release the energy in a controlled manner so that it never builds to that point?"

"That is a better idea." The Professor took another bag filled with water from the tray and made a small cut on one corner. When he pushed all the water to one side and then punched the bag, the plastic around the cut corner was the first to rip, and the flow of water was more directed.

"Now, I believe that there's one more solution that may provide the best option for you at this point in your training. Do you want to guess what it is?"

"No, I'd prefer that you go ahead and just show me."

"Fair enough."

The last bag the Professor lifted from the tray had a valve on each end. He hooked one valve to a hollow tube that was connected to another gallon of water, and the second valve to a tube that trailed into a bucket on the floor. The Professor opened all the valves, and Kaleo watched as the water began to drain from the gallon of water into the bucket by way of the bag.

He repeated the same test as with the other two bags, but this time when he punched the bag, the water only gushed out into the bucket on the floor with extra force.

"How am I supposed to provide an outlet for my abilities if I can only use them in a defensive capacity? And while we're on the subject, why is it that I can only use them defensively?" Kaleo asked

"Your shield itself is one outlet for the energy; the harder, brighter, and larger you make your shield, the more energy output is required. Don't worry, we'll be working on both your ability to draw more energy from your surroundings and your ability to drain the same energy. As for the defensive aspect, I confess that I'm not certain; before you lost your abilities, were you ever able to use them in a capacity that was only offensive?"

Kaleo cast her mind back to all the missions that the Flock had run and shook her head. "I don't know. I think so, but my abilities as Canary only showed up when my danger sense was tingling. I was never able to activate them on my own no matter how hard I tried."

"It's possible that this is simply one of the drawbacks of your abilities then, although I'm not completely certain due to the chaotic power that was released when you were overwhelmed..." The Professor seemed to lose himself in thought for a minute. When he remembered that they were in a lesson, he shook his head as if to clear it. "It doesn't matter; we'll work around it."

For the rest of their lesson time, Kaleo worked on how to better feel the energy in a room, harness it, let it flow through her, and then release it. It was slow and tedious, and Kaleo felt like she was floundering while trying to distinguish the different types of energy and only draw what she needed from the flow. When she'd used her abilities before, she had let as much energy as possible flow into her and then kept it all bottled up to use as she saw fit. Now, modulating and taking only what she needed while still immersing herself in the flow was much harder, and Kaleo realized that she had an innate urge to hoard as much energy within herself as she could and then only use it sparingly. By the end of their lesson, she still hadn't made much progress, and her frustrations were beginning to mount.

The Professor assigned her the homework of continuing to immerse herself in the flow. "Remember that you're not a dam in the river that is trying to hold back the flood; you are a single rock that is only seeking to redirect the flow of the water," he said as parting advice.

Kaleo did her best to not roll her eyes at him; for all his talk about going with the flow, she felt more like an innocent turtle being cast helplessly adrift and heading towards a series of major rapids.

# Chapter Six

The next two days passed by quickly, and before Kaleo knew it, she was getting ready for her date with Stefan. As they'd arranged the day before, he picked her up and took her to a very nice steakhouse that overlooked the lake. Once they had both eaten their fill, he leaned back in his chair and looked at her with an enigmatic expression.

"There's something that I want to share with you. Do you mind if we head back to my apartment after we're done here?" he asked softly.

Kaleo felt her heart skip several beats. They still hadn't done anything more than kiss on the cheek since their match, and now he seemed to be turning the dial up to eleven. "I'm not sure if I'm ready for that yet. I mean, it's nothing against you, it just seems kind of soon, this being our third date and all. Don't you think?" she said as soon as she could find her voice.

Stefan frowned, the look on his face the same as when she had seen him concentrating in his office on Monday. Then, as he processed what she had said, his eyes widened and a crimson flush crept across his cheeks. "Oh no, it's not like that. I would never... that's just..." He paused and took a deep breath. "You're right, and I wasn't suggesting anything of that nature. I was referring to a set of papers that a mutual acquaintance wanted me to show you."

"In that case, sure, we can go back to your apartment," she said after breathing a sigh of relief.

Once dinner was over, they drove to a part of town in which Kaleo had never spent much time before, but that she recognized as being near the building where they both worked. Stefan drove into a garage and parked next to his red bike.

He led Kaleo up to the lobby, where he picked up his mail.

"I'm sorry, I didn't have a chance to stop by after work and have been expecting several letters," Stefan said.

"It's no problem. This is really nice," Kaleo said as she looked around. There were fresh flowers on the reception desk, and several nice paintings on the walls. A small chandelier contributed to the luxurious atmosphere.

Stefan led her back to the stairs. "Yeah, it's not too bad. I mainly picked this place because it was close to work and in the middle of everything, but it has its perks."

They climbed several flights of stairs before they exited the stairway, turned a corner, and walked down a corridor. The art on the walls and gray carpet reminded Kaleo more of a hotel than an apartment building, and when Stefan stopped in front of his door at the end of the hallway, she half expected to see a stereotypical hotel room on the other side with industrial carpet and beige furniture.

Instead, she was greeted by dark hardwood floors, stainless-steel kitchen appliances, and high ceilings. At a glance, it was apparent that Stefan's apartment was decorated as spartanly as his office; there wasn't much in the large open room beyond a couple of gray couches, a coffee table, and a few stools next to the island that separated the kitchen from the living room. The main decorations consisted of several framed paintings, and the far wall was made up mostly of windows. In the fading light, Kaleo could see that Stefan had quite the view of the city beyond.

"Well, what do you think?" he asked as he closed the door behind them and locked it.

"Very minimalistic and clean," she replied honestly, and wondered what he thought about her house, which was much more cluttered in comparison.

Stefan stood behind Kaleo, wrapped his arms around her, and moved his head next to hers as if he were trying to survey his apartment through her eyes. "You're right. I think I like your place better, though; it feels more comfortable."

They stood in silence for a moment, enjoying each other's company, when Kaleo remembered why he had brought her to his apartment.

"What was it that you wanted to show me?" she asked.

"Hmm? Oh, that's right. Let me go grab it. Make yourself at home."

Stefan disappeared down a hallway and Kaleo kicked off her shoes and settled on one of the couches. As she waited for Stefan, she entertained herself by looking out the window at the setting sun. The city's downtown area was painted in various hues of orange and pink, and she could just barely make out the glint of lake water in the distance. After several minutes, she heard Stefan's footsteps coming back.

"You have quite the view; it's beautiful," she said as he entered the room.

"I agree."

Something in his voice made Kaleo tear her eyes away from the window to find him watching her. She smiled and gestured back at the window. "I was talking about outside."

"I wasn't." He sat next to her on the couch and glanced out the window, green eyes glinting in the light of the dying sun. "It is pretty nice, though. In fact, it's one of my favorite things about this place." He held a large manilla envelope, which he promptly handed over to her. "Director Stone wanted me to show you this. I'm afraid that you can't take it home; I had to show it to you here because I sweep my apartment regularly for bugs, and it contains sensitive material."

Kaleo had a feeling that she knew what it was, and her suspicions were confirmed when she opened the envelope and pulled out a sheaf of papers with a cover page of Midwestern Pact Abled Task Force.

"Take your time and get comfortable; I want you to know exactly what you're getting into if you decide to take him up on his offer. Do you want any water or anything?"

Kaleo nodded, and Stefan got a glass for each of them.

"If you have any questions, feel free to ask," he said as he settled on the couch next to her again.

Kaleo took her time reading through the papers and then looked out the window to let the information soak in. There was nothing earth-shattering, but when combined with what she already knew, it definitely helped to paint a better picture of what would be expected of her if she joined.

The task force had meetings at least once a week, another two days a week of mandatory training with the Professor, and missions that could last anywhere from several hours to a couple of days. All of that would be on top of her current job, and any extra information gathering that the task force needed. Director Stone hadn't been kidding when he said that it would take up most of her free time. However, they were paid a good base wage, plus a bonus upon each mission they went on.

Kaleo's eyes widened when she saw what her compensation would be. She glanced at Stefan. "This sounds like it would almost be another full-time job."

"For you, yes, it probably would be."

"At least I'd be getting paid well. If I went on a few missions a month, I could probably quit working for Logistics and Trade."

"The money isn't bad," he agreed in a noncommittal tone.

Kaleo turned to look at him. "What do you think I should do?"

"As one of the task force leaders, or as your boyfriend?"

"Both."

He shrugged. "As Mission Leader Strike, I think you'd be a great addition to the team. We've got a range of abilities but are lacking in those geared more towards actual action; and no one has the defensive capabilities that I believe your shield does. Plus, you've got experience working on a team, which means that we wouldn't have to train you completely from the ground up."

"And what does boyfriend Stefan think?"

"He thinks that some of the missions are very dangerous, and he doesn't want you to get hurt... and there's no guarantee of how many missions we'll need you on, which means that you shouldn't quit your day job yet."

"Would we even still be able to be together if I joined? Aren't there usually rules about dating co-workers or teammates or something?"

"Not with this task force. They'd be crazy to try banning anything like that with the amount of Saban-40 in the air when we all get together. In fact, I'm pretty sure that Dr. Saban is trying to convince Nova and Director Stone to let him study us for more proof for his group-dynamics and Abled-relationship theories."

Kaleo couldn't help herself; she looked at Stefan with raised eyebrows. He laughed when he saw her face and squeezed her hand. "Sweetheart, there's no need to get jealous; we're not animals. In fact, as far as I know, no one's paired off yet."

"I'm sure that you got lonely on some of those long missions..."

"Not particularly, and definitely not with the more recent ones now that I've known I had someone special to see when I got back."

"And before you met me?"

Stefan shrugged. "The task force wasn't fully operational until your mother announced it after Adrian's rescue. If you'll recall, I met you the very next day. However, even if it had been operational before then, you of all people should know how it is when you're the leader and in charge of planning and executing a mission—if you do it right, there's not much time for anything else."

Kaleo knew that her expression was still skeptical; Stefan apparently thought so too because he leaned in close and whispered softly into her ear, slipping his arm around her waist as he did so. "No one on that task force can hold a candle to you, my dear. I knew you were different from anyone else the moment I first laid eyes on you."

"Bold things to say for someone who's been dating me less than a week," Kaleo murmured.

"I know what I want."

"Oh? And what would that be?"

"That's for me to know and you to find out."

As Stefan's lips grazed Kaleo's cheek and traveled to the corner of her mouth, his hand lightly traced her side—and then they were both gone, their absence sending a shiver down her spine. When she turned to look at him, she saw him gulp and take a deep, shaky breath, and she wasn't sure if his reaction stemmed from kissing her or from the contents of the second manilla folder in his hands.

"Almost two weeks ago you gave me your file to read. Tonight I wanted to return the favor." He placed the folder on her lap.

"Stefan, you don't have to do that."

"Yes, I do. I want this relationship to be built on trust, and it's hard to do that when I know much more about your past than you know about mine. You've been wonderful this week by taking all of the revelations about me in stride, but I don't want you to feel like that's going to be a regular thing. Granted, I had to redact some parts pretty heavily, but you should get the main gist."

"I appreciate it."

He stood from his seat on the couch. "You don't have to stay here to read it; I'll drive you home and you can take your time. I know it's getting late, and you've got work tomorrow."

"Are you sure? You stayed to read mine..." Kaleo asked as she thumbed through the papers.

"Positive. I even took the liberty of adding in a few handwritten notes as to past relationships throughout the file so we could really be on the same page." Stefan paused and made a face. "Nothing as serious as yours, and you'll quickly realize that there aren't many of them. Historically, I haven't had the best of luck with the ladies."

"That's surprising. I would have thought the opposite. You're quite the smooth operator."

"Maybe I didn't have the right motivation before... Or maybe you're just the only person that my special brand of charm works on."

Stefan gave her a smile, and Kaleo returned it before a yawn took over.

"If you're done reading through the task force packet and have no other questions, I'll drive you home now," Stefan offered.

"I hate to take all your personal information and leave you hanging."

"It's really no problem, we can always talk about it later. I just want to make sure that you know that I'm not trying to hide anything from you. I'm as much of an open book as you care to read, and as I can legally share."

Stefan took the task-force papers back into the other room, presumably to lock them up. While Kaleo waited for him to return, she glanced at the first page of his file, which consisted of an overview of his basic information. A couple of things had been blacked out, like his Saban-40 score, but Kaleo thought that she could almost see the numbers underneath. She listened closely to see if she could hear Stefan's footsteps, and when she was sure that everything was silent, she lifted the paper up to the light to see if she could make anything out.

"You won't be able to see anything. I'd hope that by this point in my career I'd know how to redact something properly," Stefan said, startling her. She whirled around to see him standing in the hallway with an amused look on his face.

Kaleo felt her face flush. "I was just admiring the quality of the paper."

"You're a horrible liar." Stefan chuckled as he held the door open for her and escorted her down to the parking garage. Once they were in his car, he looked at his motorcycle sitting next to them and then at Kaleo. "Would you ever be interested one day in taking the bike instead of the car? We can get you your own gear."

Kaleo looked at the red sports bike and considered it before shaking her head. "I'd be worried about getting in an accident."

"Really? I would have thought that'd be one of the last worries on your mind. Wouldn't your abilities protect you?"

"Only if I'm in contact with something like solid ground under my feet. No protection in the air."

"I get that. You're missing out, though. They're a lot of fun."

"Fun that I will be content to let you enjoy on your own for now."

As they drove back to her house, Stefan entertained Kaleo with stories about his mishaps on his bike, some of which made her laugh so hard she couldn't breathe. When they pulled into her driveway and she had calmed down, Kaleo told Stefan goodnight before she gathered her things and turned to open the car door. Just as she was reaching for the handle, Kaleo felt Stefan suddenly grab her other arm above her elbow. She turned back to look at him in surprise.

"Try not to judge me too harshly for what's in there," he said with a hint of panic in his voice.

Kaleo smiled and leaned across the center console to press a gentle kiss to his lips, her good hand holding his face in place. "You entrusting me with this information already means more to me than you could ever know," she whispered as she looked into his eyes. "I don't take this lightly, don't worry."

"If I'd known that this would be the reaction, I would have done it weeks ago," Stefan whispered back before returning the kiss.

After she had waved goodbye to Stefan from her porch and watched him drive off from her living room window, Kaleo settled on her sofa to read over what his file contained.

Stefan had certainly been a busy man; directly after high school, he'd enrolled in a military academy, joined a military special forces unit called the Rangers as soon as he was able, and then been recruited into his current job once his military contract had run out.

Kaleo could easily see how Stefan had risen so quickly to his current position, and also why the handwritten relationship notes that he'd scrawled in the margins of the report were so few: It seemed that when he had not been in training, volunteering for missions, away on missions, or preparing for missions, he'd completely immersed himself into the other aspects of his work.

Even in the past several months while she'd known him, Stefan hadn't slowed down at all. Most of the operations and missions that he'd gone on were for the task force, and all of them had been heavily redacted, although she could still read most of the dates. To her surprise, there were a few dates included that Kaleo hadn't even realized he'd been out of town for. As she read through the report and realized how much Stefan worked, she wondered if he was ever lonely.

Kaleo was surprised to read that his last relationship had only lasted for a couple of months and ended well over a full year before. There was also notably no mention of Audra anywhere in the packet, and she had the distinct feeling that Stefan wasn't the type to omit any details to avoid a potentially awkward conversation.

The next day when Stefan visited her office, Kaleo handed him his file back and told him that it changed nothing about her feelings for him.

"Not even how much of a workaholic I am?" he teased.

"As long as you make some time for me every now and then, I'm sure I can manage."

"Oh, I can do that. Stone keeps on telling me that I need to take more breaks anyways, which I've always thought is rather hypocritical of him considering the hours he keeps."

Kaleo smiled and wrapped her arms around him. "I recall you telling me not too long ago that I needed to learn how to have fun and not work so much. Maybe you should take some of your own advice."

He chuckled. "Maybe I just need someone to keep me in line and remind me. Think you're up for the job?"

"I guess we'll see, won't we?"

# Chapter Seven

Part of Kaleo's job duties included biweekly meetings with her boss and Governor Hamilton to talk about the various needs of the industrial and trade sectors for both the state and the Midwestern Pact. Some of the proposed plans needed approval by the governor, and he usually had questions about how bills that were passing through either the state or federal legislature would affect his constituents.

When he'd first been selected to be Senator Johnson's running mate in the presidential election, it was assumed by many that the stresses of the campaign trail would require Governor Hamilton to step back from the minor duties of governorship. However, he'd never forgotten his job, and anyone who knew him knew he worked hard to make sure that he continued to govern the state and the Midwestern Pact as effectively as he had before the nomination. It was through these meetings that Kaleo had formed a working acquaintanceship with Hamilton and his chief of staff, Todd, whom she had first seen at the meeting after the rescue of Adrian Hamilton several months before.

After one of the meetings, Todd pulled Kaleo aside and asked her if she would be willing to help coordinate a rally that the governor was planning to hold in Chicago in a months' time. Their current assistant coordinator had resigned unexpectedly, and Todd had been impressed by Kaleo in their meetings.

Taking on the responsibility of event planning on top of her regular job meant that Kaleo's workload increased exponentially. Despite her extremely busy schedule, Stefan continued to stop by and visit Kaleo at her office almost every day. He seemed to have a peculiar sense as to when she was particularly overwhelmed, and would sometimes bring her a snack to eat, or a trinket to brighten her day. Kaleo always offered to repay him, but he waved her offers away and stated that he was simply fulfilling his duty as her boyfriend by spoiling her. Eventually, Kaleo discovered that Stefan had a terrible sweet tooth, and she made sure to always have a supply of cookies and other desserts stashed away for him when he stopped by to visit.

Life began to fall back into a routine for Kaleo. She had thought long and hard about the task force for several days and then informed Director Stone that she would have to pass on the opportunity to join. After Todd had offered her the job to organize the rally, she knew that she wouldn't have time to continue her current job, organize the event, and participate in the task force, and the rally was much less of a permanent commitment. The director graciously said that he completely understood, reiterated that the offer remained standing, and that if she ever changed her mind, she was welcome to contact him again.

Kaleo continued her lessons with the Professor and slowly began to sensitize herself to the river of energy that he had told her about. Once she was able to fully immerse herself and feel the energy flow into and out of her, they began to work on her siphoning off only what she needed for her shield. As she progressed, the Professor encouraged her to create larger shields and bubbles, and to work on decreasing the time it took to erect them.

"Good. Now that you've proven that you can control the flow of energy, it's time to see if we can increase how much energy you can hold and utilize at once," he finally said after a particularly rigorous lesson.

It wasn't easy, but Kaleo eventually learned how to create shields big enough to fill a room from wall to wall, or bubbles large enough for her and several other people. Both efforts always left her exhausted, and the Professor continued to emphasize that she not only maintain but also increase her aerobic physical fitness as much as she could to limit the strain and fatigue on her body.

Between her work, event planning, lessons with the Professor, and her work-out regimen, Kaleo sometimes felt like she hardly had the chance to sit down and breathe, let alone relax or do anything for fun. While she could never be positive, judging by how often Stefan was gone and how many times her parents and sister had to cancel and reschedule their weekly family dinner, Kaleo guessed that the task force was also keeping everyone busy. There were brief moments when she felt left out and regretted not joining, but then she'd stop and laugh at herself for wanting even more on her already overflowing plate.

The one person whose schedule seemed to lighten was Lin, and they ate lunch together almost daily. Kaleo would also see Nicole at least once every week or two to work out together, usually followed by a coffee date to catch up. Even with Katherine's help, her arm still hadn't healed enough for any more matches or sparring sessions, but Nicole provided great motivation in their workouts and would occasionally drop seemingly innocuous hints about the task force that helped Kaleo feel a little more in the loop.

Despite their busy schedules, Stefan and Kaleo stole as much time together as they could. It became a common occurrence for Stefan to call and let her know as soon as he was available so that they could make plans before anything else could claim their time. They'd occasionally go out on dates, and sometimes on double dates with Adrian and Kiana when the other couple was visiting on a rare trip away from the new American capital, Lincoln, where Adrian's job had moved them not long after their wedding. Much more often, Stefan would simply join Kaleo at her house for dinner.

As the work began to really pour in, Stefan and Kaleo settled into a comfortable rhythm of dinner, a short walk, and then spending several hours curled up together on the couch working on their different projects. While they were together the time seemed to fly by, and it was always too soon and with an air of regret that Stefan would kiss Kaleo goodnight before going back to his apartment.

As the date of the governors' rally drew closer, and Kaleo really started to feel the crunch of the mountain of work that needed to be done in a very short time, Stefan suddenly became much more available and stepped up to take some of the pressure off her shoulders.

Whereas before Kaleo had been the one cooking their meals, now their roles reversed and while Kaleo was the better cook in the relationship by far, she appreciated Stefan either cooking or buying takeout once they became tired of the rotation of the five meals that he knew how to make. After they'd eaten, he would either pick a book out of Kaleo's collection or massage her neck and shoulders when she was particularly stressed. After several such evenings, Kaleo began to feel guilty that Stefan was wasting his free time watching her work.

"I'm sorry that I can't take a break from this. I know that I'm not very entertaining company, and I'm sure that you've got plenty of things that you'd rather do. Maybe we should reschedule our evenings until after this rally is over and I can actually pay attention to you," she said one night as he finished cleaning up the kitchen.

"I don't mind, I'd much rather stay here and spend time with you than go back to my empty apartment," Stefan said as he sat next to her on the couch and put his arm around her shoulders. "I'm perfectly happy sitting with you in the quiet and distracting you when you start to look too serious. Besides, it's a nice break for me to be able to focus on you and not have to always be thinking about my own work."

"What's been going on with that? Did you catch all the bad guys and now have nothing else to do?" Kaleo teased.

Stefan shrugged. "You could say that, in a way. Sometimes these things run in cycles, and we just recently finished up some old business. Things should start ramping back up soon."

"Well, I'm glad that at least one of us has time to relax."

"At least for now," Stefan agreed, his brow creased in thought.

Kaleo waited a moment for him to say what he was thinking, but when no further explanation seemed forthcoming, she reached up to smooth the wrinkles from his skin, and then drew him down for a kiss to clear the worry from his face.

# Chapter Eight

Finally, after several weeks of preparation, the day of the rally arrived. It had been a whirlwind of activity getting it set up, but Kaleo and Lucia, Governor Hamilton's event coordinator, made an efficient team and everything was in order. The night before the rally, Lucia insisted that Kaleo take off the first half of the day while she finished attending to a few last-minute details.

When Kaleo arrived at the arena, she spent most of the final few hours walking through the security details with Governor Hamilton's team one last time. The head of security, Michael, was a rather grizzled man who appeared to be a few years older than middle-aged, and his only distinguishing feature was that he looked tougher than nails. When Lucia had first introduced them several weeks before, Kaleo had recognized him as another face from the meeting with Governor Hamilton after Adrian's foiled kidnapping, and they had been in frequent contact leading up to the event. While Kaleo would never have been so bold as to even call them acquaintances, she respected Michael's dedication to his job and stern but fair nature.

The first half of the rally hummed along. The speakers before Governor Hamilton were top-notch, and the crowd was buzzing. Kaleo privately mused that if she could have manipulated the emotional energy in the room that night, she very well might have become one of the most powerful people in the entire world. Even better: Everything behind the scenes was running so smoothly that Kaleo almost felt like her presence wasn't needed; a welcome relief from the high-pressure days and exhausting nights when it seemed like everything that could go wrong would do so.

Governor Hamilton had just walked out onto the stage to deliver his speech when the radio on her hip flared to life and her blood ran cold. *"Security here requesting backup, we've got a possible bomb threat on the northwest corner of the arena."*

Michael's gruff voice crackled over the radio. *"Sending a team over, clear the area."*

*"Explosives team Alpha on our way."* There was a tense pause of several minutes. *"Team Alpha reporting in. We've got a nasty package here. Timer has thirty minutes on it, beginning to defuse."*

*"Understood. Teams Red and Orange sweep the arena for any other threats. All other teams begin evacuation procedures."*

Kaleo had been surveying the crowd from her perch on the sidelines but started walking to the designated security area to help coordinate the evacuation. Michael had already beat her there, and she saw him looking intently at a couple of computer screens connected to the arena's camera systems. Just as she reached his side, a frantic voice came from the radio. *"This is team Orange. Cancel evacuation procedures, we've got tripwires around the external exits."*

Kaleo's heart dropped into her stomach and then did a flip-flop when a second voice came over the radio on the heels of the first. *"Red team reporting in. We've identified a second bomb with a timer of less than six minutes."*

Michael's voice was as steady as if he had been placing an order for pizza. "Team Alpha, can you disengage from the first bomb and prioritize the second?"

*"Yes sir."*

"I don't like this one bit," Kaleo said quietly to Michael.

His face was grim. "Two bombs with two different timers and no way to leave the building without possibly triggering some kind of infernal booby trap. You have any ideas? Saved the son back in April, want to go a bonus round and try to save the father and a couple of thousand people now?"

"If worst comes to worst, I may be able to provide us with some protection."

He glanced at the watch on his wrist. "Well, hurry up and explain. We don't exactly have all day, you know."

"Get me something to cover my face and clothes first, and then I can explain as I work."

Michael looked at Kaleo strangely; she sighed in exasperation and looked around. For the moment, they were standing alone in a sea of movement as various staffers scurried to enact the parts of the security protocols that they could.

"Look, I've got some abilities, but I'd prefer to not broadcast my identity to the world if I have to use them, okay?" she said.

Michael looked at her for just a moment more before he reached under the table and pulled out a duffle bag. "Take this, it's got my motorcycle gear in it. Put it on over your clothes. You're thin enough that it should fit."

Kaleo grabbed the bag and walked over to where several sets of extra drapes had been left hanging in rows for easy setup and tear down. She looked around to make sure no one was watching, and when she was satisfied that they were all more concerned with other things, she slipped between the drapes and donned the gear.

It fit terribly. Michael's shorter stature meant that the pants ended a couple of inches higher on her legs than she was used to, the arms of the jacket were too short, and she felt like she was swimming in extra fabric from her bunched-up suit—but the helmet fit fine, although she couldn't resist wrinkling her nose and wondering when he had cleaned it last. Judging from the smell, it had been a while..

She circled back to Michael's station. It was surprisingly easy to get close to him considering she was an unknown person walking around dressed in all leather with a helmet obscuring her face, but Kaleo told herself that perhaps the security teams knew what their boss's gear looked like. Nevertheless, she made a mental note to talk to him about upgrading the security protocols if they made it through the night in one piece.

"Any news?" she asked when she reached Michael's side again.

"The bomb with the shortest timer is almost defused, and the staffers have managed to move most of the crowd to the center of the room."

"Good, see if they can get everyone as close to the stage as possible without causing a panic; I think I can raise a barrier that should protect from the worst of the blast if something happens."

"You think?"

"Do we have any other backup options at this point?"

Michael nodded and spoke the new orders into the radio.

At just that moment, Governor Hamilton ended his speech and walked off the stage. Kaleo watched as his facial expression changed from a charismatic smile into a deep frown as he felt the waves of tension, desperation, and other negative emotions that permeated backstage. Todd, his chief of staff, explained the situation to him in a low voice, with Michael adding input as Kaleo stood nearby. The governor readjusted his tie and squared his shoulders.

"I'm going back out there. You need someone to keep the crowd calm and as unaware as possible," he said in a tone that brooked no argument.

Throughout the night Kaleo had allowed the energy from the heat of the crowd, the noise of the speakers and the brightness of the overhead lights to flow through her like a river just like she'd been training with the Professor. Redirecting the energy into a bubble shield to cover the crowd was a simple matter in theory, but much more difficult in practice due to the sheer size of the area, and the immediate time constraints. Whereas in her practice sessions Kaleo had taken all the time she needed to compose herself first and then slowly open the flow of energy when she was ready, she no longer had that luxury and settled for maintaining as much of a controlled gush as she could. Before she began her desperate attempt, she repeated the Professor's mantra to trust herself and to trust in her abilities, hoping that hearing his words in her mind would help convince her heart of their truth.

As Governor Hamilton walked back out onto the stage, Kaleo began to work her magic. Only a few in the crowd saw what appeared to be a gossamer-thin yellow light creep up like a rising mist from the floor, and as she raised the shield, she also sought to visualize a framework for excess energy to flow into if need be. The last thing that she wanted was to cause an unexpected electrical storm on top of everything else.

As she worked, Kaleo reflected grimly that this was the first time that her abilities were being put into practice on such a large scale, and that she had absolutely no idea what would happen if the blast from a bomb actually did hit her shield. She tried not to think about what had happened with Strike when she had been just slightly overwhelmed, or how much worse the consequences could be now if she lost control.

It wasn't easy work, and Kaleo could soon feel her heart rate increase in response to the intense effort it took to shape the energy into a usable form. As she continued to redirect energy into the barrier and weave it into the shape that she wanted, the air surrounding her began to glow faintly with the same yellow light. When the shield's walls were just over fifteen feet high and had encircled the crowd, she felt a familiar strain that signaled that she'd reached her current limit of control and resources, and focused on maintaining the smooth, balanced flow of energy in and out of the barrier. Michael had previously excused himself to a different area of the arena floor to direct the security team's response with crowd control, and Kaleo had long since turned her radio off; the influx of energy that she was manipulating had caused it to only emit an annoying static sound.

"Michael told me to check on you. How are you holding up?" When she looked to see who was asking the question, Kaleo saw an older man whose clothes identified him as another member of the security team.

"I'm holding," she growled through gritted teeth. "Can't raise the barrier any higher or we run the risk of it folding in on itself or being too flimsy to work."

The new person checked his watch. "Michael sent me to tell you that both bombs have been defused and the explosives team has identified and cleared an exit path. The team's radio broke and Michael is worried that if someone is trying to sabotage the rally and they're listening to the radios, they'll do something drastic when he gives the all clear. He wanted me to tell you to drop the barrier so they can start implementing the evacuation plan."

Kaleo nodded and began to let the barrier dissipate, but as she did so, she felt the whisper of an all-too-familiar sense of unease and impending doom flit across her consciousness—a feeling she had long since learned to not distrust, no matter the circumstances. The hairs on the back of her neck stood on end and she hastily raised the barrier once more, feeding more energy into it to restore it to its former strength.

"Something isn't right. Tell Michael that I can't lower my shield until we figure out what's wrong," she explained.

The man looked at her strangely and shrugged. "Suit yourself, it's your funeral. I'll relay the message." He turned away, presumably to take her words back to Michael.

"Hey, what was your name again?" Kaleo asked, but he didn't appear to hear her question.

He was still walking away when a blast rocked the building.

Kaleo could feel the shockwave as it hit the barrier and was absorbed. It had caught her off guard, and she wrestled with the sudden influx of energy. On the heels of the first blast followed a second, third, and fourth, with no two coming from the same direction. The steady stream of energy she had been managing abruptly transformed into a tidal wave that threatened to sweep away all that it encountered.

Kaleo had never experienced anything like the raw power now assaulting her hastily-formed shield. For a split second she was afraid that the intense barrage would rip her barrier apart like a piece of tissue paper in a tornado, but somehow it held firm.

As the energy charged her existing shield to its limits and kept on coming, Kaleo was immensely grateful that she already had made plans for the overflow. The barrier increased in height and width until it was a shining bright bubble that towered in the air.

The crowd began to scream as the air outside filled with smoke and dust from the bombs, but the barrier still held. It wasn't perfect by any means; Kaleo hadn't had time to form a truly tight weave, and a brisk wind and some small debris filtered through, but they were minor inconveniences when compared to the damage that could be seen outside of the safety of the shield. Granted, they couldn't see much to begin with—the blast had knocked out the overhead lights.

Thankfully, the explosions didn't last long, and soon only the screams from the crowd and a few groans from the building itself could be heard. While the air outside was thick with smoke and dust, and as dark as night, the barrier shone radiantly. Within its confines, it was almost as bright as noon on a cloudless day.

From her vantage point, Kaleo could see that the security team had grouped around Governor Hamilton as he walked through the crowd to make sure that no one had been hurt and calmed their fears. Kaleo breathed deeply and looked around to check her surroundings for the first time since the moment that the first blast hit. As she turned her head, she saw that Michael was leaning against a nearby table that had been used for snacks for the staff and keeping an eye on her.

"Not with your boss?" she questioned.

"Those are some of my best agents. They'll stop anything before it starts."

"Except for a bomb."

"That's why I'm watching you."

"You think I'm a bomb?"

"No, I think if whoever set those bombs has a person on the inside right now, you just made yourself a priority target." He reached for a pistachio from the table and blew the dust off it. "Like this nut here. If I try and eat this as it is currently, it'll crack my tooth and I won't get anything..." He paused and flipped open his knife. "But if I crack the shell open like so, I can get to the meat of the nut with very little difficulty."

"Are you calling me a nut?" Kaleo struggled to keep her voice even; she couldn't resist the banter, but the exertions of the day were beginning to take their toll on her.

Michael's smile was the encouragement that she needed. "I'm calling you the person who just saved all of our lives."

As the dust settled, Kaleo could see the blast had knocked down parts of the outside walls and sunlight was filtering in. She could almost make out shapes moving past the holes, but had to divert her attention as Governor Hamilton walked up to her side.

"You, whoever you are, first of all: thank you from the depths of my heart. Second, are you able to turn off whatever is creating the barrier and let us through? We've got quite a few very frightened people here who would very much like to get away from this building, and I don't like how many of the columns and walls are no longer standing."

Kaleo nodded. "Yes sir, I can lower the barrier. It may take me a couple of minutes longer to lower it than it did to raise it, so that I have something to work with if I need to raise it up again in a hurry."

Governor Hamilton nodded. "Right, I'll leave you to it then." He turned away, but then paused and turned back to her. "And I'd like you to stop by my office on Monday for a chance to better express my gratitude. You can coordinate with Michael and Todd after we get everyone out."

"Yes, sir."

Kaleo watched him walk away before she began the tedious work of letting the barrier drop by drawing the energy in as if it was a flowy dress she was gathering around herself. She was cautious and meticulous in her work; her danger sense didn't go off as it had before, but she wasn't about to take any chances and gamble with any lives. The thrum of energy that surrounded her as she worked was almost painful, but she tolerated it because it meant that if she suddenly sensed something off, she could reverse the flow and have a new shield up within seconds. This wasn't something that she'd practiced with the Professor, but after becoming so accustomed to the fabric of her shield, it felt like second nature.

Several minutes of painstaking and arduous work passed until Kaleo had reduced the existing barrier to a height of approximately six inches. She'd done her best to pack as much energy into the barrier as she could, and its color had changed from bright yellow to a near-blinding white light that crackled and sparked at the edges. Kaleo thought she could hear a faint thrum from the barrier as well, although that very well may have been her imagination.

"Everyone can step over the barrier, but make sure they're very careful and don't hit it. If they go in staggered small groups and wait until the people ahead of them are out safely, then I can maintain this just in case we have another surprise," she said to Michael, who had kept watch over her throughout the entire process. He nodded and said a few words to one of his underlings, who promptly scurried off to notify the governor.

Several members of Governor Hamilton's security detail volunteered to be the first brave souls to attempt a way out. Unfortunately, the explosives squad had perished when the bombs went off, so there would be no help if another bomb was discovered. Kaleo could only hope that the blasts had been enough to set off any other traps, and that the evacuation would proceed without a hitch.

The first team made it out of the arena safely, clearing a way for the others as they went. Governor Hamilton had stated his intention to remain behind until everyone else was out, but he was overruled by his staff, and he and the remainder of his security team were the second group out. Todd, his chief of staff, stayed behind to organize the rest of the crowd into small groups and send them out one by one after the governor had made it to safety.

When she heard the signal that the last group was safe, Kaleo manipulated the barrier one last time. She was careful to hold back a very small amount of energy from the main force before she let the leftovers dissipate in a steady stream of light that was accompanied by a low humming noise. With the strain from maintaining the barrier finally gone, Kaleo took a step forward and stumbled, completely drained.

Michael was by her side in an instant, and she grasped his proffered arm, grateful for the support. She leaned against him for a few steps until the energy that she had kept back from the barrier fully incorporated itself into her body and she felt like she had the strength to walk steadily on her own. As they made their way out of the building, a gust of wind knocked a small piece of debris loose from above and it glanced off Michael's head. He groaned and put a hand to where he'd been hit; blood was already welling between his fingers out of the cut that the debris had left. Kaleo paused mid-step, but Michael kept on walking, completely unfazed.

"C'mon, don't stop now. Let's get out of this mess, and then we'll see if my head is about to fall off," he growled.

Once they were free of the building, Kaleo and Michael were greeted by the flashing lights of emergency vehicles. The first responders rushed up to her, but

Kaleo waved them off and directed them to look at Michael's head—she wasn't injured, she didn't want to remove her helmet, and Katherine could always check her over later if something came up. Michael let them guide him to a seat where they took his vitals. Once they were satisfied that he was uninjured except for a few minor cuts and a superficial head wound, they stepped away to get bandages for his still bleeding head. Kaleo hung back, unsure of what to do. The area was swarming with people, and she couldn't exactly just return Michael's gear to him and then leave in her car. In fact, she realized that her keys and other personal items were in a locker deep within the arena. As she watched the crowd and tried to think of her options, Kaleo saw the security guard who had approached her just before the blasts went off. She pointed him out to Michael and asked what his name was.

Michael furrowed his brow and shook his head. "You're mistaken. That's not one of my men."

"Are you sure? He was wearing security tags and told me that you had said to lower the barrier."

Michael practically jumped out of his seat "I never said such a thing," he hissed, eyes searching the crowd for the man he had previously dismissed. "Do you still see him?"

Kaleo had been tracking the man in question, but had momentarily lost sight of him when Michael reacted to the news and couldn't find him again. When she told Michael that she had lost him in the crowd, the older man swore.

"You think he could have been an imposter?"

"Must have been. That timing can't be a coincidence," Michael paused when the EMTs came back with the bandages and fussed over him.

By the time the EMTs had finished with Michael, Todd joined them, his planner out and a pen in his hand. "I was told by the governor to set you up with a time for a meeting on Monday. Please remove your helmet and tell me your name so I can get you penciled in."

"I, uh, am not sure that I can do that right now," she replied sheepishly.

He raised an eyebrow skeptically. "Why not?"

"Not many people know who I am, and considering what just happened, I think I'd prefer to keep it that way."

"Well, what can you tell me?"

Kaleo was still trying to figure out what to say when a polished voice from nearby saved her by saying, "If that's who I think it is, they probably don't want to tell you anything at the moment considering the hustle and bustle around us, Todd."

The owner of the voice stood just outside of Kaleo's peripheral vision, and when she turned to see who had spoken, Director Stone stepped forward and nodded in her direction, acknowledging her presence.

"Is she one of yours, Jason?" Todd asked in an exacerbated tone. He'd obviously had a very long day and by the weariness in his tone, he seemed to have resigned himself to the fact that it wasn't going to end anytime soon.

"Not at all, though not for lack of trying," the director replied before he turned to look at Kaleo. "You okay?" Although the helmet was heavily tinted, he seemed to have no problem looking right through the plastic and directly into her eyes.

"Tired, but otherwise all right."

"Good to hear." He turned back to include Todd and Michael in the conversation. "Why don't we all go somewhere quieter for a little chat?"

"Sounds good to me. I think I'm about ready for some answers," Michael said as he rose from his seat.

Todd spoke into his walkie-talkie for a moment and nodded. "I'm no longer needed here, and Governor Hamilton said that scheduling this meeting was top priority."

They piled into Director Stone's car, and he drove them to an unassuming building on the outskirts of town that Kaleo had never seen before. The director drove to the back of the building and unlocked several complicated-looking locks before leading them in.

Inside, Director Stone led them down several hallways until stopping in front of a door.

"There's a bathroom down the hall, third door on the right. You can use it to freshen up and take the motorcycle gear and helmet off. We'll be waiting in this conference room for you once you're done. Don't worry about anyone finding out your identity; this is a very secure area, and there's no one here except for us at the moment," Director Stone said to Kaleo.

After she had used the bathroom, changed out of the gear, and wiped most of the sweat off her face, Kaleo joined the three older men in the conference room. When she sat down, Director Stone had a thoughtful look on his face.

"Welcome back, Kaleo. I hope you don't mind—I took the liberty of catching Michael and Todd here up to date on your abilities and where you currently stand with the task force."

"By that you mean you told them what you think I'm capable of doing, and how I have so far rejected your offer of joining up?"

"Exactly that. Now, Todd just asked me if the task force had advance knowledge about the bombing."

Kaleo took a seat in one of the chairs as Director Stone talked and was immediately grateful for the opportunity to be off her feet; the walk from the car to the bathroom and then to the conference room, short as it was, had fatigued her greatly. She realized that she had drifted off in thought and fought to return her attention to what the director was saying.

"... So as you see, we had no real indication that this was in the works. If we'd known, we would have either asked Governor Hamilton to cancel the rally, or would have already had a team planted there ready to work, although I'm not sure that we could have done anything half as effective."

Todd nodded. "This is very disturbing news indeed. I expect that we'll have a full report from you first thing on Monday as to possible actions we can take from here out?"

Director Stone dipped his head. "Of course."

"Be sure you look into the guy who impersonated my team," Michael added. When Director Stone and Todd looked at him, he explained what Kaleo had told him and then their attention turned to her.

Kaleo yawned and walked them through what had happened, from the first bomb threat to after she had lost sight of the imposter in the crowd. Director Stone frowned and made a note on a piece of paper. "I'll have my team look into it. If you remember anything else, please let me know."

Kaleo nodded in response. Her eyelids felt like they were being weighed down by bricks, and she struggled to stay awake. Todd, Michael, and Stone continued talking for several more minutes before Michael glanced over at her.

"Gentlemen, let's table this discussion for another time. The hero of the day looks like she's about to pass out on the table," he said with a head tilt in Kaleo's direction.

Director Stone nodded and checked his watch. "I agree; you both probably have families who want to see you, and I believe that Kaleo's ride should be here by now."

The director walked the three of them back out the same way that they had entered. Kaleo handed Michael his gear as they walked and thanked him for letting her borrow it.

"No, thank you for what you did. I'm sure that after this we'll be seeing much more of it," he replied with a wink.

Kaleo briefly wondered what he meant, but then lost her train of thought as another wave of exhaustion crashed into her and all her concentration was spent on keeping her balance.

When they exited the back door, the sun had begun to set and there was now a second car in the otherwise empty parking lot. Director Stone told the three of them to wait a second as he checked to make sure that it was who he thought, and after he had walked over to the car and spoken a few words to the driver, he called Kaleo over. She took a step forward and turned back around, suddenly remembering that she'd never scheduled the meeting with Todd.

"Todd, does Monday morning at nine work for the meeting?" she asked.

Todd pulled his planner out of his coat pocket and checked. "Nine won't; is nine forty-five okay?"

"Yeah, I can swing that." She laughed hollowly. "I'm sure my boss won't begrudge me having to take off an hour or two for a meeting with the governor after the weekend I've had." She bid Todd and Michael goodnight and walked over to the car. On her way, she passed Director Stone, who paused to shake her hand.

"You did good work today, Kaleo. I'll be in touch."

Kaleo could only nod wearily in response. As she walked closer to the waiting car, Stefan's worried face came into view and he jumped out and ran over before scooping her up into a hug.

"When I heard about what happened at the rally, I was so worried," he said.

Kaleo felt herself completely relax for the first time in days, and returned his hug.

"What are you doing here?" she asked.

"Stone couldn't get a hold of your parents or Katherine, so he called me and told me that you'd need someone to pick you up."

"I'm glad it was you."

Stefan opened the door for Kaleo, and she sank into the car. She watched as Stefan crossed around to the other side and climbed into the driver's seat.

"How are you doing?" he asked as he reached for her hand and intertwined his fingers with hers.

"Exhausted, but otherwise I'm fine. Just give me a minute to relax and I'll tell you all about what happened," she said.

"Take your time, we're not in any rush."

Kaleo told herself that she just needed a moment to rest her eyes and ears in the silence, and then that she'd feel much better and not like her head was full of cotton. She leaned her head back against the seat and closed her eyes. Stefan's presence, the feeling of his hand on hers, and the warmth from the setting summer sun all lulled her senses and cocooned her in a feeling of utter security.

She was fast asleep by the time they pulled out of the parking lot.

# Chapter Nine

When Stefan looked over to check on Kaleo and saw that she was out cold, he smiled. He certainly didn't blame her; if the limited information he had was true, that day she'd been tested in ways she'd never been tested before. He'd been at his apartment catching up on laundry when he had heard a breaking news alert about the explosion over the radio.

Immediately Stefan had tried calling Director Stone to see if he knew anything. When he'd finally gotten his boss on the line, he'd volunteered to head over to the arena to help with either the cleanup or any rescue and recovery efforts that had been started. In truth, Stefan had been looking for any excuse to go to the arena so that he could find Kaleo and make sure that she was okay when the director informed him that he was already on his way there, and that Stefan needed to stay put and await further orders.

The wait had nearly driven him crazy; hundreds of scenarios flashed through his head in the time it took for the radio to begin reporting more information, and none were good. Stefan normally considered himself to be a patient man, but when it came to Kaleo something in his brain short-circuited, and by the time that he received an update call from Stone, he had taken to pacing around his apartment. He'd even briefly considered using his abilities to burn off some of the frantic energy that fizzed through his veins, but almost immediately discarded the idea—if Kaleo needed his help, he wanted to be as juiced up and ready as possible. Then his phone rang, and he sprinted over to answer it.

The director filled him in without preamble. "Kaleo is with Michael, Todd, and me at the task force headquarters. She stopped the blasts from doing any

serious damage and I had to get her away before too many people started asking
questions. I can't reach either of her parents or Katherine, and she needs someone to come and pick her up. Don't worry, she's fine, but not in any condition
to drive."

"I'm on my way."

Stefan reached the task force headquarters in record time and was just about
to exit the car and let himself into the building when a group of people walked
out. When Stone walked over to the car to verify his identity, he leaned down to
the window and gave Stefan a quick briefing.

"She's just about asleep on her feet, but I can't blame her. Early reports are
that there were multiple blasts in quick succession, and we have some evidence
of a saboteur impersonating Hamilton's staff."

"Are you going to need me to go into the office tonight or tomorrow to help
coordinate the investigation?"

Stone paused and studied Stefan's face. "No, I've got the in-person stuff
handled, and I'd bet my house that we're about to get serious involvement from
some clowns masquerading as federal agents. It's going to be a lot of politics
and posturing. You keep yourself busy making sure that Kaleo stays safe this
weekend. I don't think that her identity was revealed, but she's quite possibly
the only person who got a good look at the imposter, which makes her both the
hero of the hour and one of our most valuable witnesses."

"I'll do that. I'll call you when I get her settled. I don't mind helping coordinate over the phone and running interference if I need to."

"Sounds like a plan," Stone said as he straightened up and motioned to Kaleo
that it was safe to approach the car.

Stefan had never seen Kaleo look so haggard; the director certainly hadn't
exaggerated her condition. When Stefan pulled her into his arms to confirm for
himself that she was okay, he was almost overwhelmed by the pungent mix of
dust and grime intermingled with the sour scent of her sweat. He wrinkled his
nose in distaste, but then he felt her melt into him and forgot all about the smell.
He was just grateful that she was alive and unharmed.

He drove her back to her house and spoke softly as they pulled into her driveway.

"Time to wake up, Kaleo. You're home."

"Uhhhh," she grunted and shifted in her seat.

Stefan reached over and shook her gently. "Kaleo, wake up. You can sleep more inside."

She awoke with a start and looked around wildly. "What happened?"

"We're at your house. I need your key to unlock the door."

She settled back into the seat and groaned. "All of my things are back at the arena, just pick the lock or break a window or something."

Stefan considered the idea and discarded it. He only had one personal lock-picking kit and it was currently with his bike. Plus, he didn't want the unnecessary attention from neighbors thinking he was trying to break in, especially with Kaleo in her current condition.

"Well, then it looks like you won't be staying here tonight." He glanced at Kaleo and saw that she was already beginning to doze off again. "I've got an extra bedroom in my apartment..." His voice trailed off, the unspoken question hanging in the air.

"I'd let you drop me off in a cave if it had a bed and a working shower."

Well, that was settled then. Stefan didn't know where else to take her, and she obviously was far past the point of caring. He drove them back to his apartment and helped her inside. She'd fallen asleep on the way, and the interruption of her nap made the normally even-tempered Kaleo more irritated and emotional than he'd ever seen, and Stefan had quite the time cajoling her up the stairs. After the third flight of near-constant insisting that her taking a nap in the stairwell wouldn't be appropriate, he simply picked her up and carried her the rest of the way.

"I'm sorry, Stefan, I promise I'm not trying to be difficult, and I really do appreciate you. I'm just so tired," Kaleo mumbled after he deposited her on the couch and told her to wait while he got things ready.

He kissed her forehead. "I know, darling. You've had a very long day. Don't worry, I'll set some things out for you and then you can have your shower and go to sleep."

"Okay, if you insist," she said as she gulped down the glass of water and practically inhaled the granola bar that he handed her.

Stefan hurried to his room and grabbed a clean t-shirt, sweatpants, and socks from the pile of unfolded laundry still on his bed. He paused and considered his choices, and then added an old sweatshirt from his closet to the pile, just in case she got cold. Next up was the guest bedroom and bathroom. His family didn't visit often, but he'd occasionally have old friends drop by unexpectedly, and it never hurt to have a few extra bars of soap and other toiletries in the closet. Stefan set the change of clothes neatly on the bed, made sure that he had set out a towel and washcloth in the bathroom, double-checked that there was soap in the shower, and then went back to the living room.

The water, snacks, and brief naps seemed to have helped revive Kaleo, and he was grateful to see that her dark brown eyes, if not as lively as usual, at least weren't as dull as they had been before.

"Everything's ready for you," Stefan said as he led her to the guest room and showed her where the bathroom was, and how to work the shower. "I left a few things for you to change into on the bed, if you want to. If you need anything, I'll be in the other room, just come and find me or give me a shout."

After leaving her, Stefan headed into the living room to make some phone calls. The first was to Caleb and Nova's home phone. On the fourth ring he heard a click, and then the gruff voice of Kaleo's father. Once he had assured Caleb that Kaleo was fine, that there was nothing to be worried about, and that she was safe and staying at his apartment for the night, he hung up and called Katherine next. She didn't pick up, but Stefan left a message on her answering machine with his apartment address and an invitation to stop by the next morning and check up on Kaleo if she so wished. He did the same with Nicole and asked her to pass on the message to Lin, whose number he didn't have.

Finally, the last phone call Stefan made was to Director Stone. He reported that Kaleo was safe at his apartment, and then they discussed the aspects of the case and coordinated what parts Stefan needed to handle.

The sound of the running shower had long since stopped, and Kaleo had wandered into the living room and found herself a spot curled up on the couch by the time that Stefan was done talking with his boss.

"What are you still doing up? You need to go to bed," he told her as soon as he had hung up the phone.

"I wanted to tell you goodnight... and thank you for letting me crash here. I didn't mean to impose and be a burden, I don't know why I didn't just tell you to drop me off at my parents or Katherine's..." Kaleo's voice trailed off and she shot up from the couch. "My parents. They're going to be so worried about me!"

Stefan walked over and hugged her. "Don't worry about it, sweetheart, I've already told them, Katherine, and Nicole that you're okay, and Nicole is going to pass the information along to Lin. And don't worry about anything else either, you're never a burden to me." He felt her sag against him and guided her back to the darkened guest bedroom where he tucked her into bed.

"Sleep well, Kaleo. If you need anything, I'll be in just the other room," he said as he kissed her forehead goodnight.

"Just a kiss on the forehead? What does a girl have to do to get a real kiss around here? I should think that I've more than earned one," she purred as she wrapped her arms around his neck to stop him from drawing himself up. Her voice was husky, and her words already slurred from sleep.

Stefan laughed softly and bent down again to press a kiss to her lips. "Goodnight, my love," he whispered, knowing that she was far too tired to remember anything in the morning.

"Goodnight, Stefan," she replied sleepily before rolling over on her side and burrowing deeper into the blankets.

After Stefan shut the door behind him, he went back to the kitchen where he made himself a cup of coffee; he had work to get to. For the next several hours, he fielded some phone calls, made others, and began to consolidate whatever information he could gather from his informants in the field. He also spent a good amount of time sitting in the darkness between calls, thinking of both the events of the day and the role the young woman in his guest room had had in them. He tried to not think too much about his own feelings for her, afraid that it would only distract him from the task at hand.

It was approaching midnight and he'd just finished up the last priority call of the night when he heard strange noises coming from Kaleo's room. He switched on his answering machine and went to investigate.

Stefan knocked gently on Kaleo's door but threw all caution to the wind when he heard her cry out in pain. He opened the door and in the dim light from the hallway saw her thrashing around wildly. Stefan hurried to the side of the bed and pulled her onto his lap to hold her and stop her thrashing before she hurt herself.

"No, no, don't go... not the conference... Reader... Polygraph... No, stop. Let me go. I have to help them!" she cried out, her face twisted in pain—and even in his arms she continued to jerk in her sleep and shake her head, caught in the grip of some terrible nightmare.

"Shhh... it's okay, Kaleo. Everything is okay. You're safe here," he whispered repeatedly as he held her close and rocked her back and forth, his heart tearing itself into pieces at the thought of the horrors that her mind was subjecting her to. Eventually, she began to calm, and just as Stefan was considering how best to settle her back on the bed, she opened her eyes and looked up at him.

"Oh, Stefan... I'm sorry. All those people, I couldn't save them, I couldn't do anything. I tried to help, but I couldn't do anything, and they all died. I failed again." A flood of tears began to run down her face.

"Kaleo, you were having a nightmare. It wasn't real. You saved everyone today. They're alive because of you," he said tenderly as he wiped away her tears.

"It felt so real," she clung to his shirt as if he were a life preserver and she was afraid of slipping back under the waves and drowning.

"I know, sweetheart, I know. It's over now, though. Let's get you back in bed."

Stefan gently helped her get under the comforter and sheets and then began to stand, but was forced to stop when she lunged towards him and grabbed his arm.

"Don't leave me, not now. I don't know what I'd do," she whispered, barely loudly enough to be heard in the still room.

Stefan wasn't sure if she was talking in a literal or metaphorical sense, but either way it wouldn't have changed his response. He sat next to her with his back partially propped against the headboard and his legs stretched out in front of him. Kaleo snuggled up next to him and put her head on his chest and her hand over his heart. Stefan placed his arm around her shoulders and ran his fingers lightly over her skin in what he hoped was a soothing manner.

"Don't worry, darling. I'm not going anywhere," he said softly, and she nuzzled in closer.

After a few minutes, Kaleo's breathing grew deeper and more rhythmical, and he knew that she'd fallen back asleep. Still he didn't move until she rolled over onto her back and he was sure that she wouldn't be having any more nightmares. Gingerly, Stefan stood up from the bed and surveyed Kaleo's sleeping form. The intense expression that she had been wearing all too often lately had been soothed by the peace of sleep, and she looked so innocent and vulnerable that it took all his willpower to not lie down next to her and hold her close. Instead, he smoothed hair that was still damp from the shower away from her face and kissed her cheek before pulling the comforter up closer to her chin and leaving her to sleep in peace.

Stefan slept fitfully that night and rose with the sun. After he checked on Kaleo and was reassured that she still slept peacefully, he sorted through the messages on his answering machine and continued his work until he was interrupted by the phone ringing. It was Katherine, asking if she could come over to check up on Kaleo. Stefan told her that Kaleo hadn't woken up yet, but that she was welcome to come anytime. A few minutes later he also fielded a call from Nicole asking something similar.

Almost before he knew it, Katherine, Nicole, and both of Kaleo's parents were standing outside his door. Stefan let them in but asked them all to be quiet, as Kaleo was still sleeping. He made everyone coffee and set out whatever breakfast foods he had available in his sparsely populated fridge while they waited. Thankfully, Katherine had the foresight to bring donuts and Nova had brought a fruit tray, and as they waited and ate, he filled everyone in on what he knew.

They were discussing the implications for the task force when Stefan looked up and saw Kaleo standing in the hallway. Her dark brown hair fell in loose waves around her shoulders, and the wan look on her face from the night before had been replaced with more of a well-rested glow, although the dark circles under her eyes told him that she still wasn't fully recovered. Stefan didn't care. To his eyes, as she stood there in his apartment in his old clothes, she was one of the most beautiful women he had ever seen, and whatever words he had been about to say died on his lips at the sight of her.

Everyone else in the room turned to see what had caused the change in his attitude, and Kaleo was promptly swamped in a group hug. As her family and Nicole peppered Kaleo with questions over how she was doing and what had happened, Stefan refilled everyone's cups and set the kettle back on the stove to heat more water in case his girlfriend wanted anything to drink.

Once Kaleo caught everyone up to speed, assured them all that she was fine, and let Katherine check her over, Nova handed her a small duffle bag. "There's a change of clothes in here for you and some toiletries; Stefan told us about how you were locked out of your place last night, and I remembered that you gave your father and me your spare key when you first moved in, so we picked some of your things up on our way over here."

Kaleo thanked her mother, yawned and looked at the height of the sun outside. "How long was I asleep for?"

"A while. It's pretty late in the morning, but I'm sure that you needed it," Stefan said.

"I don't know why I'm so tired; I hardly remember anything from last night." She yawned again.

Nova and Caleb glanced at each other. "From what I heard, it sounds like you really pushed your limits yesterday. I'm not surprised that it drained you," her mother said.

Katherine nodded. "You'll probably be feeling pretty fatigued today too; you're not injured, but your body went through a lot and needs time and rest to recover."

Kaleo grimaced and stretched her neck and shoulders. "You're not wrong about that; I do feel really sore and stiff all over. It's strange, I don't remember feeling this way last night, but when I woke up it felt like I got hit by a truck." She excused herself on the grounds of getting ready and walked down the hallway to the guest bedroom, followed by her mother, whose concerns had not yet been completely allayed.

Once his wife and oldest daughter had left the room, Caleb turned to Stefan. "I take it that with recent events, you'll be too busy to be at the family dinner tonight?"

Stefan sipped his coffee to buy himself some time to think. "Not necessarily. Director Stone is handling most of the big stuff right now; my main job is to make sure that Kaleo stays okay until we know for sure that she's not in danger, so if she's up to attending the family dinner, then it looks like I'll be tagging along as well."

Caleb nodded. "Sounds good. We'll have a plate ready for you."

To Stefan's surprise, once Kaleo had finished getting dressed, she waved off her parent's offers to drive her back to her house, hugged everyone goodbye as they left, and took a seat on one of his recently vacated kitchen stools.

"I hope you don't mind me hanging around for a little longer. I just felt like we didn't really get much of a chance to talk last night. Do you have any questions for me? I know that I did a terrible job of staying awake and answering them like I said I would," she said as she sipped her cup of tea.

He shook his head and waved his hand around the apartment. "Stay as long as you'd like. Director Stone wants me to keep an eye on you until things settle down a bit more anyways. As far as questions go, I don't have any that haven't already been answered in one way or another by now." He paused. "Actually, on second thought, I do have one. Are you doing okay? Be honest."

Her brow furrowed. "Doing okay? Of course I am. Why would I not be?"

Stefan was going to tell her about the nightmares that had woken her up the night before but was interrupted by the sound of her stomach growling.

She scrunched her nose up in the adorable way that she did when she was embarrassed, and he decided to hold off on the serious conversations until they were both more well rested and had put some distance between themselves and the traumatic events of the evening before. He checked his fridge to see what they could have for lunch, and rather predictably found it mostly empty.

"I'd offer to make you lunch, but it appears that I'm all out of food," he said as he surveyed the scattered remnants of the donut box and fruit tray.

Kaleo made a face. "I need to go grocery shopping too."

"We can stop by the store on the way to your place. Just let me tidy up first."

"Oh no, don't worry about it. I can go later today, or maybe tomorrow after work. You can just drop me off at my house whenever you have time, or I can always take the bus home if you're busy. I don't mean to impose," Kaleo replied quickly.

Stefan set the last of the coffee mugs down to dry and walked over to where Kaleo was sitting. He reached up to cup her face in his hands and traced his thumbs across the smooth skin of her cheek. "Why do you always have such a hard time letting me take care of you?" he asked softly.

Her lips parted as she looked up at him and he had to make a conscious effort to not bend down and kiss her.

"I'm a grown woman, I should be able to take care of myself. I shouldn't need you or anyone else to help me... And I don't want you to think that I'm weak and helpless," she whispered.

A low laugh escaped Stefan's throat. "Kaleo, there are many things that I could call you: smart, compassionate, and stubborn being the current top three that come to mind... but never weak and helpless. Besides, like I said, Stone wants me to make sure that you stay safe until we know that the imposter that you saw won't try and tie up loose ends."

"So I'm stuck with you for the rest of the day then?" Her eyes were lit up by the teasing light that he loved.

"Afraid you are, sweetheart."

"Well, it's a good thing that you're cute then. At least I've got some eye candy to enjoy."

Stefan laughed at her teasing and helped her to gather her things before they left his apartment. His suspicion that she still wasn't back to her full strength was confirmed when she dozed off in his car on the way to the grocery store, and then again when she fell asleep as he drove back to her place.

He spent the rest of the day at her house, alternating between helping her cook and clean. When she got too fatigued and had to lie down to rest before they went to her family's dinner that evening, he contented himself with reading a book in the overstuffed armchair she had next to the window that looked out onto her front garden. At one point in the afternoon, as he glanced over at her sleeping form, curled up on the couch with a hint of a smile on her face, he felt his heart swell once again.

At just that moment, Kaleo opened her eyes and caught him watching her. "You sure have been very attentive today."

"Just doing my job."

She sat up and stretched out her arms. "I think someone was worried about me."

"Worried? When I first heard the news, I was terrified that something had happened to you."

"That's sweet. You must really like me a lot," she said with a smile on her face that he had come to know well, and that told him not to take her too seriously.

He put the book down on the windowsill and leaned forward, resting his arms on his knees. "Kaleo, last night I was practically wearing a hole in the floor of my apartment with my pacing when I heard about the blast because I was afraid that you'd gotten hurt..." His next words came out much more softly. "Afraid that you'd been killed, and that there was nothing that I could do to help you." He paused, overcome with emotion and feeling like the next words were somehow both on the tip of his tongue, demanding to be spoken, and also stuck in his throat. "I love you, Kaleo. I love you so incredibly much. These past few months have been wonderful, and I can't imagine what my life would be like without you in it."

There was so much more that he had to say, so much that he had wanted to tell her for so long, but he just barely managed to stop himself before the words spilled out like a tsunami. He'd known that he loved her for a long time, longer even than he wanted to admit to himself, but he had been afraid of scaring her off, of making her feel like he was trying to get too serious too soon. He had tried hard to slow down and bottle up his emotions, but now he couldn't have stopped himself from telling her exactly how he felt any more than he could have stopped breathing.

Stefan braced himself to hear her gentle rebuke that it was too soon, that they had only been dating for a few months and she wasn't ready for anything more, that she still needed time to get to know him, and that her heart still belonged to another. He understood, and he would keep on loving her until she was ready to reciprocate. He just hoped that he hadn't ruined everything and scared her off; he hoped that he hadn't just lost his best friend.

His fears were unfounded. As he was speaking, he watched a radiant smile spread across Kaleo's face. "I love you too, Stefan," she said, her simple reply every bit as genuine and heartfelt as his impassioned speech.

Stefan smiled with tears in his eyes and walked across the room so that he could wrap his arms around her and hold her, immensely grateful that she was in his life and that she had chosen to give him a chance all those weeks before.

# Chapter Ten

As it turned out, Kaleo's parents had spent most of their day helping clear the arena where the rally had taken place, and they were able to pull some strings and snag her keys and belongings while they worked. Thanks to them, she found her car waiting for her in the driveway when she and Stefan went to her parents' for family dinner.

Katherine was at work, Nicole was on a date, and Mod was out on a mission, so it was just her parents, Wiper, Lin, and Kaleo and Stefan. Wiper was almost apologetic when he asked if he could take a look at her memories and report what he saw to Director Stone, but Kaleo was more than happy to aid the investigation.

Stefan helped her mother and Lin finish getting the food ready in the kitchen while she sat with Wiper and her father in the living room. On the couch next to her, Wiper placed a hand on each side of her head as he had done many years before.

"Now, Kaleo, I want you to close your eyes and do your best to remember the face of the imposter. You might hear me start talking to your father as you do so; just ignore it and try to keep the picture clear in your mind," Wiper instructed her.

She did as he asked and felt a deep pressure behind her eyes.

Wiper began talking, and while Kaleo tried her best to ignore him, she couldn't help but listen. "Short brown hair... no, not quite that short. A wide forehead, wider, still wider, okay a little more narrow there. Got it. Now, brown eyes that are normal-sized, more round than almond-shaped and set just a little further apart. Heavier eyelids, a typical nose, yeah, there you go. Lips are pretty average, thinner on the top than the bottom. The face overall is moderately wrinkled and he's clean-shaven. The sides of his hairline are a little more receded than that, and he has just a hint of a widow's peak. Add a bit of heft to the face overall, maybe a little more to the jowls? No, take it away and add it to the cheeks instead. There, now just make the ears a little smaller and the chin more narrow. Yeah, I think that's about it. Kaleo, you can open your eyes now."

When Kaleo opened her eyes, she saw her father holding up a sheet of metal with the face of the man who had impersonated the security team etched on it. It was a remarkable likeness, almost uncanny in its accurateness. Not that she was surprised; to entertain her and Katherine as children, her dad used to have them describe scenes and do his best to recreate them on metal or stone tablets, and she had many fond memories of afternoons spent dreaming up things for him to make.

"Close enough? Have I lost my touch?" her father asked with a smile, apparently thinking of the same memories.

"It's almost exactly like how I saw him," Kaleo replied.

Caleb nodded and handed the tablet to Wiper, who stowed it away in a bag. "I'll get this dropped off to Director Stone tomorrow." He paused and laughed. "Actually, I'll just give it to Stefan before I leave. I'm sure that he'll see the director much sooner than I will.

They were interrupted by Nova calling from the kitchen to let them know that dinner was ready. The meal didn't take very long and was subdued as far as family dinners went, although that could have just been because half of the family was missing.

Once Kaleo was back at her house, she kissed Stefan goodnight only to be surprised when he produced an overnight bag from his car.

Kaleo shook her head. "Stefan, this is ridiculous. Go home and get some sleep. I'll be fine here. If anything, you should get that picture that Wiper gave you back to your apartment so that you can give it to Director Stone tomorrow."

"I'm glad that you're so concerned about the investigation, but it'll be just fine here tonight."

"Oh, it will be? So if it's safe enough here for the supposedly crucial piece of evidence, it should be safe enough for me, right?" she couldn't keep the smirk off her face as Stefan struggled to come up with a good argument.

He didn't give up easily, and it was only after a lengthy debate that she was able to convince Stefan to go home and rest. They'd compromised on Kaleo allowing him to check the entire house from top to bottom for anything suspicious, make sure that everything was locked, and then him insisting that she call to check in with him and let him know that she was still safe before she went to bed.

The next morning Kaleo arrived at work early and saw Stefan waiting by his red bike next to her usual parking spot. He opened the door for her when she turned off her car, and Kaleo couldn't help but raise an eyebrow at him. "I can't tell if it's Strike or Stefan being protective, but both of you need to calm down and stop treating me like I'm a child." She glanced around to make sure that they were the only two in the area and then leaned in close to him. "Don't forget that I almost beat you in our little match; I am more than capable of taking care of myself."

Stefan chuckled. "I see that someone's feeling a little feisty this morning," he replied before giving her a good morning kiss.

Kaleo dropped off her things at her office and fielded a barrage of questions and well wishes from the co-workers who knew that she'd been involved with the rally. Even her normally taciturn boss called her into his office to let her know that if she needed to take the day off or go home early at any point, he'd completely understand given the events of the weekend. Kaleo was grateful for the offer but let him know that she was perfectly fine to continue work as usual after she'd had her meeting with the governor.

The Capitol was only a couple of blocks away from Kaleo's workplace, and she made it to Hamilton's office suite in plenty of time. After she had passed through the security checks and notified his secretary that she had arrived, Kaleo took a seat and looked around. It had been a couple of weeks since the last logistics meeting, and only a few months since the first time she had first stepped foot in the building, but it felt like a lifetime had passed.

She waited in the reception room until it was time for her meeting and was then ushered into Governor Hamilton's office. The governor was sitting at his desk, Todd in a side chair, and Michael leaned against the opposite wall. The door closed behind her, and while Kaleo suddenly felt very much like a fish out of water, she did her best to fake her confidence and sat where Governor Hamilton indicated.

Hamilton surveyed her for a moment and smiled. "So you're the person I have to thank for averting a serious disaster on Saturday."

"I am."

"I suppose this puts me in your debt twice—once for my son and now once for my own life."

She shrugged his words off. "I wouldn't think too much about it; I was only doing what anyone else would have done if given the chance. Is everyone okay?"

"Beyond a few scrapes and bruises, everyone who was within your shield is fine. Unfortunately, there were several people either in the bathroom or working to defuse the bombs who didn't fare nearly as well. So far we have estimated the casualties at approximately twenty-five dead and five missing, of which Lucia is one."

Kaleo sighed and nodded. It wasn't a small number, but when compared with how many people had been in the arena it could have been much, much worse and she knew that she had done all she could.

Hamilton sat back in his chair. "But I didn't arrange this meeting with you to break the bad news—I wanted to extend my utmost gratitude to you and offer you a job with my office."

"A... job?" Kaleo wasn't sure that she'd heard him correctly.

"Yes, a job. Before I delve into the details, I have a question for you: Why did you feel the need to borrow Michael's gear and helmet?"

Kaleo took a moment to gather her thoughts. "Honestly, sir, I'm not sure. I think that growing up with my parents, and after hearing what happened to them and what they had to do once things got political, it just seemed like a natural choice to protect my own identity."

"I see." Governor Hamilton nodded and glanced over at Todd. "In that case, I think you may appreciate the somewhat unorthodox position that we have created for you."

"I'm listening."

"First and foremost, Michael has insisted that I hire you as part of my security team. We aren't certain yet, but the bombing this weekend was well coordinated, and we're afraid that it won't be the last such occurrence. We feel that having someone who is proven in thinking quickly and deflecting the blasts will provide us with both a safety net, and a means of deterrence. It'll be up to you and Michael about how best to protect your identity and what your exact duties would be. Secondly, you will need access to my office and staff on a day-to-day basis, which is where Todd comes in."

Todd leaned forward and handed Kaleo a small booklet. "We would officially hire you as one of my aides. With your background and work experience, it wouldn't be suspicious if we made the hire, especially after your work on this most recent rally and the fact that our staff has been somewhat depleted."

"My work on the most recent rally that blew up?"

"It was very well organized, and signing off on the security for it wasn't technically part of your role."

"What exactly would the new job entail?"

"The duties would be suitably nebulous so as to give me leeway in choosing projects for you to work on and give you plenty of excuse for being away from the office for long periods of time; a perfect disguise for if you had to be out with Governor Hamilton at his events... or on other assignments."

Kaleo sighed and looked at the governor. "So to summarize, you're offering me a job working under Michael as part of your security detail where I would be accompanying you to all of your campaign events, and also a job working for Todd as one of his aides for the rest of the time? That sounds like two full-time jobs rolled into one monster package."

"Your work as an aide won't be too strenuous, more of a cover story than anything; plus, the position comes with a rather nice compensation package relative to its responsibilities if you will look at the second page of the booklet," Todd said.

Kaleo did as he directed and took note of the large salary increase that the job would give her. As she scanned the page for a summary of her compensation, duties and responsibilities, a small paragraph towards the bottom caught her eye.

"Liaison between the governor's office and the Midwestern Pact Abled Task Force?"

Todd nodded. "I spoke with Director Stone yesterday and was made aware of some of the reasons for your reluctance to join the task force. This position will enable you to have a high enough security clearance and authority to be in the room with the task force leadership while also keeping you separate from them. You will officially be reporting to Michael and me, and by extension the governor, not to Director Stone."

"How do they feel about that?"

"It's a tradeoff that they're willing to make. We've got a good working relationship with Stone and he was very keen to add you to the task force, so it shouldn't put you into an awkward position. As a liaison, you'll also have the ability to pick and choose what missions you want to go on with them; or if you would rather not go on any missions at all," Michael said.

Kaleo frowned. "So I take this job and have to alternate between stopping anyone who tries to blow Governor Hamilton up, helping Todd out, and attending task force meetings to make sure that we're all on the same page? Forgive me for my cynicism, but what's the catch here?"

"The 'catch,' if you want to call it that, is that you'll be placing yourself in potential danger fairly often," Michael said.

"It would also be good to note that as part of Governor Hamilton's security, you'll be traveling with us off and on for the next three months, until the election is over," Todd added.

"And when it is over? If we win does that mean I will need to relocate to Lincoln with everyone else?"

"We can talk about that after the election, but rest assured that we'll find you suitable employment no matter what happens."

The governor looked at Kaleo. "I understand that this is a lot to absorb—why don't you take a day or two to think about it?"

"I can do that. Thank you," Kaleo said as she shook his hand and added the booklet Todd had given her to the briefcase she'd brought to the meeting.

Michael escorted her out of the room to the entrance of the building. She appreciated that he didn't try to fill the silence with chatter, but simply walked beside her to make sure that she knew where to go. Kaleo paused on the steps to revel in the warmth of the summer sun.

"If you don't mind me saying, we're all hoping that you take this job. It will provide a much-needed sense of security," Michael said casually as he looked straight out, his eyes scanning the area in front of them.

"Are things that bad?"

"Off the record? Yeah, I think so. Both Stone and I have our teams working on this case, but the explosion knocked out all the camera footage in the arena, and we're not much closer to understanding what happened now than we were right after the blasts went off. All we know is that the attack was well planned and well executed, with several backup fail-safes. What I do know for sure is that there weren't any bombs when I did my final walkthrough before the rally. That lends credit to the theory that the people behind the bombing had a man on the inside."

"Architect made a sketch from my memories last night. Do you think that it'll help at all?"

Michael shrugged. "It might, but my gut says that whoever you saw yesterday is probably long gone by now."

"What if I'm part of the team and this is all a ploy to get me into Hamilton's inner circle?"

"If that's the case, it'll show up in the background check and psychological testing that's mandatory for all our new hires." Michael smiled. "Although the fact that you're suspicious enough to ask such a question makes me think that you'll be a great fit to my team."

"Sounds like I don't have much of a choice then." Kaleo sighed. "I should have known that Director Stone and my mother wouldn't give up on recruiting me so easily. They couldn't do it directly anymore, so they tried the roundabout way instead, through Todd."

"It was my idea to create the position." Kaleo glanced at Michael, and his face remained impassive as he spoke. "Yesterday Stone gave me the file that he had on you. It was quite impressive, but I think I understand why you didn't want to add the responsibility of the task force to your current job."

"And why do you think that would be?"

"Stone seems to think it's an aversion to nepotism... I think that you know your limits and yourself. You strive for excellence and wouldn't have been happy if you were stuck with two jobs and felt like you were only mediocre at both of them. Plus, I may be wrong, but I get the feeling that you have enough ambition to not be satisfied with a position as low man on the totem pole."

"You may be right." Kaleo shrugged. "You may both be right."

"It's not a bad thing, and this won't be a bad deal. I'd want you to work with me like you did on Saturday. Todd'll find you something to do to keep you occupied in your down time, and you can decide on your own terms how much you want to participate in the task force beyond their weekly meetings or whatever they have going on."

"You make it sound almost too laid back."

Michael chuckled. "If I thought that you were the type to take advantage of a relaxed attitude, we wouldn't be having this conversation."

Kaleo checked her watch. "I'll think seriously about your offer. I better get going."

"All right, I'll see you around then."

She had already taken a few steps down the stairs when she heard Michael call her name out. She turned to see him looking at her intently. "Now, remember that you do have a choice; if you decide not to accept our offer there won't be any hard feelings, and we'll make do," he said.

She nodded and walked back to her office, many thoughts swirling in her head.

At the office, Kaleo found that she couldn't focus. It was a slow workday; she had finished several of her projects the week before and no new ones had come across her desk yet. Anything affected by the bombing had already been given to her coworkers.

By the time lunch rolled around, Kaleo decided to go home early. She had spent several hours trying to make headway on a few lesser projects, but her mind kept on drifting back to the booklet in her briefcase. On her way out, she let both her boss and the office secretary, Stacey, know that she wasn't feeling well, and that after lunch she was heading home to try and rest more. Stacey gave her a hug and told her to not push herself too hard, and her boss nodded sagely as if he had been expecting her to go home early anyway.

Kaleo met Lin at lunch and they spent most of the time talking about Lin's weekend; they had already talked on the phone the day before about the bombing, and they knew better than to talk about confidential matters in a room full of strangers who might or might not have abilities that would allow them to eavesdrop. Kaleo kept an eye out for Stefan but wasn't surprised when he didn't make an appearance at the cafeteria, as she assumed that he was swamped with work.

Just as they were finishing their lunch, Audra walked up to their table. Lin shot Kaleo a look; Audra had so far stuck to making rude faces and snide comments in passing at Kaleo but had never made the effort to actually seek her out.

"Hello, Kaleo, I heard that you had quite the weekend. Are you doing okay?" Audra's tone was saccharine.

"I'm doing just fine, Audra, thank you for asking."

"I'm sure that must have been so scary for you—all those bomb threats and not knowing if you'd survive or not." Audra clicked her tongue. "Not to mention that I hear from the grapevine that you were the event coordinator in charge of everything. How does it feel to know that if it hadn't been for that random Abled person, your lack of attention to detail would have meant all those people's deaths would have been on your hands?"

The expression on Lin's face turned stormy, and the light over their table dimmed. Kaleo knew what the sudden change in lighting conditions meant and shook her head ever so slightly at Lin before turning back to Audra.

"To be completely honest, Audra, I felt horrible about it at first, but then I talked to Stefan afterwards and he assured me that he hadn't heard any whispers, and that there was no way I could have done anything differently to prevent it. He was so sweet to make sure that I didn't feel guilty for something completely out of my control," Kaleo said as calmly as she could, even as her hands under the table balled into fists.

"I didn't know that Stefan was at the rally." Audra studied her nails and Kaleo took note that they had been painted a deep red, a suitable color for the topic of the conversation.

"He wasn't." Kaleo decided that the color reminded her of bloody claws. She tore her eyes away from the sight and donned her sweetest and most innocent smile as she looked up at Audra. "I'm surprised your grapevine didn't tell you about how my keys were lost in the blast, so he picked me up and I spent the night at his place."

Audra's smile didn't change, but her eyes narrowed and Kaleo knew that she had scored a hit.

"That was sweet of him, but then again, he's always such a good friend to everyone." Audra's previously cloying tone now had a bite to it, and she turned on her heel to leave without another word.

Kaleo couldn't stop herself from giving one last parting shot. "Actually, he's more than just my friend, you know. He's my boyfriend." She turned back to Lin and spoke just loudly enough for Audra to still hear her. "Lin, you should have seen how adorable he was. He spent most of yesterday doting on me and making sure that I was doing okay, and I practically had to beg him to leave me alone last night."

Lin laughed. "She's gone now, Kaleo, you can lower your voice."

"That's good, I didn't have anything else to say." Kaleo took a deep breath and struggled to calm the shaking hands she had been hiding in her lap. "What kind of person just walks over and says awful things like that?"

"Apparently the kind that hasn't learned to leave you alone yet. Are you okay?"

"Yeah, I just wasn't expecting that. I'm already scheduled to head home after lunch today, and I'm sure that I'll be fine when I get a chance to decompress."

"Want to stop by my place later? I feel like we haven't had much of a chance to catch up lately between my work and your side projects. We can invite Nicole too and make a girls' night out of it."

Kaleo nodded. "That sounds perfect."

After she left work, Kaleo went to the gym to work off some steam, as the exchange with Audra had gotten under her skin more than she'd let on to Lin. The exercise helped her to clear her head a little, but no matter what she did, she still didn't feel quite like herself.

She was surprised to see Stefan's bike at her house when she pulled into the driveway. He was waiting for her on her porch and trotted down the steps at the sight of her car.

"Shouldn't you be working?" she asked him as he opened the car door for her.

"There's only so much we can do in one day. The lab is still running several samples, and our list of current suspects isn't so long that I couldn't run out for a bit."

"What are you doing here?"

"I stopped by your office only to have Stacey tell me that you went home early because you weren't feeling well. I was worried about you."

Kaleo began to get frustrated as she unlocked her front door. "How many times do I have to tell you that I'm fine before you believe me? You don't have to come running every time I get a scratch. I don't need you to hover all the time." Her voice became more heated with every word that she spoke, and she tossed her keys into their bowl with more force than necessary.

"What happened to you wasn't just a scratch. I'm just trying to make sure you don't push yourself too hard."

"You're right: thanks to my abilities it was even less than a scratch. I'm not some damsel in distress, Stefan. I can take care of myself."

He muttered something under his breath, and Kaleo turned around in a fury. She knew that she was taking her anger out on him, but she couldn't control herself; her emotions felt all off kilter. "What was that you said?" she hissed.

Stefan threw his hands in the air. "I said that the next time you're thrashing around and crying out in your sleep, I'll remember to just leave you alone because you apparently don't need me or my help!"

Kaleo stared at him. "What are you talking about?"

He leaned against the back of the couch and folded his arms across his chest. "Do you really not remember Saturday night?"

Kaleo shook her head and he sighed before explaining what had happened after she'd fallen asleep.

As he talked, her anger and aggressive feelings receded like the tide, and a sense of shame came over Kaleo. She hung her head, hardly able to look him in the face.

"I'm so sorry, Stefan. I had no idea. I've had the weirdest day, and I don't know what's come over me." Her voice had become thick with emotion.

Stefan was immediately concerned and pulled her into a hug. "Do you want to talk about it?"

As they stood like that, with his arms wrapped around her body and his presence comforting her, Kaleo told Stefan about the meeting she'd had with Governor Hamilton and the others, and how she hadn't been able to focus all day.

"And then Audra added onto all of that."

Kaleo leaned back to look at Stefan in surprise and he shrugged. "I had already stopped by to check on you right after lunch, but Stacey told me that you'd gone home for the day. Not too long after, Lin came up to my office." He grimaced at the memory. "It wasn't until after she'd been whisper-shouting at me for over five minutes that I even found out about what Audra had said to you at lunch. Why haven't you told me that Audra was making life difficult for you? Don't you know that I'd have stopped it if I had known?"

"You knew Audra and that group before you knew me, and I didn't want to be the new girl causing drama with your friends," she said.

Stefan's expression deepened into a frown. "Is it true then? That's why you haven't been eating lunch with me?"

"Who told you that?"

"Lin, in between making my office look as dark as a cave and ripping me a new one."

"She really shouldn't have done that; I'll have to talk to her later..." Kaleo said and then the full force of his words hit her. She backed out of his embrace and stood with her eyes filling with tears and her hand over her mouth.

"Kaleo? What's wrong? Don't cry, sweetheart, it's okay. There's no reason for tears. I'll talk to Audra and tell her that she's been out of line and that I won't tolerate it. No one's going to bully my girlfriend without having to answer to me." Stefan reached out to her and tried to wipe the tears away from her face.

"It's not okay! And it's not about Audra. I was so rude to you, and you were just trying to check on me."

"You were frustrated with me, and that's perfectly fine. Maybe you're right and I've been too clingy. I am sorry for that—I was just so afraid that something had happened to you when I heard about the explosions." He pulled her close again and held her. "You are strong, and capable, and I've never had any doubt at all that you can take care of yourself. I just love you so much that seeing you hurting, or thinking of you hurting, makes me hurt too."

"You're too patient with me." Her words were muffled against his chest.

Stefan kissed the top of her head. "I believe it's the other way around, actually. I'm obviously still trying to figure out the whole boyfriend thing and how to balance wanting to protect you from everything and not completely smothering you. I'll admit that it's a hard lesson to learn, especially when you look as adorable as you do." Kaleo could hear the tender smile in his voice.

Kaleo sniffed, and then realized that her nose was running. She broke away from Stefan's arms to grab a towel from the kitchen to wipe her nose. Once she was done, she eyed his suit jacket and dearly hoped the large wet spots were tears from her eyes, and not snot from her nose. "Sorry about that," she apologized.

Stefan looked down and shrugged. "Guess that's my punishment for not giving you enough space," he teased.

Her heart twisted and she gave him another hug with the snot towel still in one of her hands, just in case.

"Now tell me, what are you going to do about the new job?" he asked after a couple of minutes of silence.

"I think I have to take it. There's no reason not to. It's a good career move, and I can do more in the governor's office than in the logistics department." She looked at him with a mischievous glint in her eyes. "Will Strike be able to contain himself if Phoenix gets a little bruised and battered every now and then on a mission?"

Stefan's arms tightened briefly before relaxing, and he smiled down at her. "I think Strike can manage it as long as you let Stefan hover afterwards."

"That's a deal then," she said and sealed it with a kiss.

# Chapter Eleven

After Stefan left to go back to work, Kaleo took a long shower and still had time for a short nap before she had to go to Lin's. When she arrived at the apartment, Lin greeted her at the door dressed in sweatpants and an old t-shirt. Nicole had already arrived and was lounging on the couch, eating a slice of pizza.

"How was your day, Kaleo?" Nicole asked with a full mouth.

"Could have been better."

"I heard that Audra tried to pick a fight with you and Lin almost punched her teeth in."

Kaleo looked at Lin, who shrugged. "I just filled her in on what happened; you know that she likes to be dramatic."

"As dramatic as you storming up to Stefan's office and reading him the riot act?" Kaleo asked as she grabbed a handful of chips from the bowl on Lin's countertop.

Nicole sat up. "Lin? You didn't."

"Someone needed to tell him what was going on, and Kaleo obviously wasn't going to do it," Lin sniffed.

"I'm proud of you, Lin." Nicole raised her half-eaten slice of pizza in a toast to Lin. "How did he take it?"

Kaleo interrupted before Lin could answer, a grin on her face. "I think she may have scared him a little. He certainly seemed to waste no time in driving to my house to make sure that I was doing okay and ask me about it."

"As he should have. I can't believe that you didn't tell him *anything* about what's been going on. He was absolutely shocked when I explained in no un-certain terms exactly why you've been declining his lunch invitations," Lin said.

"Yeah, well, now it's out in the open," Kaleo said as she poured herself a glass of wine.

"Don't you worry about Audra. I'll get it taken care of," Nicole growled.

"Stefan already said he'd talk to her."

"What's he going to do? Take her aside privately and ask her nicely to stop? Knowing her, she'd probably enjoy the attention from him. I'll talk to Stefan tomorrow and tell him not to worry about it." Nicole cracked her knuckles. "He's a good guy, but he's got to be professional about things. Fortunately for you both, Audra knows better than to mess with me, and everyone on the task force knows that they need me way more than I need them."

"Nicole..."

"Nope, already made up my mind. Anyone who messes with Blast's friends should be prepared to get burned."

"Do you practice saying things like that in the mirror?" Lin teased.

"No, I do it in the shower where all my best thinking happens."

The three of them talked for several hours as they worked their way through the food. Something about being with her friends helped to center Kaleo, and as she spent more time in their company, she felt the barbs from Audra work their way out of her skin and disappear under the comforting weight of the greasy pizza and salty snacks.

When it was time to go home, Kaleo hugged Nicole and Lin goodbye, and they all agreed they should have a designated girls' night more often.

The next day, she notified Todd that she was accepting the job offer and told her boss that he would need to start seeking a replacement for her. He was a pompous old man who hadn't made things easy for Kaleo during her short time in the Logistics and Trade Division, but even he could understand the significance of the promotion, and what working directly under Hamilton's chief of staff could mean for her career prospects.

Even though she wasn't officially due to start her new job for a couple of weeks, Kaleo decided that it wouldn't hurt to start attending the task force meetings. She knew that once she started working and spending more time on the road with Governor Hamilton's campaign, it would be much more difficult to attend the meetings, and she wanted to try and get to know her new teammates as much as she could before work took her away.

Truth be told, she was nervous about her role in the task force. Kaleo knew there was nothing to worry about—out of the six people currently on the leadership board, including herself, she was dating one, sister to one, and the daughter of another, with the two unrelated members being the Professor and Director Stone. However, no matter how many times she told herself that everything was going to be okay, she still couldn't shake the feeling that she had to prove that she was worthy of the position on her own merits.

As the official representative from the Governor's Office, Kaleo had clearance to attend both the general information and the leadership planning meetings.

Fortunately, due to the timing of the meetings and her official hire date, Kaleo had the chance to dip her toes into her new role by attending one of the general information meetings required for all task force members before she would have to attend the meeting reserved for the leadership.

Once they heard she had accepted her role as liaison, Kaleo's parents gave her a tour of the former old gym the task force now called home. She had seen it before, albeit in a very limited way, when Director Stone had taken her there after the rally bombing. The building itself was medium-sized, and had more than enough room for a lobby, gym, a lecture room, a couple of interrogation rooms, a full kitchen, and a smaller wing with a few dorm rooms and bathrooms.

"Of course you won't be staying in the rooms unless you're about to go on a long mission that leaves early in the morning," her mother said. "We used to not require that... but after several incidents we came to the conclusion that it was best to make sure that everyone is at least all in one place the night before they are scheduled to depart."

"The layout is familiar."

"We modeled it after the Roost. It's not an exact replica, but some of the elements are similar."

"I see. What's security like?"

"During the day Mod usually comes in and plays receptionist if they feel like it or aren't busy with other things. At night we lock up, and that's about it. We don't keep any personnel files here and if someone breaks in they won't find much."

Kaleo's father handed her an ID badge and a key. "This is if you need to get in during the day and the doors are locked. We have very few cameras to limit what information could fall into hostile hands if something were to happen, although I'd still be careful of what you do even when you think you're alone; some of the other members have unusual abilities."

"Thanks, Dad, I'll keep that in mind," Kaleo said as she looked around the room before noticing that her parents were beaming at her. "What?"

"We're just so proud of you. I know that you've always wanted to do things on your own terms, and you did. You've worked so hard, and we know that reaching this point wasn't easy for you," her mother said.

Kaleo felt her eyes begin to tear up, and her parents enveloped her in a group hug. "I just hope that I don't disappoint you again," she whispered.

Her father released her from his embrace. "You've never disappointed us, little girl. Now hold your head up, you're a Hughes and you've earned this, carry your name well and do your job with pride."

"Speaking of your job..." Her mother led her over to a separate room that they hadn't seen yet. "This is the women's locker room and main bathroom." She unlocked the door and turned on the light to reveal a beige room with dark blue carpet and dark wooden lockers set into the wall. Half of the lockers were empty, the other half had plaques above them with names like "Sifter," "Beguile," "Silver Tongue," "Observe," and "Blast".

Kaleo's mother led her to the locker next to Blast's and told her to open the storage compartment underneath. When she did, Kaleo found another plaque with the word "Phoenix" set on top of a set of clothes in black and gray. She unfolded the jacket and saw the same patch the Professor had velcroed onto her jumpsuit for her match with Strike sewn on the shoulder. Under the clothes was a helmet of similar design to the one the Professor had given her at the match against Strike.

"Now you're an official part of the team."

"Not technically, though, right? As a liaison it's a bit different?"

Her mother shrugged. "Semantics, dear. I know that you may need time to feel comfortable with the task force before you go out on missions, if you ever want to go, but we thought that it would be best to be prepared, and you can also wear this when you're out with Hamilton, if you so choose."

Kaleo hugged her mother and then hung her name plaque over the locker.

# Chapter Twelve

Two days after her parents had given her the tour of the task force building, Kaleo walked into the general information meeting thirty minutes early. She was the first one there, but she'd done that on purpose, as she didn't want to have to deal with questioning glances from a room full of strangers right away, and she wanted to make sure she had time to grab a good seat. When she'd asked Nicole for details about the general meetings earlier in the day, her friend had given her the basic run down: they were once a week, usually lasted an hour or so, and were used by Sifter, Stefan, or one of the other task-force leaders to update the team on any evolving situations or provide new information.

Kaleo chose a seat in the back corner so that she could observe everyone as they walked in, and spent the rest of the time surveying her surroundings and mentally preparing herself. The layout and drab colors of the room reminded her strongly of several of her lecture halls in college, with the noticeable difference that the task-force chairs were at least a little more comfortable, and the attached desks were handy.

Before too long, people began arriving. Kaleo was surprised to see that several of the arrivals didn't even notice that she was there; they simply walked to their usual seats and sat down. Mod and Wiper were both present, as were Audra and Laura, but no one else from Stefan's lunch group was. Apparently, Stefan had been telling the truth when he said that not all the people he ate with were co-workers. When Nicole walked into the room, she went to the back and took a seat next to Kaleo without any hesitation. Stefan did the opposite; he scanned the room, made eye contact with Kaleo, smiled, and dipped his head in acknowledgement before taking a seat at the front and focusing his attention on a stack of papers he'd brought with him.

Kaleo smiled at his subdued greeting. She and Stefan had talked before the meeting about boundaries, and had agreed that when they were working at the task force they would do their best to keep things strictly professional.

Some aspect of Stefan's smile must have been different than usual because one of the women sitting at the front who Kaleo hadn't yet met, turned to see who Stefan had been smiling at. Once she saw Kaleo, the woman elbowed the man sitting next to her. Soon enough, everyone in the entire room—except for her boyfriend, who had caused the stir—was staring at Kaleo and whispering.

The room could have easily held thirty people, but there weren't nearly that many in attendance; yet being the intensely scrutinized object of several pairs of eyes was still more than Kaleo was used to. Audra, in particular, looked like she had just dipped a lemon in battery acid and then swallowed it whole.

No one had a chance to speak, as at just that moment Kaleo's parents swept into the room. Her mother began handing out packets of papers as her father took a seat next to Stefan and struck up a conversation with him. Kaleo watched several people talk to Sifter before glancing her way. Sifter listened to their questions, nodded, and said a few words in response.

Nicole got up to grab a packet for her and Kaleo, and once everyone had settled into their seats with the papers in front of them and the conversations had died down, Sifter stood at the front of the room and smiled. "As many of you have no doubt noticed, we have a new member joining us today who is the newly designated liaison to the Governor's office, Kaleo Hughes. Several of you may already know her as... Yes, Audra?"

Audra's hand had shot into the air before Sifter had a chance to finish her sentence. "I'm sorry for interrupting, Sifter, but I thought that these task-force meetings were for Ableds only."

"If I was you, Audra, I'd shut up before you embarrass yourself," Nicole said.

"It's an honest question; I was under the impression that Kaleo didn't have abilities anymore, if she even had them at all to begin with. She may be your friend, Nicole, but some of us have standards."

Kaleo kept an eye on Stefan during the argument, curious to see what his reaction would be. She knew that Nicole had told him that she'd talk to Audra, but as far as Kaleo was aware, the blonde girl hadn't been this open about her dislike for Kaleo in front of Stefan since her first lunch with them. At Audra's words, Stefan's face turned stormy, but as he heard Nicole's rebuttal he glanced back at Kaleo, and after seeing her calm expression, he schooled his own face into a neutral look.

Sifter cleared her throat to center the attention back on herself. "As I was trying to say before your question, Audra, many of you have either already seen Kaleo in action as Phoenix in her match against Strike, or at the very least heard of her work averting the bombing at Governor Hamilton's rally a week and a half ago."

Audra snickered. "So you're telling me that Kaleo was the Abled responsible for saving that entire arena of people? Is this a joke? What did she do? Re-route the bombs and store them somewhere they wouldn't hurt anyone like they were stacks of toilet paper?"

"Actually, yes, something like that. I take it that you weren't one of the ones watching my match with Strike?" Kaleo asked.

Audra turned and gave Kaleo a derisive look. "I was busy that day and didn't have time to watch him beat up another weakling."

Kaleo had enough of Audra's attitude. "Oh, really? That's too bad. Anytime you want to see what I can do, let me know, and I'm sure that we can get a demonstration arranged. I'll even let you pick the time and place... Unless you'd like to try your luck now?"

"Hey, let's not do this right now," Nicole said as she gripped Kaleo's arm before Audra could respond. Everyone in the room looked at her in surprise, including Kaleo; in her experience, her best friend was usually the one starting fights, not stopping them before they began. Nicole rolled her eyes when she saw that she was the center of attention. "Y'all need to stop staring at me like that; I've got my eye on a nice new apartment and it's going to take me at least a few minutes to find someone to let me bet them a large sum of money that Kaleo's going to kick Audra's—"

"Okay, we're moving on now," Sifter interjected. "I have it on good authority that the Professor is already setting up several matches for some of you against Phoenix to test out her abilities for yourself, and there will be plenty of time for everything else later. Now, if we can all keep our focus on the current meeting and turn to the information in your packets, I would like to direct your attention to the first page."

The informational meeting was true to its name. It only lasted an hour, but by the time it adjourned, Kaleo felt like she had a good handle on the current state of things in the task force. They had been making progress tracking down leads as far as the rally bombing went, but still had nothing definitive. There were other updates over prior missions and intel that Kaleo would need to ask someone about, and she added her new questions to the ever-growing list that she was making so that she could get up to speed as soon as possible. After Sifter had finished her presentation and officially dismissed everyone, Audra leaned over and spoke to Laura, who was sitting next to her, before looking back at Kaleo with a snide expression on her face.

Kaleo did her best to ignore Audra and tried to focus instead on the several people who walked back to introduce themselves to her. Stefan didn't join them; he stayed in his seat and appeared to be in a deep conversation with her father, and Kaleo appreciated the chance to get to know everyone on her own terms.

One young man seemed particularly interested, and after he had introduced himself as Trey, he asked her to get a drink with him under the pretense of getting to know her better.

"Sorry, I can't right now. I was planning on going home after this meeting and having a quiet night in," Kaleo said.

Trey brushed his light brown hair out of his face in what he must have thought was a sexy manner, but the gesture only called attention to the dark bags under his brown eyes. "Oh, c'mon, it'll be fun. If you want quiet, I know a great little bar near here that's usually not too busy. They've even got some little private booths."

Kaleo was taken aback at his insistence but tried not to let it show. "Sorry, Trey, I can't. I don't think that my boyfriend would appreciate that." She smiled nicely to take any sting of rejection out of her words.

"Really? I'm sure he wouldn't mind—it would just be just one drink between new friends, and if you decide that you like my company, I can give you the low-down on all the task-force members too; the inside scoop, if you know what I mean. I promise you won't regret it, and what your boyfriend doesn't know won't hurt him." Trey winked and reached out to put his hand on her knee.

It was obvious that Trey wasn't going to be thrown off so easily, and his too-familiar manner didn't sit well with Kaleo. She took his hand by the wrist and placed it back onto the armrest that separated them, only to have him twist in her grasp so that he was holding her hand in his. Kaleo frowned and opened her mouth to deliver a stronger rejection when she was interrupted.

"She's dating Stefan, you idiot," Nicole said with a snort. "And even if she wasn't, she'd still not be interested in you."

"Stefan's girlfriend? I see. In that case, don't worry about the drinks. In fact, forget I said anything about them. It was nice to meet you, Kaleo." Trey dropped Kaleo's hand like it had burst into flames before scurrying away without another word.

Kaleo turned to Nicole. "What was that about?"

"Trey likes to think of himself as a stud, but he's about as sleazy as they come. When he does get a date, it's always very much of the one-night stand type, and honestly? He's not even good at that."

"I assume that you know this from personal experience?"

Nicole's grin was wolfish. "Let's just say that at one point I took him up on his offer, and he wasn't quite up to my standards."

Kaleo watched as Trey hurried out of the room without speaking to anyone else. "He practically ran away when you mentioned Stefan."

"Yeah, well, you haven't had the chance to see him in action in the field, but your boyfriend over there can be a very scary man at times, and it doesn't take a genius to guess at how deep his protective streak runs." Nicole paused.

"Although I will say that it would have been very entertaining if Stefan had seen that little move Trey tried to pull."

"He wouldn't have done anything. We agreed to be professional at work."

"You haven't seen him in an interrogation yet, have you?"

Kaleo shook her head.

"Trust me, he doesn't have to be unprofessional to be intimidating."

The next day, Katherine cleared Kaleo's arm for physical combat at the Professor's. Kaleo was delighted when she reached the facility and was informed that Stefan would be her new primary sparring partner.

"I am well aware of your personal relationship, but I must ask that you both put that aside for now," the Professor said with a critical expression before he took a seat in the corner and motioned for them to begin.

"Don't worry, Professor, I won't go easy on him," Kaleo said. Stefan only shook his head and chuckled in response.

It didn't take Kaleo long to figure out why Stefan had laughed. The Professor had them start off fighting without their abilities, and within seconds Stefan had easily outmaneuvered her and tossed her to the ground. Kaleo scrambled up and tried again.

Again, she was beaten too easily. After the fourth or fifth time that she found herself on the ground or in a headlock, she admitted defeat. Stefan stepped back and looked at the Professor, who waved his hand. "Go ahead and teach her like we talked about, Stefan. Don't mind me, I'll let you know if you miss anything."

Stefan nodded at the Professor before turning back to Kaleo.

"Okay, sweetheart, I think that it's high time that you learn how to fight."

"I already know how to fight," she complained.

He shrugged. "You know how to throw some punches and some basic defense, I'll give you that, but you don't have any finesse, and if you're fighting someone experienced who has half of a brain, it'll take them about four minutes to figure you out."

"Four minutes isn't a lot of time. Why haven't I had a problem until now?"

"Remember, I said an experienced fighter. There aren't that many of us, all things considered, but if Phoenix is going to be on Hamilton's security team, you need to be prepared for everything. Don't worry, I'll start off easy on you until you get your confidence. Now, get into your fighting stance."

Kaleo settled into her natural stance, knees bent and hands at the ready.

Stefan looked her up and down before making some moderate adjustments to her form. Finally, he stepped back once more and settled into a stance of his own. "Try and hit me, but slowly. In a few minutes we'll reverse the roles, so pay attention to how I defend myself. Once you get the basic forms down and get comfortable, we'll start adding abilities in."

"What if I hurt you?"

He smiled. "If you can land a punch, it means that I've done my job."

# Chapter Thirteen

For Kaleo, the aspect of her new job that took the most getting used to was changing into and out of her Phoenix persona. Her initial onboarding week with Todd and Michael went smoothly, and they established an alibi for her disappearance from the office whenever Hamilton was out on the campaign trail: that of a fictional aunt who had been recently ill and required care. Due to her aunt's extenuating circumstances, Kaleo was given a waiver to "work from home as needed."

Granted, "working from home" really meant working as Phoenix. In fact, when she was traveling with the governor's campaign, Kaleo could only leave the hotel room or train roommette when she was in full Phoenix mode. Fortunately, one of the other members of the task force was a woman named Taylor Schmidt who worked as the deputy press secretary for Governor Hamilton for her day job. Taylor's task-force alter ego was Silver Tongue, an Abled with an extremely persuasive voice.

Rooming with Taylor meant that Kaleo didn't usually have to worry about suiting up before opening the door, answering the room phone without her voice modulator, or otherwise risk revealing her identity.

Taylor's presence also had multiple other benefits. First and foremost, having someone to talk to helped keep the loneliness at bay, even if Taylor wasn't always the best conversationalist. As Kaleo learned on the first night they shared a room, Taylor was unable to completely turn off her abilities. So as not to accidentally force people to do something against their will, she had trained herself to only speak facts unless she was truly using her persuasion on someone.

Within days of their first campaign trip, Kaleo and Taylor had settled into a comfortable routine on the campaign trail, although Kaleo began to worry that she wouldn't be able to carry her own weight in the friendship. Due to the limitations that her secret persona placed on her, Taylor had to run all the errands, as it would create more of a stir than would be worth it for Phoenix to go to the local pizza place.

A couple of weeks after starting her job, Kaleo felt like she had already been pushed to her mental limits. It had been a particularly long day, and to tie everything else off in a nice little bow of unpleasantness, there had been an anti-Abled protest outside Governor Hamilton's rally.

Interestingly enough, while the numbers of Ableds were steadily increasing each year, they were still fairly uncommon, and each Abled had abilities as unique as their appearance. Ableds who had useful abilities and good control were highly in demand, and the competition was fierce to employ them. This created a double-edged sword, as it meant that Ableds tended to rise more quickly in the ranks of whatever profession they joined and take on more high-profile jobs, with the unfortunate side effect of causing jealousy amongst their non-Abled peers.

The feelings of envy weren't helped by the increasing public perception that being Abled was synonymous with being low-class, a prejudice stemming from the beginning of the Hard Times, when just about everyone who could afford to stay inside during the flares did. The children of those people didn't gain abilities, and for the most part they grew up resenting their parents and envying their more gifted counterparts.

Whereas once Ableds were widely respected for the services they'd performed during the Hard Times, not all Ableds were good people, and some fairly recent and widely-publicized news stories highlighted Ableds who used their abilities unethically for personal gain. In a post-Savior world, Kaleo feared that the pendulum had begun to swing too far in the other direction, with people considering many Ableds to be pretentious and power-hungry.

The appearance of Phoenix—the previously unknown Abled who had sin-gle-handedly saved an arena full of people and then been hired as a personal bodyguard to Governor Hamilton's team—only served to aggravate the anti-Abled protestors.

That day in particular, tensions reached a breaking point and Phoenix was forced to raise her shield to stop several shoes thrown by the crowd from hitting Governor Hamilton. The protestors were arrested, but the fact that they had been bold enough to do such a thing was disturbing to her. Hamilton refused to cancel his last few events, and Phoenix was forced to work under high alert, always on the lookout for more threats, and always worried that the next projectile would be a bullet or a brick. She'd hoped that the protestors would realize that things were getting out of hand and leave them alone, but her hopes were unfounded, and by the end of the day she was completely exhausted.

Once she was back in the hotel room, had changed out of her work clothes, and whipped off her helmet, Kaleo threw herself face down on the bed. She didn't move until long after the autumn sun had set and Taylor had gotten back from the small press conference that Hamilton had taken to hosting at the end of each day.

"Hard day, huh?" Taylor asked as she set a bag of takeout food on the table between their two beds.

"You have no idea." Kaleo groaned before rolling over. "What's for supper tonight?"

"Thai. A local said that it's one of the most consistent restaurants around with the biggest portions, and I had a feeling that you'd need something good after today."

"What did the press have to say about the protestors?"

"More of the usual. They wanted to know if Hamilton thought that your presence was becoming too distracting, and if he thought that the protestors should be banned."

Kaleo took a bite of noodles and chewed thoughtfully. "And what did he say?"

"That he was ever grateful for you saving his life and the lives of the others in the arena, that you would remain at your post until we learn more about who was behind the rally bombing for the protection of his supporters, that he welcomes the protestors exercising their right to free speech, and that he hopes that both your example and his speeches may eventually sway them to see his point of view."

"How very Hamilton."

Taylor smiled. "He's a natural, that's for sure. He also re-emphasized his plans for Abled integration and Abled/non-Abled cooperation moving forward, and his desire to represent all Americans regardless of Abled status. He said that even in the few months the Midwestern Pact Abled Task Force has existed, he has come to appreciate just how important it is to have both types of people in an organization to maximize results and minimize costs."

"The talk of costs makes me nervous sometimes," Kaleo admitted.

"Why?"

"Because I don't know what the costs of my own abilities are yet."

"I thought it was that you had to be connected to the ground, and that you couldn't use yours in the air?" Taylor asked before taking another bite of her sandwich.

"That's more of a limitation, not a true cost. Sometimes I feel like I'm on borrowed time."

Taylor shrugged. "Who knows? Maybe you'll be one of the lucky ones without a cost. Do you want me to tell you to not worry about it and that everything will be okay?"

"No, thanks, I'll get over it eventually. It's just that hard days like today make me insecure."

"I get you. If it helps, I'd trade costs with you, whatever yours may be. It's hard to make friends and share hobbies when you don't know if the other person is actually friendly, or if it's just my abilities working."

Kaleo was intrigued. "Can anybody resist you when you start persuading them?"

Taylor took another bite of her food and chewed for a moment. "Not really. I used to not be able to moderate it at all, and no one could resist anything I said. After I joined the task force and started working with the Professor, I've been able to modulate it a little, but I don't think I'll ever be able to dial it back all the way."

"Why don't we try now? We can make a game out of it: You try to persuade me to do something and I try to resist you."

Taylor shook her head. "I don't know about this. I don't like persuading people unless I really have to."

"It'll be fun. It's good practice for both of us. You get to practice toning it down, and I get the dual benefit of having someone to talk to and the challenge of trying to hold out against your influence. It's a win-win." Kaleo smiled. "Who knows? Maybe by the time this campaign is over, we can have an actual verbal discourse with *opinions*. Besides, I have to trust you anyway, and we're teammates and friends now, right? If you can't try this with me, how else will you be able to practice?"

In the end, Taylor agreed to try.

The first week was frustrating for them. Taylor would tell Kaleo to do a simple task, like pick a pencil up or open the closet door, and Kaleo would do her best to fight against the influence of Taylor's abilities, albeit unsuccessfully.

After several weeks of daily practice, they were surprised when Kaleo ignored some of Taylor's influence, although if Taylor pressed hard enough, Kaleo eventually gave in. As the weeks passed and the campaign neared its end, Kaleo had been inoculated against the milder forms of Taylor's ability, and they were indeed able to hold a short debate over the best way to fold towels. It was a small victory, but one that had been dearly fought for, and it cemented their friendship.

The campaign schedule was grueling and usually consisted of a one- to two-week-long train ride with stops for various events and speeches that looped back to Chicago, followed by two or three days to rest and get caught up on other work and laundry before they were back on the train. Whenever they got back into town, Kaleo and Taylor would get briefed by one of the task-force leaders on what they had missed, and be given a list of things to keep their eye out for while they were on the campaign trail.

Stefan stayed true to his word, and he and Kaleo talked for at least a few minutes almost every day on the phone; no matter what time Kaleo got back to the room, she knew that she could call him on either his office or home phone, and that chances were good that he would pick up and be happy to hear her voice. Whenever Kaleo was back in town, she'd schedule all her work, appointments, and time with friends and family for one of the days and leave the second open for her and Stefan to spend together. The quasi long distance wasn't easy on their new relationship, but they somehow made it work.

Before Kaleo knew it, the day for the announcement of the official election results arrived. Since her grandmother's time, when working computers had become as rare as hen's teeth, the states had passed laws declaring an official "election week," with the results tallied throughout the seven days as people voted. The results were then announced on the evening of the first Saturday in November.

As she stood in her Phoenix uniform at the results party and watched the crowd swirl around Governor Hamilton and his running mate, Emmerson Johnson, former senator to California and now presidential candidate, it was hard for Kaleo to believe that it was already almost over. While she was out on the campaign trail, it had felt like every day dragged by, but now that she looked back on the past two and a half months, it all seemed to be a blur.

The atmosphere of the party started out tense, but quickly turned celebratory when the official results began to roll in and the Johnson/Hamilton ticket was announced as the winner. After the first feelings of joy had passed, Kaleo felt numb. She was so exhausted that she didn't even have the energy to wonder where she would fit into the new administration.

She didn't have to wait long to find out—Hamilton's campaign splurged by paying for all his staffers to fly back to Chicago from California the day after the election results were announced, and on the flight back she was summoned to a partitioned-off part of the plane that had been turned into Hamilton's temporary office.

In an almost eerie parallel to several months before, Kaleo found Hamilton, Todd, and Michael all waiting for her when she walked in. Once the door had closed behind her, Kaleo took off her helmet and set it on a side table.

The new vice presidential elect was the first to speak. "Kaleo, how do you think you've performed at your job?"

Kaleo was thrown off guard by the question and took a moment to think before deciding on the blunt approach. "Well, I haven't stopped any more bombs if that's what you're asking, so I haven't really had the chance to do what I was hired to do. I've been able to keep up with the task force information but haven't been able to do much beyond file it away for future use. Honestly, I've only been truly helpful with some of the reports and research that Todd's had me work on in the hotel room during my downtime."

Michael chuckled from his corner. "I'd say that you have more than served your purpose as a deterrent."

Kaleo shrugged. As interest in her grew, there had been several articles written about how Phoenix, the hero who had averted the "Rally bombing" was now serving as part of Hamilton's personal protection detail—but it was nothing major, and in her opinion, the anti-Abled protests had only increased the more that her role had been highlighted. As it was, at all of Hamilton's speeches and large events she'd remained hidden in the background, but when Hamilton was out with the people she had been photographed several times, and her presence had become a part of his brand and a reminder of the current state of politics in the country, albeit a somewhat polarizing one. The rival political party had run several attack ads accusing Hamilton of creating his own type of "secret police" with Phoenix and the task force, but fortunately the idea hadn't gained any traction among the general populace.

"You've done a superb job with the work that I've given you," Todd said.

"Thank you," she replied.

There was a brief pause, and Hamilton spoke again. "The purpose of bringing you into this meeting is to formally ask if you'd be interested in continuing your current job working with us. I'm aware that when we first offered this to you the end date was left up in the air due to several factors, not least being the results of the election. However, I've been very impressed with your work ethic and dedication, and Todd and Michael both agree that you'd be a great asset to the team we're aiming to build."

Kaleo wasn't sure what to say; she had tried to not think too far ahead during the campaign and now regretted not taking more time to think about what she would want once the campaign was over. "What exactly would my duties be if I remained?"

"You'd officially be one of my aides, and much of your work would be spent in the vice president's offices in Lincoln. Your presence as Phoenix would be needed much less, probably only at large events; it would be a similar arrangement to now, but you would be spending much more time working as Kaleo than you do currently," Todd said.

"And what about the task force? I can't both work for you in Lincoln and remain a member of the task force that is four hours away by train."

Hamilton and Todd shared a glance. "In regard to the task force, I'm currently weighing several options, none of which are solid enough to discuss at the moment. For now, be assured that its impressive record in investigations into corruption, combating crime, and working as positive ambassadors for the Abled community hasn't gone unnoticed by several very powerful people," Hamilton said carefully.

"You don't have to make a decision right now. You can go home, relax, and think about it for a few days," Todd added. "We have no big events scheduled at the moment, and a couple of weeks before we'd need you for transition planning."

Kaleo thanked them for the opportunity, put her helmet back on, and then excused herself from the room.

The plane touched down in Chicago late that afternoon. Mercifully, there was no need for the vice president elect to make a speech, and everyone disembarked as quickly as they could. Many of them, Kaleo included, had been promised a one-week break to recover from the stress of the campaign frenzy leading up to the election-results night, and were more than ready to get home and relax. Kaleo had left her car parked at her house while on the road and had already made arrangements for her mother to pick her up. Nova drove Kaleo-as-Phoenix to the task-force headquarters so that she could change out of her Phoenix gear and into her regular clothes.

They nodded to the young black woman talking on the phone at the front desk, who Kaleo assumed was Mod from the red and blue scarf tied around her afro, and headed back to the locker room. As Kaleo started changing out of the outer layers of her uniform, they chatted; Kaleo had tried to call her parents and Katherine at least once a week while she was gone, but it hadn't been the same as their in-person conversations.

Several minutes later, her mother stood from where she'd been sitting on her locker. "I'm so glad that you're back and that you get more of a break this time. We've all missed you. I've got to go run and do some errands, but someone else will be by to pick you up soon, and I'm sure that he'll be very excited to see you," she said as she hugged Kaleo.

After her mother was gone, Kaleo hopped in the shower and made sure to take her time getting ready; she'd been away for two and a half weeks during the final campaign push, and she wanted to look her best just in case the person who picked her up happened to be a certain young man with dark brown hair and striking green eyes.

Even with her mother's hint and her own hopes, Kaleo was still happily surprised to find Stefan waiting for her outside the locker room. She squealed in delight and ran into his waiting arms, and he picked her up and swung her around before setting her back on the ground and kissing her deeply.

"I've missed that," she said as she looked up into his warm eyes.

"I'm glad. Otherwise that would have been very awkward," he replied with a goofy smile before taking her duffle bag and carrying it to his car for her.

As they drove away, Stefan took a different route than normal to her house, and when he saw Kaleo's confused look, he laughed. "Don't worry, sweetheart, I haven't forgotten where you live. We're just going on a little detour."

Stefan drove them to Nicole's apartment, where Kaleo discovered that her friends had thrown a quasi-welcome-home party under the guise of an election celebration in her honor.

"It was mostly Taylor's idea," Nicole said when Kaleo had gotten over her surprise and asked how they'd arranged everything.

Kaleo looked at her new friend for confirmation, and Taylor shrugged and grinned. "I know that it was hard for you on the campaign trail, and I thought that this would be a great way to celebrate, especially since you didn't get much of a chance to last night."

The party was a blast; although that should have been a given, considering who the host was. Lin brought her new boyfriend Sam, and Nicole had invited several other mutual friends who were outside of the task force. Due to the presence of the outsiders, there was no temptation to talk about work., and Kaleo was able to spend the evening enjoying the good friends and good food.

The next day Stefan insisted on first taking Kaleo out to the nicest restaurant in town, and then to watch a play to celebrate the end of the campaign and her subsequent return home in a more intimate manner. When he picked her up at her house, he was dressed in his nicest suit and holding a giant bouquet of flowers and a large box of chocolates.

"Stefan, Valentine's Day isn't for several more months," Kaleo teased as she put the flowers in a vase with water.

Stefan swept her up in his arms to dance as he hummed a tune. "I've got to make up for lost time, remember?" he murmured in her ear.

She laughed. "It's only been two weeks since you saw me last, not two months, and besides, I was the one who left you here and went away on a trip. Are you hinting that I should buy you flowers more often?"

"Yes, well, it's felt more like two years to me since the last time that I saw you, and I was sure that you'd look extra beautiful tonight, so it was really the least that I could do." He held his hand up for Kaleo to twirl around in a circle and whistled when she did so. "I was right, you're absolutely ravishing. My flowers didn't nearly do you justice."

"You're pretty handsome yourself," she replied as he drew her back into his arms for one last kiss before they had to leave to make their reservation.

It was at the restaurant that Stefan asked Kaleo what the next step was. She sighed and played with the food on her plate.

"Well, Hamilton offered me a job doing pretty much the same thing, but more time with Todd and less with Michael," she said carefully, mindful of the public nature of the restaurant.

"That's awesome, congratulations!" Stefan's excitement waned when he saw the look on her face. "What's the catch?"

Kaleo stabbed one of the potatoes on her plate. "It's in Lincoln. They told me to take some time to think about it, but I'm just not sure what to do. It'd be good for my career, and I don't have any other jobs lined up right now... but it's a permanent long-distance move, and I'll have my hands full working, which means weekend trips back here would be few and far between."

Stefan's face fell. "That certainly won't make things easy for us."

Kaleo nodded and they ate in silence for several minutes before Stefan set his fork down abruptly and reached across the table for Kaleo's hand. "I want you to do what's best for yourself, and what will make you happy. Opportunities like this don't come by often, and you'll regret it if you don't take it," he said. The soft look in his eyes made Kaleo's heart skip a beat.

"You make me happy," she said quietly.

"There's nothing that says that we can't make a long-distance relationship work. We've got a couple of months before you'll have to move; I'm sure that we can figure something out. Who knows? Maybe I'll be able to find a job in Lincoln too."

"That's so far away from your family, though." Kaleo frowned. "And what about all your work here? I can't let you uproot your life to follow me."

Stefan waved his hand lazily in the air "Au contraire, *ma chérie*, I'm a grown man. I can do whatever I want to. Don't forget that I've got friends in Lincoln too—Adrian and Kiana, for one. If I decide in, say, two months that I'm sick of the lakeshore scenery and that I'd like to live in America's heartland where my girlfriend just so happens to also live, there is absolutely nothing you can do to stop me."

"Have you always known how to speak French?" Kaleo asked, raising an eyebrow.

"I just started learning. I had to have something to occupy my extra time while you were gone, and I was feeling romantic." Stefan winked at her over the brim of his glass.

Kaleo shook her head, unwilling to let the subject go. "What if we break up? If we realize in three months that it's just not working out, you're going to feel very silly for moving."

Stefan shrugged. "If you don't take this job and we break up in three months, you're going to feel very silly for not taking this chance. Plus, remember that you've already promised to meet my family in a couple of weeks for Thanksgiving. For all we know, you could absolutely hate them and break up with me on the spot."

"Or they could hate me and forbid you from ever seeing me again."

"You see? Anything could happen between now and the end of January. Take the job, we'll make everything else work out."

"Promise?" Kaleo looked across the table at Stefan. His eyes glinted with a strange magnetism in the candlelight and made her feel like they were the only two people in the room.

"Promise." His warm smile steadied her nerves and she turned her attention back to the delicious food on her plate.

After her week off, and once she had accepted the new job, Todd began to assign Kaleo more projects to work on, but she rarely had to take work home. Between task-force meetings, lessons with the Professor, and actual dates, she saw Stefan almost every day. Once a week she also had a standing dinner date with Lin and Nicole, and she ate lunch often with Taylor. For the first time in a long while, Kaleo felt as though she finally had time to live her life and enjoy what she had built for herself instead of rushing to put out one fire after another.

November slipped by like a light breeze pushing autumn leaves down the sidewalk. Kaleo and Stefan drove to his parents' house for Thanksgiving, where she met his family with no small amount of trepidation. She needn't have worried, as after less than an hour in their home she'd been accepted into the fold as though they had known her for years. Stefan's mother had never learned English fluently, and often used her husband or one of her children as interpreters, but Kaleo could easily see that Stefan had inherited her warm smile and laughing green eyes, and they got along well even without the aid of a common language.

Stefan's father was a quiet, reserved man who seemed content to let his wife organize the family while he sat at the kitchen dining table peeling potatoes or keeping an eye on his grandchildren. His presence was a calm spot in the storm of the holiday cooking, and from what Kaleo could see, anyone who needed a break from the hustle and bustle was more than welcome to sit next to him and help him with whatever task he'd been assigned. While his salt-and-pepper hair was still cut in the same severe army style he wore in his old military pictures, he spoke softly and gently, and Kaleo got the impression that if Stefan's mother was the life of the family, his father was its steady foundation.

Kaleo thoroughly enjoyed getting to know Stefan's family, and his brothers took great pleasure in telling her all his embarrassing stories while his mother made sure to show her the high-school and military-academy awards Stefan had won—as it turned out, his abilities gave him quite the edge in athletics. Stefan seemed uncomfortable with the attention, and after he ascertained that Kaleo was having fun and getting along well with his mother and sisters-in-laws, he made his escape by letting his nephews and nieces drag him outside to play in the snow.

Watching him play with the children gave Kaleo a warm feeling in her chest.

"He is good with the children, no?" His mother sidled up to her as she looked out the window.

"Very good; they all love him," Kaleo replied as she watched Stefan defend himself from the kids' snowball attacks before he was forced to admit a good-natured defeat and let them tackle him into the snow.

His mother nodded her head. "He is good son. Will be very good husband and father one day too." She nudged Kaleo gently and gave her a meaningful look before turning away to add the finishing touches to a dish that had just been pulled out of the oven. Kaleo felt her cheeks begin to redden, and mentally added the ability to leave her speechless as another trait that Stefan and his mother shared.

Later, as Kaleo and Stefan were saying their goodbyes to his family on the train platform, his mother hugged Kaleo tightly and told her that she was welcome to visit anytime. Kaleo then watched from several feet away as Stefan's mother hugged him goodbye and spoke several rapid sentences to him in her native tongue. Stefan laughed and replied before hugging her back. While Kaleo couldn't understand what his mother had said, judging from the beaming smile that Stefan gave her, she guessed that it was good news.

"So? What did you think of my family?" he asked once the train had pulled out of the station.

"They were all very nice. I had a great time. How did I do? Did your mother tell you to never see me again?"

"She told me that I'd be a fool to let you go."

Kaleo looked out the window and sighed. "That's nice. One more obstacle down then, I suppose."

Stefan's only response was to squeeze her hand.

# Chapter Fourteen

Kaleo's training with the Professor and Stefan progressed well over the course of November and into December. While she was away working on the campaign trail, every day, for hours, she'd practiced immersing herself into the different types of energy flows and tapping into and out of each flow, using it as she needed. However, she remained frustrated, as while she could manipulate the various flows into a defensive shield in any shape or form, something prevented her from using the energy offensively.

Still, though she'd quickly distinguished herself as one of the more powerful combat-oriented Ableds on the task force in practice, when it came to her sparring sessions with Stefan she was never able to repeat the success of her first match. Even with her abilities, she soon realized that whether through the element of surprise or the fact that Strike had been more distracted than he'd let on, she'd had a disproportionate advantage. Now that Stefan knew her abilities' strengths and weaknesses, and was better able to focus on the task at hand, he could almost always get past her shield before he tired.

It seemed like in every lesson with the Professor and Stefan Kaleo learned something new. She now understood that while Stefan could harness the energy from her glancing blows and use it to fuel his speed, the hits still hurt, and even his body had its limits as to how much abuse it could take and how much energy it could pump out to his muscles before he needed to rest. It was a bonus that if he happened to hit her shield instead of her, the blow drained him twice as quickly; though her shield was composed of energy, it was energy that he couldn't use.

During one especially close match, Kaleo felt like she might finally have the chance to wear Stefan down. She had been perfect in her shield placement and reactions, and as he was forced to use his abilities to land hits, she was able to use the energy in the room to manipulate and expand her shield to protect herself and drain him. However, her hopes were dashed when Stefan waited until she was manipulating her shield and in a last-ditch effort, swept her feet out from under her, caught her, pinned her arms to her side in midair, and then lifted her.

Kaleo was only a couple of inches shorter than Stefan, but when he arched his back, he was able to just barely keep her feet off the ground and thus prevent her from using her abilities.

"This isn't fair; I was about to win. Put me down right now!" Kaleo struggled in his arms, frustrated at being foiled once again.

"First you have to say that I won and that I'm the best fighter in the entire task force," Stefan gloated.

"I'm giving you one last chance before I do something drastic."

He laughed and squeezed her more tightly. "Not until you admit that I'm the winner."

Kaleo grunted and brought her knee up into Stefan's groin. He immediately groaned, let go of her, and dropped to the ground.

She paused to catch her breath and looked over at the Professor, who was sitting in his usual spot. "Are we done now?"

When he nodded, she crouched beside Stefan, who was still writhing and groaning on the ground. She waited until he had calmed down before speaking.

"Sorry about that, but I did try to warn you, you know."

"That was a cheap shot."

"Well, you kind of left yourself wide open for it."

"You could have headbutted me instead or something!"

"And risk giving myself a concussion? No, thank you."

"As hardheaded as you are sometimes, you could probably headbutt a steel post and leave a dent," he muttered as he took her proffered hand and stood up.

"Kaleo's right, Stefan; you had a good idea to get her off the ground, but you did leave yourself... rather unguarded." The Professor grimaced. "That was painful to watch. We'll call that good for today. You two are free to go."

By the time that they reached the parking lot where Kaleo's car and Stefan's bike were parked, he was mostly recovered and had almost stopped walking with a hitch in his gait.

"I really am sorry about that," Kaleo apologized again.

Stefan didn't look at her as he finished drinking the last of his water bottle and began putting his gear on. "No, you're not; you're happy that you beat me," he grumbled.

"Okay, yes, I will admit that I'm happy that I finally won for once, but I am really sorry about hurting you," Kaleo replied as she handed him his jacket.

Stefan zipped up his jacket and glanced at her with a smirk on his face. "I forgive you; just don't do that too many more times or we might never be able to have children."

"Children?" Kaleo tapped her lips with a finger before giving him a devilish grin in return. "That's at least a couple of years out. Which should give you plenty of time to recuperate from any other training incidents we have."

He laughed and kissed her. "Next time, I'll remember your legs. You won't get that chance again."

"Hey, at least I can still surprise you. I hear that's good for keeping the spark in the relationship," Kaleo teased as he put the helmet on his head.

"Yeah, well how about we try to only have good surprises from here on out?" Stefan asked.

"I suppose I can live with that. Are we eating dinner together tomorrow?"

"Probably better if we didn't. I've got a work thing tomorrow afternoon that may bleed into the evening."

"Super-spy stuff?"

"Always. I'll call you when I'm done if it's not too late, otherwise let's plan on the day after tomorrow, after the task-force meeting. Drive home safe. I love you." He embraced her one last time before getting on his bike, and waited until

Kaleo had gotten into her car and started it before he pulled out of the parking lot.

Their separate routes home started out along the same road, and Kaleo was still behind Stefan when he approached a busy intersection. She watched as he first slowed down when he saw the red light, and then sped up when the light turned green. She was still watching when an electric car with no lights on flew into the intersection and made a left-hand turn. Kaleo looked on in horror and with her heart in her throat as the car crashed into the front of Stefan's bike and his body went flying through the air, hit the ground, and rolled into the traffic-light pole where he lay still in a crumpled heap.

# Chapter Fifteen

As Kaleo later learned, the car that hit Stefan had been running low on its electric charge, and the driver had been trying to reach their nearby house before the car stalled. They'd kept their lights off to conserve energy and had been watching the level of the car's battery with such concern that they hadn't even seen Stefan's bike enter the intersection.

Kaleo was thankful that Stefan had always thought he should wear all of his safety gear every time he rode his bike. In the end, it saved his life. In fact, it did much more, and by the time Kaleo had parked her car and ran over to where Stefan lay on the side of the road, he was awake and moving his arms and legs. When the ambulance arrived, he was sitting up and able to explain what had happened. She followed his ambulance to the hospital and stayed as close to his side as the doctors would let her while they checked him over.

As they waited for the test results, Kaleo used a hospital phone to call her parents and Katherine, and Stefan called his parents and Director Stone. When he got off the phone with the latter, he frowned and sighed. "Stone is on his way up here. I'm sure that he's not going to be pleased at the timing of this."

"Is it going to affect your plans for tomorrow?"

"It shouldn't; I feel fine. I've got a small headache and my whole body hurts, but it's nothing that won't go away with a little bit of rest."

It was a busy night in the ER, and Katherine and Director Stone had ample time to arrive at Stefan's room before the doctor stopped by. As they waited, Katherine checked Stefan and frowned. "I know that I've told you that the bike would kill you one day."

There was a knock on the door, and the doctor entered as Stefan told Katherine, "I'm not dead, just a little bruised up."

"I'm afraid that you're more than just a little bruised," the doctor said before introducing himself as Dr. Ariz. He paused when he saw Katherine. "Hello, Dr. Hughes, I wasn't expecting to see you here. I assume that this is a friend of yours?"

"He is. I'm also part of his primary care team."

"I see." Dr. Ariz turned back to Stefan. "To put it succinctly, you've got a mild concussion, three broken ribs, and a partially collapsed lung. We can give you some medication for the pain, but we'll need to treat your lung and keep you for observation until tomorrow morning at least."

"I can't do that. I've got to go to work tomorrow," Stefan said.

The doctor shook his head. "You won't be working for at least a few days, maybe a week, depending on how long it takes your concussion to heal."

"What are you talking about? I've got things that need to get done!"

Katherine sighed and looked at Dr. Ariz. "I can explain everything to him, I know that you're probably swamped. Would you mind if I got a look at his test results and x-rays?"

"I don't if the patient doesn't."

Stefan waved his hand. "Let her see whatever she wants. It doesn't change anything; I'm leaving here tonight."

Katherine followed Dr. Ariz out of the room and Stefan turned to Director Stone. "I can still run the op tomorrow," he said fiercely.

Stone shook his head. "You heard the doc, I don't think you can. You know that you need to be on your A-game for something like this, and a brain injury won't even get you off the bench."

"I have to! We don't have anyone else."

The director huffed. "What am I? Chopped liver? I was running operations like these before you were even in diapers."

"You're too valuable to go."

"What kind of operation are you two talking about?" Kaleo asked from her seat beside Stefan.

"Nothing that you should worry about," Stefan said too quickly, and then wouldn't meet her eyes.

"We're following up on a lead on the rally bombings," the director said.

"Okay, fill me in."

Stefan snorted. "It doesn't concern you. Don't worry about it."

Kaleo frowned at Stefan and had a feeling that she was getting a good look at his stubborn side. "Need I remind you that part of my *job* is to act as personal security for Hamilton? If this has to do with finding out more information on the bombing that *I* stopped, I believe that it is both right up my alley and quite literally within my job description."

"She does have a point," Director Stone said. Stefan grunted, but didn't say anything more, and the director continued. "Several weeks ago, we were able to trace several materials used in the bombs to a Heinstein Transport train. We notified the owner of the company of our findings and with our help he traced the route of that specific train in the days before the bombings to a distributor with some shady connections. Last week, Brant Heinstein reached out to us and said that he had found someone who would be willing to provide us with more information about the bombings for a price."

"I see, and Stefan was supposed to meet with this source tomorrow?"

"Yes, Stefan, a representative from the Treasury Department to authorize the transfer of funds, and Brant Heinstein to confirm the identity of the source were all scheduled to fly out tomorrow afternoon to make the trade."

"Why was the task force not notified about this development?"

"We wanted to have something concrete to act on. If we notified the leadership team about every potential source or problem we ran across, our meetings would run very long and half of the information would either be outdated or useless by the following week."

"I take it that there is at least a small element of danger to all of this?"

Stone nodded. "We haven't been able to independently verify the identity of the source for ourselves, and the location of the rendezvous is a rather remote hunting lodge."

"Don't you dare even think about it, Kaleo," Stefan warned, but it was no use. Her mind was already made up.

Kaleo looked at Stefan and rubbed the back of his hand. "It seems to me that with you on the sidelines for who knows how long, we've only got one option."

Stefan turned his head to meet her gaze with a glare, but she ignored him and turned back to the director.

"With Stefan out of commission, you'll need to be there to verify the information and run the operation, and I'll need to be there to make sure that if things go south you have a decent chance of getting out unharmed."

"Is no one listening to me? I'll feel perfectly fine after a good night's rest. There is no need for either of you to do my job for me tomorrow!"

Katherine walked in again, taking care to shut the door behind her. "Stop shouting, Stefan, you're only lending more credence to the concussion diagnosis. I've just taken a look at your test results. The good news is that the part of your lung that collapsed is small enough that if you let me work my magic, allow the nice doctors to check you over one more time, and Kaleo is agreeable to keeping an eye on you, they'll let you go home tonight."

"Finally, someone who is talking sense," Stefan grumbled.

"I'm glad you think I'm being sensible, because the bad news is that you shouldn't be working for at least one week, and you won't be exercising or using your abilities until we get your ribs and lung completely healed, not to mention your head—which means that even accelerating that timeline with my treatments, it'll probably be closer to a month before I even think about letting you back into the field," she held up her hand to stave off Stefan's protests. "No more arguments. As the lead doctor for the task force, I reserve the right to pull someone off duty if I feel that they're not fit for action. Looking at those x-rays and listening to you just now, I'm declaring it official."

"It's not a task force thing, so you don't have that authority," Stefan replied triumphantly.

"But I do." Director Stone crossed his arms. "You're off the op tomorrow, and you're taking the next day off too. If Katherine is satisfied with your progress, I'll put you back on light duty part time for the rest of this week and next, or until she fully clears you to return to work, whichever comes last. Now, do you still have your set of files for the operation at your apartment?"

Stefan nodded, finally defeated.

"Good, then make sure that Kaleo reads them." Stone turned to Kaleo. "Be at my office tomorrow afternoon at four p.m. sharp, dressed and ready to go."

Kaleo nodded and Stone patted Stefan's shoulder and left the room. Katherine spent a couple of minutes working on Stefan's lung, explained to Kaleo what concerning signs and symptoms she should watch for, and then went to notify the nurse that Stefan was ready for his final checkup and discharge, leaving them alone for a moment.

"I thought that we just agreed to no more unpleasant surprises," Kaleo said as she squeezed Stefan's hand in an attempt to lift his spirits.

Stefan turned to look at her despondently. "I really don't want you on that mission tomorrow; something about it gives me a bad feeling. Stone feels it too, or he wouldn't be involving you."

"Then all the more reason for me to go. You don't want the director there without any protection, do you?"

He leaned his head back against the pillow. "If I had any choice, I'd rewind time until just before I got to that intersection, so I didn't have to watch you make the choice for me."

After Dr. Ariz had cleared Stefan to go home and gave him some medication to take for the pain, Kaleo drove them to his apartment, making a slight detour on the way to stop by her house and fill a bag with everything she would need for the night. As they slowly climbed the stairs to his apartment, she could tell that even with the pain medication he was hurting, and she supported him under one arm to help him as much as she could.

In his apartment, Stefan waved off Kaleo's offers of further assistance and limped to his bedroom to find the papers for the upcoming operation. While he was busy looking, Kaleo took a quick shower in the guest bathroom.

After she got out of the shower and put her pajamas on, she went to check on Stefan and found the door to his bedroom wide open. She could hear the shower in his bathroom running and couldn't resist the temptation to satisfy her curiosity; she peered into his room through the open doorway. The exposed brick walls were mostly bare, save for a couple of large landscape paintings and two candle lanterns that bathed the room in a warm glow. The dark gray comforter on his bed matched the dark brown side tables, and the cream-colored rug contrasted with navy curtains that imparted a decidedly masculine air to the room.

As Kaleo turned to leave, she saw several papers that had been left out on top of the comforter. Her curiosity got the better of her, and when she looked closer she recognized that it was the report she needed to read, and assumed that Stefan had left it out for her before getting in the shower. Intrigued, Kaleo absentmindedly sat on his bed and began to leaf through the document in the light of the candles.

She had read the first couple of pages while lounging comfortably on her side when the door to Stefan's bathroom opened and he stepped out with only a towel wrapped around his waist. They both froze; Kaleo hadn't heard the water from the shower turn off, and Stefan had obviously not been expecting to find her lying on his bed.

"I was, uh, coming to check on you and the door was open, and I saw the report," Kaleo said as she tried not to stare at the newly formed bruises covering half of his muscular torso and arms.

"I must have gotten distracted and forgotten to close the door," Stefan replied before readjusting his grip on his towel. "It's a good thing that I have the towel on today, sometimes I don't," he added with a small laugh, and then immediately looked like he wished he hadn't.

Kaleo felt a fierce blush creep over her cheeks at the mental image that his words conjured in her brain and sat up. "I should leave you alone and let you finish getting ready."

"No, it's fine, stay where you are and keep on reading, I just need to grab my clothes from the closet," Stefan assured her.

Once he had exited his walk-in closet dressed more comfortably in sweatpants and a shirt, Stefan glanced at Kaleo and left the room, reappearing minutes later with two glasses of water that he set on each of the side tables. He gingerly sat on the bed with his back against the headboard and patted the space next to him, his eyes on Kaleo.

Kaleo glanced nervously at the water, the candles, the bed, and finally at Stefan. "I'm sure you're tired. I better head back to the guest room and finish up reading this," she said as she shuffled the papers back into their original order.

"Why would you do that when there's a perfectly good bed right here?" Stefan asked quietly.

"Well, with the talk about children earlier... and the candles... and then you in that towel... I think it would probably be best if we just kept some space between us tonight," Kaleo stammered.

Stefan chuckled low in his throat and reached for Kaleo, but grimaced and put a hand on his bruised side before settling back. "I promise that the open bedroom door and the towel was an accident, love, not an invitation. I didn't mean to scare you. Don't worry, the doctors at the hospital banned me from all physical exercise more strenuous than walking for at least the next two weeks, remember?"

"I also remember you trying to convince them that you were perfectly fine and mission-ready."

"Yes, well that's one particular mission that I'm not quite ready to undertake yet, and I promise that I've taken their advice to heart. I also recall that your sister told you to keep an eye on me tonight. How are you going to do that if you're all the way across the apartment?"

"I can find a chair and bring it in here..."

"You'll do no such thing." Stefan patted the bed beside him once more and looked at her pleadingly. "If you really want to go to the other room, I won't force you to stay, but I promise that I'm not going to try to seduce you tonight."

"Yeah, well, you're not the only one I'm worried about," Kaleo muttered under her breath.

She thought that she said it quietly, but the Cheshire grin that spread across Stefan's face told her otherwise. "If that's what you're so worried about, I promise that I won't let you seduce me either."

"You sure are pushing hard for me to stay with you here for someone who 'accidentally' left the door to his bedroom open and the documents I needed on the bed."

"And you sure wasted no time in taking full advantage of that accident and sprawling across my bed like you owned it."

He had a point, and Kaleo had no more good arguments. She crawled across the bed to sit next to Stefan, and smiled when he sighed contentedly, rested his head against her chest, and wrapped his arms around her. Kaleo absentmindedly combed her fingers through his hair as she read the dossier. When she had finally finished it, she had a good idea of what to expect, but a couple of questions still plagued her.

"Stefan?" she asked.

He stirred. "Hmmmm?"

"Were you asleep?"

"Yes, shhhhh. It's bedtime now. Let the injured man get his rest," he replied sleepily, and held a finger up to her lips before scooting further down onto his non-injured side and resting his head on the pillow.

Kaleo smiled and got up quietly from the bed. She blew out all the candles except for one and took it with her into the living room. There, she paused; Stefan had been right—if she stayed in the guest bedroom she wouldn't be able to hear him if he needed anything. Then inspiration struck, and Kaleo grabbed one of the pillows and the comforter from the guest room and made herself a bed on the couch.

The next morning Kaleo was grateful that she hadn't spent the night in Stefan's bed when his mother opened the apartment door and bustled in at such an early hour that the sun hadn't yet risen. The unexpected activity woke up a very disoriented Kaleo and without thinking, she activated her abilities and slammed a barrier into place between the kitchen where the intruder was standing, and the rest of the apartment. The sudden adrenaline rush helped lift the fog of sleep from her brain, and once Kaleo had sat up, rubbed her eyes, and seen who walked through the front door, she felt embarrassed and immediately dropped the barrier. Stefan's mother stared at her for a couple of seconds, glanced at her makeshift bed on the couch, and gave a satisfied nod before disappearing down the hallway to the guest bathroom.

Kaleo went to Stefan's room and kissed him awake gently. He took one look at the clock on his bedside table and rolled back over onto his side. "What are you doing up so early? Go back to sleep, Kaleo. You don't have to go to work for at least a couple more hours."

"I would love to, but your mother's here."

His eyes sprang open and he bolted upright in bed, then hissed at the pain. Kaleo reached out to help him, but he waved her off and pinched the bridge of his nose. "Where is she right now?"

"In the guest bathroom."

"She has her own key. I can't believe that I completely forgot that she told me last night she was coming today." He looked at Kaleo and groaned before leaning back against the headboard. "Did she walk in on us?"

"I was in the living room."

"That's good." He saw Kaleo's raised eyebrow. "Look, I know I'm a grown man with my own place, but my mother is very traditional, and she raised me to be very traditional too, and I've got to say that there's some very good points to waiting before you sleep with someone, and neither of my older brothers really did. I know that must have disappointed her, so I'm kind of the last one who has a chance of not disappointing her in that way, and I promise that I'm not a little kid, and I have other very good reasons for waiting, but if she had walked in on us sleeping in the same bed, I'm sure that she'd probably have some questions, and it's not that she'd disapprove of you because you saw her with Louisa and Annette, and you know that she loves them both, but I'd just really like for us to be the good ones, you know? It's not just that either. I also personally believe that sex is a very special thing to share with one special person, not that I don't find you extremely special and absolutely maddeningly beautiful and sexy, because I really do, but I also just know that I get *really* attached really easily and I just really don't think  that it's a good idea for us to take that step in the relationship without being committed, like seriously committed, like rings-on-both-of-our-fingers committed, which I'll admit is very much a possibility from my viewpoint right now because I'm so incredibly in love with you..." Stefan's sleepy brain finally caught up to his runaway mouth, and he snapped his mouth shut, groaned once more, and ran his hands over his face. "I'm sorry, I know that was a lot. I didn't believe Katherine last night when she said I had a concussion, but I certainly do now. Let's just pretend I didn't say any of that, okay?"

Kaleo smiled and took Stefan's face in her hands. He froze and looked up at her, his tousled brown hair framing green eyes that were still dark with sleep.

"It's okay Stefan, don't worry. Now, I want you to repeat after me. Can you do that?" she said in a soothing voice.

He nodded.

"Kaleo loves me."

"Kaleo loves me."

"We're on the same page."

"We're on the same page."

"She thinks that my concussion ramblings are adorable, and she loves that I'm finally comfortable enough around her to let down my suave facade and tell her what I really think and feel."

"What did I ever do to deserve you?" he asked softly.

She kissed his forehead and combed her fingers through his hair. "That wasn't exactly the same, but I'll allow it. Now, I'm going to go get ready, and you need to get up and tell your mother good morning."

Once she was satisfied that Stefan was mentally competent to deal with his mother, Kaleo went to the guest bedroom where she had stored her change of clothes the night before. By the time she was done, Stefan had joined his mother in the kitchen. Kaleo sat down next to him on one of the barstools and he kissed her on the cheek. His mother walked over to give Kaleo a hug and officially tell her good morning before chattering a string of words to Stefan and returning to her cooking.

The tips of Stefan's ears turned crimson and he smiled. "She told me about the reception that you gave her this morning."

"Tell her I'm sorry about that; she woke me from a very deep sleep and I was too surprised to think."

"No, no, she was very impressed." He eyed the comforter and pillow on the couch. "Impressed in more ways than one actually, although I think that later you and I may need to talk about appropriate places to sleep. I do have more than one bed in this apartment, you know."

Kaleo shrugged. "You were right—the guest bedroom was too far away for me to hear you if you needed me." She grinned. "Don't think too hard about it; I'd hate for you to start rambling again."

Stefan opened his mouth to reply but was interrupted by his mother sliding a plate of food in front of each of them.

After she was satisfied that Stefan was eating, his mother took his car keys and some cash and told him that she was going to run to the store to stock up his groceries. She hugged them goodbye and was gone as suddenly as she had entered.

With his mother gone, Stefan turned to Kaleo and kissed her deeply. "That is for taking such good care of me."

He kissed her again. "That was for waking me up in such a delightful way this morning and being so understanding."

A third time he kissed her, and then tickled her. "And that was for sleeping on the couch last night."

Kaleo laughed and slapped his hands away before standing up. "I've got to call Todd and let him know what's going on, and then while we've got time I need you to answer some questions before I have to leave and get ready." Stefan made a face but nodded and finished eating while Kaleo made her call.

After she had talked to Todd, Kaleo took the comforter and pillow off the couch and remade the bed in the guest bedroom. She sat with Stefan on the couch and they went over the report together.

Stefan explained that the meeting place with the source would be at a remote hunting cabin late that afternoon.

"And Brant absolutely has to be there?"

"Unfortunately, yes, he's the only one who can confirm the identity of the middleman. Is that okay?"

She shrugged. "It'll be fine. I'll be Phoenix and he won't know any different. What's this about us having to hike to the cabin?"

"It's in dense woods, so the helicopter won't be able to fly you in and the only road leading to it got washed out last week. The nearest landing spot for the chopper is about a half mile out."

"Then are we skiing in?" Kaleo frowned. "I'm not even sure I remember how to ski."

"Don't worry, you'll be walking. There was a warm front a few days ago that melted most of the snow."

"Will we have any backup?"

"Not immediately nearby, no. There's a military base about thirty minutes away by helicopter from the cabin and I've arranged to have a squad on standby just in case something happens, but apparently the source in question is a bit skittish when it comes to military and police types."

Kaleo nodded and then looked at Stefan. His furrowed brow and the frown on his face gave her no doubts as to his feelings on the matter. She nudged him gently. "Hey, we'll be fine. You've planned this all out down to the smallest detail. We'll get in, make the trade, get the information, and be done. You probably won't even know that I'm gone until I'm back."

"You better." He squeezed her hand. "If anything happens to you today, I'm never going to forgive myself."

Kaleo set the report on the coffee table, cupped his cheek in her hand, and leaned in for a kiss. He wrapped his arms around her, held her close, and kissed her back, and they didn't break apart for a very long time.

# Chapter Sixteen

Once she was sure that Stefan was going to be okay, Kaleo drove to Hamilton's office to squeeze a few hours of work in and drop off several documents for Todd before heading over to the task force headquarters to get her Phoenix gear. She saw Audra and Laura sitting in the rec area, but only nodded in their direction to acknowledge them before ducking into the locker room; she didn't have the time or mental bandwidth to be distracted by feuds that she hadn't started and didn't know how to end.

Phoenix walked into Director Stone's office at exactly 3:57 p.m. and found Brant Heinstein already there. His appearance had changed in the five months since she'd seen him last: his chestnut hair now fell just below his square jaw, and he'd gained some weight, although not all of it was fat judging by the way his broad shoulders tapered down to his waist.

She took a seat on the couch and crossed her arms. Brant turned from the window where he was standing, his expression darkening into a frown when he saw her. He looked at the director.

"I said that Henry doesn't like authority figures or cops, and you assign the person who is infamous for being Hamilton's personal bodyguard to the team? Where is Stefan? He told me that he'd personally be running this operation and that he had worked everything out."

"*Assistant Director* Peters has had something detain him. Once the fourth member of our party gets here, I will explain everything."

"What about you?" Brant asked as he turned to Phoenix. "Take that silly helmet off and let me see your face."

"Sorry, can't do that," she said. The voice modulator added a deep and authoritative tone to her words.

"Phoenix will keep all of their gear on. Their true identity is a closely guarded secret for good reason."

"I can't trust them unless I know who they are!"

Director Stone pinned Brant with his eyes. "And I don't trust you even knowing exactly who *you* are, Mr. Heinstein. Don't forget that it was your company who transported the bombs that almost blew that rally apart. You should be grateful to Phoenix here for their intervention; otherwise you might be facing a much more intensive investigation that would cast a long shadow of terrorism and suspicion on your company, not to mention the public embarrassment that would follow."

Brant huffed and opened his mouth to give what Phoenix assumed would be an indignant reply when the door to Director Stone's office opened, and the Treasury representative entered the room. She paused for a moment, halfway leaning out of the doorway to speak to Brian, and Phoenix watched Brant ogle her expensive heels, shapely legs, and fitted skirt. Then she turned around and took another step into the room, letting the door shut behind her.

Phoenix glanced over at Brant and felt no small sense of satisfaction when she saw that his formerly florid face had been drained of all color, and that he had been rendered completely speechless.

"Thank you for waiting, we had a small snag at the treasury getting the funds signed over to me and prepped for travel," Lin said as she walked over to shake Director Stone's hand and introduce herself, oblivious to the other occupants in the room.

"You aren't dressed appropriately," Director Stone replied and looked pointedly at Lin's shoes.

Lin nodded towards a large bag slung over her shoulder. "I brought a change of clothes and boots. We have a very strict dress code at the treasury, and I didn't want to change before I got here and be even more tardy. It won't take me but a minute or two to get dressed."

The director nodded and cleared his throat. "Now that we're all here, I believe it is time to make some introductions and explain the change in plans."

Lin turned around. She saw Phoenix first and nodded smoothly as the director introduced them; she of course already knew who was really behind the helmet.

Then Lin looked at Brant and froze.

"It's good to see you again, Lin. It's funny how we keep on running into each other under unexpected circumstances," Brant said quietly.

"Yes, very funny. Absolutely hilarious," Lin's voice was breathless.

Phoenix hadn't seen her two former teammates together in the same room since before Puppeteer's betrayal. She remembered how Lin had told her all about how after the Betrayal she'd been in an intense relationship with Brant for almost a year, and how she had to leave him when he'd started spiraling after losing his hand in a failed operation to capture Puppeteer. Lin had also told her how she had reconnected with Brant at a fundraiser in the preceding spring, and how they'd disconnected several weeks later under somewhat painful circumstances that her friend hadn't elaborated on.

Even knowing the history between Lin and Brant, Phoenix was struck by the sizzling chemistry that filled the space between the two as they stared at each other.

"Well, it certainly seems like you two know each other, so let's skip that introduction for the sake of time," she said lightly to break the tension.

Lin shook herself out of her trance and took a seat by Phoenix. "Thanks for that," she whispered softly before glancing back at Brant, who had turned back around to look out the window again.

"Yes, well, with that part over, I believe I need to give you all an update," Director Stone said as he shuffled his papers. "As you can see, my assistant director is not here at the moment. He had an unfortunate accident last night and will be on medical leave for the next several days—"

Lin interrupted. "That's horrible. Is Stefan okay? Poor Kaleo, does she know? She must be worried sick."

Brant snorted from the window and Phoenix struggled to contain a laugh. Lin was playing the part of the clueless friend almost too well.

The corner of Director Stone's mouth twitched. "Stefan is fine, he just sustained a couple of injuries that require him to rest. His girlfriend was with him at the time of the accident and kept an eye on him last night. I have it on good authority that they are both doing well. Now, if I may finish what I was going to say?"

"Sorry," Lin murmured.

"As I was saying, he won't be available for this particular operation. As such, I will be stepping in for him, and Phoenix has agreed to join both for our protection and because, as the person who averted the more serious side effects of the bombing, they have an invested interest in the case. Everything else will be following the plan that you each received in your dossiers, aside from the personnel change. Miss Parks, I take it that you have the correct funds on your person?"

"In here," Lin replied as she patted the briefcase at her side.

Director Stone nodded and checked his watch. "In that case, Phoenix will show you where the restrooms are so that you can get changed. We're due on the roof in fifteen minutes."

Phoenix led Lin to the women's restrooms and followed her in. Once the door had shut behind her, Lin collapsed against the wall and groaned.

"Did you know Brant was going to be here?"

Phoenix checked the stalls to make sure that they were alone. "I didn't even know about this operation until late last night."

"That's right; how's Stefan? What happened?" Lin went into the largest stall and began to change out of her clothes as she talked.

"A car hit him on his bike after our training last night. He's got a concussion and several broken ribs, but the doctors said that he'd be okay with plenty of rest."

"And how did your first real night sleeping over at his apartment go?"

"I slept on the couch."

"Ouch."

"His mother, who may actually be more traditional than I am, made a surprise visit early this morning that he forgot to tell me about, so it turned out to be a very good decision. How are you feeling about Brant?"

Lin forcefully exhaled. "I had no idea he was going to be here. My dossier was all about the financial side of things and only said that a Heinstein representative would be present. I was expecting someone from middle management, not the owner of the company himself. We didn't part ways on the greatest of terms last time, and I honestly thought that I'd never see him again."

"What happened?"

"I've told you about the gala, right?"

"Yes."

"And how after that disaster he made an account at the investment firm I worked at so that he could apologize to me and ended up becoming basically my only client?"

"Also yes."

"Did I tell you that after a couple of weeks of working with him we got into a fight, and he implied that he could essentially buy me like a prostitute, and that in a fit of rage I passionately kissed him and then told him he wasn't man enough to be with me?"

"... No. You left that part out."

Lin opened the stall door and bent over to tie her hiking boots. "Yeah, that's what happened. The last time I saw him, I had just broken the news that I was transferring his account to one of my associates and moving up here. Then I walked away and left him alone on a park bench."

"I certainly don't envy the situation you're in."

"Me either." Lin straightened. "But then again, I don't envy your position either. Don't think I didn't hear that disrespectful little snort he gave when he heard your name."

"At least I've got a helmet on, so he can't see when I roll my eyes or stick my tongue out at him."

"Very true. Want to trade?"

"Not on your life." Phoenix paused. "Are you going to be okay? Things seemed a little tense in there."

Lin finished folding her work clothes and placed them in her bag with her high heels, then checked her makeup in the mirror as she pulled her long, straight black hair into a high ponytail. "I'll be fine now that I've had a chance to recover." She looked at Phoenix in the mirror, her dark almond eyes set with a resolute expression. "I've got a great job, great friends, and a boyfriend who treats me far better than I deserve. Brant's just a distraction—no, he's even less than a distraction. What's not to love about my life right now?"

"If you're sure..." Phoenix didn't say that it sounded like Lin was trying to convince herself more than anything else.

"I'm positive." Lin smiled and slung her bag back over her shoulder. "Now, let's go get this thing done. The faster we get there and make the trade, the sooner we can get back and I can move on with my life once and for all."

# Chapter Seventeen

Phoenix and Lin walked back to the office to rejoin the two men, and they made their way as a group up several flights of stairs to a waiting helicopter on the roof that had "Heinstein Transport" painted on its side. Director Stone was the first in and sat against the far wall.

"I'll need you to sit next to me so we can make sure we're on the same page going into this, Phoenix," he shouted over the whirr of the blades.

Phoenix climbed in after him and looked around the space before taking a seat next to the director. There were more than enough seats for the four of them; seven at a brief count, but three seats were piled high with boxes. She watched as Brant gestured for Lin to get in next, and saw Lin's face fall as her friend realized there were only two seats open, and that they were right next to each other. Lin glanced at Phoenix and chose the seat closest to the window. Brant was next and had a similar reaction. He closed the door behind him, looked at the boxes strapped to the other seats, and seemed to seriously consider moving them out of the way so that he wouldn't have to sit next to Lin. Director Stone shook his head.

"Some of the things in those boxes are a bit touchy, and from what I hear it took the loading crew quite a bit of time to get them strapped down appropriately earlier."

Brant's shoulders slumped forward slightly and he took the seat next to Lin before letting the pilots in the front know that they were ready to go.

After Brant had closed the door, the noise of the helicopter blades faded considerably and while the thrum of the electric engine was loud, headphones weren't needed. Still, Phoenix was sure that Lin and Brant wouldn't be able to hear her over the faint background noise and turned to Director Stone.

"What was it that you wanted to talk about?"

"I assume Stefan briefed you and answered any of your questions?"

She nodded.

"Then I have nothing else to add, I just wanted an excuse to make those two sit together. They looked like they might appreciate the chance to get reacquainted earlier."

"That's not what it looked like to me."

The director shrugged. "They may thank me later. I could have cut the atmosphere in my office with a butter knife."

"They had a bad breakup several years ago and she's got a serious boyfriend now."

"Ah, what a pity. Oh well, can't say that I didn't try. If nothing else, maybe this will provide us with some entertainment for the next hour."

"You're not a very nice man sometimes, you know that?"

Director Stone snickered and leaned his head back. The rest of the flight was spent in silence. Phoenix watched as Brant tried to ask Lin something, but after a few terse replies, he gave up and let the conversation stall into an awkward silence.

When the helicopter touched down over an hour later, it couldn't have been soon enough for Phoenix— being so high up in the air for so long made her nervous, and she was grateful to get her feet back on solid ground.

Director Stone and Brant stepped over to speak to the pilots for a moment and left Phoenix and Lin standing alone briefly.

"Quiet ride?" Phoenix asked.

"Did the director even talk to you at all?"

"Nope, he just wanted to make sure that you two had the chance to sit together."

Lin sighed. "Just what I need, someone to play matchmaker between my ex and I."

Phoenix was prevented from replying when Brant and the director walked back over to where she and Lin were standing.

"Everyone ready?" Stone asked.

"I'm good." Lin patted the briefcase.

Phoenix checked that she had her baton on her belt and gun on her hip and nodded. She wasn't a great shot by any means, but sometimes having a gun was better than nothing at all.

"The only thing I need is my wits," Brant said.

"Too bad you drank those away a long time ago," Lin muttered under her breath. In the calm of the forest, she might as well have shouted, and when Lin realized that everyone had heard her, her cheeks flooded scarlet.

"Yes, well, Mr. Heinstein you may lead the way now," Director Stone said dryly.

Brant nodded. "All right then, Lin will be in the front with me and Phoenix can bring up the rear. It'll be best for Henry to see a pretty face carrying a large amount of cash before he's confronted with the terror in black."

The walk was relatively short. The path took them through the woods and down a steep hill before leveling out along a partially frozen, sluggishly gurgling stream and then leading up another small hill to the lodge. Phoenix stayed open to her surroundings and kept an eye out for anything unusual, but everything seemed completely benign.

They rounded a bend in the trail, and the lodge came into view. It was a two-story log cabin with a large stone chimney and wrap-around front porch. As they approached the lodge, a middle-aged man stepped out onto the porch and scrutinized the group. "I thought I told you not to bring any cops, Brant," he called out.

"Phoenix here isn't a cop."

"You think I don't know who that is? Bodyguard to the new vice president is close enough. Are you trying to play games with me?"

Phoenix didn't like the hostile attitude of the man and began to open herself up to the flow of energy in her surroundings in preparation to raise a shield in an instant if she needed to. To her dismay, the only energy she could find was the rapidly fading sunlight and the faint burbling sound of the nearby stream. Some heat was radiating from the bodies of her teammates, but she would have to be in a truly desperate situation to tap into that source and risk giving them hypothermia.

She made a small bubble in the palm of her hand to test out how the energy flow felt.

Just as she suspected, the cold immediately began to sap away the strength of her shield. Even as heat sources bolstered her shield and made it stronger, cold dulled the edge of her abilities and sapped away her strength, making it much more difficult for her to maintain a shield. She shivered, unsure whether it was from fear or the freezing air. The energy drain was a phenomenon that she had encountered before under the tutelage of the Professor, but she'd never had to deal with it on such a large scale.

"No one is here to play games with you," Director Stone said smoothly, and raised his hands. "We don't mean any harm to you; we're only here to make a trade for the information that you have. Phoenix is here for our protection. Surely you can understand that we had to take precautions considering the delicate nature of the situation."

"We have your money, Henry. This isn't a trick," Brant added.

The man who Phoenix assumed was Henry shrugged his shoulders. "Fine. You three can come inside to discuss, but Phoenix stays out."

"Phoenix will do no such thing. I don't trust you any further than I can throw you, and they're here to ensure that you don't try any funny business," Brant replied firmly.

Henry frowned but stepped to the side and opened the door of the hunting lodge. The quartet trooped inside, Phoenix first, followed by Lin, the director, and Brant bringing up the rear.

The inside of the hunting lodge was warm and inviting, a stark contrast to the bitter wind and cold they had just been standing in. The warm tones of the wooden interior reminded Phoenix of the cabin that she'd lived in with her parents after the Betrayal and her subsequent year-long recovery. The muted brown and green decor mimicked the forest outside and created a relaxing atmosphere. A merry fire danced in a hearth made of large river stones, and its heat filled the room. The door shut behind them, and the only sound in the room was the crackling of burning wood in the fireplace. Phoenix took advantage of the energy that the warmth of the fire and the soft electric lights provided and began storing up as much as she could to replenish what the cold outside had drained.

"Oh good, I see that our guests have arrived."

A voice that clawed at Phoenix's memory cut through the silence, and she momentarily forgot how to breathe as a young man with sandy blond hair and blue eyes swiveled around in one of the large recliners that had been positioned around the fire. It had been almost six years since she'd last seen him in person, but his face wasn't one that Phoenix could have ever forgotten—it had been irrevocably burned into her brain and forever linked with the feeling of a gun in her hand and the image of Polygraph and Reader lying still on the blood-stained concrete, bullet holes in both of their heads.

Puppeteer sat in front of them.

In the back of her mind, the part of Phoenix that had formerly been Canary began to scream, but she shoved down the rising feelings of panic and rage and took several deep breaths. She had grown. This time would be different. She wouldn't let her teammates down today.

She was drawn from her internal conflict by the sound of a roar, and then was pushed aside as Brant rushed past her. Whatever his plans were, they were thwarted when he hit the barrier that Phoenix hastily erected. He was knocked off his feet, rolled, and bounced back up as if he were made of rubber before glaring at Phoenix.

"Take this barrier down and let me at him," he growled, his face flushed such a dark crimson that it was almost purple and his fist clenched at his side.

"No." Phoenix didn't trust herself to say more, but the last thing she needed to worry about was Brant under Puppeteer's sway. She turned to look at Lin and the director. Lin's face was as white as the snow that had begun to swirl outside and her chest rose and fell rapidly, her breathing shallow. In contrast, Director Stone remained as impassive as his name.

Brant turned to see what Phoenix was looking at before taking a step away from the barrier and towards Lin, angling his body slightly so that he was standing between her and Puppeteer. As he did so, Phoenix began to absorb as much of the energy in the room as she dared. She remembered well the lessons from the Professor about being a stone in a stream and not a sponge soaking up water, but she had no choice in the matter. Puppeteer had been waiting for them, and she would have to store up as much as she could if they were to have any chance of surviving whatever he had planned.

As she concentrated on stocking up her abilities, Brant growled low in his throat. "What do you want, Puppeteer? Finally decided to crawl out of whatever hole you've been hiding in so that I can end you?" He turned to the older man who was now standing at Puppeteer's side. "And you, Henry, why? We had a deal."

Understanding dawned on Director Stone's face at the mention of Puppeteer's name, and he surreptitiously cut his eyes towards Phoenix.

At the same time, Henry raised his hands in a shrug. "The deal was to connect you with someone who had information about the bombing, nothing more. I'll take my payment now and be on my way to let you two figure out whatever your problem is."

"If you get paid, it'll be for helping us kill this pathetic excuse of a human being."

"And here I thought that you'd be happy to see me. I'm hurt," Puppeteer sneered before glancing over the rest of the group. "Ah, the illustrious Phoenix that I've heard so much about, and who's been causing my colleagues so much trouble lately. I must say that I wasn't expecting to see you today, but it's no matter." His eyes slid over her and settled on Lin. "And Lens, what a surprise to see you here. Oh, this is almost poetic! We're just missing Canary and it would be just like old times."

"I think you're missing a couple of names there, or did you forget about what you did, you—"

Puppeteer held up an airhorn and the resultant sound drowned out Brant's tirade. In the confines of the room, it was a near-deafening noise, but Phoenix was able to use it to her advantage to fill her energy stores as much as she dared. After Brant's mouth had stopped moving, Puppeteer stopped the horn and stood from the chair. He walked forward until he was only a few inches from the barrier and smiled. Phoenix had wished many times before that she could use her energy shield to attack, but now the desire to wipe the smile off his face was almost a physical need.

Puppeteer's warm smile was offset by his cold eyes and gave the impression of a shark opening its mouth to devour its prey. "Please, watch your language old friend. Remember that there's a lady present, and we must mind our manners. There's no reason to get so upset; of course I didn't forget about dear Polygraph. She and I had more than our fair share of nights together, you know."

Brant made a sound that sounded like a cross between throwing up and gagging.

"Oh, so you didn't know? Yes, your sister and I had quite the special relationship." Puppeteer licked his lips as if savoring the memories.

Brant was practically foaming at the mouth. "I'm going to kill you." He took a step forward, and Puppeteer held up a finger and wagged it.

"Yes, yes, I'm sure you'd love to do that, but now that we've got all of the posturing out of the way, let's get down to business, shall we?"

"We have no business with you."

Puppeteer sighed and turned to walk back to his chair. "Oh, but you do. You see, Brant, you've brought me a very special gift today; the assistant director of the Midwestern Pact's Intelligence Agency, the same person who is also rumored to be an important part of their little 'task force.'" Puppeteers' words dripped with disdain as he used air quotes on the last words. "Hand him over to me for five minutes and leave the money here and perhaps I'll let you and Lens return to your helicopter safely." Puppeteer paused and cocked his head. "Actually, hand over Phoenix too. Two lives for two lives; I'll regret not finishing what I started with you and Lens, but the money helps to make up the balance."

"I will have you know that I am Jason Stone, Director of the Midwestern Pact Intelligence Agency. I would think that my distinguished position would be worth more than just an even trade," Stone said indignantly.

Puppeteer's full attention was drawn to the director for the first time, and after pausing to assess the situation, he sighed. "That's too bad then. If the assistant director isn't here as promised, then I'm afraid I'll have to kill all four of you. You see, Director, the problem is that you don't have the same connections your assistant does. I hear that his best friend is particularly well connected, and the icing on the proverbial cake is that his girlfriend is quite a beautiful little bird who I have some unfinished business with... Excuse me? Am I boring you?"

Phoenix couldn't suppress a snicker when she saw that Director Stone had made a great show out of checking the time on his watch.

"Not at all, your monologue has been riveting and I'm absolutely dying to hear more. I'm definitely not checking my watch to see how long it takes before one of us falls asleep," Stone said, his voice dripping with sarcasm before turning to Phoenix. "This has been rather disappointing, although at least we now have a face and a new suspect. I believe that we're done here."

"I'm not leaving until I have his head on a platter," Brant snarled.

Director Stone started walking towards the door. "Heinstein, see to Miss Parks please. I believe that she's in need of some assistance," he said over his shoulder.

With a start, Phoenix realized that Lin's hands had begun to shake, and her still pale face had broken out into a sweat despite the moderate temperature of the room. Brant took in Lin's condition at a glance and moved to her side. He positioned himself directly in front of her so that he was completely blocking out the sight of Puppeteer and leaned down to whisper something in Lin's ear. Whatever he said had the intended effect, as Lin looked up at him and nodded weakly before turning and walking to the door. Brant followed closely with his hand on the small of her back, and Phoenix brought up the rear while maintaining the barrier between them and Puppeteer.

When she walked out into the cold air, Phoenix drew the energy from the barrier back into herself, while keeping the mental scaffolding up in case she needed to raise another shield quickly.

They had made it down the steps of the lodge and were halfway across the small clearing when their path forward was blocked by several men who stepped out from the shadow of the woods and formed a half-circle around them. The others stopped, and Phoenix took several steps forward to put herself in the path of the new threat. As she did so, the sound of slow clapping rang out from the porch of the lodge.

Phoenix turned slowly, unsure of where she should be placing her shield and what threat to take on first. As darkness began to settle, she watched as several more men stole out from behind the house and completed the circle. Next to her, Director Stone frowned and Brant left Lin's side to take a step towards Puppeteer, who was now leaning against the stairs. A few of his men had guns they kept trained on the group.

"More of your puppets?" Brant spat.

"Puppets?" Puppeteer looked confused before understanding dawned on his face. "Oh, you mean am I using my abilities on these men? No, not really, they're working for me completely of their own volition."

Director Stone laughed hollowly. "Evil henchmen? Are you a walking cliche? Are there any original thoughts in your head? I bet that if you could have convinced a cat to sit on your lap back in the lodge as you turned around, you would have."

As the director spoke, Phoenix watched Brant put his hand behind his back and fiddle with his prosthetic arm. He removed something from a compartment and stared at her intently before cutting his gaze back to Stone. When she saw what he had in his hand, Phoenix dipped her head in acknowledgement.

"Now, hold on a minute and show me some respect, you old fool. I'll have you know that—" Puppeteer never got to finish his sentence.

Brant reared back and threw a small cylinder towards the men blocking the path. At the same time, Phoenix tackled Director Stone. As soon as her body hit the ground, she raised a barrier just in time to protect the four of them from the effects of the flash-bang grenade. As soon as he'd thrown the grenade, Brant had knocked Lin off her feet and covered her body with his while gunshots rang out in the brief pause before the flash-bang went off. Then Phoenix was on her feet and pulling up the director, with Brant doing the same for Lin. She released the barrier, reformed it into a shield, and settled into a fighting stance. Her shield had absorbed enough of the energy from the flash-bang to fill her to her limits and give her hope that they would be able to win a fight, but Brant shook his head and shoved Lin at her.

"We don't have time and we're too outnumbered. I'll hold the others off. Get them both out of here," he said as he turned back to face Puppeteer's men.

"Brant, no!" Lin shrieked. "Don't do this!"

"Go now!" he bellowed.

Phoenix wasted a precious second to look searchingly at him and then nodded. She grabbed Lin's arm and pulled her away from Brant. Thankfully, the men blocking their way were disoriented, and Director Stone had been able to knock them to the ground. With a firm grip on Lin's elbow, Phoenix followed him down the path.

# Chapter Eighteen

For someone who professed to care so little about Brant Heinstein, Lin sure didn't leave him easily. Phoenix had to practically drag her down the trail until they were out of sight before Lin got hold of herself. Director Stone had taken the lead and Phoenix kept a hand on Lin's back, pushing her forward for fear that if she let go, her friend would turn around and run back into danger. On top of everything else, Phoenix also kept an ear open for any signs of pursuit behind them and reached out with her senses to search for energy sources. There were none of either.

They ran as fast as they could, and reached the helicopter in record time just as the last of the light faded from the sky. Phoenix threw the door open and shoved Director Stone in. "Get it started!" she shouted at the pilots.

Lin threw her briefcase in after the director and turned to Phoenix. "We can't leave Brant behind, please. We have to go back for him," Lin pleaded.

Phoenix ignored her and gestured at the boxes on the seats. "Are these the kits that I think they are?"

The director nodded once. Phoenix grabbed a knife from her belt and slashed the ties holding the boxes in place before lifting the top two boxes down from the helicopter onto the ground.

"We're going back for him," she told Director Stone, as if he didn't already know.

He nodded again. "Once we're in the air, we'll radio for help. If you can hold them off for thirty minutes, you'll have plenty of backup."

"We'll do that." Phoenix clasped Stone's arm and then released him and slammed the helicopter door shut.

There was no time to watch the helicopter lift off; they had a mission to accomplish. Phoenix ripped one of the boxes open and tossed a package to Lin. "Put these on," she ordered. Lin looked at her with wide eyes.

"NOW!"

They were running out of time. Brant had given them a head start, but the precious seconds were ticking away. Lin nodded and slipped the bulletproof vest and helmet on. Silently, Phoenix thanked Stefan for his meticulous planning and foresight.

"Do you know how to shoot a gun?" Phoenix asked.

"No. If we're going to be in close quarters, I won't need one."

Phoenix shrugged and considered the gun she'd drawn from the holster on her hip. She removed both the holster and the gun, and set them in the box. Canary was long dead, but Phoenix had no intention of doing anything that would cause a repeat of history, and the feeling of the gun in her hand after seeing Puppeteer made her nauseous.

They were ready.

"Just like old times," Phoenix said sardonically. Lin grunted in response as she finished buckling on a pair of gloves. They turned back to the trail and ran like Brant's life depended on them. To Phoenix, time seemed to lose all meaning; it had both sped up and slowed down, the seconds rushing by like a mighty flood and then slowing to a trickle.

They crested the top of the hill and paused for a moment to observe the situation. Below, where the path ran off to the side, Brant was standing with his back to a bluff within a small circle of light, facing a shadowy figure that could only be Puppeteer. A group of men surrounded the two figures but seemed to be holding back from attacking at the moment. Phoenix sensed the heat radiating from the torches and then her attention was caught by a strange type of energy that swirled around and within Brant's left hand and arm. The implications hit her immediately.

"He's prepping his summer hand," she whispered to Lin.

"Without his winter hand he can't protect himself from the heat for longer than a second or two. His abilities will burn him. He's going to turn himself into a human torch and take Puppeteer out with him." Lin swore under her breath. "I'm going to kill him if we make it out of this alive."

"If I can get to him, I think I can redirect the buildup of energy, but we'll need to get past Puppeteer's men. Can you give us a shadow screen?"

"You know I can."

They raced down the path and across the open ground to where Brant was standing. As they got closer, Lin began to weave the shadows and light around them until it felt as though they were running through a tunnel of darkness. Finally, they sprinted through a gap between two of the henchmen and then were birthed into the torchlight. At their sudden appearance, Puppeteer stumbled out of the circle of light.

They were almost too late.

The energy swirling around Brant's hand had turned into a vortex and Phoenix felt, rather than saw, him release it. With a last burst of speed, Phoenix threw herself on top of him and cupped his hand in her own, absorbing the energy and allowing it to flow through her body. She let the momentum carry her as she hit the ground, rolled, sprang to her feet with an activated shield ready, and stood next to the prone Brant, swinging away with her baton at anyone who dared venture close. Once she was satisfied that they wouldn't try all rushing her at once, Phoenix allowed herself a moment's rest. Right away she noticed that many of the men now had the blank, glass-eyed expressions that she had seen all too often in her nightmares. It seemed that she was not the only one whose abilities had grown in strength.

Phoenix watched from the corner of her eye as Lin took the concept of shadow boxing to a whole new level by first using a shadow to feint and then deliver a solid punch coming from the opposite direction. Despite her diminutive size, the puppets who tried to attack her never knew what hit them and were driven back from Brant's other side.

The entire surprise attack had taken less than a minute, and before their opponents could recover, Phoenix raised a solid barrier over the three of them.

"I told you to take Lin and get out of here," Brant growled at Phoenix once he'd peeled himself off the ground. His badly bruised and swollen face looked grotesque in the torchlight, and several small streams of blood cascaded from various cuts. His prosthetic arm had been ripped off, leaving only the docking portion that encased the small stump that was now his forearm. He looked terrible—Puppeteer must have only allowed the face-off after letting his men give Brant a good beating.

"I don't leave teammates behind," Phoenix said.

"How sweet, they came back for you after all, Brant," Puppeteer said. He had moved to just within the torchlight, the shadows of the nearby flames dancing over his face.

The puppets charged the barrier, but their attacks only served to energize it more. Finally, Puppeteer bade them stop when he realized that they were in a standoff.

"Keep your little shield up for now; it's no matter to me. You three are vastly outnumbered, and I can wait all night. You'll have to drop that barrier sometime." He sneered.

Phoenix took great pleasure in rolling her eyes even if Puppeteer couldn't see it. "Shut up, puppy dog, or whatever your name is."

"It's Puppeteer!"

"I really don't care."

Puppeteer turned away and sat on a log at the edge of the woods, seemingly content to fume while he waited.

"Puppy dog... I like it. He sure whines like one." Brant looked up at the barrier surrounding them. "So what happens now?"

"We wait until backup gets here," Phoenix said.

"Which is going to take how long?"

"Thirty minutes. Did you even read the dossier that Stefan sent you?" Lin huffed as she sat down beside Brant and pulled a small first-aid kit out of one of the pockets in her vest. "Now sit still and let me get a look at your face."

"I'm sorry that it's not nearly as pretty to look at as yours." Brant's words were followed by a hiss of pain as Lin began to work on cleaning the worst of the cuts with rubbing alcohol.

Phoenix chuckled to herself; they might all have grown up, but some things seemed to never change. She moved to the back of the bubble and sat against the wall of the bluff so that she could better keep an eye on the entire barrier and their surroundings. Once she had gotten settled, she checked her watch. Twenty-five minutes to go.

Snow fell thickly, and a biting wind sprang up. With a sinking feeling, Phoenix felt the cold, wet weather leach the energy from her barrier faster than she had originally anticipated. She stood and moved closer to the front of the barrier. Usually, the more contact her body had with the ground, the more powerful she felt, but now the cold soil only served to steal the warmth from her body.

Several more minutes passed, and her energy reserves drained away at an alarming rate. Phoenix placed her hands against the barrier and funneled as much of her body's energy into it as she dared. In response to the new stress, her heart began to pound and her breathing sped up. She told herself that she only needed to maintain the barrier for fifteen more minutes, but in her current state that small amount of time might as well have been years. Her hands and feet felt like blocks of ice, and her heart beat within her chest like a drum. For the first time that night, Phoenix wondered if she'd be able to hold up under the strain. The cold crept further up her legs and she began to tremble. Wherever the snow made contact with her barrier, it melted into water and ran off in cooling rivulets. Whereas once her barrier had felt rock-solid, now as she pushed against it she could feel the energy bend slightly under her weight. She'd already wicked away all the heat that Lin's and Brant's bodies gave off, but her abilities wouldn't let her pull any away from their core temperature, despite the danger that they were all in.

"Lin, Brant, we need to have a talk," she said quietly. Apparently she had been too quiet for them to hear her, as Lin was completely wrapped up in caring for Brant's injuries and he had happily submitted to her attentions.

"Hey, lovebirds! Can you spare a minute?" her words had the desired effect, and Lin and Brant jumped apart as if struck by lightning. Lin shot an irate glare at Phoenix, but took in the drooping of her head and the sagging of her shoulders, and her expression turned concerned. The two of them moved to stand next to her.

"Is everything okay?" Lin asked.

"Can't keep this up for much longer. Maybe a minute or two is all I've got left," Phoenix gasped.

She dearly regretted not bringing the gun with her; even firing bullets into the barrier to regain some energy would be preferable to the slow, cold, life-sucking drain she was fighting against. She knew that she could ask Lin and Brant to hit the barrier, but it wouldn't be enough to replenish what the freezing cold was wicking away, and they would need everything they had to escape

Brant frowned. "How long do we have now before backup arrives? Five? Ten minutes?"

Phoenix nodded. Talking took too much effort; she had severely underestimated the effect that the energy drain from the freezing cold would have on her. She steeled herself and chose her next words carefully. "When I release the barrier, you two run. Lin, use your shadow screen and get Brant out of here. He's too injured to help fight and he'll need you to keep him safe. I should be able to use the last of the energy to hold them here and give you enough time to hide until our backup arrives."

Lin's eyes flashed in the fading yellow light of the shield. "First Brant, now you. We're not playing this game again," she hissed.

Phoenix felt the last of her excess energy begin to drain away. She looked up to see that the water streaming down the barrier was slowing and that at the top, the part with the least amount of energy, her shield had already begun to freeze. Once the ice started, it began to creep inexorably onwards, compounding the energy drain. As if they sensed the change in the situation, the puppets moved closer to the dying light of the shield like a pack of ravenous hyenas circling their injured prey. She prayed that they wouldn't make another attempt on the barrier. If they attacked now, she feared they would be able to break through before the barrier regained enough strength to hold them off.

"No other options. Get ready," Phoenix warned, and closed her eyes as she prepared to snap the barrier into the best shield that she could muster. Her entire body was ice, and try as she might, even her thoughts felt like they had slowed down. "You'll have to move fast."

At just that moment, Brant placed his hand against the barrier and released a raging torrent of heat. Phoenix's eyes snapped open as she felt the rush of energy, and she immediately wicked it away from his hand and channeled it up and around them. The sudden influx turned the ice and water on the barrier into steam, and the faint glimmer of yellow brightened until it looked like they were standing within the sun. Phoenix laughed as she felt the excess energy that overflowed from her shield rush through her and warm her body. She looked over at Brant.

"Thank you."

He smiled and winked through his swollen black eye. "There's only room for one of us to play at being the hero tonight, and I called it first."

They stood side by side, working in synchrony until they heard the deep thumping sound of a helicopter in the distance.

Judging from the reactions of the puppets, Puppeteer had heard the helicopter too. Suddenly, every single puppet was attacking the barrier, shooting at it with guns, slashing at it with knives, or beating on it with their bloody fists. Not that it made much of a difference; with the energy provided by Brant the barrier had been sufficiently strengthened, and Puppeteer had missed his window of opportunity.

A spray of bullets mowed down several of the puppets, and the others melted back into the dark night. Not long after, a small team rappelled down from the helicopter and introduced themselves as the backup. Once they had cleared the area, Phoenix released her barrier and the backup team surrounded her, Lin, and Brant and escorted them back to the clearing where the helicopter had landed.

After they'd reached the clearing, half of the backup group peeled off and trotted down the pathway. Phoenix watched them go from her seat on a box next to the helicopter. At some point, someone had wrapped a heavy blanket around her, and as she began to warm up, she truly realized just how cold she had been before—the heat from Brant's hand had most likely been the only thing keeping her from hypothermia.

As she sat, the leader of the backup group explained to her that Director Stone had read them into the situation, and that they had orders to investigate, arrest everyone they came across, and secure the hunting lodge until a team from the Midwestern Pact Abled Task Force could be mobilized due to the threat of the powerful Abled in the area.

The minutes ticked by, and then Phoenix heard a large explosion and saw a bright glow through the trees. Not long after, the rest of the backup group jogged through the trees and reported that they'd found the lodge, but that it had blown up before they could get close and there had been no sign of hostiles remaining in the area.

The soldiers had already secured a perimeter around the clearing as they began to ready the chopper, but Phoenix still felt uneasy. It may have just been an echo of adrenaline from the fight earlier, but something still felt off, and all her senses were on high alert.

Then a gunshot rang out, and time slowed down.

Phoenix felt rather than saw a bullet exit a gun and begin moving through the trees. She turned her head to extrapolate its destination and traced its general trajectory to the helicopter. It was then that she realized that Brant was sitting several feet away, with his back to the chopper. The medic who had been checking his wounds was inside, digging through what Phoenix assumed was first-aid bags. There was no one else in his immediate vicinity; it was obvious who the intended target was.

The bullet was still moving slowly in the air, but Phoenix could feel it beginning to speed up. There wasn't enough time to create a shield around him, and even if there were, she didn't have the energy reserves to make one strong enough to stop a bullet on such short notice. The bullet, which had started out moving at a snail's pace from the gun, was now on par with the speed of a galloping horse and still getting faster.

Without thinking, Phoenix launched herself into its path.

She was just in time, and felt her body jerk backward and her ribs flare with pain before she hit the ground with a thud. She could hear answering gunfire and faintly feel other bullets in the air, but her main focus was on catching her breath. After what felt like forever, air finally entered her lungs and she gasped greedily for the oxygen. Then she registered that the medic and Brant were kneeling beside her.

"Are you okay?" the medic asked as he unzipped her bulletproof vest. His fingers probed around where the bullet had hit, but there was no blood. "You saved my life," Brant said at the same time.

"Yeah, don't get too excited. The bulletproof vest made it an easy decision," she gasped as she struggled to calm her breathing.

"You still didn't have to put yourself in harm's way."

"And give Puppeteer the satisfaction of actually accomplishing something today? No, thank you."

The leader of the backup team strode over as Phoenix sat up and tried not to wince. Getting shot had felt like getting hit with a very large hammer. She wouldn't be surprised if it left a nasty bruise later. "Hostiles are still in the area. We're going to stay behind and coordinate with a team sent from your task force, but we need to get you three out of here ASAP," he said curtly.

"That's fine with me. I think that I've had enough excitement for tonight. What's the plan?" Phoenix asked.

"Chopper'll fly you to a location about fifteen minutes north of here to rendezvous with the other member of your party, you'll switch over there and then be on your way back home."

Phoenix nodded and gingerly climbed into the chopper. Brant and Lin had already strapped themselves in, and she found a seat in the middle of the row, furthest away from the windows. She'd already had several shocks to her system and felt no desire to be reminded of how high up in the air they were. The flight to the rendezvous was boring in comparison to how the rest of the operation had gone, and she was grateful that it was almost over. So much had happened it seemed insane that just that morning she'd been eating breakfast with Stefan, and that they had left Director Stone's office less than three hours before. She was just beginning to drift off into a dreamless sleep when the helicopter touched down.

The three of them transferred back into Brant's helicopter, where they found Director Stone waiting for them. Brant was the first one in and sat beside the director, ostensibly to fill him in on what had happened after Stone had left, leaving Phoenix and Lin to pick between two of the three empty chairs left.

"I'm going to shut my eyes for a bit. Wake me up if anything interesting happens," Phoenix told Lin, who nodded.

It felt like she had only closed her eyes for a couple of minutes when someone was shaking her awake.

A very discombobulated Phoenix tried to create a protective shield around herself but couldn't summon the energy. The panic woke her fully, and she bolted upright in her chair.

"Is everything okay?" she asked Lin, who was watching her with wide eyes.

"I think that you started having nightmares. You were talking to yourself, and your hands were twitching. I thought it'd be better to wake you up sooner rather than later before you gave anything away," Lin said with a subtle head nod towards where Brant and Director Stone were sitting.

Phoenix sighed and leaned her head back against the chair. "Thanks, I appreciate it."

As if sensing that he had been the object of their discussion, Brant excused himself to Director Stone before making his way across the cabin to them. He sat carefully on the open seat next to Phoenix.

"They worked you over pretty good, didn't they?" she asked when he winced as he sat down.

"Yeah, well, you should have seen the other guy."

"I did. I still think you got the short end of the stick. Frankly, I'm surprised you can even talk or walk right now."

"Winter clothes with layers helped the body, and I've been in a bulking phase for my weight training lately, so I had some extra padding... as for the face, I guess you could say that I have a very hard head." He chuckled and then grimaced. "I never did tell you thank you for the rescue, did I?"

"Nope."

"Well, thank you for saving my sorry hide then." He leaned past Phoenix to look at Lin and waited until he had made eye contact before speaking again. "Thanks to *both* of you. You were amazing out there, Lin."

"I've been working on some new tricks," Lin said primly before she nodded at his stump. "I'm sorry that you lost your prosthetic. Did it hurt? Are you going to be able to get another one?"

He frowned. "It got pulled off before you two got there. Thankfully, I was able to release it fast enough that they didn't dislocate my arm when they were yanking at it. I've always got a backup or two lying around, and after a doctor checks it over tomorrow, it'll be as good as new."

Lin gestured at his gloved hand. "What about the hand? Any more burns?"

"None at all, although I suppose that I am indebted to Phoenix for that."

Lin's eyes flashed. "If you ever try something like that again, I'll make you regret it."

His eyes widened into an innocent expression. "Try what? Reinforcing a teammate's shield?"

"No. You know what I'm talking about, and Phoenix can sense energy patterns. We all know what I'm talking about."

Brant's face fell. "I didn't have any other option, Lin. I had to take him out once and for all."

"What's the story there?" Phoenix asked carefully, hating how she had to pretend to be completely clueless.

"It's a long story."

"We've got like ten minutes, right?"

Brant sighed. "Puppeteer used to be part of a team that both Lin and I were on. He betrayed us, killed my sister and another one of our teammates, and tried to kill a third. A few years ago, I tracked him down and he cut my arm off. I had to use my summer hand to get away from his ambush and... well... there's a reason I keep the glove on." Brant turned to look at Lin. "Did you know about him and Ashley?"

"Ashley?"

"Polygraph, sorry."

Lin shook her head. "I knew he was closer with her than anyone else, but not that they were *that* close."

Brant shuddered and leaned his head back against the seat. "Just more fuel for my nightmares, I guess."

"You're preaching to the choir there," Lin agreed.

Several minutes later when they landed on the same spot where they had taken off only a few hours before, Phoenix was surprised to see that besides the fact that night had fallen, it almost looked as though they'd never left.

Katherine was waiting for them on the roof, and Phoenix assumed that Director Stone had arranged for her to be there to look over Brant; she couldn't blame him—Brant was putting on a brave metaphorical face, but his actual face looked awful, and he walked with a very noticeable limp.

Phoenix nodded at Katherine before walking over to the director, who was talking to several people she didn't know. He waved them off when he saw her approach.

"I'm assuming we're having a meeting about this tomorrow?" she asked.

"Correct."

"Are you and Katherine going to clear Stefan to be part of it?"

"Considering how this operation might have turned out if he'd been on the mission today, I think he has a right to attend."

She nodded in agreement and handed him the bullet from her vest. He promised to pass it along to his ballistics people, and they told each other goodnight. Katherine was still checking Brant over while Lin stood at his side and Phoenix allowed herself to smirk in the safety of her helmet. No matter what Lin said, watching her and Brant had been very telling. It was obvious that there were still feelings there on both sides, but she could also sense a deep pain. Besides, Brant still hated Kaleo, and Lin was in love with Sam, making things very messy indeed. Phoenix shrugged to herself as she walked away. They were both grown-ups, and they could work it out themselves.

She waved goodbye to Brant and Lin but was positive that neither saw her leave. Her next stop was at the task force headquarters. An older man dressed in a dapper gray suit with Mod's red and blue silk scarf stuffed into their front pocket looked up from where they was overseeing the front desk when she walked in.

"Rough day?" Mod asked as they eyed the damaged vest slung over her shoulder.

"You have no idea."

"Bet I do. We got an alert from Stone about an hour and a half ago, and Sifter led a team out not too long after. Didn't get much detail, but it sounds like you had quite the time."

"Yeah, well everyone is still alive, so it wasn't a total failure." Phoenix leaned against the desk where Mod was sitting and removed her helmet. They were at an angle that did not allow anyone from the outside to see her, and it was beginning to feel claustrophobic, not to mention rude, to keep it on.

"How was your day?" she asked. Their schedules always seemed out of sync enough for her to rarely see Mod outside of the occasional family dinner and task-force meeting. She didn't say anything about the re-emergence of Puppeteer; she knew that Mod would find out eventually, and she was too exhausted to think about the deeper implications of the day.

"Not too bad. It's been pretty quiet, but that all changed once Stone sent out the alert." Mod grinned. "Not two minutes later, I got a call from a certain concussion patient who asked me to tell you to call him as soon as you could. He sounded just a tad bit panicked."

Kaleo sighed. "Thanks for letting me know."

"Anytime. Glad that you made it back in one piece."

Kaleo called Stefan from the phone next to the locker room and wasn't surprised when he picked up directly after the first ring.

"Hello?" his voice sounded breathless.

"You didn't just sprint to the phone, did you?"

"Where are you? Are you okay? Is everything all right?"

He hadn't answered her question, which was answer enough, and she smiled. "We're all okay, although some of us are a bit more beat up than others. Have you eaten dinner yet?"

"No, I wasn't hungry."

"Well, I'm starving. Do you want me to drive over and pick some takeout up on the way?"

"Is that even a question?"

"Yes? I'm tired. I can always go straight home and you can see me tomorrow at the task-force meeting."

Stefan snorted on the other end. "You know what I meant."

After Kaleo took his order and hung up the phone, she hopped in the shower and changed into her street clothes. Phoenix's gear went into the laundry hamper for cleaning, and she wiped down her helmet and checked it over for any wear and tear before putting it away in her locker and leaving the facility.

Once she got to Stefan's apartment and knocked, Kaleo didn't have to wait long before he opened the door, dragged her inside, and scooped her up into a hug.

"Ouch... Watch the ribs," she protested.

"They're fine, don't worry about them." His deep voice was muffled as he buried his face into the junction of her neck and shoulder.

"Not yours, mine."

Stefan immediately released her and stepped back. Kaleo took the opportunity to move further into his apartment and set the food on the countertop. He followed her, worry lines creasing his face. "Your ribs? What happened?"

"Is your mom still here?"

"Out Christmas shopping. She goes home tomorrow morning. I told her that she didn't have to stay, but she insisted and said something about me still being her baby even when I'm grown." He shrugged and narrowed his eyes at Kaleo. "Don't dodge the question."

In response, Kaleo lifted the left side of her shirt up to show off the red and purple patch that had begun to form over her bottom ribs. "I just got a little shot. Isn't my bruise super pretty?"

Stefan looked horrified. "You got shot?"

"It was either that or Brant's brains getting blown out, and I was wearing body armor, so I think I made the right choice."

He shook his head and set out plates and silverware on the counter. "I will never understand how you get shot more than anyone else I know. What is this? Twice now in less than a year? You'd think that with your particular abilities it'd be the other way around."

Kaleo shrugged. "I guess the bullets just love me."

"Hard for them not to, when you keep on jumping in front of them."

"Better me than someone who isn't as well equipped to deal with them."

Stefan huffed and sat next to her at the countertop. As they ate, she filled him in on everything that happened. When she was done, he leaned back and frowned. "So this was all a set up then."

"Looks that way." Kaleo began clearing away the dishes and he rose to help her.

"Seeing Puppeteer again must have been quite the shock," he said carefully.

"It was."

"How are you feeling?"

Kaleo shrugged. "Part of me, a small part, mind you, wants to curl up and cry in a corner. Hearing his voice again and seeing him control those people was like something out of one of my nightmares... But looking back, it's not so bad. It felt good to foil his plans, it's just all so much to process." She yawned before leaning on the countertop, suddenly feeling very tired.

"You've got that right." Stefan finished putting the leftovers into the fridge and hugged her from behind, his mouth beside her ear. "I don't like the idea of you being all alone in your house tonight knowing that he's still out there and holding a grudge."

"I'll be fine. I wasn't the one that he was targeting. Besides, where would I go? My parents? Katherine's?"

"You could sleep here."

"On the couch again? Or with your mom?"

He chuckled. "No, in my bed."

She made a big show of taking his left hand in hers and holding it up to examine it. "Perhaps your concussion has affected your short-term memory, but I distinctly recall a very agitated Stefan making quite the speech earlier today about why that wouldn't be a good idea... and unless I'm missing something, I don't see any rings on either of our fingers."

Stefan snorted and nuzzled her neck. "Don't worry, I'll take the couch."

She shook her head. "I'm not kicking you out of your bed, Mr. Concussion."

"How else am I supposed to comfort you if the nightmares come again?"

"I'm a big girl, Stefan. I've had nightmares before, and I'm sure I'll have them again. It's whatever, at this point. Besides, you're the injured patient. The last thing you need is to wake up in the middle of the night because I'm having nightmares." She shrugged and checked the time on her watch. "I'm exhausted. I better go. The faster I get home, the sooner I can go to bed."

"Any chance I could convince you to nap here until you're not so tired?"

"No dice. I had a nap or two in the helicopter on the way back, so I think I'll be okay. If I nap here right now, I might not want to wake up until tomorrow morning."

He squeezed her again. "That sounds like a great plan to me."

"It'd be absolutely horrible. I might never leave."

"You say that like it's a bad thing."

"Stefan, I need to go home."

"We had a deal: Phoenix is on the task force, but I get to hover after you get off a mission. It's not fair that you got to hover yesterday, but won't let me return the favor now," he said.

Kaleo smiled and turned around to kiss him. "It's going to happen whether you like it or not. Don't worry about me, I'll be fine. We can go out to eat after the meeting tomorrow and then you can have plenty of time to hover."

Stefan caressed Kaleo's cheek gently and studied her face. Then he broke their eye contact and pulled off the sweater that he had been wearing before thrusting it into her hands. "Take this home with you. I may not be able to be there physically, but maybe I can be there in spirit."

That night Kaleo fell asleep with her face buried in Stefan's sweater. She dreamed of being chased through the woods by faceless men, of Puppeteer's cruel smile and cutting voice, and of watching her friends be killed in front of her. It was a fitful night, but when she woke up in the wee hours of the morning frightened and covered in sweat, Stefan's scent surrounded her and helped to calm her mind, and she fell back into a dreamless sleep.

# Chapter Nineteen

The emergency task-force leadership meeting the next day was scheduled for later in the evening than usual, so Kaleo and Stefan agreed to grab a bite to eat before the meeting. They stopped at Stefan's favorite hole-in-the-wall hamburger joint and sat down to enjoy the deliciously greasy burgers and fries.

Kaleo had just finished telling Stefan about her day helping Todd coordinate the transition for Hamilton's office when she had a sudden realization and made a face. "I'll need to take the train up to Lincoln next week to start apartment hunting."

"So soon?" Stefan asked.

"The inauguration is just over a month away, so if I wait any longer I may not have any time to actually move and get settled before the real craziness starts." She paused to eat another fry. "Anyways, how was your day? Still having a hard time just sitting and resting?"

"More or less. My mother picked up some sculpting clay from the store yesterday on a whim as something for me to do. I tried my hand at it."

"How did it turn out?"

"Like a piece of garbage that looks worse than what my three-year-old nephew could do. She also got a set of watercolors, so I think I'm going to take up painting instead."

Kaleo laughed and a sly look crossed Stefan's face. He nonchalantly looked down and dragged one of his fries through the ketchup on his plate. "I also received a very interesting phone call from Hamilton's office today."

She raised an eyebrow. "Aren't you supposed to be off work and recovering?"

"This doesn't really count as work. Don't you want to know what it was about?"

"Are you even allowed to tell me?"

"I didn't want to tell you earlier because I didn't want to get your hopes up, and you can't share this with anyone yet..." Stefan looked around. They had picked a table for two in the back corner of the small space and were the only ones in the dining area. From the kitchen, Kaleo could hardly hear the cooks over the blaring music of the radio. Stefan leaned forward conspiratorially. "If all goes well, you may be looking at the new assistant director for a national Abled Task Force."

Kaleo's jaw dropped. "National? You're joking."

"Not in the slightest."

"Stefan, that is so exciting!" She had to fight to keep from squealing.

He laughed and reached for her hand. "It's a big step, but they wanted Stone to lead it since he's done such a good job with the task force here, and he told them that he would accept on condition that he could have total control over his team. And I haven't even told you the best part yet—we'll be based out of Lincoln, so it looks like you won't be the only one moving."

As she heard his words, Kaleo's eyes began to fill with tears, and she could see that Stefan's eyes were just as watery as her own. They looked at each other for a long minute, no words needed to communicate the feelings they shared.

They finished eating, and then Kaleo drove them to task-force headquarters. As they walked through the door they greeted Mod, who was engrossed in a book.

"Oh, Kaleo, you had a delivery today." Mod pointed at an enormous floral arrangement sitting on the table behind their desk.

"These are for me?" Kaleo asked as she walked over. She had never seen so many flowers in one place outside of a florist shop.

"They're addressed to Phoenix, so I would assume so. Apparently, they were sent to Director Stone's office and he had someone bring them here."

Stefan whistled. "That thing is huge. Do you have a secret admirer that you never told me about? Should I be concerned?"

Kaleo found the card nestled amongst a dozen orchids. She read it out loud.

*Phoenix—*

*I could send you an arrangement twice as large as this one every day for the next ten years and it still would not even begin to make up for how much I am in your debt. Thank you from the sincerest depths of my heart. If you ever need anything, don't hesitate to call.*

*Brant Heinstein*

She turned the card around. "He wrote his phone number on the back here."

"It's from Heinstein? Well, that's good. I was worried for a split second that I had competition," Stefan said with a twinkle in his eyes. "I was trying to figure out how I could outdo this, and it was making my poor concussed head hurt."

Kaleo giggled and turned to Mod. "Would you mind if I take the card and we keep this here? I think it brightens up the lobby, and it would be a pity to take it back to my place and only have me enjoy it."

"Sounds good to me. I'll think of it as a consolation prize for you not giving me the scoop about Puppeteer and the reunion yesterday. Ungrateful kids. I spent almost an entire year babysitting you three, and no one tells me when our new archnemesis shows back up unexpectedly. Wiper was the one who had to fill me in." Mod scoffed before the skin around their eyes crinkled in concern. "Are you doing okay? What about Lin and Brant?"

"I'm doing fine, but I haven't heard from the others yet. I'm really sorry, Mod. I thought about telling you, but it felt like too big of a deal to talk about when I saw you yesterday. It was too fresh," Kaleo said.

Mod walked over and hugged Kaleo. "I understand. Just know that if you ever want someone to talk to, I'm here."

"Thanks, I appreciate it. We should have dinner together sometime soon," Kaleo said as she returned the hug.

Kaleo and Stefan moved on into the main part of the building and went directly to the conference room usually reserved for the leadership meetings. They were still fifteen minutes early and the only other person in the room was Katherine, who insisted on checking over Stefan to see how his injuries were progressing and then giving Kaleo a quick screen to make sure that she hadn't been hurt the night before. By the time she was satisfied, everyone else had arrived and it was time to begin.

As usual, Director Stone started the meeting and informed everyone of what had happened the day before. Most people in the room already had a good idea of events, by being there in person or through the task force grapevine, but Stone believed in consistency and recounted the entire tale with input from Kaleo for the parts he had not witnessed, and then turned the floor over to Nova to talk about what her team had uncovered after they had investigated the site.

"Not much, I'm afraid," Nova said. "We found several dead bodies, guns, and explosive residue from the crater that had been the lodge, but so far all we're turning up is dead ends. Perhaps Puppeteer should change his name to Ghost; he disappears easily enough."

Stone looked at Nova over the tips of his interlaced fingers. "Any ideas on how he got away?"

"We found hoof prints leading in the opposite direction from the lodge, but Sniffer wasn't with us and we lost the trail."

"Hoof prints from a horse?" Stefan asked.

"I've never met the man, but I would think that he would be too big to be riding a goat," Katherine snapped. Kaleo shot her sister a look, and Katherine sighed. "Sorry, I've had a rough day at the hospital, still have another six hours to go on my shift, and this is eating up my dinner break," she told Stefan.

Director Stone ignored Katherine's outburst and checked his list of questions. "Was Puppeteer acting alone, Nova? I assume from his posse that he still has the support of the Pure?"

Nova shook her head. "When I say that we keep on hitting dead ends, I mean it. We're going to have to wait for the lab results to come back on the samples from the explosive residue that we collected; maybe that will provide a lead." She looked from the director to Stefan with narrowed eyes. "Now, what have you two been up to that would cause Stefan to become a target?"

Stefan and the director exchanged glances, and Stone sighed. "I suppose now is as good of a time as any. The incoming Johnson/Hamilton administration has been toying with taking the idea of the task force and making it national. They're still ironing out the details as to how exactly it would enmesh with other federal agencies and get funding, but at this point it's looking very likely. If everything works out, I will be leading it and Stefan will be one of the people directly under me."

"Could yesterday be related to that?"

"It's not impossible... but if there's a leak, it's not coming from Hamilton's office, and I'd hate to think of the consequences of someone in Johnson's circle being compromised. I think it is more likely to have to do with Stefan's personal connections."

Katherine frowned. "His personal connections?"

"Puppeteer mentioned, and I quote, 'his particularly well-connected best friend and his beautiful little bird of a girlfriend who he has unfinished business with.' It sounds to me like he made the connection between Canary and Kaleo, and he was going to use Stefan to both gain access to Hamilton for political reasons and to get to her for personal ones."

"I'm not sure I like the implications of either of those ideas. I suppose it wouldn't take much to connect me and Adrian, considering the press coverage that the wedding had, but how would he know about Kaleo and me? We're not exactly celebrities," Stefan said with a frown.

Kaleo nodded in agreement. The media flurry that had surrounded her family at the announcement of Sifter's and Architect's return had died down within weeks; starved by the lack of information from her parents and the privacy that she and Katherine had demanded.

"Are we positive that Stefan was the only target last night? From what you've told me, this Puppeteer sounds more than a little devious and the shot taken at Brant Heinstein worries me. Why would a shooter not attempt to take out Phoenix instead? Her death would have caused the most destabilization and opportunity for further attacks."

The Professor's question made everyone turn to look at him.

"Perhaps it was a personal vendetta against Heinstein," Stone volunteered.

Kaleo frowned and shook her head. "If he was trying to cause the most hurt, Lin would've been the one he shot. He likes playing mind games with Brant too much to pass that opportunity up."

"Unless he had only made plans for Brant because he hadn't realized that Lin would also be there. Even I didn't know who the Treasury Department would send," Stefan replied.

Nova scowled in thought. "He may not have even been aware of the personal connection between Lin and Brant. From what I understood of it, their romantic relationship began several months after the Betrayal."

"If he didn't before, he probably suspects something now," Kaleo said.

"She's right; Heinstein and Miss Parks had the chemistry of a baking-soda volcano. Speaking of Brant Heinstein, he has suddenly become very interested in the task force. He contacted me today to see how he could become involved," Stone said.

"He'd probably change his mind when he realized who one of the members was," Kaleo said sourly. Stefan shot her a sympathetic smile and squeezed her hand briefly under the table.

Director Stone nodded. "Yes, I can see how that would cause a problem. Still, with the kind of money that he likes to throw around, and his connections in politics, he could be a very strong ally for us. Does anyone have any ideas?"

"Give him my contact information. I've heard a lot about this young man and am intrigued that he was able to use his abilities with Phoenix's help," the Professor said. "I'll evaluate him and perhaps he'll be content to train with me either until we can think of a more permanent solution, or he loses interest."

Director Stone nodded and turned back to his list. For the next half hour, they talked through several other urgent matters, including the possible need for a security detail for those who had been on the mission until more information about Puppeteer could be obtained, and what to tell the general task-force members at the next informational meeting. By the time they were done, Kaleo felt drained again, and Stefan's face had begun to look pale.

After the meeting, Kaleo drove Stefan to his apartment and helped him up the stairs. He had long since given up pretending to be fine and had to pause several times in the stairwell to catch his breath. Finally, after what felt like several miles of stairs, they were back in his apartment and sitting on the couch. Stefan pulled Kaleo into his arms and held her close, and for a few minutes they sat in silence, simply enjoying each other's company and mulling over recent events.

"How are you feeling?" Stefan asked as his fingers brushed lightly over Kaleo's bruised skin.

"A little tired and sore, but I'll manage. What about you?"

"About the same. More sore than tired, and more worried than sore." He kissed the top of her head.

Kaleo turned to look up at him. "So what happens next?"

Stefan took the opportunity to kiss Kaleo's lips gently before replying to her question. "I haven't talked to Stone yet to finalize everything, but judging from the tone of the meeting tonight, I'm guessing that you, Brant, and I will probably be getting security details for a little while just in case Puppeteer tries anything funny. Other than that, I don't know."

"Better add Lin to that list."

"Lin? Do you really think she's at risk too?"

"I think that it was glaringly obvious that there was something between her and Brant, and she'd be an easy target for Puppeteer. If it's a funding issue, take the detail off me and give it to her, I can take care of myself well enough."

"You're insane if you think that I'd consider that for even a second."

Kaleo turned back to look out the window. "Lin is a pressure point for Brant and me, Brant is too powerful and well connected to not keep protected, and your job makes you too valuable. It makes the most sense that if someone has to have their detail cut, it be mine."

"Is that what you really think? That you're so unimportant you don't need a security detail because if something happened to you it wouldn't matter?"

Kaleo shrugged.

Stefan squeezed her more tightly. "Kaleo, I love you more than I've ever loved anyone else. How could you even suggest that I wouldn't make absolutely certain that you're safe?" He kissed her again before continuing. "If you want to talk about pressure points, let's talk about your parents. Let's talk about

Lin, and therefore Brant by proxy, or about Nicole, and Taylor, and Katherine. That's not even mentioning your proximity to Hamilton and his entire staff, or Phoenix's role in protecting him. Darling, you're not alone anymore; you've never been alone, and you're far too important to too many people for us to leave you unguarded when there's a threat."

"But Lin..."

"We'll get something figured out about Lin. If nothing else, if what you said about her and Heinstein is true, it shouldn't be too hard to convince him to help us foot the bill for her protection. Don't you worry, and don't you ever pretend again like you aren't absolutely vital to your family, and to the task force, and to me."

Kaleo was speechless. They sat for a long time in the darkened room and listened to the radio until the nightly news was over and soft classical music began playing.

"I didn't mean to overwhelm you," Stefan said quietly.

"You didn't. I just don't know what else to say."

"Say that you love me too."

Kaleo laughed and turned her head to nuzzle the hand resting on her shoulder. "Of course I love you too, Stefan, that should be a given by now."

"Perhaps, but I never get tired of hearing you say it."

Kaleo sat up from the couch and stretched her arms. "It's getting late and I should be heading back home. I'll stop by tomorrow after work and bring your sweater back."

"Keep it as long as you need it, or you can bring it back and switch it out if you want. I don't mind." Stefan kissed her goodnight and looked deep into her eyes. "Don't worry about Puppeteer or anything else. You and I are a team now, and I promise you that together we're going to be able to get through whatever is thrown our way."

That night Kaleo slept better than she had in a very long time.

**PART TWO**

# Chapter Twenty

It was the day of the presidential inauguration. The decorations had been hung, security protocols had been finalized, and everything had been planned down to a T. Still, the large crowds made Kaleo uneasy. It wasn't a question of power; the Professor had released her as his full-time student and moved her to a maintenance program, which meant that she was currently only seeing him on an as-needed basis. She had been hesitant at first, but the Professor had insisted that she was ready, and that while there was always room for improvement, she would benefit the most from more real-world experience and less classroom lessons. It was true—the more Kaleo practiced her abilities, the more she learned to trust them, and the more powerful she became. After Phoenix's faceoff against Puppeteer and his minions the month before, she no longer felt like she was always on the threshold of losing control.

As she gained trust in herself, her abilities had another shift. First and foremost was that the color of her shield, which had once been yellow, changed into a deep blue in the days after the operation—named Operation Cuckoo due to Puppeteer's unexpected influence. The color change had been surprising at first, but Kaleo soon appreciated the new beauty of her shield.

The second, and more concerning part of the shift, was that Kaleo's danger sense hadn't made much of an appearance since the operation. At first, she'd questioned why she'd had so little warning as to the precarious situation that she and the others had been walking into. However, the Professor had assured her that, in his opinion, her abilities were so defense-oriented that when she hadn't known how to use them, they had subconsciously worked as her "danger sense":

a protective mechanism, or a way for her brain to warn her when it sensed that something was off. He believed that as she grew more confident in her abilities, the danger sense would continue to decrease until it was possibly nothing more than an uneasy sensation at the worst of times. Unfortunately, in a trifecta of bad luck, Operation Cuckoo occurred as her danger sense was waning, in winter, when her abilities were at their weakest, and on such a short timeline that she hadn't had the chance to process any signals that might have warned her that all was not well.

Either way, danger sense or not, Phoenix hadn't been invited to the inauguration, as the presence of the mysterious figure that the press had dubbed "Hamilton's shadow" had been deemed far too distracting and intimidating for the first day of a new administration. So it was that Kaleo Hughes, one of the top aides to the new vice president, attended the inauguration and afternoon festivities with Stefan Peters, the man who was rumored to soon have a high-ranking position in the new Abled Task Force that had been proposed.

The moratorium against Phoenix went away with the setting sun as Vice President Hamilton and his wife, Lucy, attended several inaugural balls with President Johnson and the First Lady.

At the third ball of the night, Phoenix found herself a convenient spot backstage, where she could keep an eye on the Hamiltons, the Johnsons, and the large crowd. As she watched the two couples dance, Phoenix felt a small pang of loneliness in her heart; the song currently playing had been one that she and Stefan had danced to at Adrian Hamilton's wedding over six months before.

Then a hand slipped into hers. She turned her head to see that Strike was standing next to her, and she realized that she wasn't the only one reflecting on simpler times.

"Careful there; if anyone snaps a photo and connects Strike to Stefan, we're going to have a scandal on our hands. I can just see the headlines now," she said.

He laughed softly and squeezed her hand before letting go and taking a step to the side to put some distance between them. "You're probably right. I don't know if even Silver Tongue could persuade the press out of that one."

The dance was over. The music stopped, the lights lifted, and the hairs on the back of Phoenix's neck began to rise. President Johnson embraced his wife, turned to wave to the crowd, took two unsteady steps, and collapsed to the ground.

For a heartbeat, there was dead silence in the event center as the attendees of the ball watched in disbelief. The silence was shattered by the sound of the First Lady's screams. Immediately, Vice President Hamilton and his wife rushed forward to help. Phoenix was still trying to process the scene in front of her when she heard Strike curse at her side, and then he was a blur racing towards the crowd.

Phoenix looked where Strike was heading and saw a man standing with a gun in each hand, pointing at the stage. She turned back to see that Hamilton was so distracted by President Johnson's condition that he wasn't paying attention to anything else, and there were no Secret Service agents within the immediate vicinity. Phoenix gauged the distance between herself and Hamilton and judged that he was too far away for her to reach him in time. She ran onto the stage and was still evaluating her options when the gunman fired off several shots.

Time slowed down. She wasn't ready. She was too slow.

She immediately stopped in her tracks and felt, rather than saw, the first of the bullets exit one of the guns and make its way across the room.

Without thinking, she planted her feet and gathered all the energy she could feel swirling around her in preparation for a desperate bid to save the vice president.

The first bullet was beginning to speed up as it carved its deadly path directly to Hamilton's head. Phoenix pushed at the energy in the room and used it like a hammer, smashing the bullet to the side until it buried itself in the wall behind him. She used the same technique for the second bullet by pulling a particularly strong wave of energy towards herself and timing it so that it hit the bullet in midair and diverted it to the outside of his right shoulder. The bullet had sped up rapidly, and there had not been enough time to knock it away so that it completely missed him.

Two down, several more to go. Phoenix turned her attention to the final three bullets. They too had begun to speed up, and she didn't have enough time to divert them in the same way that she'd done the first two. The cluster of three was far too close to Hamilton for her to effectively push it off course, and the bullets were spread far enough apart that she wouldn't have been able to hit all three at once.

Acting more out of instinct than any type of conscious thought, and knowing she was otherwise all out of options, Phoenix harnessed all the energy she could reach and brought it down in a crashing wave directly between Hamilton and the bullets now speeding towards him. In her overzealousness, she knocked out the lights, and even through her helmet the roar of the crowd reached an earsplitting pitch.

Fortunately, she didn't need the light to feel the bullets. They slowed down considerably when they passed through the loose barrier she'd created, but not enough to make them any less dangerous. In a last-ditch effort, Phoenix reached deep within herself and focused on the bullets. She felt the way they slid through the air like sharks swam through the ocean: beautiful and deadly. Then she took the energy the bullets were carrying, wrapped it around the front of each bullet as though she were wrapping a special present for a loved one, and pressed against them as hard as she could.

The lights flickered back on, and for a second everyone saw the bullets hanging in midair, less than a foot away from John Hamilton's body, engulfed in a bright, electric-blue light. The room was silent.

The bullets dropped to the ground with a soft "clink" and chaos erupted.

# Chapter Twenty-One

After she'd stopped the bullets, Phoenix sprinted out onto the stage and erected a barrier over the president, vice president, and their wives. Lucy Hamilton, a nurse by training who'd only recently retired from practice, was already assessing President Johnson's vital signs. Within seconds they were surrounded by Secret Service agents and Phoenix snapped her barrier into a large shield to cover their backs as they were hustled away.

She stayed on high alert and kept her shield up as they were rushed through the back of the event center and into a waiting car, letting it fade away naturally as her feet left the ground when she sat down next to the Hamiltons. One of the Secret Service agents began to apply a makeshift dressing to Hamilton's profusely bleeding shoulder wound as their driver pulled out into traffic.

Minutes later, they reached the hospital designated for Hamilton's care, and several doctors and nurses ran out to meet them. Phoenix was the first out of the car, her shield at the ready just in case there was another attempt on Hamilton's life. A judge was waiting for them in the parking garage, and they paused briefly for him to swear Hamilton in as acting president.

As they made their way further into the hospital, Phoenix kept her shield up, and it was only once they were safely ensconced inside the presidential medical suite that she let it dissipate, although she still insisted on staying as close to the new president as possible.

Hamilton was whisked back to get a CT scan, and while he was in the machine Phoenix managed to grab a catnap in the observation room; using her abilities had drained her, and she succumbed briefly to the wave of exhaustion while she had the chance to recharge.

When the scan was completed, one of the imaging techs gently shook Phoenix and she awoke with a start, feeling somewhat refreshed and ready to get back to work. As it turned out, President Hamilton's shoulder wound had been comparatively minor and required only a small surgery, but Phoenix didn't want to take any chances and waited right outside the operating room— a stance that, surprisingly, no one begrudged her.

"That's what? Three times now that I owe you?" Hamilton said to her when they were back in his suite.

"More like eight if you could each of those bullets separately. I think I'm due for a raise."

Hamilton chuckled and reached for his wife, who had taken up station beside him, and held her hand. Lucy smiled at Phoenix. "Thank you for all that you did today. I'm not sure that we can ever repay you."

"It was just part of my job, ma'am," Phoenix replied, afraid that even with the voice modulator, they'd be able to hear the exhaustion that had crept in; the brief recharge from her catnap had already begun to run out. She turned back to President Hamilton. "If it's all right with you, Mr. President, I'll go see if I can track Todd down. I think that I heard him in the next room trying to corral everyone and coordinate everything."

"That sounds fine with me. Best get to work as quickly as possible and minimize the damage." Hamilton shrugged and winced. "Let's just pray that by the end of tonight my shoulder is the only thing that's broken."

Phoenix nodded and got up to get Todd.

When she walked in, Hamilton's chief of staff glanced over at her and immediately dismissed everyone else in the room.

"How's he doing?" Todd asked as he offered her a seat.

Phoenix sat and turned off her voice modulator so they could speak quietly. "He's fine; he even refused general anesthesia for the surgery so there wouldn't be any question about his competence to lead if something comes up in the next few hours. He's ready for you and other visitors now." She took in Todd's relatively disheveled appearance: his tie was loosened and he had taken off his suit jacket and rolled up the sleeves of his shirt. "How big is the fire out here? What's the news?"

Todd sighed heavily. "President Johnson is currently receiving treatment at the hospital across town, but from what I hear, it sounds like he's had a horrifically bad stroke and is still in surgery. Eric Leland, the speaker of the House, has been secured but wasn't sworn in as acting president."

"Why not?"

"The doctors here never ruled that Hamilton was out of commission."

"I see. What do you need from me?"

"Right now? Only for you to keep on doing what you've been doing."

Once Todd had spoken to Hamilton to get his stamp of approval on a game plan, things moved rapidly. Within ten minutes, President Hamilton was out of his hospital bed and changing into a suitable outfit for an emergency national address. Within thirty, the face of the new president was being broadcast to every TV in America, and his voice dominated the radio waves.

His speech was one of sadness over the loss of a friend and colleague, of anger for the terrorist flaunting the ideals of American democracy, of vowing revenge on those who sought to destabilize the country. It was also a speech of hope and promise, reminding the public that though there had been great tragedy, America was a resilient country and he would lead her into a bright future.

From what she gathered later, it was possibly the best speech that Hamilton had ever made, although Phoenix heard very little of it as she drifted in and out of consciousness. Everyone in the crowded room had been vetted and cleared by security several times over, and no matter how hard she fought, staying awake and alert was a losing battle.

Finally, the president's speech was over and the room cleared of all except his innermost circle. His head of security, Michael, walked over to where Phoenix leaned against the wall.

He clapped her on the shoulder and spoke with his characteristic brusqueness. "You did good tonight, kid. Go home and get some rest while you can."

"I can't leave until we know more about what happened. How can we be sure that there won't be another attempt on his life here at the hospital?" Phoenix asked.

Michael shook his head. "You're not fooling me. I saw the way that your head was nodding off just now during that speech. You've already done enough from this end for tonight, the rest of us can handle it from here. You know that our security protocols are good—you helped write them."

"Not good enough considering what almost happened," Phoenix complained.

Michael shook his head. "You've done your job. Go home."

Behind her visor, Phoenix frowned. "How exactly am I supposed to get home without revealing my identity? From the bits and pieces I've heard on the radio, it sounds like half the country wants to know who I am. In fact, it almost looks like daylight from all the cameras and press outside."

"We've already got that taken care of." Michael gestured to one of the men on Hamilton's security team, a tall, beefy man Phoenix had worked with before on the campaign trail. "Gerald'll escort you to the parking garage where your arranged ride will take you home."

Phoenix followed Gerald down to the basement garage where the president and other VIPs had a secured parking area. The path to the garage took them through a hallway that was strangely dark, had several blind corners and made the hair on the back of her neck stand on end. After one such corner, Gerald stopped suddenly in front of a plain-looking door with a restroom sign on it, knocked three times, and turned to Phoenix.

"Don't freak out," he said.

She didn't have the chance to ask him what he was talking about before the door swung open and he shoved her inside.

# Chapter Twenty-Two

The room was dark, and Phoenix found herself being grabbed and pulled in several directions. She lashed out with a fist, and felt it hit something soft with a satisfying thwack.

"For the love of God will you stop? We're trying to help you," a familiar voice complained. Someone turned on a light, and she saw Stefan, Adrian, and Kiana standing around her in a small corridor. Adrian was rubbing the side of his shoulder.

"Stefan wasn't kidding when he said that you packed a mean punch." He grimaced.

"We don't have much time. Take your helmet and jumpsuit off and hand them to me," Kiana said as she started taking off her own shoes.

"What are you talking about?" Kaleo asked.

Stefan sighed. "Did Gerald not tell you the plan?"

Kaleo removed her helmet and handed it over to Kiana. "All he said was to not freak out, and then he shoved me in here."

"Typical. That's probably more words than he's said all week," Adrian said.

"How do I look? Suitably Phoenix-like?" Kiana asked as she buckled Kaleo's belt over her own hips.

Stefan looked her up and down critically and pressed the button on the side of her helmet to turn the voice modulator on. "It'll do. You remember the rest of the plan?"

"Of course; unlike Kaleo and Gerald, I had quite the chatty Kathy to make sure I had all the steps committed to memory."

"I was just trying to be thorough," Adrian grumbled.

"I know you were, dear, and I appreciate it. I'll see you in a little bit. Be safe," Kiana said as she tenderly brushed a lock of Adrian's hair behind his ear before turning and walking out the door.

Kaleo had an uncomfortable out-of-body experience as she watched her own persona leave without her. She was distracted by a jingling sound and turned to see Stefan toss a pair of keys to Adrian. "You remember how to ride?"

"It's not been that long, and don't forget who got you started in the hobby."

"Does Kiana know that you'll be driving it?"

Adrian snorted. "Of course she does. She wasn't too happy until I told her about the role she'd be playing. We negotiated that if she's okay with playing the part of Phoenix's body double for a little bit and all the dangers that might present, she should be just fine with me taking your bike the short distance to the White House, especially if I use all your gear."

"Just making sure our stories are straight. I didn't want to let something slip and accidentally snitch on you."

"Thanks, I appreciate that."

"Can someone fill me in on what's actually happening? I'm feeling very out of the loop," Kaleo said.

"Phoenix's role in preventing the assassination of Hamilton is already starting to circulate, and we're trying to be proactive about protecting your identity," Stefan said as they reached the end of the corridor. He paused and motioned for Kaleo to wait a second, then cracked the door and checked outside. Once he was satisfied that it was safe, he opened the door fully into a narrow, dark alleyway where Adrian's car was parked next to Stefan's motorcycle.

"You two take care. Kaleo, try not to beat any more of Stefan's friends up tonight, they may not take it as nicely as I did," Adrian teased.

"Yeah, yeah, yeah, I'll try not to let anyone else know that you got beat up by a girl," Stefan shot back. Then he smiled. "Are we still good for trivia night tomorrow?"

"Of course."

"Good. Mod will drop your car off later tonight."

"No need for them to rush. I don't mind keeping your bike for a couple extra days," Adrian said. He started up Stefan's bike and drove it out of the alleyway before Stefan could respond.

"I don't think I'm getting that back until next week," Stefan said with a sigh.

"Where are we going?" Kaleo asked as she climbed into the passenger's seat of Adrian's car.

"Back to your place. If you remember, Mod's been masquerading as you for the evening after you made the switch to Phoenix. Once Michael called to let us know that Phoenix was almost done for the night and that you'd need to get changed back, Mod 'accidentally' spilled a shrimp cocktail all over the front of your dress. The official story is that you're heading back to your house for a change of clothes before going to the White House to help Todd out tonight."

"I really liked that dress. I hope they didn't stain it permanently."

Stefan glanced at Kaleo, and she could see the concern on his face. "Are you feeling okay?"

She nodded. "Tired, but I got a little nap in. What about you? Were you able to get hold of the shooter?"

"I'm fine, the would-be assassin isn't." Stefan grimaced. "Even moving as fast as I could, he still had time to slip himself some cyanide after firing off those shots and was already foaming at the mouth by the time I got to him. Last I heard, Homeland, the Secret Service, and the FBI were fighting over who had priority in the investigation."

"Well, that sucks. Is Stone going to try and make a play too?"

"He's going to let the big dogs duke it out for now, although he's about as pleased as could be considering it was his task-force members who averted the assassination."

"I see. What are you going to do for the rest of the night? Work?"

"I'm crashing at your place."

"Just invite yourself over then, why don't you."

Stefan chuckled softly. "I'm keeping an eye on it while you're gone."

"With Adrian's car? If anyone sees his car at my house tonight while Kiana is at the White House, doesn't that look suspiciously like Adrian and I are cheating on you and Kiana? But that doesn't even make sense because Adrian doesn't have a disguise and is going to show up to the White House on your bike, so what even was the thinking behind switching vehicles with Adrian?" Kaleo groaned. "It's been too long of a day for me to have to unravel all your intelligence cloak-and-dagger things."

"I had to give Adrian something to do so he'd let Kiana be your body double. Plus, if rumors do start circulating about you and Adrian, we'll know that someone was following at least one of you around tonight, and we can take precautions for the future... Don't worry, I've already made all the arrangements. You don't have to think about anything else for a little bit, I've got it covered."

"You always think of everything, don't you?"

Stefan looked at her out of the corner of his eye. "One of us has to keep you safe. I'm surprised you didn't try to jump in front of any of those bullets today."

"There wasn't enough time." Kaleo shrugged.

"I thought you'd say something like that." He smiled and glanced at the clock on the dashboard. "Why don't you try and catch another nap? With all of this traffic we've still probably got at least thirty minutes until we get back to your house."

"That's not a bad idea. I am exhausted," Kaleo said as she leaned her head against the seat.

Almost as soon as she closed her eyes, it seemed like Stefan was shaking her awake. She sat up and looked out the window to see that they had parked on the side of her house, away from the prying eyes of her neighbors. Once he was satisfied that Kaleo was awake, Stefan reached down to pop the trunk of Adrian's car. "I've just got to get my stuff out really quick. You wait here for a second," he said by way of an explanation.

"Do you need help? Doesn't his trunk have a tendency to get stuck?" Kaleo asked, thinking back to when they first met.

"No, I don't think it's ever had a problem with that." Stefan smirked before he exited the car to grab his things. Kaleo watched him close the trunk to Adrian's car and turn to survey the neighborhood in the darkness for a moment. He stood to the side as he opened the door for her, shielding her from the street.

Kaleo felt like she was having a second out-of-body experience when she saw Mod-as-Kaleo relaxing on the couch in her living room.

"Oh, good, you're here. I was beginning to wonder if something had happened to you," Mod said. Kaleo wondered if that was what her voice actually sounded like and cringed internally.

Stefan checked his watch. "You were supposed to already be transformed, Mod."

"You think that this is easy? I'll have you know that it's quite draining, and occasionally very painful. I've had to do what? Two so far today? With another two coming up? It's starting to push my limits."

As Mod spoke, Kaleo tried not to look too much at her own face. She had always been insecure when looking at pictures of herself, and had justified it by believing the camera lens did different things than a mirror. Now she had an exact replica of her own face standing in front of her, and she didn't want to look too closely for fear that her self-esteem would tank if she didn't like what she saw.

"I'm sorry. Thank you for doing this again," Stefan said to Mod.

"Yeah, well it's what friends are for, right? And the Hughes are practically family." Mod shrugged before turning to the mirror in the hallway, and Kaleo watched their face begin to subtly shift. "Kaleo, I'm sorry about your dress, hopefully you can get the stain out. Also, Todd called and left a message on the answering machine." Mod's voice deepened as their vocal cords shifted.

"Don't worry about the dress, I'll get it cleaned or get a new one," Kaleo replied as she walked over to the machine to listen to her messages.

*"Hey Kaleo, it's Todd. I'm sure that you've heard the news by now. I need you to come in and help me out. We're getting slammed right now, and due to the festivities we're a little understaffed."*

Kaleo sighed. "Guess there's my official summons. If you two will excuse me, I'm going to go get freshened up and changed before part two of this nightmare circus starts."

# Chapter Twenty-Three

After Kaleo had shut the door to her room, Mod glanced at Stefan through the mirror. "How's the plan gone so far?"

"No complications beyond Adrian getting punched."

"Michael's security didn't warn Kaleo ahead of time?"

"That would be correct." Stefan sat on the couch and leaned his head back, mulling through the events of the day now that he had a quiet moment to think and no urgently pressing matters.

After he'd tackled and subdued the would-be assassin, answered the questions of the Secret Service and other investigating agents, and been released from their custody, Stefan had an emergency meeting over the phone with Stone. Unsurprisingly, Stone had somehow already been read into the situation and expected his call.

Stefan wasn't quite sure how his boss did it. Director Stone had spent several decades working in the capital for various intelligence departments before moving back to the Midwestern Pact Intelligence Agency in what had probably seemed to many at the time like a step down before retirement. Stefan had never formally asked what had precipitated Stone's move from the near center of the national intelligence community to the relatively backwater agency. Now, though, he wondered if it wasn't a careful move on Stone's part to attach his name to that of one of the country's rising stars, Governor Hamilton.

Nevertheless, Stone's time in Chicago had done nothing to dull his instincts or his skills, and both his mind and his connections were just as sharp as ever. After Stefan's contract had ended with the Rangers, he'd been approached by recruiters from several government agencies and military contractors, some offering very lucrative compensation packages. When Stefan had decided to accept Jason Stone's offer, it had been with some trepidation; the pay, while nice, was still substantially less than the other offers he'd received, and the job came with much more responsibility, and thus more work. The weight that had tipped the scale in favor of the Midwestern Pact Intelligence Agency was that Director Stone had presented it as an opportunity for Stefan to get a foot in the door of the formal intelligence community and to have the chance for more on the job mentoring and learning than he would anywhere else.

It had been a good choice. Director Stone stayed true to his word, and over the two years that Stefan had worked for him, he'd learned far more than he'd ever dreamed. Not to mention that when he accepted Stone's offer, Stefan could never have imagined that it would have led to meeting the love of his life, or such a fast promotion from a pact-run agency to a national one.

Working with the Saviors in the early days of the new Midwestern Pact Abled Task Force had also been like something out of a dream, and he and Caleb Hughes had become good friends. In the smaller missions leading up to Adrian's rescue the summer before, Architect had even begun to hint to Stefan that he had two very single daughters, and that he wouldn't mind Stefan taking one of them out just to see if anything happened. At the time, Stefan had laughed it off; he hadn't been looking for a new relationship, and he certainly didn't want to endanger his friendship with Caleb and Nova if things didn't work out with one of their daughters.

Then, a month after Caleb had tried to set him up, and the day after Adrian's rescue, Stefan had seen Kaleo walk into the conference room, and all his plans and resolutions had gone out the window. He might still have escaped somewhat unscathed, except Adrian, ever the politician's son, somehow picked up on Stefan's interest and decided to play matchmaker.

It had been a wild eight months, but Stefan wouldn't have traded a single second of it for anything.

Well, that wasn't necessarily true. He would have gladly traded the motorcycle accident that he'd been in the month before so that Kaleo wouldn't have had to deal firsthand with the reemergence of Puppeteer.

At the thought of Puppeteer, Stefan's mind turned down a different track. Since Operation Cuckoo, Director Stone and Stefan had placed the Pure and its sister organizations at the top of their priority lists. Considering the history of the kidnapping attempt, the nature of the rally bombing, and Puppeteer's own stated interest in using Stefan to get to Adrian, they had been suspicious that something was going to be attempted at the inauguration and had prepared accordingly.

Of course, Director Stone had tried to warn the appropriate authorities, but they'd brushed him off and told him to stay in his lane, and an assassination attempt the night of the inauguration was something that the two of them couldn't have prepared for given their current limited resources.

His stomach suddenly grumbled, and Stefan remembered that he hadn't eaten much for dinner earlier. He stood and moved into the kitchen to take stock of what was available in the pantry. "Are you hungry, Mod?" he called out.

"Not at the moment. I already had to eat quite a bit in preparation for this transformation. It's a good thing that Adrian is taller than Kaleo, so I only have to worry about inputs and not having to get rid of any extra mass."

Stefan chuckled softly as he rifled through the fridge, reminded of how grateful he was that his girlfriend always kept a fully stocked kitchen. He wasn't a terrible cook and had a healthy love of food, but try as he might, he rarely seemed to have more than a day or two's worth of provisions in his own apartment.

As he finished up making two roast beef sandwiches, Mod joined him in the kitchen. "How do I look?"

Stefan appraised their face. It was remarkably like Adrian's, especially considering the time constraints that Mod was currently under.

"It'll do as long as you don't let anyone get too good of a look at you," he said as he handed Mod the keys to Adrian's car.

Mod nodded, took the keys, and left the house. A few minutes later, Kaleo emerged from her bedroom. Her navy suit contrasted nicely with the pink and white patterned blouse and simple silver necklace she wore. Stefan eyed her outfit and nodded in approval; she looked beautiful in dresses, but she was powerful in her suits.

"Hungry?" he asked as he held out the second sandwich that he'd wrapped in paper.

"Starving. Are you sure? I can probably find something to eat at the White House."

"I made an extra for you. I know how much you like roast beef."

Kaleo smiled at him and slid the sandwich into her purse. "Thank you," she said as she wrapped her arms around Stefan and pressed a kiss to his lips.

"Be safe," he whispered.

"I'm always safe," she quipped before turning to head out the door. "Now, feel free to make yourself at home; you know where everything is. Also, don't you dare even think about touching the dishes in the sink or I'll make you regret it."

"Is that a promise?" he retorted, and was rewarded with her faint laughter. It was a running joke between them—while Stefan kept his apartment immaculately clean, Kaleo's could be described as comfortably cluttered, and she seemed borderline allergic to having a kitchen sink with no dirty dishes in it.

Stefan smiled to himself as he finished his sandwich before pulling a laptop out of his bag. He was thankful that the move to Lincoln had precipitated a forward-looking tech upgrade for the task force. Computers were still uncommon, but being able to download the information from several databases at once and then peruse through it without going into the office was priceless on a night like tonight.

After almost an hour, the screen began to get blurry. Stefan grabbed a cookie from the drawer in the pantry and wandered around the house to double check that all the entry and exit points were secured. Once he was satisfied, he made his way back to the living room and blew out the candle lanterns before he lay back on the couch. He checked his watch and calculated that Kaleo would probably be gone for at least another couple of hours, giving him plenty of time to get some sleep before she got back.

Stefan had no difficulty falling asleep and awoke easily when he heard a car turn into the driveway outside. He sat up and checked his watch again—he'd been asleep for three hours and it was now in that awkward time between very late night and very early morning. He'd just opened his laptop to look busy when Kaleo walked through the side door.

"Have a good nap?" she asked as she set her bag down on the countertop and lit a couple of candles in the kitchen before snuggling up next to him on the couch.

"Nap? I have no clue what you're talking about. I've been awake this entire time, you know, for solidarity."

"You can pretend all you want, but the hair on one side of your head is standing up and I think I see the imprint of the seam of my couch on your face," Kaleo paused and giggled. "And you've gone and drooled all over the couch cushions."

"All right, fine, you caught me. I thought that one of us might as well get some quality sleep tonight," Stefan growled playfully, and leaned back into the couch with her in his arms.

She kissed his cheek before wriggling out of his grasp and walking back to her room. After several minutes, she rejoined him on the couch and pulled his arms around her, but not before blowing out all of the candles that she'd previously lit so that the only light left in the room came from the bright moon outside, shining through the window curtains.

Silence fell between them as they reflected on the night. "Stefan... I've been thinking, and the expression on Johnson's face when he walked to center stage right before he collapsed... I've seen that look before," she said quietly.

"I was afraid that you'd say that. Maybe it was just a coincidence." He sighed before trying to change the subject; Kaleo didn't know just how involved he and Stone had gotten into tracking down the Pure, and he didn't want to open that can of worms when they were both stressed and exhausted. "How were things up at the White House?"

"They could have been worse. I think Todd wanted me up there to help him keep everyone under control, more than anything. We're already getting a flood of interview requests for President Hamilton, and more than a few for Strike and Phoenix. Tomorrow you and Stone are going to be invited to a meeting about the events of the night, and my mother is already on her way with the results from the lab that compared the rally bombing residue with the explosion at Operation Cuckoo."

"It certainly took them long enough to get those samples processed."

"I didn't get all the details, but I believe that's one of the reasons that she's coming up."

"I'm sure that we'll hear all about it tomorrow," Stefan said as he ran his fingers through her loose hair and marveled not for the first time at how soft the waves felt.

She looked up at him. "You're distracted."

"Just thinking about some things at work."

"Don't want to talk about it?"

"Not really. At least, not right now."

"I understand; me either." She nuzzled her head closer to his chest and yawned.

Stefan held her as her breathing slowed and evened into the deep and rhythmic pattern of sleep. He waited a few more minutes, and then shifted them both to the side so that they were lying on the couch together. Gently, he pulled the couch cushions from behind his back and tossed them onto the floor to give them more room before nestling back and pulling her against him.

Two months ago, he would have been hesitant to do such a thing, but something fundamental about their relationship had changed after his accident and the subsequent mission on which Kaleo had replaced him. She was more confident, more self-assured, and had opened up to him more. They'd had several long discussions about their boundaries and beliefs, and he had been surprised to learn that one of the reasons Kaleo had been so reluctant to initiate more physical contact with him was that she was afraid he would want more from her than she was willing to give.

She hadn't been only trying to calm him down after his embarrassing word-vomit concussion speech so that she could get out of the room and away from the awkward situation; she'd actually been relieved. He'd never brought the topic up before out of fear, as several of his past girlfriends hadn't been so understanding about his no-sex-before-marriage rule, and by the time that he and Kaleo had started getting serious, he'd fallen so deeply in love with her that he didn't want to risk driving her away.

In the days after her encounter with Puppeteer, Kaleo openly sought out the comfort of his touch once she knew that he wouldn't mistake it for her trying to start something or lead him on. As it was, Kaleo's increased desire for physical touch had been a comfort that he was all too willing to provide, especially after he had a long discussion with Brant Heinstein and gained some very informative insight. In fact, when Brant had heard that task-force budget concerns might preclude Lin from getting the same amount of security as he or Stefan, he'd insisted on paying half of the total bill and also offering a piece of advice to Stefan.

"Now, you make sure that whoever you hire knows that sometimes she has nightmares. If they hear her screaming in the middle of the night, it doesn't necessarily mean that someone's attacking her," Brant had warned. Their meeting unofficially occurred at the Heinstein Company's offices in Chicago the day after the task-force leadership meeting and two days after Operation Cuckoo. While Stefan hadn't been technically cleared to return to work in the office, Director Stone had made an exception and allowed him to personally make arrangements for the security details.

"Screaming nightmares?" Stefan had repeated, and leaned back in his chair.

Brant nodded. "I take it that Kaleo's told you her version of what happened with Puppeteer's betrayal?"

"I am aware of exactly what happened," Stefan replied evenly, his tone brooking no argument or invitation for Brant to insert any of his own unwelcome judgments.

"Yeah, it was extremely traumatic, to say the least, and it affected Lin pretty bad. For as long as we were together, she'd have those nightmares pretty regularly, and they'd wake us both up. It's been several years, and she told me yesterday that she's been on some medication that helps most of the time, but things like that don't really just go away, you know?"

Stefan had nodded and assured Brant that he'd pass the information on.

Lin wasn't the only one who'd had nightmares after Operation Cuckoo. Kaleo might have gained confidence in herself, her abilities, and their relationship, but the dark circles under her eyes made it obvious that she wasn't sleeping well. When he'd asked, she'd insisted that she was fine, but she hadn't stopped switching out his sweaters, and it took her a couple of weeks to stop jumping at any unexpected noise.

For those reasons, Stefan had decided to keep an eye on her personally after the assassination attempt that night. His suspicions were confirmed when Kaleo's body started jerking as he had begun to nod off to sleep. Thankfully, his arms were still wrapped around her, and when he hugged her tightly she stopped moving as much, although the little that he could see of her face in the moonlight was still twisted in pain.

With a sigh, she turned around so that her head was buried in his chest, and it was only then that she finally calmed. At first Stefan thought that the worst was over when her body relaxed against him, but then a faint blue light appeared over her hands. It was hardly more than a glimmer, but he watched in fascination as it spread from her skin to his and started to cover his arms where she was touching him.

The light increased in intensity and spread further up their arms, and was soon accompanied by a faint vibrating feeling.

"Sweetheart," he hissed, hating to wake her, but also very wary of letting her power up in a dark house with windows facing the street.

She didn't wake, and as the light grew brighter, he picked her up and took her to her room, carefully shutting the door behind him. It took a minute or two of fumbling in the dark to get the bed in order, but Stefan was eventually able to lay Kaleo down and get her settled. By the time he finally let go of her, half of his body was covered in the light—and the tingling sensation, while unsettling, wasn't completely unpleasant.

Once he had completely disconnected himself from her, the blue light faded and Kaleo slept peacefully, not having woken once in the entire transition. Satisfied that there wouldn't be any more drama, Stefan made his way back to the living room to keep vigil for the night.

# Chapter Twenty-Four

When Kaleo opened her eyes and found herself in her bedroom, she was quite disoriented. The last that she remembered, she'd been cuddling with Stefan on the couch.

She dragged herself into the kitchen to start the water boiling for her morning cup of tea, and saw Stefan stretched out on the couch, a blanket draped haphazardly over his body and soft snores issuing from his mouth. With a smile, Kaleo sat next to him and began to run her fingers through his dark brown hair.

"It's time to wake up, sleepy head."

Stefan groaned and reached up with his hand to pat her face. "Where's the snooze button?"

"I don't have one."

He pulled the blanket over his head. "No snooze button? You must be defective. I'm taking you back to the store and trading you in for a newer model."

Kaleo snorted. "Good luck with that. I'm a Hughes original."

Stefan's arm snaked around her, and he pulled her against him. "You're my Hughes original, and don't you forget it," he whispered as he nuzzled into her side.

"Oh, I'm yours?" Kaleo made a big deal out of examining her hands. "I believe that that's a perk of the fiancée package, and unless I slept through the engagement and then lost the ring, I do believe you're currently only subscribed to the girlfriend-level of benefits."

"It's too early in the morning for your sass," Stefan said. "We've only been dating for six months and you're trying to upsell me already?" He cracked open one eye to look at her. "Although I will say that you've made a very convincing argument. With a face like that, you're wasted in politics. I think you could have had a stellar career in sales."

Kaleo heard the water boiler click off and laughed as she tousled Stefan's hair before extracting herself from his arms. "I don't have any coffee; do you want some tea instead?" she asked over her shoulder.

Stefan stood from the couch and cracked his neck. "No, thanks, I'm good. I actually slept pretty well... that couch is surprisingly comfortable."

"You do know that I have more than one bed in this house, right? The couch isn't an appropriate place to sleep." Kaleo put her hands on her hips and deepened her voice as much as she could for her best Stefan imitation.

"I'm just learning from the queen of stubbornness."

"And don't you forget it," she called after him as he walked down the hallway to the bathroom.

After they'd both gotten ready, Kaleo drove them to the president's office for their joint meeting. Years before, when the country's capital had been moved to Lincoln, one of the many topics of debate was where the president should live and work, and what such a building should be called. In the end, tradition had won out, and once a suitable building in the middle of town had been picked, renovated, and refurbished, it had been dubbed the "new" White House. However, the general public's memory was short, and after a couple of years the newness had worn off and everyone had reverted to calling it by its historic name.

Once they arrived at the White House, they went their separate ways: Stefan to the Lake Room where he would wait for Director Stone and Kaleo's mother, and Kaleo directly to the president's office to finish the preparations for the day.

She'd done most of the prep work the night before, but a couple of details still required her attention, and when she was done it was time to go get the others and let them in.

As she made her way from her desk to the Lake Room, she crossed paths with Todd, who was walking towards Hamilton's office. He stopped her briefly in the hall to ask how she was doing.

"I'm fine," she said before a traitorous yawn gave the lie to her words.

"I know it's early, but after this meeting, take some time to make a list of things for Sabrina and James to handle, and then take the rest of the week off. You've more than earned it," he said.

Kaleo glanced around at the busy hallway that they were standing in and shrugged. "If you're sure. I still feel like I could have done more if I'd had more time."

Todd smiled. "Don't we all feel that way sometimes. Take the break; it's only a couple of extra days. If you really start to get bored, talk to Michael and perhaps he can come up with something for you to do. Now that we've got our talking points in order and the first phase of the crisis is averted, it'll take a couple of days for the impact from the waves last night to really start being felt, and I'll need you on your A-game next week."

"I'm sure I can find something to do with my very long weekend. Is the president ready for the meeting? I was just on my way to the Lake Room to get everyone."

"Yes, he is. I'll meet you in his office."

Kaleo guided her mother, Director Stone, and Stefan back to the president's office where Hamilton, Todd, and Michael were waiting. She closed the door behind them and sat in a chair at the edge of the room with her back to the wall.

"Hello, you three, please take a seat anywhere you like," Hamilton said with a wave of his hand around the room.

"This is a smaller meeting than I was expecting to find, Mr. President," Nova remarked as she settled onto a couch and looked around.

"Please, Nova, call me John. You've more than earned that right." Hamilton sighed and loosened his tie. "Truthfully, the events of last night have me rather shaken, and even though I no longer have any authority over the Midwestern Pact Abled Task Force, I trust you all and wanted to get everyone's read on the situation before I'm officially briefed by Homeland and the FBI later. Now, if you'd be so kind as to share the results that you got back from explosives with everyone before we delve into the other matters at hand, I'd be very grateful."

Kaleo's mother nodded before launching into what they had found.

"I have good and bad news. First of all, the lab that the task force uses finally got back to me yesterday. The samples that we took from the explosion at the site of Operation Cuckoo matched those of the residue samples from the bombing at your rally, and after reading the reports Nicole told me that she wouldn't be surprised if they'd been set by the same person. Apparently, different explosives experts have their own types of signatures when setting bombs up, and from the similarities she could see on the ground at Operation Cuckoo and what she read in the file from the rally bombings, she seemed to think there was a pretty good likelihood that they were placed by the same person. The implication of course is that Puppeteer is linked to the people who set up the rally bombings."

"And the bad news?" Todd asked.

Nova frowned. "The reason it took so long for the samples to be processed is that they had been conveniently misplaced. We had to send Beguile in to convince them that it was in their best interest to get us the results as soon as possible."

Kaleo felt her eyes narrow, but otherwise kept a straight face. Beguile was Audra's codename, and no matter what Kaleo did, Audra seemed determined to needle her whenever she could. In the days after Operation Cuckoo, there had been more than a couple of passing comments about how much she must need to keep on working with the Professor if Phoenix still wasn't strong enough to handle only one Abled adversary and a handful of non-Ableds.

As Nova spoke, Stefan, Michael, and Director Stone all shared a series of furtive glances that didn't escape the president's notice.

"You three look suspicious. Care to share with the rest of us what's going on?" Hamilton asked.

"We have news. The venue yesterday where President Johnson suffered his stroke had a security camera located outside the back entrance where the presidential party made their entry. We were able to obtain footage from that camera and found something," Director Stone said as he pulled several full pages out of his briefcase.

Michael pulled a computer out of his own bag and turned it on before plugging it into the large TV in Hamilton's office. Everyone's attention was glued to the screen as they watched the footage of Johnson's convoy pull up to the backdoor of the venue. As Johnson's security moved around his car, an FBI agent stepped forward to hand him a small package. After Johnson took the package from the agent, he shook the man's hand, paused to speak a few words with him, and continued inside with his security team.

The agent watched Johnson go inside before removing a second package from under his jacket and turned back to the driveway. He began making their way towards Hamilton's car but paused when Phoenix stepped out and raised her shield. At her appearance, the stranger backed out of the frame, and Hamilton made his way inside with his security detail without any further interruption.

"We've taken the liberty of blowing up some stills from the video. I think that some of you will recognize the young man," Stone said. Stefan passed a series of pictures around for everyone to look at.

When Kaleo was handed one of the pages, her heart rose in her throat. The composition of the picture was nothing special, but even the grainy quality didn't keep her from recognizing Puppeteer. She looked up to see Director Stone studying her face. "I thought you, in particular, might recognize him, Kaleo," he said.

"I told Stefan last night that I thought the look on President Johnson's face just before he collapsed was familiar," she said quietly.

The room fell silent and Director Stone nodded. "I recognized his picture too." He glanced around at the other people in the meeting. "For those of you who haven't had the dubious pleasure of meeting him, the young man in this picture is David Rockhill, also known to most in this room by his alias, Puppeteer."

"And this is who?" Hamilton asked.

"Puppeteer is a member of an Abled supremacist cell. He was the man who caused the trouble for us during Operation Cuckoo, and he and Kaleo had prior dealings several years ago. If Nova is correct, it sounds like he, or his group, may have also played a role in the rally bombings."

"I see. And what is the status of the situation?" Hamilton asked.

Director Stone frowned. "As things currently stand, I've tasked Stefan with tracking down more information about these groups since what we have is either sadly lacking in specifics or woefully outdated. He's not had much luck, although I'm hoping that they overextended themselves this time around and we'll have a couple of new leads."

Kaleo shot Stefan a look, but he didn't meet her eyes as he leaned forward to address the room. "From the little that I've been able to uncover for certain, it appears that the Pure, the group that Puppeteer was a part of when Kaleo first came into contact with him several years ago, has swallowed several other groups in the intervening time and has now become a dominant force in that particular part of the political spectrum. Unfortunately for us, they're very careful about covering their tracks, and have a rather annoying predilection for manipulating other groups into doing their dirty work for them to maintain their innocence."

"Which means, if our suspicions are correct, that last night wasn't this group's first attempt on your life. We've noticed a disturbing pattern; first they try to gain control of you, and when that fails, they try to kill you," Michael added.

President Hamilton groaned. "Well, isn't that lovely. Just for curiosity's sake, I have to ask: how exactly would this Puppeteer try and manipulate me?"

"He can control the bodies of anyone he comes into direct physical contact with. If he touched you for even a few seconds, he might have had complete physical control," Kaleo said.

"What stopped him from trying last night? And what was in that box?" Todd asked.

Michael rewound the video and played it again. As Kaleo watched Puppeteer walk up to President Johnson and shake his hand, she remembered what it felt like to be under Puppeteer's control and fought back a rising tide of nausea. For the second time she watched as Puppeteer walked towards Hamilton's car, only to pause and then back away as Phoenix exited from the car and created her shield.

"It definitely looks like the investment that we made into using Phoenix as a deterrent was worth more than its weight in gold," Michael said.

Stefan nodded. "We now believe that the assassin inside the building was there as both a backup plan and a scapegoat."

"Do we know anything else about the actual assassin, or are we still waiting on that?" Hamilton asked.

Stefan and Director Stone exchanged glances. "We're making progress, but that's outside the scope of what Stefan and I can currently inquire into. If you'll remember, sir, we're in a little bit of limbo at the moment as we stepped down from the Midwestern Pact Intelligence Agency and the National Abled Task Force has not been approved by Congress yet. Strike was able to make a couple of observations about the nature of the assassin before the FBI and Homeland took over, but we don't have the resources or influence to do much more. We also don't know what was in the box, as that falls under the Secret Service's jurisdiction," the director said carefully.

"Sir, you've got a meeting with those agencies later today. Hopefully they'll have more information for us," Michael added.

Hamilton nodded and wrote something down on the legal pad in front of him. "Speaking of which: Todd, Kaleo, how has this affected the public sentiment for the National Task Force?"

"It's created a large amount of good publicity for the plan. Strike and Phoenix are hot topics right now, and the fact that they saved your life in such a televised way is almost guaranteed to increase favorable public sentiment. I don't think that it would be unwise to grant some of the requests for more information, but I'm not sure who we want the public face of the task force to be. Phoenix of course would be the most obvious answer," Todd said.

Kaleo felt all eyes in the room turn to her and shrugged. "I can talk to Phoenix about it. I'm sure that she'll understand and be open to discussing revealing her identity for a good cause." She was careful to only speak in the third person; it never hurt to be extra cautious when discussing such sensitive matters.

"I'm not sure that that would be the best idea," Stefan said. Kaleo frowned at him, but he ignored her. "Keeping the identity of Phoenix secret can only help us in the long term. We still don't know as much about Puppeteer's group as they seem to know about us, and I don't like how close they've gotten to causing major damage multiple times." He turned to address President Hamilton. "Sir, you should know that we believe Puppeteer was targeting me specifically during Operation Cuckoo with the goal of getting closer to Adrian, and thus to you. If it's true that his group was also behind the rally bombings, it appears that so far Phoenix is the main person who has been able to stand against them and foil their plans. If we reveal Phoenix's identity now, it makes it all that much easier for them to take out a vital layer of security."

"If not Phoenix, who will be the public face of the task force?" Todd asked.

"I'll do it," Nova volunteered. "At least for a year or two; I've got my eye on a Senate seat that's opening up the next election cycle, and by then we should be at a more stable place and more fully staffed so someone else can take over the public relations duties for me."

"Sounds good to me. That's settled, then," Todd said.

"I have one more question: Do we have any theories as to how Puppeteer got hold of an FBI jacket and clearance to be back in the security staging area?" Hamilton asked.

Director Stone shrugged. "Various possible ways, the most benign being that he simply seduced one of their field agents, and the most sinister being that the Pure has managed to infiltrate the government."

"That's just what we'd need, isn't it?" Hamilton sighed and ran his free hand over his face. "Thank you all for this information and for your continued support, it gives me a lot to think about. Jason and Stefan, we'll be in touch to keep you updated as things with the task force progresses. Nova, Todd will coordinate the interviews and public relations side of things with you until we can make the task force official."

Todd took the cue from his boss and stood, buttoning his suit jacket as he did so. "I'm afraid that's all the time we have right now. Kaleo, please show them out. Nova, if you'll hang around for a minute, we can discuss a meeting time to get you caught up on our strategy for the media blitz before you go back to Chicago."

# Chapter Twenty-Five

After they had all left President Hamilton's office, Michael turned to Kaleo. "I can show Jason the way out from here. I believe that he and I still have some things to discuss. Did Todd already tell you to take the day off?"

"Yes, he actually told me to take the rest of the week off. Why? Do you need something?" Kaleo asked.

"Not at all, I just wanted to make sure that you had some time to relax. I know that the two of us have been running you pretty ragged lately with all the preparations leading up to yesterday, and the events from last night were the icing on the proverbial cake."

"You too, Stefan, take it easy for a couple of days. Don't forget that you're using your paid vacation days to be here, so you might as well take advantage of that," Director Stone added.

When Stefan opened his mouth to protest, Stone shook his head. "I won't hear any arguments out of you, young man. Take some time off; I'm going to be handing all the information we've gleaned over to Homeland for them to take the lead on this investigation and see if I can't get some political capital and a couple of favors in return. Rest up now, you'll be glad that you did when we hit the ground running in a couple of weeks."

"You want me to take the next couple of weeks off? With everything that's going on?" Kaleo struggled to not laugh at the shocked look on Stefan's face and the disbelief in his voice.

"Not the next two weeks, just the next few days. I'll be busy with networking and the political side of things for a bit, and it sounds like our replacements have things under control up in the Midwestern Pact. Check back with me tomorrow and we'll discuss the next steps we need to prepare for, and a more solidified timeline for your return to work."

"If you're sure..." Stefan replied.

Kaleo laced her fingers through his as they walked away. "Try not to look so glum, Stefan. He told you to take some time off, not shoot your grandmother," she teased.

He smiled and glanced over at her. "I suppose you're right."

"Of course I am, I'm always right."

As they walked to the office that Kaleo shared with the other vice-presidential aides, she told Stefan that she needed to delegate a couple of things to her co-workers before she could leave. "It may take me a little bit. If you want to pick up your keys from wherever Adrian left them, we can always meet up for lunch later," she offered.

"Mod dropped the bike off at my apartment last night. I was planning on calling a taxi after the meeting this morning, but if you've got the rest of the day off and just need to tidy up a few loose ends I don't mind waiting. Why? Are you trying to hide me from your coworkers? I've not forgotten that you still haven't introduced us yet," he said as they paused directly outside her office.

"Not at all, although I'll warn you that they can be a lot sometimes." Kaleo shrugged. "I just didn't know if you had anything else that you needed to do."

"Not at the moment. I'm on vacation now, didn't you hear? All I'm missing is a floppy hat, some sandals, and a truly atrocious Hawaiian shirt."

Kaleo raised her eyebrow and looked him up and down. Stefan's navy suit was impeccably tailored as always, and his brown shoes had that kind of soft, supple shine that spoke of quality without fuss. The mental image of a sunburnt Stefan in flip flops and a straw hat made her laugh softly. She was still smiling when they walked into the office, and her two co-workers, Sabrina and James, looked up when she entered.

"Sabrina, James, this is Stefan. Stefan, these are my co-workers, Sabrina and James," she said by way of introduction before turning back to Stefan. "It'll take me a few minutes to get some things written down and make sure everything is in order. Make yourself comfortable." As she spoke, she grabbed an extra chair and moved it next to her desk before sitting down to look over a few of the morning reports that she hadn't had time to get to before the meeting.

"Did I miss the 'bring your significant other to work' memo? Sabrina asked from her desk.

"Stefan was here for a meeting and Todd just gave me the rest of the week off and told me to pass anything pressing off to you two, so I thought that if Stefan wouldn't mind waiting a bit while I wrapped things up, we could go grab brunch." Kaleo said.

"It'd be just like Todd to do something like that. I always knew that he played favorites. I'd kill for a couple of days off," Sabrina complained.

"Don't be jealous; it's not my fault that I was doing all three of our jobs last night while you two were out getting hungover."

She'd worked with Sabrina and James for the past several months, as they had all been hired at approximately the same time when their predecessors had been among the casualties in the rally bombing. Usually they got along well, but the other woman's entitled attitude could grate on her nerves on the best of days. Sabrina had been noticeably absent from the chaos the night before, and Kaleo hadn't had nearly enough sleep to have the patience to deal with her at the moment.

"She's got you there, Sabrina. I don't think that there's been a day in the past month when Kaleo got here later than us or left earlier. Todd's probably worried that if he lets her keep working at her current pace, she'll find somewhere else with better hours and much better pay, and then we'll really be up a creek." James snickered from his chair across the room, where he was weaving a pencil through his fingers, before swiveling to look at Stefan. "So you're the Stefan that we've heard so much about."

"I hope it's been all good things," Stefan said.

"Only the best of things. James and I were starting to wonder if you were even real. Is it true that you hung the moon on your lunch break and then cured cancer in your free time?" Sabrina asked.

Stefan looked at Kaleo with a grin and a slightly raised eyebrow, and she redoubled her efforts to get everything done faster, suddenly thinking that perhaps she should have tried a little harder to discourage him from meeting her coworkers.

"Maybe you two should focus on your jobs; I'd hate for Stefan to distract you," she said as she picked up her phone to listen to any new voicemails.

"He's not a distraction at all. Speaking of jobs, what do you do for work, Stefan?" James asked.

"I work in intelligence, although at the moment I'm kind of in between jobs."

"In between jobs? What, are you letting Kaleo pay for everything and be your sugar mama?"

Stefan laughed. "Something like that." He lowered his voice to a stage whisper and cupped a hand around his mouth. "Don't let her know that I told you that, or she'll make me sleep on the couch again. Last night was rough enough as it is."

"Kaleo, you made him sleep on the couch? That's cold. A man like this obviously needs someone to keep him nice and warm." Sabrina shook her head in disgust before glancing at Stefan and biting her lip.

After she hung up the phone, Kaleo turned in her chair and pointed at Sabrina with the pen in her hand. "Stop thinking what I know that you're thinking."

"She's right, Kaleo. I'm just a cold little man who needs my sugar mama to keep me warm," Stefan said with a wide grin on his face.

Kaleo rolled her eyes and relaxed, fighting back a grin of her own at the absurdity of the words coming out of the tall, lean man sitting beside her. "Not that I have anything to defend, or that it's any of your business, but for your information, Sabrina, Stefan made his own choice to sleep on the couch," she said.

"Yeah, Sabrina, he was just trying to be a gentleman. You wouldn't know anything about that because all of your boyfriends have been losers," James piped up.

"Not all of them!"

"Name one who hasn't."

Sabrina opened and shut her mouth a couple of times before returning to her work with a huff.

Kaleo checked her watch. "Not that this hasn't been extremely fun and all, but I think that I've got my loose ends together and am under strict orders to delegate all of my other responsibilities for the rest of the week to you two." She handed a piece of paper to each of her coworkers and ignored the complaints and grumbling that issued forth from their corners.

As Stefan and Kaleo got ready to leave, the good-natured grumbling stopped. "It was nice to meet you, Stefan," James said before returning to his work. Sabrina waved at them as she picked up a ringing phone.

As they walked out of the offices, Kaleo frowned. "Cold little man? I'm not going to hear the end of that for at least a week."

"I was just trying to show off my impeccable sense of humor to your coworkers, sweetheart. Didn't want them to think that I was a stick in the mud."

"No fair. I can't be ridiculous around your coworkers to embarrass you and then leave without repercussions," Kaleo said.

"You could always join the task force full-time, you know. I'm sure we could find a role for you now. Then you could commiserate with everyone else about your crazy boss."

"I think I'll pass, and you better keep your voice down and not let Michael or Todd hear you trying to lure me away."

Stefan lowered his voice to a conspiratorial whisper. "I would never."

"Anyways, what do you want to do with the rest of the day since we both have it off? Or for the rest of the week for that matter?"

"It's trivia night tonight, so Adrian and I will be at that..." Stefan paused. "This may seem very off the cuff, but do you want to try and go skiing this weekend? There's supposed to be a great place only a few hours away from here by train. It'd be fun."

"I haven't skied in years, and you can call me crazy, but something about the thought of flying downhill on a pair of flimsy boards in the snow just doesn't seem all that appealing to me. Besides, what if something else happens and they need me? It's probably best if we just hang around Lincoln," Kaleo said as they walked to her car.

Stefan made a face. "Where's your sense of adventure? You've got to live a little."

"I think that I've had more than my fair share of adventure in the past several years."

"Those were all for work, you never have any adventures just for fun."

"Katherine's warned me about what happens to people who ski. I don't think either of our jobs could afford for one or both of us to blow out our knees on the slopes and be out of commission for who knows how long." She paused what she was saying as they got into her car. "Besides, I was kind of looking forward to finishing up getting settled into my house. I haven't had time to do much beyond unpack the basic necessities. Speaking of Katherine, I don't think that she'd be very happy to hear that you went skiing with your ribs in the state that they're in. Have you already forgotten just how much work it took to convince her to clear you for duty yesterday?"

"Fine, you win." Stefan buckled his seatbelt.

"Of course, you're more than welcome to help me unpack if you're bored out of your mind. Maybe we could go shopping for a few things while we're at it? We can make a day of it; I've heard that there's an ice-skating rink somewhere around here."

"So you won't go downhill on perfectly stable and strong wooden boards, but you're totally okay skating around on six-inch razor blades?"

"Yep. You know, you can always go skiing on your own, or take Adrian or one of your other friends. I don't have to go with you."

"But then who'll be there to drink hot chocolate and cuddle with me at the end of a long day out on the slopes?" Stefan asked as he rested his hand on Kaleo's leg. She took one hand from the steering wheel and interlaced her fingers with his.

"If that's all that you want, we can always go skating and then go on a nice, long, cold walk before heading back to one of our places for cuddles and hot chocolate. We've had a very big twenty-four hours, and I don't know about you, but I've had an insane couple of months ever since you got into that accident. A restful long weekend sounds like just what I need."

"Fine, I give in. We'll have your restful weekend this go around, but next time I want to go skiing or do something extra fun." Stefan pouted.

Kaleo smiled and squeezed his hand in agreement.

# Chapter Twenty-Six

Kaleo drove them to a local brunch spot that she'd heard good things about but hadn't had the chance to try yet. Unfortunately, the reviews seemed to have been mostly hype, and the only good things about the cafe were that it wasn't busy and the mediocre service meant they were left completely alone.

"So, when exactly were you planning on telling me about your new little work project?" Kaleo asked as she sipped her overpriced tea.

Stefan frowned as he struggled to cut his waffle into bite-sized pieces with only the fork he'd been provided. "Whenever it became relevant and we had actual solid information to go from... so today." He glanced around the nook they were sitting in before looking at her meaningfully and then glancing back at his waffle with a raised eyebrow.

Kaleo shrugged. "We're the only ones here. I don't mind as long as you aren't obvious about it."

With a nod, Stefan reached under the table and pulled out a small knife, which he used to quickly cut his waffle into pieces before wiping it off with his napkin and then sequestering it away again. "Thanks, I really wasn't having any luck with the fork."

"Don't change the subject," she said as she started on her bacon and eggs.

"I'm not. It's true, I've been doing a deep dive into whatever we can find about any of the Abled supremacist organizations whenever my time hasn't been taken up by the transition. It's not been easy, and there hasn't been a lot of information. The good news is that most of these groups are fairly young, relatively small, and usually disorganized. The bad thing is that because of those three factors they've been hard to keep track of."

"And Puppeteer himself? Anything about him?"

"We know his supposed name, his date of birth, and his face. Other than that, we don't have much, especially not what he's been up to in the past few years."

"That's unfortunate."

"It's not good, that's for sure." Stefan shook his head. "I have a sneaking suspicion that he's got some friends in high places, and that he knows how to use them. The most important thing that we need to figure out now is if he's truly the only puppet master, or if someone else is pulling his strings."

An idea suddenly struck Kaleo. "Do you think that his attempt to make contact with you back in December was related to last night?"

Stefan took a bite of his waffle and chewed thoughtfully before speaking. "Certainly could be. Let's see... if it had only been me, Brant, and Lin, what would have happened?"

"Brant would have attacked him, you would have stopped Brant, Puppeteer would have tried to take control of you, and once Lin had snapped out of it, she would have done whatever she could to help," Kaleo said.

"What if Lin hadn't been there?"

"What do you mean?"

"No one knew that Lin would be there. What if it had just been some random guy from the treasury? And what if I hadn't had time to use my abilities, or if Brant had beat me to the punch? What do you think Puppeteer would have done? You know him far better than I."

Kaleo scowled in concentration before realization hit like a train. "He wanted Brant to attack him. He loves his backup plans; the bullet that Phoenix saved Brant from was the backup. He would have somehow killed Brant either 'accidentally' or in a claim of self-defense, and the Treasury representative would have been a reputable witness. You may have never even known who he was, or what he could do." She set down her fork and began winding her cloth napkin through her fingers. "Then, through you, he'd have had access to the task force, the entire Hamilton family, my parents, and the Midwestern Pact Intelligence Agency. He'd have had the option of backups for his backups."

"And the cherry on top would be that he'd remain at his leisure to exact whatever kind of revenge he wanted on you as well," Stefan added quietly.

"What's his endgame, though?"

"Perhaps to move someone else into Hamilton's place?" Stefan frowned. "There's too many layers to this. It's like trying to figure out a thousand-piece puzzle in the dark."

"Maybe now that he's made his move and it's gained national attention, we can finally start unraveling parts."

"You know, I love a good challenge as much as the next person in my line of work, but I think that I prefer my bad guys to be dumb."

"You and me both."

It had been the right decision to stay in Lincoln for their long weekend, as Kaleo and Stefan hadn't had much recent quality time together. Only a few days after Operation Cuckoo, Kaleo had taken the train to Lincoln to go house-hunting for a place to rent, and as soon as she'd signed a lease Todd asked her to move ahead of schedule so she could help him coordinate the transition for Hamilton's team.

In a mad dash of adrenaline-fueled packing, even with the help of Stefan and her family Kaleo had barely been able to relocate on time. For three long weeks she'd lived in Lincoln with only Taylor Schmidt, and Adrian and Kiana Hamilton to keep her company while Stefan had been kept busy back in Chicago helping Director Stone turn the reins of the Midwestern Pact Intelligence Agency over to their successors, and her family worked with the task force planning their own potential moves.

When Stefan finally moved to Lincoln the week before the inauguration, Kaleo had picked him up from the train station with a small bouquet of flowers and a large box of cookies. He'd already signed the lease on an apartment downtown sight-unseen, and she, Adrian, and Kiana had helped him move in.

After their long weekend, Kaleo and Stefan hit the ground running. Todd's predictions and Director Stone's hopes had proved true, and with the huge boost in publicity and goodwill that Phoenix and Strike had elicited, along with the media blitz that Sifter went on, it was almost laughably easy to get the bill creating the National Abled Task Force, or NAT, as it came to be called, through Congress.

The goodwill from the events of the inauguration night was also aided by the long list of accomplishments of the Midwestern Pact Abled Task Force. When she'd first started working in Chicago, Kaleo had never had the time or inclination to truly pay attention to all that the task force had done before she had joined, but in the past several months, the force had shut down several large-scale drug operations, child-pornography rings, taken down two of America's most wanted criminals and Mafia bosses, and even assisted the Secret Service in busting a very productive counterfeiting operation.

While being a part of the NAT was certainly exciting, the nice thing about her day job as one of President Hamilton's aides was that, for all intents and purposes, it let her fly completely under the radar. Very few people noticed the presence of a lowly aide at the security briefings, and anyone who both noticed and dared to question the president received a gracious explanation that she was taking notes for him to reference later. The excuse worked like a charm, and within a couple of weeks her presence was as accepted in the meetings as that of the president's dog.

# Chapter Twenty-Seven

In hindsight, Stefan was glad that Kaleo had convinced him to use their time off as a chance to rest and recharge because the next two months passed in a dizzying blur of activity.

Fortunately, most of the members of the Midwestern Pact Abled Task Force had agreed to relocate. Even better, the new National Abled Task Force was funded with an extremely robust budget, and they'd been able to find a full-time position for everyone on the previous task force who wanted one. Most of the former members had taken him up on the new job offer, with the exception of Kaleo and Taylor Schmidt, who chose to continue working for Hamilton's office.

The investigation into the inauguration assassination attempt moved at a glacial pace. The FBI and Homeland had managed to identify the assassin, but hadn't seemed particularly motivated to do much else than chalk it up to the product of a single man's deranged bid for infamy.

It was Director Stone and Stefan who eventually linked the assassin to a fledgling group of anti-Ableds that called themselves the Snakeheads, and who had discovered the insignia of the group, the fanged head of a viper, was also a patch that several of the killed puppets at Operation Cuckoo had been wearing on their jackets.

When the president had casually asked the director of the FBI what his agent had handed then-President Johnson on the night of the inauguration, the FBI director had denied any knowledge of the event. When confronted with the pictures and tape, and then given several days to conduct an internal investigation, the director had theorized that perhaps one of the Snakeheads had managed to put a type of poison powder onto the package that subsequently had caused Johnson's stroke. There hadn't been a satisfactory answer as to how the Snakehead in question had managed to get his hands on an FBI jacket and believable enough credentials to sneak past security, and the box that had been handed to Johnson had somehow gotten lost. Thus, President Hamilton quietly delegated any further investigation into the Snakeheads and their link with Puppeteer to the NAT.

Former president Johnson remained critically ill. His stroke caused massive bleeding throughout his brain that required a very delicate surgery, and his recovery had been very slow. From the whispers that he'd heard in hallways after meetings, Stefan gathered that the prognosis for Johnson wasn't good, and that he'd most likely need full-time care for the rest of his life.

After several weeks, the stress had given the former First Lady a heart attack while she had been out of town visiting her family, and she'd passed away before anything could be done.

President Hamilton's new vice president was a young senator from one of the New England states. He wasn't particularly bright, but he held strong convictions mostly in line with Hamilton's, and more importantly, he held a healthy suspicion of other politicians and distrust of newcomers. Stefan had met the man on a couple of occasions and privately thought that it was a wonder he had ever managed to win one election, let alone rise to the distinguished position of senator, but family money still went a long way in politics, and the new vice president's family was swimming in it.

During one of their first official NAT meetings, Director Stone had gone over the government hierarchy structure, and while Stefan had listened and committed it to memory in case he needed to know for the future, he didn't particularly care about the politics looming over the task force; that was Stone's job. In fact, as the days passed, Stone took on most of the political and administrative side of things and left Stefan to start handling the intel and missions with minimal oversight.

"Bro, are you going to lift more or just check yourself out in the mirror?" Brant Heinstein's voice broke through Stefan's reverie.

"Chill out, I'm taking a break," Stefan said.

"Then hurry it up, I'm starting to get cold."

Goaded on by Brant, Stefan stepped back underneath the loaded barbell for another punishing set of squats.

After the events of Operation Cuckoo, the Professor had stayed true to his word and taken Brant Heinstein on as an occasional student. While Heinstein no longer was able to use his abilities to any real degree, apparently Kaleo had reported to the Professor that his combat skills were still good, and the Professor had paired him with Stefan several times to spar.

Stefan had to admit that he'd been surprised at just how good Brant was. Of course, Stefan's abilities would have placed him miles ahead of Brant in any type of real combat, but the other young man was more than capable of helping him keep his fighting skills sharp.

It was after one of their sparring sessions, when they were recovering in the locker room, that Stefan and Brant discovered a mutual shared interest in fitness. Stefan had gone home that evening feeling conflicted. Adrian wasn't much the gym type, and Stefan hadn't had time to form the same connections in Lincoln that he'd had in Chicago to help him with his lifting routine, but Brant had made his dislike of Kaleo obvious, and even considering hanging out with him seemed disloyal.

Kaleo had picked up on his mood when they had met for dinner that night, and he'd hesitantly explained his conundrum.

"So, what's the problem?" she had asked in between bites of her fried chicken.

"Well, he's been pretty clear about what he thinks of you..."

"You need someone to help spot you, and these chicken wings of mine aren't anywhere near strong enough to fill that role," she said with a self-deprecating smile and a shake of her arm before continuing. "I really don't mind, just promise me that you won't let him talk so poorly about me that you reconsider our relationship."

"I promise that if he tries anything, I'll club him over the head with one of the barbells," Stefan had replied in a tone that was only half-joking.

After he had received the green light from Kaleo, it wasn't too long before he and Brant were meeting up a couple of times a week to work out. Brant was more than wealthy enough to afford his own private gym, and once the task force was up and running, they could have also used that gym space, but Heinstein had insisted on working out at a very popular fitness club on the wealthy side of town. The facilities hadn't quite been Stefan's cup of tea—too flashy and posh for his taste, but he hadn't needed to get his own membership as Brant's guest, and the weight area was top-notch, so he didn't complain.

It didn't take Stefan very long to figure out why Brant preferred to go to that particular gym; he was very popular with the female clientele, some of whom Stefan thought he recognized as models from several national advertising campaigns.

"You know, Stefan, I'm sure that if anything ever happens between you and Kaleo, you could probably find plenty of girls here willing to help you get over the breakup," Brant remarked offhandedly.

Stefan was trying to rep out his max, and the only response that he was capable of was a scowl and grunt at Brant as he finished the set. Brant shrugged, racking the weights. "Just an observation: The last girls who talked to us seemed way more interested in you than me. You realize that there are other fish in the sea, right? Why settle for canned tuna when you could have a dolphin?"

"I am more than content with what I have right now." Stefan wiped the sweat off his face and shot Brant a cocky grin. "Besides, if I was single you'd never be able to get a date because all the girls would be flocking to me, so you better be glad that I'm a happily taken man."

Brant grumbled, but otherwise left the issue alone for the time being. However, Stefan suspected that the matter wasn't completely closed, and when Brant repeated something similar the next week, Stefan took great care to shut down any of his suggestions swiftly and in such a way that the topic was not brought up again.

Still, once Stefan made his boundaries clear and Brant understood that anything about Kaleo in general, and her relationship with Stefan specifically, was
solidly off-limits, they got along well.

Adrian and Stefan had taken to meeting up every other week for trivia night
at one of the local bars in town, and it wasn't too long before Stefan invited
Brant along. As it turned out, Brant's knowledge of all things sports and pop
culture was unparalleled, and the three of them made a pretty good team.

Then, one night a couple of months after Stefan had first invited Brant out,
disaster struck in the form of a large water pipe break, and the bar that usually
hosted the trio's favorite trivia night had to shut down. They'd just gotten to
the bar when it flooded, and instead of calling it a night Brant suggested they
try out a new place he'd heard some of his employees talking about. The bar in
question was a little further down the road, across a set of train tracks, and gave
off more of a gritty vibe than their usual spot, but Adrian had seemed almost
excited to be "slumming it," and his two Secret Service agents didn't appear too
apprehensive, so Stefan went along without protest.

They had fun at first. There were several pool tables towards the back of the
dive bar, and Stefan thoroughly enjoyed beating Brant in a couple of games.
Then, halfway through their third game, Stefan noticed that Brant wasn't playing quite as well as he had before, and that a busty redhead sitting at the bar was
claiming the lion's share of his friend's interest.

"You okay there, man? You seem a little distracted," Stefan said.

"She wants me, I just know it," Brant replied as he focused on the ball in front
of him. Stefan glanced at the woman surreptitiously. It was true, she certainly
was keeping a close eye on them.

"You sure that she doesn't just want a chance to play?" Adrian teased from
his station leaning against the table. "Maybe she thinks that she can hustle you
for the cash in that huge wallet of yours."

"She can hustle me all she wants if she lets me take her home and show her
something else huge," Brant said. He missed his shot, and Stefan easily took the
next several to win.

"Another game?" Stefan asked.

Brant glanced back at the woman and smiled. "Yeah, but give me a minute. I think I may need to recruit some help. You two need another drink?"

Stefan finished the last of the beer he had been nursing and held it up. "Yeah, I'll take another one of these."

"I'll take another one as well," Adrian added.

When Brant came back from the bar with their drinks, it was with the redhead on his arm. She shook Stefan's hand limply and introduced herself as Breona.

"I'm really not looking forward to getting beat by you again Stefan, but Breona here told me that she's never had the chance to see a game up close, and she promised me that she'd be my good luck charm for tonight," Brant said as he handed Stefan and Adrian their beers before wrapping his arm around her waist.

"As I recall, I actually said that if you showed me how to play you might get lucky tonight," Breona purred as she leaned into Brant's touch and rested her hand against his stomach.

Brant's grin widened. "Ah, that's right. I must have forgotten the exact phrasing, how careless of me."

Stefan and Adrian exchanged amused looks as Brant badly flubbed the beginning shots and told Breona that perhaps if she took a turn, her beginner's luck would turn the game around for him.

"I sure hope you're better at other activities than you are at pool, Brant, or the lady may be very disappointed later," Adrian quipped from his station at the side of the table as he watched Stefan line up his shot. Stefan chuckled, missed, and stepped aside for Brant, who handed his cue to Breona.

"Remember, I've never played before. Can you show me where to put my hands?" Breona asked Brant innocently over her shoulder as she bent forward at the hips and rested her ample bosom on the table with all the subtlety of a cat in heat. Stefan didn't need to be on the same side of the table to guess how far up her leather skirt, which had been almost scandalously short to begin with, had slid when she bent forward, and from his vantage point Breona's low-cut shirt left little to the imagination.

Brant looked more than happy to help. He stretched himself out over her back and placed his arms on top of hers to give her guidance. He whispered something into her ear, and Breona giggled and wiggled her hips before looking up at Adrian. "Don't worry, dear, I don't think that there's any chance that I'll be disappointed later," she said as she expertly sank the ball into the pocket.

Stefan saw Adrian open his mouth to reply, but didn't get a chance to hear what he was about to say due to a commotion that broke out across the bar. A large man dressed in a leather biker's vest stormed across the room and shoved Brant off Breona.

"What are you doing messing around with my girl?" the biker spat at Brant.

"Shut up, Billy, we broke up two days ago. You don't have any right to tell me what to do," Breona huffed as she flipped her hair behind her shoulder and put her hands on her hips.

Stefan watched Brant size Billy up. Even though the biker was at least six inches taller and probably close to a hundred pounds heavier, Brant didn't back down.

"Sounds like she's not your girl after all, so how about you go back to whatever hole you slithered out of," Brant said snidely with a pointed look at the large snake patch on the leather vest of his opponent. The biker shoved him again, and Brant returned the shove.

The snake patch made Stefan's eyebrows rise a fraction. For several weeks, he'd had his agents out on the streets searching for more information about the Snakeheads, but they had returned little information in the way of members, size of the group, or anything remotely tangible or helpful. He smiled inwardly at the irony of meeting a member here on one of his nights off.

The evolving situation quickly called for his attention, and Stefan's thoughts snapped back to the matter at hand. "Aww, look at this, the cripple wants to lose both of his hands," Billy mocked Brant as several other men dressed in leather jackets and vests filed in behind him.

"You better be glad that I've only got the one hand because if I still had both you'd have already gotten a block of ice in your face to cool you down, hothead," Brant growled.

"Oh? So you're one of those Ableds then?" Billy cracked his knuckles. "I'm glad you mentioned that. Now we can have some real fun."

Ever the politician's son, Adrian stepped between Brant and Billy to defuse the situation. As he did so, Stefan's inward smile turned into a groan. He made eye contact with Adrian's plainclothes Secret Service detail, who hadn't been paying attention as closely as they should have been, and a quirk of his eyebrow alerted them to the dangerous nature of the situation. They immediately stood from their table near the wall and made their way over to the standoff.

"Hey, how about everyone calms down right now? I'm sure that the lady can make her own choice between the two of you. Besides, we were just leaving anyway," Adrian said lightly.

"No, we weren't." Brant scoffed and crossed his arms across his chest with a glare at Billy.

"Leaving just as the party is getting started? I don't think so," Billy replied.

His eyes moved from Brant to Adrian, and a flicker of recognition crossed his face. Stefan, who'd been standing on the opposite side of the pool table, began to move towards his friends. It appeared that while Billy was large and brash, he unfortunately wasn't dumb, and when he saw the plainclothes agents join the standoff and got a good look at Adrian's face, he put two and two together and came up with the right answer.

"Hold on, you're Hamilton's son," Billy said, his eyes narrowing.

Yep, there it was. The president had managed to so far maintain a high popularity rating across most of the country, but some groups seemed opposed to him no matter what he did or the policy stances he took. After the inauguration, it hadn't been much of a surprise to learn that the Snakeheads were one such group.

Stefan sighed. He'd been looking forward to a nice, somewhat quiet guy's night out, and a chance to unwind from work and get caught up on life with his friends. The last thing he wanted to be worrying about was Adrian getting into yet another situation. He loved Adrian like one of his own brothers; in fact loved him more than at least one of them, but his friend seemed to attract trouble like cheese attracted rats. Or, in the context of the current situation, like mice attracted snakes.

He continued moving forward and sized up their opponents as he did so. Even with the addition of Adrian's agents, they were still outnumbered almost two-to-one. When the agents removed Adrian from the situation, that number would go up much closer to four-to-one, and the odds looked worse when he saw the suspicious bulges under the jackets of the Snakehead members who'd joined Billy. Stefan could only hope they were carrying knives and not guns. Knives he could work with; guns would really make things difficult.

Oh well, whatever they had couldn't be helped at this point, and Stefan knew that Brant had a couple of tricks squirreled away in his prosthetic. He just hoped that Heinstein didn't open his big mouth and say anything stupid.

As it turned out, it wasn't Heinstein that Stefan should have worried about.

Adrian looked Billy in the eye and crossed his arms, mirroring the larger man's posture. "Perhaps I am. What's it to you?" Stefan wasn't fooled by Adrian's posturing. He could see the vein standing out on his forehead, and the way that his fists clenched nervously.

"We don't much like Hamilton around these parts." Billy cracked his knuckles again and looked around at his friends. "In fact, I think that maybe we can send him a message of exactly what we think about him."

The bully swung at Adrian, but his brief glance at his friends had bought Stefan enough time to get within striking distance. He stepped forward and caught Billy's fist in his hand as easily as if he was back in school playing ball. Out of the corner of his eye, Stefan saw Brant step up to Adrian's right side, arms still crossed and eyes spitting fire.

"That's enough. Stop this and go home before someone gets hurt," Stefan said into the silence that had fallen over the bar.

Unfortunately, Billy might have recognized Adrian's face and the plainclothes agents for what they were, but his intelligence didn't extend to recognizing who was the real threat in the room. He pulled his hand back from Stefan's, turned away as if to back down, and then with the force and speed of a bull, he turned back to deliver a sucker punch.

Stefan was ready for him.

He stepped to the side and dodged Billy's punch deftly. Then, while Billy reared back for another try, Stefan reached into his pocket, withdrew his taser, and plunged the two contact points into his arm. The resulting electricity that coursed through his body created a sensation that was just slightly too intense to be called pleasant, although the minor discomfort was more than worth the tradeoff.

Now that he was juiced up, Stefan sped himself up just enough to make sure that his hand and foot placement was perfect. With remarkable ease, he danced just out of Billy's reach, grabbed the neck of his shirt and the back of his pants, and threw Billy across the pool table and to the floor on the other side.

"Nice throw, man!" Brant shouted, and Stefan turned to see his friend squaring up to another Snakehead.

Brant caught his eye and bared his teeth in a wild grin. "I told you that this place would be fun, didn't I?" he called out as he knocked his adversary to the floor.

"Trivia night is supposed to be relaxing. I'm never inviting you again," Stefan shot back.

"And miss out on all my movie knowledge? You and Adrian can kiss that championship cup goodbye."

"Fine, but you're not allowed to pick the backup bar ever again."

In the fight that ensued, Stefan was careful to not rely on his abilities in any noticeable way, only utilizing half a second here or there to dodge the worst of his attackers' punches. The last thing he wanted was to make himself more of a target, or to risk triggering the cost of his abilities. He knew his muscles would utilize the electricity from the taser before they began to work under their own power and really begin pumping out the lactic acid, but he hated taking risks.

Fortunately, the Snakeheads smelled like they were already several drinks in, so it wasn't hard to make the fight look like his opponents were just slightly more uncoordinated and unlucky, and he didn't have to truly tap into his full strength.

Stefan did have to admit that he enjoyed himself. As Strike he was responsible for a team and accomplishing the mission; as Stefan in a bar brawl, there wasn't much to worry about beyond not getting beat up too badly. However, he couldn't relax completely—he was still mindful of his current job and position in the Hamilton administration and leadership role in the new NAT, and headlines reading "Assistant Director of National Abled Task Force Attacked by Terrorist Group" were preferable to "National Abled Task Force Leader Beats Up Critics."

Despite all the fun that he was having, Stefan still had to be careful; some of the Snakeheads packed quite a mean punch. When he heard the sound of police sirens outside, one of the bikers took advantage of his momentary lapse of concentration and was able to land a solid hit that knocked Stefan off balance. The hit couldn't have come at a better time. As Stefan was struggling to regain his footing and defend himself from the worst of the blows, several officers burst into the bar and began breaking up the fight.

Even though the Snakeheads were the ones who started the brawl, both Brant and Stefan were also taken into the station. Adrian had long been removed from the scene by his security team, something that Stefan was more than grateful for—the last thing he wanted was the president in hot water because his son had been in a bar fight. Actually, no; he reflected that if Adrian had stayed and gotten arrested or hurt, Kiana's wrath was the one he really didn't want to face.

At the station, Brant and Stefan shared a holding cell. When he was given the chance to make his one phone call, Stefan checked the time and called Kaleo at her house. She'd told him earlier that she was going to enjoy a quiet night in and go to bed early, and part of him hoped she wasn't already asleep. The other part prayed she wouldn't hear the phone ring. He hadn't had a chance to drink anything immediately after the fight, and he'd only been provided one small cup of water at the station. He feared that his little taser hadn't been enough to prevent the worst side effects of his abilities, and that if Kaleo picked him up, she'd see a side of him that she hadn't been privy to yet.

# Chapter Twenty-Eight

The ringing phone next to her bed woke Kaleo from a deep sleep. With a grumble she rolled over to pick it up.

"Hello?" she said, struggling to keep the annoyance out of her voice.

"Hey Kaleo, it's Stefan. I'm at the police station. Can you come and pick me up?"

She groaned and rolled back onto her back, rubbing at her eyes with her free hand. "What are you doing at the police station?"

"I may have gotten into a small altercation at the bar."

That helped her wake up a bit. The thought of her mild-mannered Stefan getting into a bar fight was not something that she'd ever thought to worry about. "Is everyone okay? Do I need to call Phoenix and tell them to suit up?"

She thought she heard Stefan chuckle softly on the other side of the line. "No need to disturb anyone else, sweetheart, everyone is fine. Now, my time is almost up on this phone. Do you need the address?"

Kaleo listened as Stefan told her where he could be picked up, and then dressed quickly as soon as she hung up. When she got to the station, she gave the receptionist her name and settled into one of the chairs in the waiting room. The room was mostly empty, although not too long after she had arrived, a young man approximately her own age walked through the door and up to the receptionist desk. Kaleo's ears perked up when she thought she heard him mention the name Brant Heinstein, but she couldn't be sure and didn't think that she had any business asking when he settled in a chair across the room.

She didn't have to wait for long. A couple of minutes later, Stefan walked through the double doors. He certainly looked like he'd been in a fight; his shirt was rumpled, there were splatters of blood on his jeans, and he had a new cut on his cheek that looked like it had only recently stopped bleeding.

"You're looking a bit the worse for wear," she remarked dryly as Stefan drew near before pulling him into a hug.

"You can blame Brant for that. I don't think he's ever backed down from a fight in his life... especially when the fight in question is over a woman," Stefan said as he squeezed her tightly.

Kaleo looked up at him and smiled. "That does sound like him. Does he need a ride too? I'll put a paper bag over my face and we can pretend that I'm just an average taxi driver if you think it'll help."

"That won't be necessary." The man that Kaleo had noticed earlier spoke up. "I'm Mr. Heinstein's assistant, here to pick him up."

As if he was summoned by the sound of his own name, Brant walked through the doors. "Oh good, Enrique, I hope you brought the spare set of keys. I think I lost my other set sometime during the fight," Brant said as he strolled over, before stopping when he saw Kaleo.

"I was going to offer to give you a ride home, Peters, but apparently you've already made other arrangements. I'm surprised you showed up, Kaleo, considering what happened the last time that you had a boyfriend in trouble."

Kaleo felt Stefan's grip tighten on her arm at Brant's barbed words. "Say that again, Heinstein, and I'll make you regret it, even if it puts us both back in those holding cells. Remember what the deal was," Stefan snarled before she could respond.

She squeezed his hand and shook her head when he looked at her. "As I recall, the last time that I had a boyfriend in trouble, Stefan had just been hit by a car and I followed him to the hospital," she said coolly to Brant before offering an olive branch. "Thank you for having his back tonight... you've always been good about that."

Brant's eyes narrowed, but he only gave the smallest nod before turning towards the door and gesturing for Enrique to follow him. Kaleo sighed in relief at his lack of a scathing response, hopeful that perhaps one day he would be able to forgive her. She felt Stefan pull her into another embrace, and her melancholy thoughts fled as she basked in the warmth of his arms.

They were halfway to Stefan's apartment when in a panicked voice he ordered Kaleo to pull the car over. She did so immediately, and as soon as the car rolled to a stop, Stefan opened the door, leaned out, and threw up. After he was done, he closed the door and leaned back against the seat.

"Get me to my apartment as quickly as you can and I'll explain," he said before she could say anything.

Kaleo pulled out into the street again and glanced over at him. "Are you okay?"

He shook his head. "Remember when I said that one of my abilities costs is that if I go too fast I feel like I'm about to have a heart attack?"

She nodded.

"Yeah, well the other cost is that if I don't drink enough water in time to dilute the waste products from my muscles, the lactic acid makes me sick."

"How sick?"

"Have you ever had the stomach flu?" He glanced at the clock on the car dashboard. "I really was hoping you wouldn't see me like this, but I think that we have enough time to make it to my apartment before the next wave hits as long as you don't drive like a grandma. I thought I'd be okay, but it's been a while since I didn't have enough water after using my abilities, and I must have overestimated myself."

They did indeed make it to his apartment complex in time, although just barely. While Stefan threw up in the trashcan by the stairwell, Kaleo grabbed his jacket from the car before locking it and joining him.

"You don't need to help me up. You can go now, Kaleo. I'll be fine," he said weakly as he leaned against the top of the trashcan.

Kaleo shook her head and looped one of his arms over her shoulders. "C'mon, honey, let's get you home."

Once she had helped Stefan into his apartment, Kaleo did her best to make him comfortable. He refused to let her in the bathroom with him, which she appreciated, as it sounded like his distress wasn't limited to only vomiting. However, in between bouts of his symptoms, he joined her in the living room and let her sponge away the sweat from his forehead and refill his glass while he guzzled as much water as he could and gave her the rundown on the events of the night. After an hour had passed, he came back from his most recent bathroom trip and refilled his own glass of water.

"That should be the worst of it now," he said.

"That's it? That wasn't too bad. I thought that it would take you all night."

Stefan shook his head. "Normally it would have, but I was careful to only use my abilities when I needed to, and my taser helped. This was easy mode."

"I see. Well, if that's it, I'll head home now." Kaleo yawned and grabbed her things.

He frowned and looked down at the floor. "I'm sorry that you had to see that. I was hoping to spare you."

She hugged him and kissed his cheek. "Don't worry about it, sweetheart. I'm just glad that I could help. Maybe one day you can return the favor."

He smiled down at her. "I look forward to it."

The next morning Kaleo went into the presidential offices early to report to Todd and Michael about what had happened the night before. She knew that the current plan was for the Snakeheads in police custody to be taken to the task-force headquarters, where Audra and Taylor would interrogate them as their alter egos of Beguile and Silver Tongue.

By the time she was able to tear herself away from the mountain of work at the office and head over to NAT headquarters for an update, the interrogation had already occurred.

She found Stefan in his office, leaning back in his chair with his hands over his face.

"Feeling okay?" she asked as she settled herself in the seat across from him.

"Much better than the last time that you saw me, that's for sure."

"I take it that the interrogation didn't go so well then?"

"The interrogation went off without a hitch. You know how convincing Audra and Taylor can be, especially when they're working together. We wrung them dry of information and got enough to get a warrant for a raid."

"So what's the problem?"

"Stone's made it clear that all the planning and execution for any future missions is solely my responsibility from here on out."

"Isn't that what you wanted? That he's letting you help him out with more things?"

"Yes, of course, but this is the new task force's inaugural operation and it's just a little intimidating," Stefan grumbled, but removed his hands from his face and sat upright in his chair.

"I'm sure that you'll do great with it. You've planned and run plenty of these before, and they've all gone off without a hitch."

"Not the most recent one."

"I'd say that saving the life of the vice president and subduing his would-be assassin was a pretty good result of the last one."

One corner of Stefan's mouth lifted in a small smile at her attempts to lighten his spirits. "You know as well as I do that you and Michael were the main planners for the inauguration. I was just there for backup."

"Very helpful backup, as it turned out. Besides, no one, least of all you, could have predicted what happened with Operation Cuckoo, and thanks to your foresight we were all relatively unharmed."

"Only because you and Brant had to take unnecessary risks."

She shrugged. "Occupational hazard in our line of work. Besides, Puppeteer doesn't know what kind of abilities you have. If you hadn't gotten hurt you probably could have taken him out easily."

The smile on Stefan's face widened. "You're not going to let me feel bad at all, are you?"

Kaleo returned his smile with one of her own. "Nope. You've had long enough to enjoy your pity party; time to get back to work."

"You're quite the slave driver. Do Sabrina and James ever complain?"

"All the time, I just ignore them and give them something else to do. If they've got time to complain, then they aren't working hard enough."

"I'm dating a monster."

"Yes, you are, and you love me anyways."

"Very true." Stefan frowned and looked back at the papers in front of him. "We may need some of that monster before it's all said and done. This isn't going to be an easy mission."

"The Kaleo monster or the Phoenix monster?"

"Possibly both. Like I said, we've got enough for a warrant, but I want to make sure that we're above reproach. I certainly wouldn't mind a second set of eyes on the game plan before we put it into action."

Kaleo frowned. "You want a little of Canary and a little of Phoenix then."

"Is that going to be okay?"

Kaleo looked down at her hands and shrugged one shoulder. For so long she had told herself that that chapter in her life was closed. Now Stefan was not only asking her to voluntarily open that part of herself up again but also to use it.

She had always drawn a distinction between what Canary had done and her own current job. The logistics side of planning events and evaluating supply and trade was different enough from mission planning that it hadn't brought up any old ghosts. Of course, the rising anxiety in her gut wasn't helped by the knowledge that the last person she had planned a mission with had been Reader, and she tried not to let her mind go down that particularly dark path.

Stefan gave her time to think, and after the ticking of the clock had denoted the passing of several minutes she sighed, came to a decision, and made eye contact with him. For anyone else, she would have declined without a second thought. For Stefan, she would walk through fire. "I'll be fine. I can help if you need me," she said.

He didn't seem to believe her. "Are you sure? I don't want to force you into anything or open any old wounds, and I know that this is a sensitive topic for you. I'm sure that I'll be fine on my own. You really don't have to help me."

"I said that I'll be fine, Stefan. Don't try and talk me out of it now or I'll think that you weren't being serious to begin with." The attempt at humor helped to lift her spirits, even if it felt a little forced.

"If you're really sure..." He still didn't sound convinced.

"I'm positive. Just let me know what you need me to help with." She paused. "And this should go without saying, but I'll be on the mission too."

"I thought you'd say something like that." he looked down at the papers in front of him. "I'll start coordinating with Homeland and see if we can get some reconnaissance teams in the area or to infiltrate the organization. Hopefully it won't take us too long to get the information that we need."

"Didn't you just say that you had a warrant for a raid?"

"Yeah, but I want to make sure that we get the most bang for our buck. With Mod's help we may be able to infiltrate faster than through conventional means."

"Whatever you say, boss."

Stefan raised an eyebrow and Kaleo saw his nose twitch. "Boss?" He rolled the word around on his tongue, savoring it like it was a piece of hard candy. "I like it. You should definitely start calling me that more."

"I thought that we agreed to be professional," she said coolly, attempting to hide her suddenly flustered state of mind.

"We did. What's unprofessional about calling me 'boss'? You could also call me 'sir' if you wanted to; that is what some of our newest recruits call me after all," Stefan deadpanned before a wicked grin spread across his face. "What did you think that I was implying?"

"Oh, nothing." She gathered her things and stood. "Now, if that's all you need, I'll head back up to the White House for the rest of the day. Let me know when you want me to help you with the mission planning."

"C'mon now, don't let me scare you off so easily." He chuckled before also standing. "You know that sometimes I enjoy messing with you and trying to poke holes in that unflappable professional demeanor of yours, darling. If you've got a few minutes to spare, I've actually got several people that I'd like for you to meet."

"I suppose I don't have to go back to the office immediately if you promise to behave yourself."

Stefan raised one hand up in a mock pledge. "Scout's honor. If I break my word, you have my full permission to tell everyone all the disgusting details about how you had to take care of your weak, helpless, sick boyfriend last night."

# Chapter Twenty-Nine

Stefan led Kaleo down several hallways until they reached what had formerly been a storage room. As they walked, Stefan gave Kaleo an update on their newest coworkers.

"Director Stone feels that we need to grow the force so we can have a range of abilities to choose from when deciding who to send out on mission, and so that no one has to pull double duty. He's been working with your mom and putting out feelers to get some new recruits, and we've got a couple of bites so far."

"What kind of bites?"

"The serious kind. We've got two new hires onboarding this week. One for our new lab, and one for the field. Granted, they're both on the younger side of the spectrum, but I have been assured that they know how to behave themselves and that we won't be having to babysit."

"But I thought you loved children."

"Yes, but I don't love depending on children in life-or-death situations. This is where our lab guy is setting up. By all accounts, he's a wizard when it comes to everything tech, both creating and repairing."

Stefan held the door open for Kaleo and she smiled at him as she walked through, only to stop dead in her tracks at the sight of the young man standing in front of her. Stefan opening the door must have interrupted the new recruit's work, as he was straightening up from peering at something under a microscope. When fully standing, he was just slightly taller than Kaleo, although his thin build seemed to add several inches to his height. A corner of his mouth tipped up to welcome his new visitors, and the warm light in his chocolate eyes made her heart drop to the floor.

Her mind heard Stefan say, "This is our newest recruit, Jeffery," but her eyes only saw a young Reader standing before her.

"Hello, Assistant Director Peters, to what do I owe this visit?" Jeffery asked as he shifted from one foot to another, and the spell was broken. His nasal voice sounded nothing like Reader's, and as Kaleo took a closer look she saw that the cast of the nose and jaw and the shade of his brown hair were slightly off.

"Jeffery, this is Kaleo Hughes. She's our liaison with the president's office, which means that she's the one who tells President Hamilton if we're doing a good job, and she coordinates his security for big events with us."

"Kaleo Hughes? It's good to meet you." Jeffery smiled at her briefly without making full eye contact while continuing to shift his weight between his feet. "I heard that you worked with my cousin, Nicholas, for a long time. He used to tell me all about you and what your team did."

"Nicholas?" Kaleo asked, her voice a higher pitch than normal and her face warm.

"Oh, that's right. He said that you all used your codenames all the time. His was Reader."

"I can certainly see the family resemblance," Kaleo said as neutrally as she could, still struggling to maintain her composure.

"My uncle Max always told me that Nicholas and I looked like twins. It is funny though that you and I never met until now. Nicky used to talk about you all the time back when he was alive, and my dad still mentions you every now and then when he has dinner with you and your family."

"Your dad?"

Jeffrey had transitioned to running his hands over various metallic wires sitting on his workbench, and only seemed to be partially listening to her. "Yeah, you probably know him by his old Savior-name though; he's Sniffer. It's funny that he's blind and I'm not. Wouldn't you think that I'd be blind too, especially since I have abilities of my own? I guess you don't know about my abilities, though. I can think of an idea, and then use my sense of smell to tell me the best way to combine different types of metals and chemicals to engineer what I want. My dad says that it's like I'm cooking, but with electronics instead of actual food." His back was now to Kaleo and Stefan, but from the angle at which she was standing, Kaleo could see him twisting several wires together. "It was nice to meet you, but I'm really busy right now, come back another time and we can talk," he said.

Kaleo looked at Stefan, who shrugged and motioned for them to leave the room. Once he shut the door safely behind them, Kaleo sagged against the beige wall and shuddered. Stefan was by her side in an instant.

"Kaleo, sweetheart, I promise that I had no idea. If I knew, I would have at least warned you. I'm sorry that you walked into that," he said softly.

She sniffed back the tears that threatened and opened her mouth to reply, but was cut short.

"Assistant Director Peters? The lady at the front desk said that you wanted to see me?"

Stefan turned around to face the new voice, blocking the person from Kaleo's view and giving her just enough time to compose herself, only to be knocked off her emotional footing once again when she heard the next words out of Stefan's mouth.

"Hey, Trevor. I wanted you to meet Kaleo Hughes, the liaison for the president's office. I've told you before about her."

"That's right; she's the one who coordinates the President's security detail with us and lets you know if Phoenix or anyone else is needed."

"Correct. Kaleo, this is Trevor Hartley, our newest field rookie," Stefan said and stepped to the side as he made the introduction.

Trevor paused mid-step and stared at Kaleo, appearing to feel almost as much shock as she. "Canary, is that you?"

"Hi, Trevor. It's certainly been a long time," she said carefully, swallowing down both her emotions and the rising feeling of nausea.

"It really is you!" He jogged down the hallway to close the distance between them. "How have you been? How's the rest of the Flock? Do they all work here now? I almost didn't recognize you because of the hair. I've sure missed you guys. My sisters are going to be so excited when I tell them that I'm going to be working with you!"

Kaleo couldn't see Stefan's expression, but she could have sworn she heard him groan. She guessed that he was already kicking himself for not having known more about Trevor and Jeffery's backgrounds, and she knew that if she had a meltdown he would feel terrible. That knowledge gave her strength, and she plastered a gentle smile onto her face before responding to Trevor's questions.

"Unfortunately, not too long after we rescued you the Flock ran into some issues. It's a long story, and I'm sure that eventually you'll be debriefed considering recent events, but it's probably best that I broke the news to you." She paused to take a deep breath, and Trevor's smile faded away. "Puppeteer betrayed the Flock and Reader and Polygraph were killed. Like I said, it's a long story, but from everything I've heard Lens and Divide are doing well, although Divide and I are no longer on speaking terms."

Trevor's eyes were practically bugging out of his head. His face still had a scattering of acne over it, and she was reminded that he hadn't been much out of childhood when she had last seen him several years before.

He opened and shut his mouth several times without making a sound before finally finding his voice. "I'm so sorry, Canary. I can't imagine how that must have felt."

"Please, call me Kaleo. No one has called me Canary in a very long time." She continued smiling, afraid that if she stopped the tears would come. "How is your family? Are your sisters okay?"

"They're all good, still living near my grandma. Dad got a job working as a mechanic at one of the shops around the town and does pretty well. Alicia hasn't shown any abilities yet, but she's still young and has some time, and my mom stays busy all day running after Savannah, who can't ever sit still."

"I'm glad to hear that. Preventing your abduction was the last full mission that the Flock completed before everything fell apart, so it's comforting to know that at least you and your family had a happy ending." Kaleo checked her watch. "I better be getting back to the president's office now, there's still a few things that I need to get done by the end of the day. It was good to see you again, Trevor. I'm looking forward to working with you."

"Yeah, you too," Trevor said.

"I'll walk you out Kaleo. Trevor, can you wait here for me until I'm back? I'm sure that you probably have several questions," Stefan said.

"Don't worry about it, Stefan, I can walk myself out. You can stay here with Trevor," Kaleo replied as she took a step down the hallway.

"No, I insist. Trevor doesn't mind waiting. Right, Trevor?"

"Not at all. If anything I may pop in and see what Jeffery is up to."

"You've met Jeffery?" Kaleo couldn't stop herself from asking.

Trevor nodded. "The family resemblance is pretty crazy, isn't it? I thought that it was so cool that Reader's cousin and I are working at the same place... I just can't believe that he didn't tell me..." He paused and grimaced before opening the door to Jeffery's lab. "I'm going to stop talking now and let you get back to work."

Stefan was quiet as he walked Kaleo down to the parking garage, and she appreciated the silence and space to think. When they got to her car, she turned to face him. "What are you going to tell Trevor?"

"I was thinking I'd probably just tell him the basics. It's not really my story to tell."

"Tell him everything. I don't mind, and if we're going to be working together on the same team he needs to know."

"Everything?" Stefan repeated.

Kaleo nodded. "Everything. The good, the bad, and the ugly. He's probably bursting with questions, and he certainly needs to know that not only is Puppeteer not a friend, but what lengths he'll go to get what he wants."

Stefan hugged her tightly, but Kaleo couldn't let herself relax, afraid that doing so would allow the dam to break and the tears to flood. She returned his hug but extracted herself from his arms when she felt her emotions welling up again.

"Dinner tonight?" she asked.

"Of course. Your place? Don't worry about cooking, I'll pick something up on my way."

"I've got a chicken that needs to be cooked soon…" Her voice trailed off and she frowned, trying to remember when exactly she had bought the chicken, and if it was even still safe to eat.

"No cooking. My treat; the chicken can wait." He kissed her forehead before opening the car door for her. "We'll talk about everything else later. Don't work too hard at the office, you've had a very emotionally intense day and probably not enough sleep last night. I love you."

"I love you too," Kaleo said as she got into her car. Stefan shut the door and stepped back to let her pull out of the parking space.

The rest of the afternoon passed in a blur. Kaleo refused to let herself think of Jeffery, or Trevor Hartley, or anything that she and Stefan had talked about before meeting the two new recruits, and instead focused on getting as much of her work done as she could. Fortunately, Todd always had plenty for her to work on.

It wasn't until early that evening, as she walked through the door to her house, changed into her non-work clothes, lit a fire for the comforting warmth, and had gotten settled that Kaleo let herself begin to feel. She reclined on the couch, burrowed under a heavy blanket, and stared into the fire as tears rolled down her face and the memories came flooding back.

She was still in that position almost an hour later when Stefan let himself in. Apparently, he'd been expecting something of the sort judging by the large bouquet of flowers in his hands, and the even larger sack of food that was hanging off of his arm. He put the flowers and food on the coffee table wordlessly, and sat down on the couch next to her.

"Rough day, huh?" he asked softly as he ran his fingers lightly over her skin.

She sniffed and shifted around so that she could lean her head against his shoulder, glad for the comfort of his presence as the tears threatened to well up again. "You could say that it was certainly unexpected."

"Yeah, I'm sorry about that. Like I said, Stone was the one doing the recruiting. I had no idea that Jeffery or Trevor had connections to the Flock. If I knew, I would have warned you."

Kaleo's stomach growled and she hugged Stefan one more time before standing to get plates and silverware for them. "I know you would have. Don't worry about it, it really shouldn't be that big of a deal. You must think I'm a little baby for letting something like that make me cry after so long."

"You're definitely not little... maybe more of a big baby," he teased, and then ducked when she threw a wadded-up cloth napkin at him.

"So how did Director Stone even find them?" Kaleo asked as they settled down to eat.

"When Sniffer heard about NAT's formation, he contacted Stone to let him know it was something Jeffery was interested in. Apparently he's some kind of genius, so Stone was more than happy to jump on that opportunity." Stefan paused to take a bite of his food and made a face. "I called Sniffer to ask him why he didn't give us more of a heads up about Jeffery's background, and his resemblance to his cousin, especially considering your history with Reader, and Sniffer told me in no uncertain terms that Jeffery and Nicholas had completely different smells and that we shouldn't blame the blind man for not knowing what his nephew looked like... and Stone had never seen a picture of Reader, so he was no help. If anything, I should have been the one to pick up on it. Jeffery looked familiar but I couldn't place him—I've only ever seen that one picture of the Flock, so I suppose it just slipped my mind."

"That's fair," Kaleo conceded. "What about Trevor?"

Stefan chuckled. "You and the others in the Flock must have rocked his world when you saved him because when he heard about the Midwestern Pact Abled Task Force, he wrote Stone an unprompted letter asking when he'd be able to join up. When Stone let him know that the National Task force was hiring, he jumped at the chance."

"You're so desperate for people that you're hiring untested teenagers just barely out of school?"

"Not quite. Technically he's an intern who's also going to college."

"A paid intern? I'm not going on missions with a new person who isn't paid to at least not mess things up."

"Of course, and we're paying him a very nice educational stipend on top of his base compensation." Stefan shrugged. "Honestly, we've lucked out so far with the force. You know as well as I do how abilities go. It's pretty amazing that we've already got the kind of power that we do, and if it wasn't for your parents helping us out, we'd have probably struggled with getting even half of the people signed onto the task force last year."

Kaleo nodded. While her family, the Flock, and most of the members on the task force had very powerful abilities, they were by far the exception rather than the norm. Abilities were as varied as people, and having both the potential for powerful abilities and the mental fortitude it took to practice and hone their skills made truly powerful Ableds very uncommon.

"We did tell Trevor the last time that we saw him that if he practiced his abilities he'd get better, and even back then he was pretty strong," she said.

"He's very strong now. I was there when the Professor did his evaluation. Speaking of which, it sounds like he may want to match you two up and see what happens."

"I appreciate the heads up," Kaleo replied with a frown, fully aware that Trevor's telekinetic ability could present quite the problem for her.

"Something to think about. Just thought I'd give you a fair warning and try to make up for earlier today."

"No need for that... although I do appreciate the flowers," she said with a gesture at the bouquet still sitting on the table.

"Got to keep my girlfriend happy, you know. I'd hate for Heinstein's infatuation with Phoenix to outdo mine," Stefan teased.

Kaleo giggled. Ever since Operation Cuckoo, Brant had continued to send Phoenix a large flower arrangement every couple of weeks as a thank you for saving his life. When Stefan had told Brant that Phoenix would be moving to Lincoln to continue working for NAT, Brant had simply changed the florist. Ironically, Brant remained completely unaware that Kaleo and Phoenix were the same person, and she felt zero desire to correct his lack of knowledge.

"I still don't quite understand how you and Brant got to be so buddy-buddy, but I'm glad that you two get along well. He probably needs more good, stable friends like you and Adrian."

Stefan raised an eyebrow. "Good, stable friends who let themselves get pulled into bar fights because he couldn't keep his hands off a girl?"

"At least you had his back. I don't think that he's had too many people in his life like that."

"You had his back."

Kaleo shrugged. "Not when it mattered. I get why he hates me now; I'm just happy that Lin doesn't feel the same way."

"Don't worry, he'll come around eventually," Stefan assured her before changing the subject. "How is Lin doing lately anyways?"

"Better. You remember that she broke up with Sam around a month or two ago because she caught him cheating on her?"

Stefan nodded as he took another bite of his food.

"She met a new guy recently, and it sounds like they've hit it off pretty well. She's not as happy with her job, though—something about her old boss retiring and the new one being too uptight and expecting too much."

"Lin's boss has expectations that she can't deliver on? What are they wanting? Her to solve every single economic issue in the Midwestern Pact by tomorrow?"

"Something like that."

"You should tell her to move here. I know that you miss seeing her every day, and she'd probably enjoy the change of scenery."

"She just moved to Chicago less than a year ago, I doubt she wants to make another big move so soon."

"Wouldn't hurt to ask."

"Maybe. I'll mention it next time we talk. Did you learn anything else about the Snakeheads after I left?"

"Not really."

"Just keep me updated and let me know when you need my help."

"You're sure that you're really okay with helping me? I don't want you to do something that's going to cause you any pain. You've been doing so well lately."

Kaleo blew her nose. "Doing so well that you walked in on me curled up in the fetal position and dehydrated from all the tears."

Stefan shifted his body to look at her better. "Hey, now. It's been what, several months since you last had a problem, and longer since you've had a true meltdown, right?"

"The last meltdown was after Adrian and Kiana's wedding," Kaleo admitted, wincing at the memory. "So you'd think that I should be completely over it now. It's been over six years, and yet sometimes it still feels so fresh."

"Exactly. It still feels fresh, but it's taking more to trigger you. I'm surprised that seeing Puppeteer back in December didn't send you into more of a spiral."

"A spiral? It felt good to get one over on him. If it hadn't been in the worst possible weather conditions, Brant and I could have easily taken him out." She snorted.

"I know that it gave you nightmares, and I know that the inauguration did too," Stefan replied quietly. "That tells me that you're still processing through things... Which is fine, I know how it is. There are still some things that happened to me back with the Rangers that make me wake up in the middle of the night in a sweat too."

Kaleo's mood sobered. Stefan rarely talked about his time spent in the military, and when he did it was almost always with a dark look in his eye.

"Do you want to talk about it?" she asked.

It was Stefan's turn to stare into the fire and shiver. "Not really. We were the good guys, I know we were... but we saw a lot of ugly, and sometimes we had to do some not so good things to prevent even worse consequences."

Kaleo rubbed his shoulder and arm while he was lost in thought, giving him plenty of space to think. After several minutes he shook himself out of his reverie and turned back to her. "But that's enough brooding. Needless to say, once my contract ended I had no intention of renewing and was more than happy to take the job that Director Stone offered me."

"Not least of all because you happened to meet a very special someone while working at that job, right?" Kaleo asked with a smile.

"Yeah, I mean, I guess Laura is a good friend and coworker. I wouldn't necessarily call her special, though." Stefan's face was serious before breaking into a grin when Kaleo tried to hit him with one of the couch pillows.

"You jerk," she said as she wound back to throw another pillow at him.

He laughed, and before she could release the pillow, Kaleo found herself being tackled backwards against the couch. Her heart skipped a beat as she looked up at Stefan. He supported himself with one hand while the other traced the curve of her face and his eyes burned into hers. Then his hand began to move lower, and for a brief moment Kaleo's breath caught in her throat. She reached up to grab a handful of his hair to pull him into a kiss as a wave of desire washed over her.

The hungry look on Stefan's face transformed into a boyish grin and he began to tickle her. Kaleo screeched and tried to fight him off, unable to focus enough to even use her shield. Fortunately for her, she wasn't the only ticklish one, and after several minutes of all-out war, they collapsed back onto the couch together.

"Normal boyfriends would have tried to seduce their girlfriend just now... it would be just my luck that I'm dating someone who thinks that the better option is a tickle fight," Kaleo grumbled good-naturedly.

Stefan chuckled and kissed her temple. "If that's all you want from a relationship, you should probably be looking elsewhere. I think that I've got Trey's number written down somewhere. If you call him right now, you may even be able to score tonight."

Kaleo faked gagging and smiled up at him before snuggling closer. "The flowers you bought were pretty. Maybe I won't break up with you today."

"Oh, good, I was so worried. It's a good thing I got the deluxe arrangement instead of the standard one."

They lay in each other's arms for several more minutes until the clock chimed at the hour and Stefan frowned. "I've got to go back to the office to finish some things up tonight."

Kaleo sat up and yawned. "Do you want me to go with you? I'm sure that I can find something to do."

"No need. It won't take me too long, just another hour or two."

"I'm sorry for keeping you from your work. You could have just called and told me that you were running behind."

"And miss eating dinner with such a beautiful woman? You're out of your mind."

After Kaleo walked Stefan to the door, she pulled him close to plant a kiss on his mouth, and he hugged her and kissed her back before getting into his car and driving away.

As the days passed, Kaleo gradually got to know the new recruits, and while she still wasn't quite sure what to think about Jeffery, Trevor's sunny personality and willingness to please broke down any walls that she might have tried to build up.

With the addition of the new recruits, how to best maintain the secrecy around Phoenix's identity once again became a topic of debate at the NAT leadership meetings. Stefan remained adamant that the fewer people who knew that Kaleo was Phoenix, the better, but even he admitted to the need to increase the number of task-force members.

It was up to Director Stone to make the call. "The people that we'll be recruiting will also be going out on missions, and you may very well be putting your life into their hands, and theirs into yours. If we can't trust them to keep the identity of one of their teammates secret, they shouldn't be on the team to begin with," he said with an air of finality.

Everyone agreed, and Stefan had then updated the rest of the board on the progress being made with the Snake head investigation. Now that they had a better idea of what they were doing and a more concrete target, NAT was making inroads into tracing the leadership structure all the way up to the top. Once he was done sharing what he'd found, Kaleo read off a list of President Hamilton's events, along with making the weekly formal request for the assistance of various task-force members for the president's office.

After the meeting was over, the Professor made his way over to Kaleo. "I have someone who I think would provide a good challenge for you in a match."

"Is this one of the new recruits?" Kaleo asked, careful to avoid looking at Stefan so as not to give away how much she knew.

Despite her efforts, the Professor wasn't dumb. "I see that you've already been forewarned about my plans," he said with a glare at Stefan.

"More of a suggestion than a warning. It's not like I wouldn't have suspected anyways, considering what Trevor's ability is and what my own weaknesses are."

"That may very well be true, but I see that I'll have to have a long talk with a certain assistant director about not letting his personal feelings get in the way of my training regimen."

"Stefan was just trying to be helpful. You of all people should know just how much meeting Jeffery and Trevor would have thrown me off."

"And you think that one day you won't have any issues meeting David Rockhill, the man who you all call Puppeteer, in the field again? Make no mistake Kaleo, if everything that I've heard of him is true, and if he's truly the one behind President Johnson's current condition, you will encounter him again."

Kaleo frowned. "I've already gone up against him once without any issue."

"No, *Phoenix* went up against him. He didn't know that it was you, and he certainly didn't know how to manipulate the new variable in the equation. I may not have any personal experience with him, but I fully believe that he chose the name Puppeteer for a reason—that it's how he sees himself. You must prepare yourself for the eventuality that when you, as Kaleo, encounter him next he's going to do whatever he can to hurt you and manipulate you. He's had several years to think of how to get revenge for his foiled plans, and it sounds like he's still holding a grudge against you."

"I'll think about it. Do you know when my match with Trevor will be?"

"Two weeks from now?"

Kaleo was surprised. "That soon? Didn't he just join up recently?"

The Professor nodded. "He did, but you have to remember that you were an exceptionally complicated student. Mr. Hartley apparently took your Flock's advice and has been practicing his abilities ever since you rescued him. If anything, I think that he requires a little convincing that he still needs some formal instruction."

"You want me to knock his ego down a peg or two?"

A rare smile flitted across the Professor's face. "Exactly."

"Anything you feel that I should do to prepare?"

He shook his head. "I think that you already have all the tools you need at your disposal; it's just going to be up to you to figure out how to use them."

"Nothing is ever easy with you, is it?"

"Life isn't easy. You of all people should know that."

# Chapter Thirty

Though Kaleo had gained a lot of experience with both her abilities and her fighting skills, she still felt somewhat apprehensive for her upcoming match with Trevor. Granted, she'd come a long way since her first match against Stefan, and had already participated in several matches against others on the task force, but she knew that Trevor's basic abilities had the potential to render her own useless.

As it had turned out, her first match with Strike all those months ago wasn't necessarily the way that the Professor liked to conduct his matches. The second match the Professor had scheduled her for was just after everyone had moved to Lincoln and against Mod. The setting was at a crowded festival, and the goal to tag the other person before being tagged, with the best out of five winning.

Mod had won easily the first two times, but their limited ability to undergo a complete transformation in the crowded public space gave Kaleo enough of an edge to survive for longer than a couple of minutes the third time, although she still lost in the end without being able to even score a point.

That weekend was memorable for more than one match, as the next day the Professor pitted Strike against Mod. Watching them stalk each other from a distance had been a thrilling treat for Kaleo and the rest of the task force. The Professor had given each of the contestants a tracker that would show up on a scanner, so even when they were out of sight behind buildings or completely lost in the crowd, the NAT spectators could still see Stefan and Mod circling each other in what would have been a beautiful and deadly dance if it hadn't been a training exercise.

To Kaleo's surprise, while Mod still won the match, Stefan had a good showing with two out of five points.

Fortunately, Kaleo hadn't made a habit of her defeats at the hands of Strike and Mod. At one point she'd been matched against Trey, also known as Specter, who had the ability to create multiples of himself for a short period of time. However, splitting himself into clones also split his strength, and even with multiple attackers, Kaleo didn't have too much trouble subduing him.

When the day came for her match with Trevor, Kaleo was optimistic that even with his abilities as they were, she could improve her overall match record. When it was time, Kaleo drove to the warehouse that housed the match facility in the outskirts of Lincoln. She had already confirmed with the Professor that Trevor would be entering through the back way, so she had no compunction about walking in through the front door and heading directly to the changing room to don her Phoenix gear.

As she put on her gear, Kaleo's nerves evened out and she felt herself standing taller and walking with more confidence to the large room that doubled occasionally as an arena. When she reached the reinforced door, she found the Professor waiting for her.

"Your usual helmet won't work today. Put this one on," he said.

She did as she was told, taking note that a screen overlaid where the visor would normally be. She didn't have time to ask why the change was necessary before the door swung open and she entered the room.

Immediately she noticed that the room was empty except for her and Trevor, and there were none of the boxes or other obstacles that had been present in her match against Strike or Specter. Her opponent was also in a matching black jumpsuit and full face helmet, and a band containing several knives was strapped across his chest.

"No way. Phoenix? You've got me going up against Phoenix, Prof?" Even with the voice modulator on, the excitement in Trevor's voice was palpable. "I'm going to get to beat up Phoenix? Hi, Phoenix, my name is Lift! It's nice to meet you!"

"Can you tone it down and at least try to be more professional, Lift? This is supposed to be a serious match," Phoenix said. As she took stock of the situation, she reached out with her senses to see what energy sources were available in the room and immersed herself into the flow, taking care to draw a small amount of energy into herself just in case the Professor had any tricks up his sleeve. In her experience, it certainly never hurt to have a buffer. With some of the excess energy, she created a small shield.

At her words, Lift's body stiffened. "Well, fine, if that's the way that you want to play it." His voice crackled and he shifted into a stance that looked remarkably similar to that of a powerlifter.

At just that moment, the bell tolled to signal the start of their match. Before its clear tones had faded away, Lift shifted his feet and shoved his hands towards her, and Phoenix immediately felt herself flying backwards, her shield completely useless. She hit the nearby wall with a heavy thud and slid to the floor.

She had to get moving soon; Lift was already walking her way. Before she could stand, he stepped into a lunge and pulled with his hands as if trying to rip a tablecloth off a table. Once again she felt herself tumbling helplessly through the air, this time towards him.

Phoenix came to a stop fifteen feet away from Lift.

"I'm not trying to be rude, but I hope that you don't mind me saying how disappointed I am right now. I thought that this would be more of a challenging match," he said as he unsheathed one of the knives on his chest, took another step forward, and with hardly a flick of his wrist, sent the knife speeding her way.

Phoenix released some of her pent-up energy, and the knife skidded off her shield. She breathed half a sigh of relief before Lift moved his hand again and she remembered that he could both push and pull. Without turning her head, she made her shield into a bubble, and was rewarded with the sound of a soft clang as the knife hit the shield behind her back and fell to the ground.

Lift tilted his head, but didn't say anything. Instead, he took two more knives from his belt and bent his knees into a squat stance. Phoenix looked around desperately for anything to hold on to so he couldn't toss her in the air, making it impossible for her to use her shield—but the floors were bare.

Then the world went black.

Phoenix quickly rolled away from her previous spot. As she did so, she heard Lift's cry of frustration.

"What's going on? I can't see, and this stupid helmet won't come off!"

The Professor's voice crackled over the speaker system. "That is correct, Lift. Now that you two have had a chance to get acquainted, I thought that a little added challenge was called for. The visors in your helmets have been set so that once you are within ten feet of each other the vision screen will gradually turn back on. It will reach normal brightness when you are within five feet of your opponent. If you are more than ten feet apart, it will remain off."

As the Professor spoke, Phoenix quietly moved away at a diagonal. She reached out with her senses and found that while she couldn't see anything with her visor, the lights in the room felt like they were still on. She scowled in concentration and pushed her hands against the ground. Across the room was an energy source with a consistent pulse; she had found Lift.

She stood and took a hesitant step, becoming more comfortable when she didn't stumble or fall. She couldn't see his features, but judging from the halting, indecisive steps that he took, she could imagine the unsure expression on his face.

Had Lift been any more experienced, he would have immediately put his back to the nearest wall so that she couldn't sneak up on him. Unfortunately for him, while his abilities were indeed formidable, he didn't seem to have very much practical knowledge when it came to adapting to changing conditions in a fight.

Phoenix stalked Lift in the darkness like a lioness stalking its prey.

"Are you even still out there, Phoenix? Please tell me that the Professor isn't just playing some sick joke on me right now." It might have just been the modulator, but his voice sounded sharp with fear.

"Oh, believe me, I'm still here," Phoenix said after circling around to his left. She was moving away even as the words came out of her mouth, which proved to be a good decision when Lift turned and sprinted several steps to get closer to the sound of her voice. However, she was already outside of the ten-foot radius.

He paused for a moment; she was sure he was listening for any sound that she might make that would give away her position. The pause provided inspiration, and within the confines of her helmet Phoenix grinned diabolically. The Professor wanted her to humble Lift a little, and she had just thought of the perfect way to do it.

She crept towards him until she was just beyond the ten-foot mark. Then she slid off her gloves and slipped her baton out of its holder before tossing them to the side. Lift whirled around to face the perceived threat, but before he had time to react she was already rushing him.

Phoenix made sure to close her eyes tightly before starting her plan, reasoning that the last thing that she needed was to be blinded by the screen in her helmet going from total black to full brightness. She knew that it was the right call when she heard Lift screech in pain as his eyes struggled to adjust to the new stimuli.

Fortunately, Phoenix hadn't needed her eyes to accomplish her goal. As Lift was still reeling from the sudden bright light directly in his eyes, she tackled him to the ground, drew one of the knives out of his chest belt, and rolled to her feet. She was running away before he could see well enough to pull her back with his abilities.

She watched from the cover of darkness as Lift scrambled to his feet and turned in a circle. He was scared and frustrated; she could feel his heart pounding frantically in his chest. Lift took a couple of steps forward and paused again, but the fate of the match had been sealed as soon as she knew which side was his front. This time she didn't bother with a distraction; she simply circled around to his back side, clutching his knife in her hand.

"C'mon, Phoenix, where'd you go? How about next time you don't do a sneak attack. Face me head-on and let's see who's truly the strongest," Lift said.

The sound of his voice provided the perfect cover for her to make her final move. With three quick, large steps she was standing directly behind him and pressing the dulled edge of the knife against his throat. Lift froze and a buzzer sounded, signifying the end of the match.

"Me. I'm the strongest," she said into the quiet room after the harsh noise of the buzzer had faded. She stepped back and removed her helmet. "Although I will say that you're the most talkative opponent I've had by far."

Lift whirled around. "Kaleo? Is that you?"

"The one and the same. Are you surprised?"

"No way, you're Phoenix? That is so crazy!" He reached up to undo his helmet, but struggled to get it off.

"Here, let me help you," Kaleo volunteered, but she couldn't seem to remove it either.

One of the doors opened, and the Professor strode in. "I locked that helmet on his head to prevent him from removing it when the screens went black," the Professor said as he fiddled with a latch at the bottom of the helmet before pulling it off to reveal Trevor's face.

"I hope that you've learned your lesson," the Professor said to Trevor.

The young man sniffed. "If by 'lesson' you mean that I'm good enough to have beaten Phoenix if the game hasn't been rigged, then I think I did."

The Professor's eyebrows drew together in a frown. "It is foolish to assume that the game will be fair. My job is to train you to win even in unfair circumstances."

"Doesn't change anything," Trevor said with a shrug.

"You could have still won today, darkness or not," Kaleo said.

"I don't see how. If I can't see, I can't use my abilities. I assume that you can still use yours in the dark and that gave you the advantage," he said with a frown.

"My abilities helped me to know where you were, but all I could really feel was your heart beating, nothing else. You should have assumed that I had the advantage, found the nearest wall and preferably the nearest corner, kept a knife in each hand, and waited there for me to make my move. At that point it's simply a game of seeing who's faster, and I'm not particularly known for my speed. If you'd have stayed on your toes, you'd have had a much better chance. Instead you got cocky, stopped trying to think strategically, and you lost."

"I see," Trevor said before rolling his neck. "That's a lot to think about, thanks. Professor, do you have anything else you wanted to tell me?"

"We'll discuss the entire match much more in-depth in your next lesson. Go ahead and get changed back," the Professor said, dismissing him with a nod.

Trevor trotted off. As he passed through the door, Kaleo saw Stefan lurking on the other side. She smiled, sure that her boyfriend would be very careful in making sure that Trevor understood *exactly* how vital it was that he tell no one about the real identity of Phoenix.

"I'd say that that was a successful match. Thank you for your help," the Professor said.

"Thank you for setting it up." Kaleo paused before sighing. "And you should know that I understood the lesson that you tried to teach me as well."

"And what sort of lesson would that be?" the Professor asked, the corners of his mouth lifting just slightly.

"That I'm not invincible, and that even though I'm strong, there are others out there that can make me as weak as any non-Abled."

"What an interesting lesson. Wish I had thought of that beforehand." The Professor winked at her and they began walking towards the exit door together. "Did you learn anything else?"

Kaleo shrugged. "Not unless it's that if I'm ever faced with a situation like that again, it doesn't hurt to think a bit outside of the box. In a real fight I could have tried to blind Trevor to even the playing field a bit."

"Clever girl."

The Professor bid her adieu as they left the match arena, and Stefan joined her from the seat he had taken against the wall.

"Have a productive conversation with Trevor?" she asked.

"You could say that. I certainly don't think that we have to worry about him being the one to spill the beans about Phoenix."

"Sounds good to me." Kaleo crossed her arms across her chest and leaned against the wall. "What's the plan for the rest of the day?"

Stefan rubbed his neck with one hand. "Would you mind looking over my plans for the Snakehead operation?"

She wrinkled her nose. "Is it coming up that soon?"

"In a couple of weeks, yeah."

"Sure I can. Is it sensitive enough that we have to keep the documents here? Or can we go out to eat and I can review them after that?"

Stefan frowned. "You want to take work home?"

"You know that I think best in sweatpants."

He chuckled. "Your house or mine?"

"Definitely mine. You never have enough snacks for really serious thinking."

# Chapter Thirty-One

A week later, Kaleo walked into the NAT headquarters an hour ahead of the general task-force meeting. She planned to use the time to squeeze in a workout at the small but well-equipped NAT gym. Due to the traffic patterns in Lincoln, it was much easier for her to drive to the meeting straight after work than to go home, change, and eat a quick dinner before having to rush in and risk being late. Besides, usually the meetings didn't take long, and if Stefan was too busy with work, she knew that she could count on Nicole or Taylor to be willing to grab a bite with her afterwards.

It was a weights day, which meant that Kaleo probably had just enough time to finish her workout before the meeting started. She wasn't the only one in the gym; Audra was across the room on the stationary bike. When Audra had first walked in, Kaleo had already been lifting for several minutes and nodded at her in the mirror, but Audra didn't so much as even acknowledge her. Kaleo sighed; she kept on hoping that one day Audra would stop feeding into the petty feud that had sprung up between them, but it seemed that no matter what Kaleo did, there was no change in the level of hostility that Audra insisted on throwing her way. Out of the corner of her eye she saw Audra move from the bike to the bench press area.

She was just starting her last set of deadlifts when she saw Stefan walk through the door through the mirror. He nodded at her and waited for her to finish before approaching.

"Light day today?" he asked, a hint of a smile on his face.

"Oh, shut up. Do you really think that these twig legs are that strong? Light day. Hmpf." Kaleo wiped the sweat out of her eyes.

"I don't know about strong, but they certainly provided a *very* nice view from where I was standing."

"I bet you say that to all the women who work out here."

Stefan's eyes sparkled. "No, just the really attractive ones."

Her sarcastic response was cut short by the sound of a large clang followed by a scream. Both Stefan and Kaleo whirled around to see Audra struggling to hold up her bench-press bar. She had apparently been lifting without the safety bars, no spotter, and had overloaded herself. She was currently struggling to keep the weight off her chest but the bar was dropping lower, and if she didn't receive help, it looked like the bar and weights would crush her chest.

Stefan rushed to Audra's side, but Kaleo's abilities beat him there. Without thinking, she reached out and erected a small shield around Audra's body. It was an instinctual move, not born out of any conscious thought, and no one in the room was more surprised than Kaleo when the edges of the shield sliced through the two ends of the barbell like a hot knife through butter. The sudden lack of weight made Audra's straining arm muscles practically throw the rest of the bar up in the air, and Kaleo immediately released the barrier so that Audra's hands didn't hit the top and Stefan could assist her.

Stefan helped Audra rack the weights and sit up, only to look shocked when she threw herself into his arms in tears.

"Oh, Stefan, thank you so much for saving me. I was terrified," Audra sobbed.

Kaleo had begun walking over to make sure that Audra didn't need any more help, but stopped suddenly and felt her eyes narrow when she saw the other woman hugging her boyfriend.

Stefan awkwardly patted Audra's back before trying to extract himself from her arms. "That's all right Audra, I really didn't do much anyways. If you want to thank someone, you should thank Kaleo."

"Thank her?" Audra screeched. "She just tried to kill me. You saw her raise her shield so that you couldn't help me. She wanted me to get hurt!"

Kaleo gritted her teeth, but it was Stefan who replied. "You know that she'd never want that. She probably was trying to catch the bar in the air like she caught those bullets at the Inauguration." He stood from the bench and straightened his tie. "Now, if you two will excuse me, I need to finish up a couple of things before the meeting. Audra, if you want to lift any more weights I'd suggest asking someone else to help you; I'm sure that Kaleo would be more than willing to spot you to prevent any more accidents." And with that, he walked out of the room.

"I'm sorry if it scared you, Audra. I really was trying to help. The barrier was a knee-jerk reaction, and I'll try to be more careful next time." Kaleo apologized in the chilly silence, trying to take the high road even if it left a bitter taste in her mouth.

Audra huffed and stood. "Yeah, well, maybe you should spend more time trying to work on your control and less on lifting silly weights. I can't believe that the Professor said that you were good enough to not be meeting with him regularly."

"And maybe you should learn that being rude shouldn't be your only personality trait," Kaleo said.

"At least I'm pretty. I bet Stefan has to close his eyes to kiss you to keep himself from feeling nauseous." Audra brushed past Kaleo and began walking out the door, lobbing the insult over her shoulder like a grenade.

"You're just jealous that I'm the one that he's kissing," Kaleo retorted.

Audra paused at the doorway and turned around, her eyes narrowed into slits. "Enjoy it while you can, Kaleo; we both know that he's too good for you. Once the glitter of dating Sifter and Architect's daughter wears off and he gets tired of slumming it with you, he'll come running back to me."

"He was never yours to begin with."

"You keep on believing that, but never forget that I was here first," Audra said before turning on her heel and letting the door shut behind her before Kaleo could fire off another response.

"I'm Audra, I'm all that, and I was here first," Kaleo mimicked into the empty room as she racked the weights that she'd been using. She looked over at the barbell that her barrier had chopped into pieces, and with a sigh moved it against the wall so that someone else could deal with it later.

After the little spat with Audra, Kaleo checked the clock and saw that she wouldn't have time for a full shower, so she settled for wiping herself down with a wet towel, putting on extra deodorant and a change of clothes, and hoping that it would be good enough for the short meeting.

As usual, she walked into the meeting room approximately fifteen minutes early in order to grab "her" seat in the very front row, furthest away from the door. She doubted that someone else would take it even if she had arrived late, but it never hurt to be prepared.

Before too long the others began to file in and take their usual seats. Taylor sat next to Kaleo and leaned over. "Oatmeal raisin cookies are vastly superior to chocolate chip," she murmured.

Kaleo hadn't been prepared for the sudden persuasion, but was still able to resist nodding her head in agreement. "I prefer lemon sugar cookies, actually," she whispered back, and Taylor smiled.

Stefan stood at the front of the room and coughed to signal that he was ready to begin. "As several of you already know, the task force has been asked to investigate the circumstances behind the attempted assassination of President Hamilton at the inaugural ball several months ago. We've now identified a group that we believe has played a large role in both the events of the inauguration and the rally bombings, and have gathered enough information to justify sending a team to apprehend the leaders and hopefully take one more step towards a solution for this rather convoluted problem.

"We have solid intel that the top leadership of the Snakeheads will be meeting next week. For the past month, we have been carefully infiltrating their operation, and I believe that we have good enough intel to make a move at their annual meeting."

Stefan lifted a large series of posters up and set them on a tall easel so that everyone could see them clearly.

"As you can see—"

"I've always meant to ask: Why are you using those silly papers? That must have taken forever to print. I know that you have a laptop. Do we not have a projector for you to make actual presentations?" Jeffery interrupted.

"No, we've always used the posters." Stefan seemed to be thrown a little off guard at being so casually interrupted.

Jeffery nodded.

"Now, as I was saying—"

He was interrupted him again by Jeffery. "Would you rather have a projector, or a large screen? Oh, What about a hologram? I've always wanted to try to make one of those."

"Let's talk about this tomorrow, Jeffery." Stefan turned back to the posters, only to be interrupted again.

"Well, I need to know now so I can get started on it."

Kaleo watched Stefan raise his eyes to the ceiling and take a deep breath. At the same time, she saw Trey stand from his seat and walk over to Jeffery.

"We'll talk about it later, Jeffery. I need to update the rest of the task force on the upcoming mission first so that they know what's going on," Stefan said.

Jeffery opened his mouth to argue, but was distracted by Trey's hand on his shoulder. He flinched and shrugged off Trey's hand, but when the other man handed Jeffery a notebook and a pen, and whispered something in his ear, Jeffery settled down and began talking to himself. As he wrote furiously, his left hand began pulling at his hair in a mannerism that reminded Kaleo of a frustrated Reader years before, in what she assumed was a family trait.

Stefan nodded at Trey in thanks before continuing on. "The good news is that we have an in. Timothy Miller, who is the chief operations officer of Heinstein Transport, has graciously accepted to be our mole. The plan is simple: Tim'll be attending the annual meeting as a very important but disgruntled employee tired of being under the thumb of an arrogant Abled, who thinks that Heinstein Transport could be better run with someone else at the helm. Now, this meetup also doubles as a way for the current leaders to posture and show off, so Tim's going to need a date to impress. That's where Beguile comes in. Audra, you'll be Tim's date for the night... Yes, Nicole?"

"Why does Audra get to be the arm candy? Her abilities are going to be next to useless if things go south."

Kaleo had ignored Audra's triumphant look when Stefan announced that she'd be Tim's date, but Nicole's question made her want to smile. She hadn't yet told Nicole that she had been working with Stefan on the plan, and that they'd spent several long hours ironing out all the details. She might not have liked Audra as a person, but the other woman's abilities were definitely useful at times.

"That brings me to the next part of my plan: Once we have sufficient information, we're calling in FBI agents to help us make the arrests. If all goes well, Tim and Beguile will both be kept in the same holding area with the rest of the Snakeheads, giving her a chance to use her abilities and gain more information."

"What do you mean 'if all goes well'?" Laura asked.

Stefan frowned. "The meeting is at an older, very exclusive country club. We haven't been able to scout it out as thoroughly as I would like, and there are several variables that we've not been able to account for completely. It's for that reason that I will also be accompanying Tim and Beguile as Tim's bodyguard."

"That brings me to the fourth member of our team: Kaleo will be waiting in a nearby van and acting as the link between us and the outside world. I will be wearing a very small transmitting device, and as soon as I judge that we have enough evidence, I'll be sending a signal to her to notify our friends at the FBI to make their move."

"Why not just have Jeffery rig you a button that you can press so that you can notify them yourself? Isn't having Kaleo there overkill? I'm sure that she has better things to do with her time," Audra asked sweetly.

"It's not overkill at all. Some of you may not be aware, but Kaleo came to the task force with an extensive prior history of running operations and missions. In fact, she's been my second set of eyes on this mission plan. I've tasked her with being our outside point person and coordinator, and if things do go south and a rescue is needed, she'll have her Phoenix gear nearby to suit up at a moment's notice and lend a hand." Stefan's tone was completely professional, but Kaleo couldn't help but feel a warm glow at his words and the trust he placed in her.

If she had any growing doubts in her mind about the mission, his confidence in her abilities helped soothe them away.

Well, helped soothe most of them away. She made a mental note to talk to the Professor and perhaps take a couple of extra lessons before it was time for the mission. The situation with Audra in the weight room earlier had shaken her, and she felt that it would be better safe than sorry to have an abilities check-up and make sure that everything was okay. Kaleo had never stopped practicing her control of her abilities, and the fact that they had seemingly reacted of their own accord in such a strange manner didn't quite sit right with her, especially because Audra did have a point earlier: If Kaleo hadn't released the barrier when she did, it could have caused serious harm.

"And that about wraps up the plan. Anyone have any questions?" Stefan's voice broke through her thoughts, and Kaleo set her mind back on the task at hand.

"Yeah, so how big did you want the projector image to be? Are we going to keep on using this room, or do I need to make it adjustable?" Jeffery asked.

Stefan sighed and looked around to make sure that no one else had raised their hand. "All right, meeting dismissed. The rest of the information is in your weekly packets. Anyone with any questions about the newest mission can ask Kaleo or me. Anyone with questions about anything else can also ask Sifter." He stepped away from the front of the room and almost immediately was accosted by Jeffery, who had rushed down the center aisle to begin bombarding him with questions.

Kaleo stretched and turned to Taylor. "Have you eaten yet?"

Taylor shook her head. "I had to rush here straight from work, and I'm starving. Why?"

"I didn't get a chance to eat before the meeting either. I was thinking that if Stefan's busy, then you, Nicole, and I can go find somewhere to eat."

"Oh, lovely. I love being the second-choice dinner companion. What if Stefan manages to tear himself away from the bulldog? You going to ditch us?"

They both turned to look at Stefan and Jeffery, and Kaleo had to smile—the nickname of "Bulldog" was accurate for Jeffery. Once the young man got his teeth into a problem or challenge he *had* to solve it before he could move on to anything else.

"Let me see if I need to go rescue Stefan. If I can tear him away from Jeffery, then maybe all four of us can go get something together, if you don't mind."

"Nah, the more the merrier. You go talk to Stefan, I'll round up Nicole and see if she's interested. It looks like she's talking to Trey again, so who knows."

"Not again," Kaleo groaned. "Hurry, go save her from herself."

"You mean save him from her." Taylor chuckled.

"Do you remember what happened the last time they hooked up? I don't know about you, but I don't want to either deal with the dramatic aftermath when she's inevitably disappointed or have to put up with Trey's puffed-up ego for another week."

"Good point."

Kaleo walked up to Stefan and Jeffery and put her hand on Stefan's arm. "Hey, Jeffery, I've got a quick question for Stefan. Can you give us a minute?"

Jeffery checked his watch. "Yes, I can. I need to go get my sketches so I can show him what I've been talking about." He turned to walk back to his seat, where he had left his papers and bag.

Kaleo turned to Stefan. "Taylor, Nicole, and I were about to go out to eat. Do I need to rescue you, or are you going to be okay?"

He shrugged. "I'll be fine. The last time I tried to get away from Jeffery before he was done explaining his ideas, he called me at two a.m. to ask if we had the money in the budget for our own radio tower."

"Sounds to me like you need to set some boundaries."

"We're working on it. Trey's brother is pretty similar and he's helping me understand; it's just taking time to get the young one trained."

"Okay, if you're sure..."

"I'm positive. Are you still crazy busy tomorrow?"

Kaleo nodded and Stefan frowned. "Okay, then how about we plan on dinner the evening after? We haven't had an actual date in a while. I'll pick you up at seven?"

"Seven seems a little late if you're going to do a full date," Jeffery interjected, back from grabbing his things. "I mean, an hour or so for dinner puts you at eight, and then what are you going to do for entertainment? A play or concert would take another two or three hours, and then that'll be ten or eleven before you even got back into the car, and I remember that Kaleo told me that she likes to wake up early." His eyes widened. "Unless you're assuming that you're going to be each other's entertainment. That'd make much more sense. It would only take what? Ten minutes? Thirty minutes max from start to finish?"

The sharp look that Kaleo shot Stefan held the weight of an entire conversation, and he winced. "Boundaries. Got it. We'll work on it." He squeezed Kaleo's hand. "Have fun with Nicole and Taylor, I'll handle things from here and see you the day after tomorrow."

Kaleo returned the hand squeeze before walking outside the doors of the meeting room to rejoin her friends. "Nicole, did Taylor convince you to eat with us, or have you already made plans?" she asked with only a hint of a grin.

Nicole frowned. "I was going to make plans, but you know how persuasive Taylor can be. Let's go eat and then maybe I can salvage the rest of my night."

The restaurant that they agreed to eat at was close to NAT headquarters and was one of the favorite spots for post-meeting meals. The family that owned the restaurant had passed down their recipes for several generations, and their homemade enchiladas and salsa had turned many who worked at NAT into regular customers.

After they had ordered, Kaleo looked at Nicole. "I distinctly remember you telling me multiple times that Trey wasn't any good. Why do you keep on going back for more?"

"He's getting a little better with practice." Nicole grinned and sipped her margarita. "Plus, he's almost laughably easy, and it's about as no-strings-attached as you can get."

"I'll take your word for it," Kaleo replied.

"Are you actually allergic to commitment, or have you just not met the right person yet?" Taylor asked as she dipped another chip into the salsa.

"Who knows? Besides, you're one to talk, Taylor. When was the last time that you even went on a date?"

"It's different for me, you know that."

"Yeah, well I know several guys who are either mostly deaf or completely deaf. If you learn sign language I can set you up with them. I'm pretty sure that your abilities won't work if they can't hear anything."

"I don't want your sloppy seconds."

"Well, that eliminates what? Half the guys in Lincoln by now?" Kaleo teased.

Nicole huffed. "Be nice, or I'll set my eyes on Brant Heinstein next. He sounds like he'd be fun."

"Do whatever you want to, just remember that Lin may not appreciate you hooking up with her ex. Besides, last I heard they were friends again and have even been hanging out occasionally."

"How is Lin doing anyways? I haven't heard from her in a while."

"When I talked to her a couple of weeks ago it sounded like she's doing well. She's got a new boyfriend that she just moved in with."

"New boyfriend? Moving in? Didn't she just break up with Sam like a month ago?"

"It was back in January, so around four months now. She's known the new guy for about a month and a half or so."

"Wow, and I thought that I moved fast." Nicole shrugged. "If she's happy, good for her." She paused as the waiter served them their food and looked at Kaleo with a raised eyebrow. "So when are you and Stefan moving in together?"

Kaleo shook her head. "We've been through this before, Nicole."

"You've been together how long? Ten months? You're obviously madly in love with each other. I just don't understand what's stopping you two."

"You don't have to understand. I love you, Nicole, but you know that you and I have very different views on these things," Kaleo said firmly.

Taylor sighed. "C'mon, you two, stop it. My enchiladas are already spicy enough. Nicole, how's working for the task force full-time been? Exciting enough for you, or are you missing the demolition part of your last job?"

Nicole shrugged. "It's fine. When Stefan doesn't have me doing things he lends me out to consult for other agencies. I still don't understand why you didn't join up full-time, Taylor. With your abilities, you could have been the main publicity person, or at least helped Sifter out."

"The president needs my help now, and I don't think I've got quite the experience yet to be in charge of all of the NAT publicity. Besides, Sifter's the best public face that we could have; she's a household name, and I still get to work with her and the director. It's a win/win situation." Taylor glanced at Kaleo. "And this way Phoenix has a friend in the president's office that she can room with if he needs her to go to any out-of-town event."

"I guess that's a good point." Nicole frowned. "I shouldn't be selfish. It's just weird with me and Audra being the only two full-time women on the task force."

"I thought that Laura was also full-time?"

"Yeah, but she's out consulting even more than I am." Nicole glanced at Kaleo. "Don't worry, though, I'm keeping an eye on Audra and her thirsty self, especially around Stefan."

"I'm not worried," Kaleo replied as she finished up the last of her fajitas. She briefly considered filling the others in on what had happened that day in the gym, but decided against it. The last thing that she wanted to create was more drama. She was a big girl, and could handle Audra herself. "I trust Stefan."

"You can trust him all you want, but I certainly wouldn't trust Audra."

"I never said that I did."

"Trust or not, I've got your back, don't you worry," Nicole said as she shook part of her half-eaten taco at Kaleo.

"Yeah, and I may not be nearly as violent as Nicole, but you know that I'm here if you need me," Taylor added.

Kaleo smiled at her friends. "I know that I can count on you both."

# Chapter Thirty-Two

The town where the Snakeheads had chosen to host their yearly meeting, Aspen, was as wealthy as it was small. It was no wonder that the leadership of an organization that so hated Ableds had chosen a town where a large majority of the population lived seasonally, had no abilities, and came from old money that didn't like feeling less than the poor people that they'd had been raised to looked down on.

Nevertheless, it was supposed to be a quaint town set in a particularly beautiful and majestic valley in the mountains. The train ride from Lincoln had taken almost eight hours, and Kaleo, Stefan, and Audra had left early that morning so that they'd have plenty of time to get mission-ready. Tim had already arranged to fly into Aspen directly and had said that he'd meet the others at a house Brant owned. While Stefan originally planned for them to stay at a local hotel, Tim had assured Stefan that the house was much safer than a hotel or other rental, and that there was no chance that they'd be interrupted in their preparations.

Most of the train ride had gone by without interruption. Audra mostly napped quietly on one of the couches while Kaleo and Stefan each focused on their own separate projects for work. Then, a couple of hours before they were due to arrive at their destination, Audra woke up.

Kaleo had finished as much of her work as she could, and had moved over to sit next to Stefan at the table he was working at. Fortunately, he seemed to prefer the aisle seat in their private cabin, so she was free to take the window seat and lean against him while looking out at the scenery rushing past.

When Audra got up and announced that she was going to do a trial run of her outfit for that night, Kaleo thought it strange, but otherwise ignored her.

Forty-five minutes later, Stefan and Kaleo looked up when the sliding door to their private cabin opened, and Kaleo understood exactly what game Audra was playing. The other woman sashayed into the room dressed to the nines in a black satin cocktail dress with a halter neckline that plunged down almost to her belly button, and that hugged every one of the curves on her thin frame. The width of the neckline made it obvious that she wasn't wearing a bra, and the length of the dress was scandalously short. For a brief moment, Kaleo wondered if the main reason Audra had chosen that dress specifically was so she could have an excusable wardrobe malfunction in front of Stefan.

"What do you think of my dress, Kaleo?" Audra asked sweetly as she twirled slowly in her stiletto heels before striking a pose, seemingly unaffected by the swaying of the train on the tracks. Her long blonde hair had been styled into beach waves, and her makeup only accentuated her innocent baby blue eyes and pink lips.

And just like that, the gauntlet was tossed and the challenge issued. If Kaleo was unkind to Audra, she looked bad in front of Stefan and, worse, jealous of the other woman. If she chose to take the high road, she would have to admit out loud and in front of Stefan that Audra was indeed very beautiful. With the firing of the opening salvo, Kaleo felt like Audra had already won the battle.

"You look great, Audra," Kaleo said with as much conviction as she could muster, but couldn't resist tossing a barb in. "Although I don't think that it's an outfit that I'd ever be comfortable wearing."

"It's not?" Audra looked Kaleo up and down critically. "No, you're right, it's not something that just anyone could wear. It's good that you know your limits, though. I wouldn't want you to embarrass yourself." She twirled a lock of hair around one of her fingers. "When I saw it in the store the other day, I just *had* to buy it so that I'd have it on hand when the perfect occasion presented itself. What about you, Stefan? Do you like it?"

Kaleo looked at Stefan and fought the desperate urge to put her hand on his arm, or his leg, or do anything that would both stake her claim and tip Audra off to just how insecure she was feeling. She tried not to think of her own outfit that consisted of jeans, a bulky sweater, and her hair tied up in a ponytail. She'd worn her usual amount of makeup that morning, but it was nothing compared to Audra's evening look, and Kaleo was sure that, next to Audra, she looked as frumpy as an old spinster.

Stefan was wearing the poker face that he only displayed when he really didn't want anyone to know what he was thinking. He casually looked Audra up and down, eyes not lingering on any one specific part and shrugged, nodded, and grinned faintly. "I'm sure that Tim is going to think that he hit the jackpot. You'll have to be careful that you don't give any of the old geezers at the club a heart attack tonight before you convince them to give you some information."

Audra took a seat across from Stefan and leaned forward, resting her head on her hand, her eyes soft. "That's what Tim and the others will think...But what do *you* think?"

"I think that you look very nice, and I have no doubt that you'll do your job well tonight," Stefan said, his eyes never dropping below Audra's nose. As he spoke, his hand reached for Kaleo's, which was resting on top of the table. "Now, if you'll excuse me, Audra, I wanted to get a good handle on this report before we get to the station and we've only got an hour or so left."

He kept holding Kaleo's hand as he returned his attention to the papers in front of him, and Kaleo felt her heart swell. She fought back a smile as she saw Audra's mouth twist into a pout, and then she too followed Stefan's example and turned away from Audra to look out the window again, squeezing Stefan's hand as she did so.

Audra stayed where she was until the announcement was made that they were ten minutes from the station. She sighed and stood up. "I'm going to go get changed back now," she announced.

"Sounds good," Stefan replied, keeping his eyes studiously on the papers in front of him. When the door to the cabin slid shut and signaled that Audra was gone, he sighed heavily, closed his eyes, and leaned back in his chair while pinching the bridge of his nose.

"Do you know where Audra bought that dress from?" he asked.

Kaleo felt a rock form in her stomach. "No, but if I asked nicely she'd probably tell me," she said carefully.

"Do me a favor?"

"Depends on the favor."

He opened one eye and looked at her. "Find out the store, and then make sure that you never buy anything from there. If you ever showed up to my apartment wearing a dress like that, I'm not sure if I could stop myself from ripping it off and throwing you onto my bed like a caveman."

"Well you certainly seemed to be doing a great job with your self-control just now." Kaleo couldn't keep the bitterness out of her voice.

Stefan laughed softly and pressed her hand to his lips. "First of all, Audra isn't the woman I'm in love with, and second of all, I much prefer brunettes."

Kaleo looked down at her sweater and frowned, picking at imaginary pieces of lint. "She was gorgeous."

"Well, yes, I should hope so considering that a large part of her role in this mission is to be beautiful."

"You didn't ever ask me to take on that role."

"Of course I didn't. You think that I could stand by at the country club tonight and pretend to not care as all the other men there undressed you with their eyes? We wouldn't make it five feet past the door before I started causing a scene."

Kaleo couldn't help herself; she smiled and looked back at Stefan. His eyes were shining, and his mouth curved into a tender smile. He wrapped his arms around her and rested his head on her shoulder. "Besides, it's much easier to cuddle with you when you're dressed like this, all soft, and comfortable, and safe. Why would I ever want to give that up?"

She kissed the top of his head. "You're just trying to make me feel better about my competition."

He turned to look up at her. "No, I'm trying to make sure that you understand that in my eyes, you don't have any competition."

Tim's driver picked them up from the train station and drove them to Brant's mansion just outside of town. Later, when it was approaching time for them to leave on the mission, Audra disappeared to get ready once again. When she had returned to the living room where the others were waiting, she was dressed in a classic red evening gown that had a thigh-high slit and a neckline that showed off just enough of her cleavage to be enticing without making her look trashy.

"You look absolutely ravishing," Tim said as he looked up at her from his wheelchair. He was dressed impeccably in a designer tuxedo, and looked every part of the young C-level executive.

"That's not the same dress that you were wearing earlier," Kaleo said as innocently as she could.

Audra smiled. "I decided that for such a formal occasion it would be better to dress up, and I'm sure that there will be plenty of other women there in a black dress. I wanted to make sure that I stood out."

"And stand out you will," Tim said. "I would offer you my arm, but I'm afraid that I'll need both of them to manage the wheelchair. You are more than welcome to use one of the handles to rest your hand on, if you'd like."

"I would be delighted." Audra replied, already turning up the charm in preparation for the mission.

Kaleo looked over at Stefan. He was in a black suit and tie, and Kaleo thought he looked every bit of the stern, intimidatingly handsome bodyguard.

"I think that we're ready then. Tim, I don't need to remind you that no matter what happens tonight, whatever you see or hear is a matter of national security and that you've been sworn to secrecy, do I?" Stefan asked, his voice deepening as he seemingly transitioned into Strike in front of Kaleo's eyes.

Tim nodded. "Not at all. As I recall, if I tell anyone anything about this mission it could mean a felony and jail time, or worse. Don't worry, I know how to keep my mouth shut."

Strike drove Tim and Audra to the country club, where the Snakehead meeting was to take place. Twenty minutes later, Kaleo followed them in the NAT van that Jeffery had tricked out, and parked at the edge of the golf course in a secluded area where she was within range of both NAT and FBI communication devices.

She'd been waiting for almost an hour when one of the screens sitting in front of her suddenly blinked green, interrupting her thoughts. Strike had gotten what they needed—it was go time. She picked up the radio and contacted the FBI team on standby.

"This is Starling reporting in; we've got the green light. You're good to go," she said into the speaker.

"*Roger that. Team Bravo on our way*," crackled the response, and she sat back, the most important part of her assignment done. She and Stefan had already decided that for this mission, if she was acting as Kaleo she would go by the name Starling instead of Phoenix to minimize any potential leaks.

Several minutes later, the green screen suddenly turned into one with green and black vertical stripes, and adrenaline flooded her veins. Green meant that they had the information they needed and she was to send in the backup team, red meant to call the team off, and black stripes were a distress signal. She immediately picked the phone up again.

"Starling here. Team Bravo, we just received a distress signal. You're still good to go, just keep your eyes open and stay on your toes."

"*Roger that, Starling.*"

Kaleo checked the cameras that surrounded the van and frowned when she saw movement in the bushes. As she continued watching, she spotted several men emerging from the woods in tactical gear. They approached the van covertly; it would have been almost impossible to see them in the dark night if it hadn't been for an infrared camera that Jeffery had thoughtfully added when he'd outfitted the van.

She stood before pulling a duffel bag out from under the small desk that she'd been sitting at. Kaleo sat the duffel bag on the table and unzipped it, revealing her black NAT uniform with the Phoenix emblem embroidered on the shoulder patches, and her new custom-made helmet with a stylized blue and yellow flying phoenix on each side.

Kaleo took one last look at the screen blinking with its green and black stripes and then at the cameras to see that the men were now halfway across the clearing before turning away.

She grabbed her gear. It was time for Phoenix to suit up.

The men had crept to within twenty feet of the van and were getting closer when she opened the door and jumped out.

As soon as her feet hit the ground, Phoenix's blue shield blossomed to life, and the light cast strange shadows throughout the clearing.

Canary might not have been as dead and buried as Kaleo had originally thought because when given the choice, she'd naturally gravitated towards the type of weapon that had been her trusty sidearm so many years before. Her new baton was around nine inches when in its collapsed form, but could extend out to almost three feet, and thanks to Jeffery's skill with tech and fabrication, it packed a hefty battery that enabled it to deliver a taser-like electric current for up to fifteen minutes.

"I don't know what would bring you guys out to this deserted area right now, but how about you turn around, go back to wherever you came from, and forget that you saw me?" she asked.

One of the men shined his flashlight at her. "It's Phoenix. Someone radio into the base and tell them that we found out where the signal was sent and that we're under attack," he said as he drew a knife.

"There's no need for that, you're not under attack. I was just out for a drive in my van and thought that I'd park here for the night," she said in a lame attempt to diffuse the situation.

Her de-escalation talk definitely needed some work because the nearest man rushed at her, and Phoenix threw away any hope of getting out of the situation without a fight. With a flick of her wrist she extended her baton before swinging at the man. He raised his arm to protect his face and was rewarded with a broken bone. In the same motion, Phoenix angled the baton down and across, and a sickening crunch upon impact informed her that she'd just broken one of his kneecaps.

Another two men were running at her back, and Phoenix whirled around to face them. She pressed the button on her baton to trigger the electric charge, and while she tased the first man in the chest, a kick to the groin took care of the second.

There was only one man left, and he took one look at his colleagues groaning on the ground before turning and running away. Phoenix ran after him for a few steps, but then decided that securing the van and checking in with the others on the team was far more important than chasing after loose ends.

She zip-tied her three assailants together and left them sitting in the clearing, fearing that something had happened to Strike and the others if the appearance of the Snakehead security was anything to go by.

As she started the van, Phoenix turned off her voice modulator and spoke into the comms system.

"Team Bravo, Starling reporting in. We've run into unexpected trouble on this end with some uninvited visitors. What is your situation?"

"We were able to enter following the original plans, but they knew that we were coming and locked down the inner sanctuary. We think that our mutual friends are still inside, but we've heard some yelling and gunshots."

"I see. Phoenix and I are on our way. They'll join you outside the inner sanctuary. Due to the rapidly evolving nature of the situation, I'm turning all future decisions and coordination with you over to them. Understood?"

"Understood."

Phoenix sat behind the wheel and rolled her shoulders before putting the van into drive. Her team needed her.

# Chapter Thirty-Three

Phoenix knelt in front of the large metal doors and readied her shield.

The detonators that Team Bravo had placed against the door frame blinked faster and turned red.

An explosive blast blew the doors open, and Phoenix ran through into the smoke. Her shield, which stretched almost from one wall to the other, protected her and the others on Team Bravo from any side effects of the blast.

She'd been the first one through for many reasons; the most important involved the sound of gunshots and the bullets bouncing off of her shield, which had now been charged to full capacity and gave off a brilliant neon blue light.

The gunshots stopped, and Phoenix decreased the area of her shield until it was just large enough to cover her entire body. She could have waited until the smoke cleared and Team Bravo had a chance to set up, but she chose instead to keep the momentum going and hamper the Snakeheads before they had a chance to regroup.

A large hand swung at her out of the smoke and she ducked, then dropped into a crouch and swept her assailants' feet out from underneath them. From across the room she thought she could hear more fighting, but the lion's share of her attention was taken up in defending herself.

The man was already rolling over onto his side, and she took the opportunity while he was still on the floor to kick him over onto his stomach, pin him down with her knee, and tie his hands together behind his back.

The smoke was rapidly clearing, and Phoenix stood up and looked around the room to take stock of the situation.

As the visibility increased, one of the women began screaming unintelligibly. The screech broke her concentration, and in the chaos she didn't hear or feel the second security guard sneaking up behind her until he had looped a thin strand of wire around her neck and started pulling. At the same time, he kicked the back of her legs, and Phoenix fell to her knees.

"Everyone stand down, or I'll strangle her," he ordered.

Phoenix tried to grab at the wire looped around her throat, but her attempts were futile. Across the room she saw Strike hold his hands up and take a step forward, but then the man behind her tightened his grip and she let out an involuntary groan.

"Not another step, and drop your weapon. You new arrivals can set your weapons down too. You're going to let us all out of here, or I'll kill her right now."

Strike bent to set his knife on the ground, and then knelt and kept his hands up. His eyes were wide, although Phoenix wasn't foolish enough to think that he was only afraid. Even from across the room she could see the clench of his jaw.

She had to think; there was no getting away by conventional means, and her former attempts to struggle had only served to induce her captor to tighten the wire around her neck. As it was, her suit gave her only the slightest bit of protection, and her vision was rapidly fading.

One of her hands dropped from her neck to her side, where her collapsible baton was attached to her belt, and inspiration struck.

"We are willing to negotiate. Just be aware that if you harm Phoenix, you will be murdering a federal agent, which will entail very harsh consequences for you," Strike said.

"You think that I don't know what's in store for me... for all of us if we don't escape now? It'd be just like an Abled to think that I'm dumb because I don't have your fancy abilities."

In one fluid motion, Phoenix disengaged the baton from its holder, punched the electric button, and pushed the contact points at the end into the man's thigh. Immediately, the pressure on the wire around her neck abated, and Team

Bravo took advantage of the opening and surged further into the room, enveloping her in their midst as they did so.

Phoenix heard a familiar whistle and whipped her head around to look at Strike. He was surrounded by four men and holding one of his hands up in the air. "Mind giving me some assistance?" he called out.

With a flick of her wrist, Phoenix collapsed the baton and threw it at him. In one smooth motion, Strike jumped up into the air, caught the baton, shoved the engaged electric prods into his leg, tossed her baton back, and hit the ground in a blur. He was fast and efficient, and with the efforts of Team Bravo, the rest of the security and bodyguards had been taken care of within a handful of minutes.

After they'd taken the Snakehead leadership and their dates out to the front of the country club, Phoenix, Strike, and Eddie, the leader of Team Bravo, had a hushed discussion about the next step.

"The people in that group, while still important, aren't the big fish. The real leaders were taken into a separate room further in the club when they got word that someone had transmitted a signal," Strike said as he took another drink from the pitcher of water in his hand.

"How did they get wind about that?" Eddie asked.

Strike shrugged. "Wish I knew. It's possible they were on the lookout for signals because minutes after I'd sent the signal to Phoenix that we had what we needed, someone came into the room and hustled away the VIPs. The good news is that Beguile was chatting one of them up at the time, and went with their group. The bad news is that they could be anywhere on the country club grounds, and that we can't let them get away."

"Could they have escaped by now?" Phoenix asked.

"The other teams secured the perimeter before we received the go-ahead from Starling. It's unlikely that they were able to slip off of the club grounds," Eddie said.

"Well, that's a relief at least."

"So now the issue is how to keep our current captives secure while going after those who slipped our grasp," Strike said.

"That part is easy. I'll keep an eye on them, and the rest of you can go play hide and seek with the remaining Snakeheads. It should be easy enough with my barrier, and Eddie can leave a man or two to watch my back just in case things get hairy."

Strike frowned and loosened his tie. "Eddie, would you mind giving us a chance to discuss things for a second?"

"Sure thing, I'll go talk to my team and let them know what the plan is so far," Eddie said. After he walked away, Strike turned back to Phoenix.

"How are you feeling?"

"Fine, never better. Why do you ask?"

He rolled his eyes. "Oh, I don't know... maybe because you were almost strangled back there?"

"I had it under control. If anything, I should be the one asking how you're doing, considering what happens when you don't get enough water after using your abilities," she said.

He held up the pitcher of water. "Your baton gave me the energy boost I needed. Besides, even if it hadn't, I've had more than enough."

"Great, so we're good to go with the plan then?"

Strike sighed. "Yeah, I guess. Just promise me that you'll tell me if you start having any issues or run into any more trouble."

"Sure, I can do that. You do the same. This is a two-way street, you know."

"I know," he said with a smile.

It took almost two hours for Strike and the others to locate the last group of Snakeheads. During that time, Phoenix kept up a bubble shield around the Snakeheads that they'd already captured, only lowering it when a new fugitive was added to the group. It was hard, tiring work not helped by the dark night sky. Still, with the occasional aid of her baton, she was able to complete her end of the job without giving away just how tired she was, and after Strike, Eddie, and the rest of Team Bravo had rendezvoused with her, she helped them load the captives, including both Beguile and Tim, into waiting buses, said her goodbyes, and retreated to the task-force van for some much deserved rest.

Ten minutes later, Strike entered the van and plopped onto one of the seats with a groan.

"Everything okay?" Phoenix asked. She'd removed her helmet and started to eat a granola bar.

"Apparently Eddie's supervisor got his wires crossed somehow and didn't arrange for appropriate security at the county jail. Not only that, but we suspect that someone was able to call for Snakehead backup, and now there are valid concerns that the top dogs are going to be broken out almost as soon as we get them in a holding cell."

"That is a problem. Are they going to need more assistance from us?"

Strike nodded. "For at least four more hours."

"Four hours?" Phoenix checked her watch. The club meeting had started late, and it was already well past midnight. When combined with their early-morning departure from the train station, by the time they were done she would have been up for almost twenty-four hours.

"We can take it in shifts, if you want. I know that you're probably already really tired," he said.

She shook her head. "I'll be fine. Hopefully they have good coffee at the jail."

"No tea?"

"I'm going to need something strong."

Phoenix ate another granola bar as they drove to the county jail. Once there, she followed Strike inside to where the Snakehead prisoners were being temporarily held. Fatigue was beginning to weigh down her limbs, but she refused to give in. She made herself a pot of coffee, and proceeded to drink it all.

Even drinking a cup of coffee to keep herself awake wasn't simple due to her helmet, and Phoenix was forced to take her cup into the nearest bathroom, make sure that it was empty, and turn off the light before removing her helmet to chug her drink. It was a convoluted process, and she decided to not make another pot, reasoning that she'd had enough to keep her awake for quite some time.

Finally, just as the sun was beginning to rise, reinforcements from the FBI arrived and Strike and Phoenix were able to leave.

As Kaleo buckled her seatbelt into the driver's seat of the van, she could feel an impending crash as the caffeine began to wear off.

"How far are we to Brant's house?" she asked Stefan.

"Should be twenty-five or thirty minutes. Why? Are you feeling okay?"

"I'm fine, just a little sleepy," she said with a yawn.

"Once we get back to the base, we can take a nice, long nap. Taylor's on her way up to Denver to help me with the interrogations, but you can head back to Lincoln tonight."

Kaleo nodded and pulled out onto the street. Traffic was heavier than she would have expected in such a small town, but she didn't mind–it helped keep her mind focused. As they drove out of the city and began climbing the mountains, the twisting roads created a hypnotic effect, and she found herself fighting to stay awake. The urge to close her eyes was strong, but she'd been tired plenty of times before and reasoned that they were so close to Brant's house that there was no use in pulling over and asking Stefan to drive.

She closed her heavy eyes in a slow blink.

"WATCH OUT!"

Her eyes snapped open and her head jerked up at Stefan's shout. At the same time, she felt the steering wheel jerk out of her hands.

They skidded to a stop on the shoulder of the road.

"What just happened?" Kaleo asked as she shifted the van into park.

"I was about to ask you the same thing. One minute I'm looking out the window, and the next thing I know, you're asleep at the wheel and the van is swerving into oncoming traffic," Stefan said as he unbuckled his seatbelt and opened his door. "Now get out. I'm driving."

Kaleo fought back a yawn. "I'm feeling much better. I don't know what came over me. We're only a few minutes from the house; we don't have to switch."

"Are you kidding me? No dice. I don't have a death wish," he huffed.

Kaleo groaned, but did as he said, and they drove the next few minutes in stony silence.

She turned in her seat to look at him. "I'm sorry, I didn't realize that I was that tired. If I'd have known, I would have told you."

"You should have told me anyway. You could have gotten us killed," he said through gritted teeth.

"You're right. I wasn't thinking straight."

"Obviously."

"I already said that I was sorry."

He sighed and glanced at her. "I know, sweetheart. I'm not only angry at you, although I am upset that you didn't tell me sooner. I could have driven us. In fact, more than anything, I'm angry with myself for not telling you to sleep and let me drive. That was my fault. I should have known better."

"I was just trying to help out. You risked your life in the mission last night, I thought that I could at least drive us back," she said.

He reached out and held her hand against her thigh. "We both risked our lives last night, and then we pulled double duty as prison guards. I just wish you'd be more open with me when you're struggling. I love you, but when you bottle everything up so much, you make it hard to help you."

"That's because I don't think I need help–" Kaleo trailed off and then cracked a small smile when she heard Stefan's derisive snort "Okay, sometimes I'm wrong. I'll try to work on that."

"You know that you don't have to put that strong front up around me by now, don't you? I've got your back, no matter what."

She leaned her head against his shoulder and looked out the window to the sun rising over the tops of the mountains, painting the sky in a glorious riot of warm colors. "I know."

# Authors Note

Thank you for reading *Knight*. I sincerely hope that you enjoyed reading this book as much as I enjoyed writing it. Self-published books live and die by word of mouth, so if you have time, (and especially if you liked the story), I would greatly appreciate it if you could leave a review on Amazon.

*Knight* is the second book in a planned series of six: *Pawn, Knight, Bishop, Rook, Queen,* and *King.*

*Bishop,* and *Rook* have already been written and are in varying stages of editing, *Queen* is currently being written, and *King* is roughly outlined. My current publication schedule is to release *Bishop* in late Fall 2022, and to release the last three books in early and mid 2023.

For publication updates you can sign up for my newsletter at my website www.rghurleybooks.com. Signing up will also give you access to a FREE bonus chapter from *Pawn* detailing what happened at Broadman University from the perspective of Strike.

Have extra questions? Comments? Reactions? You can contact me directly at rghurleybooks@gmail.com

Made in the USA
Las Vegas, NV
01 September 2022